The GRAIL QUEST Series

HARLEQUIN

VAGABOND

GALLOWS THIEF

STONEHENGE: A NOVEL OF 2000 BC

The STARBUCK Chronicles

REBEL
COPPERHEAD
BATTLE FLAG
THE BLOODY GROUND

The WARLORD Chronicles

THE WINTER KING
THE ENEMY OF GOD
EXCALIBUR

VAGABOND

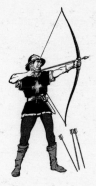

BERNARD CORNWELL

HarperCollins*Publishers*

HarperCollins*Publishers*
77–85 Fulham Palace Road,
Hammersmith, London W6 8JB

www.**fire**and**water**.com

Published by HarperCollins*Publishers* 2002
1 3 5 7 9 8 6 4 2

A catalogue record for this book
is available from the British Library

ISBN 0 00 225966 4 Hardback
ISBN 0 00 715146 2 Trade Paperback

Map by John Spencer

Set in PostScript Linotype Meridien with Photina display by
Rowland Phototypesetting Limited, Bury St Edmunds, Suffolk

Printed and bound in Great Britain by
Clays Ltd, St Ives plc

VAGABOND
is for
June and Eddie Bell
in friendship and gratitude

Durham
Neville's Cross
York
ENGLAND
LONDON
Dorchester
Hookton
Dunkirk
Calais
English Channel
Abbeville
Somme
Rouen
Seine
PARIS
Caen
Evecque
Poissy
Treguier
Lannion
NORMANDY
La Roche-Derrien
Guingamp
Fougères
BRITTANY
RENNES

CONTENTS

PART ONE

England, October 1346

Arrows on the Hill

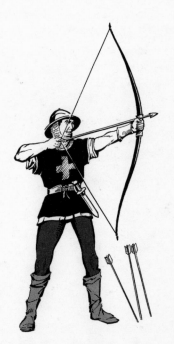

It was October, the time of the year's dying when cattle were being slaughtered before winter and when the northern winds brought a promise of ice. The chestnut leaves had turned golden, the beeches were trees of flame and the oaks were made from bronze. Thomas of Hookton, with his woman, Eleanor, and his friend, Father Hobbe, came to the upland farm at dusk and the farmer refused to open his door, but shouted through the wood that the travellers could sleep in the byre. Rain rattled on the mouldering thatch. Thomas led their one horse under the roof that they shared with a woodpile, six pigs in a stout timber pen and a scattering of feathers where a hen had been plucked. The feathers reminded Father Hobbe that it was St Gallus's day and he told Eleanor how the blessed saint, coming home in a winter's night, had found a bear stealing his dinner. 'He told the animal off!' Father Hobbe said. 'He gave it a right talking-to, he did, and then he made it fetch his firewood.'

'I've seen a picture of that,' Eleanor said. 'Didn't the bear become his servant?'

'That's because Gallus was a holy man,' Father Hobbe explained. 'Bears wouldn't fetch firewood for just anyone! Only for a holy man.'

'A holy man,' Thomas put in, 'who is the patron saint of hens.' Thomas knew all about the saints, more indeed than Father Hobbe. 'Why would a chicken want a saint?' he enquired sarcastically.

'Gallus is the patron of hens?' Eleanor asked, confused by Thomas's tone. 'Not bears?'

'Of hens,' Father Hobbe confirmed. 'Indeed of all poultry.'

'But why?' Eleanor wanted to know.

3

'Because he once expelled a wicked demon from a young girl.' Father Hobbe, broad-faced, hair like a stickleback's spines, peasant-born, stocky, young and eager, liked to tell stories of the blessed saints. 'A whole bundle of bishops had tried to drive the demon out,' he went on, 'and they had all failed, but the blessed Gallus came along and he cursed the demon. He cursed it! And it screeched in terror' – Father Hobbe waved his hands in the air to imitate the evil spirit's panic – 'and then it fled from her body, it did, and it looked just like a black hen – a pullet. A black pullet.'

'I've never seen a picture of that,' Eleanor remarked in her accented English, then, gazing out through the byre door, 'but I'd like to see a real bear carrying firewood,' she added wistfully.

Thomas sat beside her and stared into the wet dusk, which was hazed by a small mist. He was not sure it really was St Gallus's day for he had lost his reckoning while they travelled. Perhaps it was already St Audrey's day? It was October, he knew that, and he knew that one thousand, three hundred and forty-six years had passed since Christ had been born, but he was not sure which day it was. It was easy to lose count. His father had once recited all the Sunday services on a Saturday and he had had to do them again the next day. Thomas surreptitiously made the sign of the cross. He was a priest's bastard and that was said to bring bad luck. He shivered. There was a heaviness in the air that owed nothing to the setting sun nor to the rain clouds nor to the mist. God help us, he thought, but there was an evil in this dusk and he made the sign of the cross again and said a silent prayer to St Gallus and his obedient bear. There had been a dancing bear in London, its teeth nothing but rotted yellow stumps and its brown flanks matted with blood from its owner's goad. The street dogs had snarled at it, slunk about it and shrank back when the bear swung on them.

'How far to Durham?' Eleanor asked, this time speaking French, her native language.

'Tomorrow, I think,' Thomas answered, still gazing north to where the heavy dark was shrouding the land. 'She asked,' he explained in English to Father Hobbe, 'when we would reach Durham.'

'Tomorrow, pray God,' the priest said.

'Tomorrow you can rest,' Thomas promised Eleanor in French.

4

She was pregnant with a child that, God willing, would be born in the springtime. Thomas was not sure how he felt about being a father. It seemed too early for him to become responsible, but Eleanor was happy and he liked to please her and so he told her he was happy as well. Some of the time, that was even true.

'And tomorrow,' Father Hobbe said, 'we shall fetch our answers.'

'Tomorrow,' Thomas corrected him, 'we shall ask our questions.'

'God will not let us come this far to be disappointed,' Father Hobbe said, and then, to keep Thomas from arguing, he laid out their meagre supper. 'That's all that's left of the bread,' he said, 'and we should save some of the cheese and an apple for breakfast.' He made the sign of the cross over the food, blessing it, then broke the hard bread into three pieces. 'We should eat before nightfall.'

Darkness brought a brittle cold. A brief shower passed and after it the wind dropped. Thomas slept closest to the byre door and sometime after the wind died he woke because there was a light in the northern sky.

He rolled over, sat up and he forgot that he was cold, forgot his hunger, forgot all the small nagging discomforts of life, for he could see the Grail. The Holy Grail, the most precious of all Christ's bequests to man, lost these thousand years and more, and he could see it glowing in the sky like shining blood and about it, bright as the glittering crown of a saint, rays of dazzling shimmer filled the heaven.

Thomas wanted to believe. He wanted the Grail to exist. He thought that if the Grail were to be found then all the world's evil would be drained into its depths. He so wanted to believe and that October night he saw the Grail like a great burning cup in the north and his eyes filled with tears so that the image blurred, yet he could see it still, and it seemed to him that a vapour boiled from the holy vessel. Beyond it, in ranks rising to the heights of the air, were rows of angels, their wings touched by fire. All the northern sky was smoke and gold and scarlet, glowing in the night as a sign to doubting Thomas. 'Oh, Lord,' he said aloud and he threw off his blanket and knelt in the byre's cold doorway, 'oh, Lord.'

'Thomas?' Eleanor, beside him had awoken. She sat up and stared

into the night. 'Fire,' she said in French, *'c'est un grand incendie.'* Her voice was awed.

'C'est un incendie?' Thomas asked, then came fully awake and saw there was indeed a great fire on the horizon from where the flames boiled up to light a cup-shaped chasm in the clouds.

'There is an army there,' Eleanor whispered in French. 'Look!' She pointed to another glow, farther off. They had seen such lights in the sky in France, flamelight reflected from cloud where England's army blazed its way across Normandy and Picardy.

Thomas still gazed north, but now in disappointment. It was an army? Not the Grail?

'Thomas?' Eleanor was worried.

'It's just rumour,' he said. He was a priest's bastard and he had been raised on the sacred scriptures and in Matthew's Gospel it had been promised that at the end of time there would be battles and rumours of battles. The scriptures promised that the world would come to its finish in a welter of war and blood, and in the last village, where the folk had watched them suspiciously, a sullen priest had accused them of being Scottish spies. Father Hobbe had bridled at that, threatening to box his fellow priest's ears, but Thomas had calmed both men down, and then spoken with a shepherd who said he had seen smoke in the northern hills. The Scots, the shepherd said, were marching south, though the priest's woman scoffed at the tale, claiming that the Scottish troops were nothing but cattle raiders. 'Bar your door at night,' she advised, 'and they'll leave you alone.'

The far light subsided. It was not the Grail.

'Thomas?' Eleanor frowned at him.

'I had a dream,' he said, 'just a dream.'

'I felt the child move,' she said, and she touched his shoulder. 'Will you and I be married?'

'In Durham,' he promised her. He was a bastard and he wanted no child of his to carry the same taint. 'We shall reach the city tomorrow,' he reassured Eleanor, 'and you and I will marry in a church and then we shall ask our questions.' And, he prayed, let one of the answers be that the Grail did not exist. Let it be a dream, a mere trick of fire and cloud in a night sky, for else Thomas feared it would lead to madness. He wanted to abandon this search; he

wanted to give up the Grail and return to being what he was and what he wanted to be: an archer of England.

Bernard de Taillebourg, Frenchman, Dominican friar and Inquisitor, spent the autumn night in a pig pen and when dawn came thick and white with fog, he went to his knees and thanked God for the privilege of sleeping in fouled straw. Then, mindful of his high task, he said a prayer to St Dominic, begging the saint to intercede with God to make this day's work good. 'As the flame in thy mouth lights us to truth' – he spoke aloud – 'so let it light our path to success.' He rocked forward in the intensity of his emotion and his head struck against a rough stone pillar that supported one corner of the pen. Pain jabbed through his skull and he invited more by forcing his forehead back against the stone, grinding the skin until he felt the blood trickle down to his nose. 'Blessed Dominic,' he cried, 'blessed Dominic! God be thanked for thy glory! Light our way!' The blood was on his lips now and he licked it and reflected on all the pain that the saints and martyrs had endured for the Church. His hands were clasped and there was a smile on his haggard face.

Soldiers who, the night before, had burned much of the village to ash and raped the women who failed to escape and killed the men who tried to protect the women, now watched the priest drive his head repeatedly against the blood-spattered stone. 'Dominic,' Bernard de Taillebourg gasped, 'oh, Dominic!' Some of the soldiers made the sign of the cross for they recognized a holy man when they saw one. One or two even knelt, though it was awkward in their mail coats, but most just watched the priest warily, or else watched his servant who, sitting outside the sty, returned their gaze.

The servant, like Bernard de Taillebourg, was a Frenchman, but something in the younger man's appearance suggested a more exotic birth. His skin was sallow, almost as dark as a Moor's, and his long hair was sleekly black which, with his narrow face, gave him a feral look. He wore mail and a sword and, though he was nothing but a priest's servant, he carried himself with confidence

and dignity. His dress was elegant, something strange in this ragged army. No one knew his name. No one even wanted to ask, just as no one wanted to ask why he never ate or chatted with the other servants, but kept himself fastidiously apart. Now the mysterious servant watched the soldiers and in his left hand he held a knife with a very long and thin blade, and once he knew enough men were looking at him, he balanced the knife on an outstretched finger. The knife was poised on its sharp tip, which was prevented from piercing the servant's skin by the cut-off finger of a mail glove that he wore like a sheath. Then he jerked the finger and the knife span in the air, blade glittering, to come down, tip first, to balance on his finger again. The servant had not looked at the knife once, but kept his dark-eyed gaze fixed on the soldiers. The priest, oblivious to the display, was howling prayers, his thin cheeks laced with blood. 'Dominic! Dominic! Light our path!' The knife span again, its wicked blade catching the foggy morning's small light. 'Dominic! Guide us! Guide us!'

'On your horses! Mount up! Move yourselves!' A grey-haired man, a big shield slung from his left shoulder, pushed through the onlookers. 'We've not got all day! What in the name of the devil are you all gawking at? Jesus Christ on His goddamn cross, what is this, Eskdale bloody fair? For Christ's sake, move! Move!' The shield on his shoulder was blazoned with the badge of a red heart, but the paint was so faded and the shield's leather cover so scarred that the badge was hard to distinguish. 'Oh, suffering Christ!' The man had spotted the Dominican and his servant. 'Father! We're going now. Right now! And I don't wait for prayers.' He turned back to his men. 'Mount up! Move your bones! There's devil's work to be done!'

'Douglas!' the Dominican snapped.

The grey-haired man turned back fast. 'My name, priest, is Sir William, and you'll do well to remember it.'

The priest blinked. He seemed to be suffering a momentary confusion, still caught up in the ecstasy of his pain-driven prayer, then he gave a perfunctory bow as if acknowledging his fault in using Sir William's surname. 'I was talking to the blessed Dominic,' he explained.

'Aye, well, I hope you asked him to shift this damn fog?'

'And he will lead us today! He will guide us!'

'Then he'd best get his damn boots on,' Sir William Douglas, Knight of Liddesdale, growled at the priest, 'for we're leaving whether your saint is ready or not.' Sir William's chain mail was battle-torn and patched with newer rings. Rust showed at the hem and at the elbows. His faded shield, like his weather-beaten face, was scarred. He was forty-six now and he reckoned he had a sword, arrow or spear scar for each of those years that had turned his hair and short beard white. Now he pulled open the sty's heavy gate. 'On your trotters, father. I've a horse for you.'

'I shall walk,' Bernard de Taillebourg said, picking up a stout staff with a leather thong threaded through its tip, 'as our Lord walked.'

'Then you'll not get wet crossing the streams, eh, is that it?' Sir William chuckled. 'You'll walk on water will you, father? You and your servant?' Alone among his men he did not seem impressed by the French priest or wary of the priest's well-armed servant, but Sir William Douglas was famously unafraid of any man. He was a border chieftain who employed murder, fire, sword and lance to protect his land and some fierce priest from Paris was hardly likely to impress him. Sir William, indeed, was not overfond of priests, but his King had ordered him to take Bernard de Taillebourg on this morning's raid and Sir William had grudgingly consented.

All around him soldiers pulled themselves into their saddles. They were lightly armed for they expected to meet no enemies. A few, like Sir William, carried shields, but most were content with just a sword. Bernard de Taillebourg, his friar's robes mud-spattered and damp, hurried alongside Sir William. 'Will you go into the city?'

'Of course I'll not go into the bloody city. There's a truce, remember?'

'But if there's a truce . . .'

'If there's a bloody truce then we leave them be.'

The French priest's English was good, but it took him a few moments to work out what Sir William's last three words had meant. 'There'll be no fighting?'

'Not between us and the city, no. And there's no goddamned English army within a hundred miles so there'll be no fighting. All we're doing is looking for food and forage, father, food and forage. Feed your men and feed your animals and that's the way to win

9

your wars.' Sir William, as he spoke, climbed onto his horse, which was held by a squire. He pushed his boots into the stirrups, plucked the skirts of his mail coat from under his thighs and gathered the reins. 'I'll get you close to the city, father, but after that you'll have to shift for yourself.'

'Shift?' Bernard de Taillebourg asked, but Sir William had already turned away and spurred his horse down a muddy lane that ran between low stone walls. Two hundred mounted men-at-arms, grim and grey on this foggy morning, streamed after him and the priest, buffeted by their big dirty horses, struggled to keep up. The servant followed with apparent unconcern. He was evidently accustomed to being among soldiers and showed no apprehension, indeed his demeanour suggested he might be better with his weapons than most of the men who rode behind Sir William.

The Dominican and his servant had travelled to Scotland with a dozen other messengers sent to King David II by Philip of Valois, King of France. The embassy had been a cry for help. The English had burned their way across Normandy and Picardy, they had slaughtered the French King's army near a village called Crécy and their archers now held a dozen fastnesses in Brittany while their savage horsemen rode from Edward of England's ancestral possessions in Gascony. All that was bad, but even worse, and as if to show all Europe that France could be dismembered with impunity, the English King was now laying siege to the great fortress harbour of Calais. Philip of Valois was doing his best to raise the siege, but winter was coming, his nobles grumbled that their King was no warrior, and so he had appealed for aid to Scotland's King David, son of Robert the Bruce. Invade England, the French King had pleaded, and thus force Edward to abandon the siege of Calais to protect his homeland. The Scots had pondered the invitation, then were persuaded by the French King's embassy that England lay defenceless. How could it be otherwise? Edward of England's army was all at Calais or else in Brittany or Gascony, and there was no one left to defend England, and that meant the old enemy was helpless, it was asking to be raped and all the riches of England were just waiting to fall into Scottish hands.

And so the Scots had come south.

It was the largest army that Scotland had ever sent across the

border. The great lords were all there, the sons and grandsons of the warriors who had humbled England in the bloody slaughter about the Bannockburn, and those lords had brought their men-at-arms who had grown hard with incessant frontier battles, but this time, smelling plunder, they were accompanied by the clan chiefs from the mountains and islands: chiefs leading wild tribesmen who spoke a language of their own and fought like devils unleashed. They had come in their thousands to make themselves rich and the French messengers, their duty done, had sailed home to tell Philip of Valois that Edward of England would surely raise his siege of Calais when he learned that the Scots were ravaging his northern lands.

The French embassy had sailed for home, but Bernard de Taillebourg had stayed. He had business in northern England, but in the first days of the invasion he had experienced nothing except frustration. The Scottish army was twelve thousand strong, larger than the army with which Edward of England had defeated the French at Crécy, yet once across the frontier the great army had stopped to besiege a lonely fortress garrisoned by a mere thirty-eight men, and though the thirty-eight had all died, it had wasted four days. More time was spent negotiating with the citizens of Carlisle who had paid gold to have their city spared, and then the young Scottish King frittered away three more days pillaging the great priory of the Black Canons at Hexham. Now, ten days after they had crossed the frontier, and after wandering across the northern English moors, the Scottish army had at last reached Durham. The city had offered a thousand golden pounds if they could be spared and King David had given them two days to raise the money. Which meant that Bernard de Taillebourg had two days to find a way to enter the city, to which end, slipping in the mud and half blinded by the fog, he followed Sir William Douglas into a valley, across a stream and up a steep hill. 'Which way is the city?' he demanded of Sir William.

'When the fog lifts, father, I'll tell you.'

'They'll respect the truce?'

'They're holy men in Durham, father,' Sir William answered wryly, 'but better still, they're frightened men.' It had been the monks of the city who had negotiated the ransom and Sir William had advised against acceptance. If monks offered a thousand

11

pounds, he reckoned, then it would have been better to have killed the monks and taken two thousand, but King David had overruled him. David the Bruce had spent much of his youth in France and so considered himself cultured, but Sir William was not thus hampered by scruples. 'You'll be safe if you can talk your way into the city,' Sir William reassured the priest.

The horsemen had reached the hilltop and Sir William turned south along the ridge, still following a track that was edged with stone walls and which led, after a mile or so, to a deserted hamlet where four cottages, so low that their shaggy thatched roofs seemed to swell out of the straggling turf, clustered by a crossroads. In the centre of the crossroads, where the muddy ruts surrounded a patch of nettles and grass, a stone cross leaned southwards. Sir William curbed his horse beside the monument and stared at the carved dragon encircling the shaft. The cross was missing one arm. A dozen of his men dismounted and ducked into the low cottages, but they found no one and nothing, though in one cottage the embers of a fire still glowed and so they used the smouldering wood to fire the four thatched roofs. The thatch was reluctant to catch the fire for it was so damp that mushrooms grew on the mossy straw.

Sir William took his foot from the stirrup and tried to kick the broken cross over, but it would not shift. He grunted with the effort, saw Bernard de Taillebourg's disapproving expression and scowled. 'It's not holy ground, father. It's only bloody England.' He peered at the carved dragon, its mouth agape as it stretched up the stone shaft. 'Ugly bastard thing, isn't it?'

'Dragons are creatures of sin, things of the devil,' Bernard de Taillebourg said, 'so of course it is ugly.'

'A thing of the devil, eh?' Sir William kicked the cross again. 'My mother,' he explained as he gave the cross a third futile kick, 'always told me that the bloody English buried their stolen gold beneath dragons' crosses.'

Two minutes later the cross had been heaved aside and a half-dozen men were peering disappointedly into the hole it had left. Smoke from the burning roofs thickened the fog, swirled over the road and vanished into the greyness of the morning air. 'No gold,' Sir William grunted, then he summoned his men and led them southwards out of the choking smoke. He was looking for any

12

livestock that could be driven back to the Scottish army, but the fields were empty. The fire of the burning cottages was a hazed gold and red in the fog behind the raiders, a glow that slowly faded until only the smell of the fire was left and then, suddenly, hugely, filling the whole world with the alarm of its noise, a peal of bells clanged about the sky. Sir William, presuming the sound came from the east, turned through a gap in the wall into a pasture where he checked his horse and stood in the stirrups. He was listening to the sound, but in the fog it was impossible to tell where the bells were or how far away they were being tolled and then the sound stopped as suddenly as it had began. The fog was thinning now, shredding away through the orange leaves of a stand of elms. White mushrooms dotted the empty pasture where Bernard de Taillebourg dropped to his knees and began to pray aloud. 'Quiet, father!' Sir William snapped.

The priest made the sign of the cross as though imploring heaven to forgive Sir William's impiety in interrupting a prayer. 'You said there was no enemy,' he complained.

'I'm not listening for any bloody enemy,' Sir William said, 'but for animals. I'm listening for cattle bells or sheep bells.' Yet Sir William seemed strangely nervous for a man who sought only livestock. He kept twisting in his saddle, peering into the fog and scowling at the small noises of curb chains or hooves stamping on damp earth. He snarled at the men-at-arms closest to him to be silent. He had been a soldier before some of these men had even been born and he had not stayed alive by ignoring his instincts and now, in this damp fog, he smelt danger. Sense told him there was nothing to fear, that the English army was far away across the sea, but he smelt death all the same and, quite unaware of what he was doing, he pulled the shield off his shoulder and pushed his left arm through its carrying loops. It was a big shield, one made before men began adding plates of armour to their mail, a shield wide enough to screen a man's whole body.

A soldier called out from the pasture's edge and Sir William grasped his sword's hilt, then he saw that the man had only exclaimed at the sudden appearance of towers in the fog which was now little more than a mist on the ridge's top, though in the deep valleys either side the fog flowed like a white river. And across the eastern river, way off to the north where they emerged from

13

the spectral whiteness of another hill crest, was a great cathedral and a castle. They towered through the mist, vast and dark, like buildings from some doom-laden wizard's imagination, and Bernard de Taillebourg's servant, who felt he had not seen civilization in weeks, stared entranced at the two buildings. Black-robed monks crowded the tallest of the cathedral's two towers and the servant saw them pointing at the Scottish horsemen.

'Durham,' Sir William grunted. The bells, he reckoned, must have been summoning the faithful to their morning prayers.

'I have to go there!' The Dominican climbed from his knees and, seizing his staff, set off towards the mist-shrouded city.

Sir William spurred his horse in front of the Frenchman. 'What's your hurry, father?' he demanded, and de Taillebourg tried to dodge past the Scotsman, but there was a scraping sound and suddenly a blade, cold and heavy and grey, was in the Dominican's face. 'I asked you, father, what the hurry was?' Sir William's voice was as cold as his sword; then, alerted by one of his men, he glanced over and saw that the priest's servant had half drawn his own weapon. 'If your bastard man doesn't sheathe his blade, father' – Sir William spoke softly, but there was a terrible menace in his voice – 'I'll have his collops for my supper.'

De Taillebourg said something in French and the servant reluctantly pushed the blade fully home. The priest looked up at Sir William. 'Have you no fear for your mortal soul?' he asked.

Sir William smiled, paused and looked about the hilltop, but he saw nothing untoward in the shredding fog and decided his earlier nervousness had been the result of imagination. The result, perhaps, of too much beef, pork and wine the previous night. The Scots had feasted in the captured home of Durham's prior and the prior lived well, judging by his larder and cellar, but rich suppers gave men premonitions. 'I keep my own priest to worry about my soul,' Sir William said, then raised the tip of his sword to force de Taillebourg's face upwards. 'Why does a Frenchman have business with our enemies in Durham?' he demanded.

'It is Church business,' de Taillebourg said firmly.

'I don't give a damn whose business it is,' Sir William said, 'I still wish to know.'

'Obstruct me,' de Taillebourg said, pushing the sword blade away,

14

'and I shall have the King punish you and the Church condemn you and the Holy Father send your soul to eternal perdition. I shall summon—'

'Shut your goddamned bloody face!' Sir William said. 'Do you think, priest, that you can frighten me? Our King is a puppy and the Church does what its paymasters tell it to do.' He moved the blade back, this time resting it against the Dominican's neck. 'Now tell me your business. Tell me why a Frenchman stays with us instead of going home with his countrymen. Tell me what you want in Durham.'

Bernard de Taillebourg clutched the crucifix that hung about his neck and held it towards Sir William. In another man the gesture might have been taken as a display of fear, but in the Dominican it looked rather as though he threatened Sir William's soul with the powers of heaven. Sir William merely gave the crucifix a hungry glance as if appraising its value, but the cross was of plain wood while the little figure of Christ, twisted in death's agony, was only made of yellowed bone. If the figure had been made of gold then Sir William might have taken the bauble, but instead he spat in derision. A few of his men, fearing God more than their master, made the sign of the cross, but most did not care. They watched the servant closely, for he looked dangerous, but a middle-aged cleric from Paris, however fierce and gaunt he might be, did not scare them. 'So what will you do?' de Taillebourg asked Sir William scornfully. 'Kill me?'

'If I must,' Sir William said implacably. The presence of the priest with the French embassy had been a puzzle, and his staying on when the others left only compounded the mystery, but a garrulous man-at-arms, one of the Frenchmen who had brought two hundred suits of plate armour as a gift to the Scots, had told Sir William that the priest was pursuing a great treasure and if that treasure was in Durham then Sir William wanted to know. He wanted a share. 'I've killed priests before,' he told de Taillebourg, 'and another priest sold me an indulgence for the killings, so don't think I fear you or your Church. There's no sin that can't be bought off, no pardon that can't be purchased.'

The Dominican shrugged. Two of Sir William's men were behind him, their swords drawn, and he understood that these Scotsmen would indeed kill him and his servant. These men who followed

the red heart of Douglas were border ruffians, bred to battle as a hound was raised to the chase and the Dominican knew there was no point in continuing to threaten their souls for they gave no thought to such things. 'I am going into Durham,' de Taillebourg said, 'to find a man.'

'What man?' Sir William asked, his sword still at the priest's neck.

'He is a monk,' de Taillebourg explained patiently, 'and an old man now, so old that he may not even be alive. He is a Frenchman, a Benedictine, and he fled Paris many years ago.'

'Why did he run?'

'Because the King wanted his head.'

'A monk's head?' Sir William sounded sceptical.

'He was not always a Benedictine,' de Taillebourg said, 'but was once a Templar.'

'Ah.' Sir William began to understand.

'And he knows,' de Taillebourg continued, 'where a great treasure is hidden.'

'The Templar treasure?'

'It is said to be hidden in Paris,' de Taillebourg said, 'hidden for all these years, but it was only last year that we discovered the Frenchman was alive and in England. The Benedictine, you see, was once the sacrist of the Templars. You know what that is?'

'Don't patronize me, father,' Sir William said coldly.

De Taillebourg inclined his head to acknowledge the justice of the reproof. 'If any man knows where the Templar treasure is,' he went on humbly, 'it is the man who was their sacrist, and now, we hear, that man lives in Durham.'

Sir William took the sword away. Everything the priest said made sense. The Knights Templar, an order of monkish soldiers who were sworn to protect the pilgrims' roads between Christendom and Jerusalem, had become rich beyond the dreams of kings, and that was foolish for it made kings jealous and jealous kings make bad enemies. The King of France was just such an enemy and he had ordered the Templars destroyed: to which end a heresy had been cooked up, lawyers had effortlessly distorted truths and the Templars had been suppressed. Their leaders had been burned and their lands confiscated, but their treasures, the fabled treasures of the Templars, had never been found and the order's sacrist, the

man responsible for keeping those treasures safe, would surely know their fate, 'When were the Templars disbanded?' Sir William asked.

'Twenty-nine years ago,' de Taillebourg answered.

So the sacrist could yet be alive, Sir William thought. He would be an old man, but alive. Sir William sheathed his sword, utterly convinced by de Taillebourg's tale, yet none of it was true except that there was an old monk in Durham, but he was not French and he had never been a Templar and, in all probability, knew nothing of any Templar treasure. But Bernard de Taillebourg had spoken persuasively, and the story of the missing hoard was one that echoed through Europe, spoken of whenever men gathered to exchange tales of marvels. Sir William wanted the story to be true and that, more than anything, persuaded him it was. 'If you find this man,' he said to de Taillebourg, 'and if he lives, and if you then find the treasure, then it will be because we made it possible. It will be because we brought you here, and because we protected you on your journey to Durham.'

'True, Sir William,' de Taillebourg said.

Sir William was surprised by the priest's ready agreement. He frowned, shifted in his saddle and stared down at the Dominican as if gauging the priest's trustworthiness. 'So we must share in the treasure,' he demanded.

'Of course,' de Taillebourg said instantly.

Sir William was no fool. Let the priest go into Durham and he would never see the man again. Sir William twisted in his saddle and stared north towards the cathedral. The Templar treasure was said to be the gold from Jerusalem, more gold than men could dream of, and Sir William was honest enough to know that he did not possess the resources to divert some of that golden trove to Liddesdale. The King must be used. David II might be a weak lad, scarce breeched and too softened by having lived in France, but kings had resources denied to knights and David of Scotland could talk to Philip of France as a near equal, while any message from William Douglas would be ignored in Paris. 'Jamie!' he snapped at his nephew who was one of the two men guarding de Taillebourg. 'You and Dougal will take this priest back to the King.'

'You must let me go!' Bernard de Taillebourg protested.

Sir William leaned from his saddle. 'You want me to cut off your priestly balls to make myself a purse?' He smiled at the Dominican, then looked back to his nephew. 'Tell the King this French priest has news that concerns us and tell him to hold him safe till I return.' Sir William had decided that if there was an ancient French monk in Durham then he should be questioned by the King of Scotland's servants and the monk's information, if he had any, could then be sold to the French King. 'Take him, Jamie,' he commanded, 'and watch that damned servant! Take his sword.'

James Douglas grinned at the thought of a mere priest and his servant giving him trouble, but he still obeyed his uncle. He demanded that the servant yield his sword and, when the man bridled at the order, Jamie half drew his own blade. De Taillebourg sharply instructed his servant to obey and the sword was sullenly handed over. Jamie Douglas grinned as he hung the sword from his own belt. 'They'll not bother me, uncle.'

'Away with you,' Sir William said and watched as his nephew and his companion, both well mounted on fine stallions captured from the Percy lands in Northumberland, escorted the priest and his servant back towards the King's encampment. Doubtless the priest would complain to the King and David, so much weaker than his great father, would worry about the displeasure of God and the French, but David would worry a great deal more about Sir William's displeasure. Sir William smiled at that thought, then saw that some of his men on the far side of the field had dismounted. 'Who the devil told you to unhorse?' he shouted angrily, then he saw they were not his men at all, but strangers revealed by the shredding mist, and he remembered his instincts and cursed himself for wasting time on the priest.

And as he cursed so the first arrow flickered from the south. The sound it made was a hiss, feather in air, then it struck home and the noise was like a pole-axe cleaving flesh. It was a heavy thump edged with the tearing of steel in muscle and ending with the harsh scrape of blade on bone, and then a grunt from the victim and a heartbeat of silence.

And after that the scream.

*   *   *

18

Thomas of Hookton heard the bells, deep-toned and sonorous, not the sound of bells hung in some village church, but bells of thunderous power. Durham, he thought, and he felt a great weariness for the journey had been so long.

It had begun in Picardy, on a field stinking of dead men and horses, a place of fallen banners, broken weapons and spent arrows. It had been a great victory and Thomas had wondered why it left him dulled and nervous. The English had marched north to besiege Calais, but Thomas, duty bound to serve the Earl of Northampton, had received the Earl's permission to take a wounded comrade to Caen where there was a doctor of extraordinary skill. Then, however, it was decreed that no man could leave the army without the King's permission and so the Earl approached the King and thus Edward Plantagenet heard of Thomas of Hookton and how his father had been a priest who had been born to a family of French exiles called Vexille, and how it was rumoured that the Vexille family had once possessed the Grail. It was only a rumour, of course, a wisp of a story in a hard world, yet the story was of the Holy Grail and that was the most precious thing that had ever existed, if indeed it had existed; and the King had questioned Thomas of Hookton and Thomas had tried to scorn the truth of the Grail story, but then the Bishop of Durham, who had fought in the shield wall that broke the French assaults, told how Thomas's father had once been imprisoned in Durham. 'He was mad,' the bishop explained to the King, 'wits flown to the winds! So they locked him up for his own good.'

'Did he talk of the Grail?' the King asked, and the Bishop of Durham had answered that there was one man left in his diocese who might know, an old monk called Hugh Collimore who had nursed the mad Ralph Vexille, Thomas's father. The King might have dismissed the tales as so much churchly gossip had not Thomas recovered his father's heritage, the lance of St George, in the battle that had left so many dead on the green slope above the village of Crécy. The battle had also left Thomas's friend and commander Sir William Skeat wounded and he wanted to take Skeat to the doctor in Normandy, but the King had insisted that Thomas go to Durham and speak with Brother Collimore. So Eleanor's father had taken Sir William Skeat to Caen and Thomas, Eleanor and Father Hobbe

19

had accompanied a royal chaplain and a knight of King Edward's household to England, but in London the chaplain and the knight had both fallen sick with an early winter fever and so Thomas and his companions had travelled north alone and now they were close to Durham, on a foggy morning, listening to the cathedral's bells. Eleanor, like Father Hobbe, was excited for she believed that discovering the Grail would bring peace and justice to a world that stank of burned cottages. There would be no more sorrow, Eleanor thought, and no more war, and perhaps even no more sickness.

Thomas wanted to believe it. He wanted his night vision to be real, not flame and smoke, yet if the Grail existed at all he thought that it would be in some great cathedral, guarded by angels. Or else it was gone from this world, and if there was no Grail on earth then Thomas's faith was in a war bow made of Italian yew, painted black, strung with hemp, that drove an arrow made of ash, fledged with goose feathers and tipped with steel. On the bow's belly, where his left hand gripped the yew, there was a silver plate engraved with a yale, a fabulous beast of claws and horns and tusks and scales that was the badge of his father's family, the Vexilles. The yale held a cup and Thomas had been told it was the Grail. Always the Grail. It beckoned him, mocked him, bent his life, changed all, yet never appeared except in a dream of fire. It was mystery, just as Thomas's family was a mystery, but perhaps Brother Collimore could cast light on that mystery and so Thomas had come north. He might not learn of the Grail, but he expected to discover more about his family and that, at least, made the journey worthwhile.

'Which way?' Father Hobbe asked.

'God knows,' Thomas said. Fog shrouded the land.

'The bells sounded that way.' Father Hobbe pointed north and east. He was energetic, full of enthusiasm, and naïvely trusting in Thomas's sense of direction, though in truth Thomas did not know where he was. Earlier they had come to a fork in the road and he had randomly taken the left-hand track that now faded to a mere scar on the grass as it climbed. Mushrooms grew in the pasture, which was wet and heavy with dew so that their horse slipped as it climbed. The horse was Thomas's mare and it was carrying their small baggage and in one of the sacks hanging from the saddle's pommel was a letter from the Bishop of Durham to John Fossor,

the Prior of Durham. 'Most beloved brother in Christ,' the letter began, and went on to instruct Fossor to allow Thomas of Hookton and his companions to question Brother Collimore concerning Father Ralph Vexille, 'whom you will not remember for he was kept closed up in your house before you came to Durham, indeed before I came to the See, but there will be some who know of him and Brother Collimore, if it pleases God that he yet lives, will have certain knowledge of him and of the great treasure that he concealed. We request this in the name of the King and in the service of Almighty God who has blessed our arms in this present endeavour.'

'*Qu'est-ce que c'est?*' Eleanor asked, pointing up the hill where a dull reddish glow discoloured the fog.

'What?' Father Hobbe, the only one who did not speak French, asked.

'Quiet,' Thomas warned him, holding up his hand. He could smell burning and see the flicker of flames, but there were no voices. He took his bow from where it hung from the saddle and he strung it, bending the huge stave to loop the hemp string over the piece of nocked horn. He pulled an arrow from the bag and then, motioning Eleanor and Father Hobbe to stay where they were, he edged up the track to the shelter of a deep hedge where larks and finches flitted through the dying leaves. The fires were roaring, suggesting they were newly set. He crept closer, the bow half drawn, until he could see there had been three or four cottages about a crossroads and their rafters and thatch were well ablaze and sending sparks whirling up into the damp grey. The fires looked recent, but there was no one in sight: no enemy, no men in mail, so he beckoned Eleanor and Father Hobbe forward and then, over the sound of the fire, he heard a scream. It was far off, or perhaps it was close but muffled by fog, and Thomas stared through the smoke and the fog and past the seething flames and suddenly two men in mail, both mounted on black stallions, cantered into view. The horsemen had black hats, black boots and black scabbarded swords and they were escorting two other men who were on foot. One was a priest, a Dominican judging by his black and white garb, and he had a bloodied face, while the other man was tall, dressed in mail, and had long black hair and a narrow, intelligent face. The two followed the horsemen through the smoky fog, then paused at the crossroads

21

where the priest dropped to his knees and made the sign of the cross.

The leading horseman seemed irritated by the priest's prayer for he turned his horse back and, drawing his sword, prodded the blade at the kneeling man. The priest looked up and, to Thomas's astonishment, suddenly rammed his staff up into the stallion's throat. The beast twitched away and the priest slammed the staff hard at the rider's sword arm. The horseman, unbalanced by his stallion's jerking motion, tried to cut down across his body with his long blade. The second horseman was already unsaddled, though Thomas had not seen him fall, and the black-haired man in mail was astride his body with a long knife drawn. Thomas just stared in puzzlement for he was convinced that neither the two horsemen nor the priest nor the black-haired man had uttered the scream, yet no other folk were in sight. One of the two horsemen was already dead and the other now fought the priest in silence and Thomas had a sense that the conflict was unreal, that he was dreaming, that in truth this was a morality play in dumb show: the black-clad horseman was the devil and the priest was God's will and Thomas's doubts about the Grail were about to be resolved by whoever won and then Father Hobbe seized the great bow from Thomas. 'We must help!'

Yet the priest hardly needed help. He used the staff like a sword, parrying his opponent's cut, lunging hard to bruise the rider's ribs, then the man with the long black hair rammed a sword up into the horseman's back and the man arched, shivered, and his own sword dropped. He stared down at the priest for a moment, then he fell backwards from his saddle. His feet were momentarily trapped in the stirrups and the horse, panicking, galloped uphill. The killer wiped the blade of his sword, then took a scabbard from one of the dead men.

The priest had run to secure the other horse and now, sensing he was being watched, he turned to see two men and a woman in the fog. One of the men was a priest who had an arrow on a bowstring. 'They were going to kill me!' Bernard de Taillebourg protested in French. The black-haired man turned fast, the sword rising in threat.

'It's all right,' Thomas said to Father Hobbe and he took the black

22

bow away from his friend and hung it on his shoulder. God had spoken, the priest had won the fight and Thomas was reminded of his night vision when the Grail had loomed in the clouds like a cup of fire. Then he saw that under the bruises and blood the strange priest's face was hard and lean, a martyr's face, with the look of a man who had hungered for God and achieved an evident saintliness and Thomas almost fell to his knees. 'Who are you?' he called to the Dominican.

'I am a messenger.' Bernard de Taillebourg snatched at any explanation to cover his confusion. He had escaped from his Scottish escort and now he wondered how he was to escape from the tall young man with the long black bow, but then a flight of arrows hissed from the south and one thumped into a nearby elm trunk while a second skidded along the wet grass, and a horse shrieked nearby and men were shouting in disorder. Father de Taillebourg called to his servant to catch the second horse, which was trotting uphill and, by the time it was caught, de Taillebourg saw that the stranger with the bow had forgotten him and was staring south to where the arrows flew.

So he turned towards the city, called his servant to follow him and kicked back his heels.

For God, for France, for St Denis and for the Grail.

Sir William Douglas cursed. Arrows were hissing all about him. Horses were screaming and men were lying dead or injured on the grass. For a heartbeat he felt bewildered, then he realized that his forage party had blundered into an English force, but what kind of force? There was no English army nearby! The whole English army was in France, not here! Which meant, surely, that the citizens of Durham had broken their truce and that thought filled Sir William with a terrible anger. Christ, he thought, but there would not be one stone left on another when he had finished with the city, and he tugged the big shield to cover his body and spurred south towards the bowmen who were lining a low hedge. He reckoned there were not so many of them, maybe only fifty, and he still had nearly two hundred men mounted and so he roared the order to charge.

Swords scraped from scabbards. 'Kill the bastards!' Sir William shouted. 'Kill them!' He was savaging his horse with his spurs and thrusting other confused horsemen aside in his eagerness to reach the hedge. He knew the charge would be ragged, knew some of his men must die, but once they were over the blackthorn and in among the bastards they would kill them all.

Bloody archers, he thought. He hated archers. He especially hated English archers and he detested traitorous, truce-breaking Durham archers above all others. 'On! On!' he shouted. 'Douglas! Douglas!' He liked to let his enemies know who was killing them, and who would be raping their wives when they were dead. If the city had broken the truce, then God help that city for he would sack, rape and burn the whole of it. He would fire the houses, plough the ashes and leave the bones of its citizens to the winter blight, and for years men would see the bare stones of the ruined cathedral and watch the birds nesting in the castle's empty towers and they would know that the Knight of Liddesdale had worked his revenge.

'Douglas!' he shouted, 'Douglas!' and he felt the thump of arrows smacking into his shield and then his horse screamed and he knew more arrows must have driven deep into its chest for he could feel the beast stumbling. He kicked his feet from the stirrups as the horse slewed sideways. Men charged past him, screaming defiance, then Sir William threw himself out of the saddle and onto his shield that slid along the wet grass like a sledge, and he heard his horse screaming in pain, but he himself was unhurt, hardly even bruised and he pushed himself up, found his sword that he had dropped when he fell and ran on with his horsemen. A rider had an arrow sticking from his knee. A horse went down, eyes white, teeth bared, blood flecking from the arrow wounds. The first horsemen were at the hedge and some had found a gap and were spurring through and Sir William saw that the damned English bowmen were running away. Bastards, he thought, cowardly bloody English rotten whoreson bastards, then more bows sounded harsh to his left and he saw a man fall from a horse with an arrow through his head and the fog lifted enough to show that the enemy archers had not run away, but had merely joined a solid mass of dismounted men-at-arms. The bowstrings sounded again. A horse reared in pain

and an arrow sliced into its belly. A man staggered, was struck again and fell back with a crash of mail.

Sweet Christ, Sir William thought, but there was a damned army here! A whole damned army! 'Back! Back!' he bellowed. 'Haul off! Back!' He yelled till he was hoarse. Another arrow drove into his shield, its point whipping through the leather-covered willow and, in his rage, he slapped at it, breaking the ash shaft.

'Uncle! Uncle!' a man shouted and Sir William saw it was Robbie Douglas, one of his eight nephews who rode with the Scottish army, bringing him a horse, but a pair of English arrows struck the beast's quarter and, enraged by pain, it broke away from Robbie's grasp.

'Go north!' Sir William shouted at his nephew. 'Go on, Robbie!'

Instead Robbie rode to his uncle. An arrow struck his saddle, another glanced off his helmet, but he leaned down, took Sir William's hand and dragged him northwards. Arrows followed them, but the fog swirled thick and hid them. Sir William shook off his nephew's grip and stumbled north, made clumsy by his shield stuck with arrows and by his heavy mail. God damn it, God damn it!

'Mind left! Mind left!' a Scottish voice cried and Sir William saw some English horsemen coming from the hedgerow. One saw Sir William and thought he would be easy pickings. The English had been no more ready for battle than the Scotsmen. A few wore mail, but none was properly armoured and none had lances. But Sir William reckoned they must have detected his presence long before they loosed their first arrows, and the anger at being so ambushed made him step towards the horseman who was holding his sword out like a spear. Sir William did not even bother to try and parry. He just thrust his heavy shield up, punching it into the horse's mouth, and he heard the animal whinny in pain as he swept his sword at its legs and the beast twisted away and the rider was flailing for balance and was still trying to calm his horse when Sir William's sword tore up under his mail and into his guts. 'Bastard,' Sir William snarled and the man was whimpering as Sir William twisted the blade, and then Robbie rode up on the man's far side and chopped his sword down onto his neck so that the Englishman's head was all but severed as he fell from the saddle. The other horsemen had mysteriously shied away, but then arrows flew again

and Sir William knew the fickle fog was thinning. He dragged his sword free of the corpse, scabbarded the wet blade and hauled himself into the dead man's saddle. 'Away!' he shouted at Robbie who seemed inclined to take on the whole English force single-handed. 'Away, boy! Come on!'

By God, he thought, but it hurt to run from an enemy, yet there was no shame in two hundred men fleeing six or seven hundred. And when the fog lifted there could be a proper battle, a murderous clash of men and steel, and Sir William would teach these bastard English how to fight. He kicked his borrowed horse on, intent on carrying news of the English to the rest of the Scottish army, but then saw an archer lurking in a hedge. A woman and a priest were with the man and Sir William put a hand to his sword hilt and thought about swerving aside to take some revenge for the arrows that had ripped into his forage party, but behind him the other Englishmen were shouting their war cry: 'St George! St George!' and so Sir William left the isolated archer alone. He rode on, leaving good men on the autumn grass. They were dead and dying, wounded and frightened. But he was a Douglas. He would come back and he would have his revenge.

A rush of panicked horsemen galloped past the hedge where Thomas, Eleanor and Father Hobbe crouched. Half a dozen horses were riderless while at least a score of others were bleeding from wounds out of which the arrows jutted with their white goose feathers spattered red. The riders were followed by thirty or forty men on foot, some limping, some with arrows stuck in their clothes and a few carrying saddles. They hurried past the burning cottages as a new volley of arrows hastened their retreat, then the thump of hooves made them look back in panic and some of the fugitives broke into a clumsy run as a score of mail-clad horsemen thundered from the mist. Great clods of wet earth spewed up from the horses' hooves. The stallions were being curbed, forced to take brief steps as their riders took aim at their victims, then the spurs went back as the horses were released to the kill and Eleanor cried aloud in anticipation of the carnage. The heavy swords chopped down. One or two of the fugitives dropped to their knees and held their hands up in surrender, but most tried to escape. One dodged behind a galloping horseman and fled towards the hedge, saw Thomas and his bow and turned straight back into the path of another rider who drove the edge of his heavy sword into the man's face. The Scotsman went onto his knees, mouth open as though he would scream, but no sound came, only blood seeping between the fingers that were clasped over his nose and eyes. The horseman, who had no shield or helmet, turned his stallion and then leaned out of the saddle to chop his sword into his victim's neck, killing the man as if he were a cow being pole-axed and that was oddly appropriate because Thomas saw that the mounted killer was wearing the badge

27

of a brown cow on his jupon, which was a short jerkin-like coat half covering his mail hauberk. The jupon was torn, bloodstained and the cow badge had faded so that at first Thomas thought it was a bull. Then the horseman swerved towards Thomas, raised his bloody sword in threat and then noticed the bow and checked his horse. 'English?'

'And proud of it!' Father Hobbe answered for Thomas.

A second horseman, this one with three black ravens embroidered on his white jupon, reined in beside the first. Three prisoners were being pushed towards the two horsemen. 'How the devil did you get this far in front?' the newly arrived man asked Thomas.

'In front?' Thomas asked.

'Of the rest of us.'

'We walked,' Thomas said, 'from France. Or at least from London.'

'From Southampton!' Father Hobbe corrected Thomas with a pedantry that was utterly out of place on this smoke-stinking hilltop where a Scotsman writhed in his death agonies.

'France?' The first man, tangle-haired, brown-faced, and with a northern accent so thick that Thomas found it hard to understand, sounded as if he had never heard of France. 'You were in France?' he asked.

'With the King.'

'You're with us now,' the second man said threateningly, then looked Eleanor up and down. 'Did you bring the doxie back from France?'

'Yes,' Thomas replied curtly.

'He lies, he lies,' a new voice said and a third horseman pushed himself forward. He was a lanky man, maybe thirty years old, with a face so red and raw that it looked as though he had scraped his skin off with the bristles when he shaved his sunken cheeks and long jaw. His dark hair was worn long and tied at the nape of his neck with a leather lace. His horse, a scarred roan, was as thin as the rider and had white nervous eyes. 'I hate goddamn liars,' the man said, staring at Thomas, then he turned and gave a baleful glance at the prisoners, one of whom wore the red heart badge of the Knight of Liddesdale on his jupon. 'Almost as much as I hate goddamn Douglases.'

The newcomer wore a padded gambeson in place of a hauberk or haubergeon. It was the kind of protection an archer might wear if he could afford nothing better, yet this man plainly outranked archers for he wore a gold chain about his neck, a mark of distinction reserved for the gentry and above. A battered pig-snouted helmet, as scarred as the horse, hung from his saddle's pommel, a sword, plainly scabbarded in leather was at his hip, while a shield, painted white with a black axe, hung from his left shoulder. He also had a coiled whip hanging at his belt. 'The Scots have archers,' the man said, looking at Thomas, then his unfriendly gaze moved on to Eleanor, 'and they have women.'

'I'm English,' Thomas insisted.

'We're all English,' Father Hobbe said firmly, forgetting that Eleanor was a Norman.

'A Scotsman would say he was English if it stopped him from being gutted,' the raw-faced man said caustically. The other two horsemen had fallen back, evidently wary of the thin man who now uncoiled the leather whip and, with a casual skill, flicked it so that the tip snaked out and cracked the air an inch or so from Eleanor's face. 'Is she English?'

'She's French,' Thomas said.

The horseman did not answer straightaway, but just stared at Eleanor. The whip rippled as his hand trembled. He saw a fair, slight girl with golden hair and large, frightened eyes. Her pregnancy did not show yet and there was a delicacy to her that spoke of luxury and rare delight. 'Scot, Welsh, French, what does it matter?' the man asked. 'She's a woman. Do you care where a horse was born before you ride it?' His own scarred and thin horse became frightened just then because the veering wind blew a sour gust of smoke to its nostrils. It stepped sideways in a series of small, nervous steps until the man drove his spurs back so savagely that he pierced the padded trapper and made the destrier stand shivering in fear. 'What she is' – the man spoke to Thomas and pointed his whip handle at Eleanor – 'don't matter, but you're a Scot.'

'I'm English,' Thomas said again. A dozen other men wearing the badge of the black axe had come to gaze at Thomas and his companions. The men surrounded the three Scottish prisoners who seemed to know who the horseman with the whip was and did not

29

like the knowledge. More bowmen and men-at-arms watched the cottages burning and laughed at the panicked rats that scrambled from what was left of the collapsed mossy thatch.

Thomas took an arrow from his bag and immediately four or five archers wearing the black-axe livery put arrows on their own strings. The other men in the axe livery grinned expectantly as if they knew this game and enjoyed it, but before it could be played out the horseman was distracted by one of the Scottish prisoners, the man wearing Sir William Douglas's badge who, taking advantage of his captors' interest in Thomas and Eleanor, had broken free and run northwards. He had not gone twenty paces before he was ridden down by one of the English men-at-arms and the thin man, amused by the Scotsman's desperate bid for freedom, pointed at one of the burning cottages. 'Warm the bastard up,' he ordered. 'Dickon! Beggar!' He spoke to two dismounted men-at-arms. 'Look after those three.' He nodded towards Thomas. 'Watch 'em close!'

Dickon, the younger of the two, was round-faced and grinning, but Beggar was an enormous man, a shambling giant with a face so bearded that his nose and eyes alone could be seen through the tangled, crusted hair beneath the brim of the rusted iron cap that served as a helmet. Thomas was six feet in height, the length of a bow, but he was dwarfed by Beggar whose vast chest strained at a leather jerkin studded with metal plates. At the giant's waist, suspended by two lengths of rope, were a sword and a morningstar. The sword had no scabbard and its edge was chipped, while one of the spikes on the big metal ball of the morningstar was bent and smeared with blood and hair. The weapon's three-foot haft banged against the giant's bare legs as he lurched towards Eleanor. 'Pretty,' he said, 'pretty.'

'Beggar! Down, boy! Down!' Dickon ordered cheerfully and Beggar dutifully twitched away from Eleanor, though he still gazed at her and made a low growling noise in his throat. Then a scream made him look towards the nearest burning cottage where the Scotsman, stripped naked now, had been thrust in and out of the fire. The prisoner's long hair was alight and he frantically beat at the flames as he ran in panicked circles to the amusement of his English captors. Two other Scottish prisoners were squatting nearby, held on the ground by drawn swords.

The thin horseman watched as an archer swathed the prisoner's hair in a piece of sacking to extinguish the flames. 'How many of you are there?' the thin man asked.

'Thousands!' the Scotsman answered defiantly.

The horseman leaned on his saddle's pommel. 'How many thousands, cully?'

The Scotsman, his beard and hair smoking and his naked skin blackened by embers and lacerated by cuts, did his best to look defiant. 'More than enough to take you back home in a cage.'

'He shouldn't say that to Scarecrow!' Dickon said, amused. 'He shouldn't say that!'

'Scarecrow?' Thomas asked. It seemed an appropriate nickname for the horseman with the black axe badge was lean, poor and frightening.

'He be Sir Geoffrey Carr to you, cully,' Dickon said, watching the Scarecrow admiringly.

'And who is Sir Geoffrey Carr?' Thomas asked.

'He be Scarecrow and he be Lord of Lackby,' Dickon said in a tone which suggested everyone knew who Sir Geoffrey Carr was, 'and he be having his Scarecrow games now!' Dickon grinned because Sir Geoffrey, the whip coiled at his waist again, had dropped down from his horse and with a drawn knife, approached the Scottish prisoner.

'Hold him down,' Sir Geoffrey ordered the archers, 'hold him down and spread his legs.'

'*Non!*' Eleanor cried in protest.

'Pretty,' Beggar said in his voice that rumbled deep inside his huge chest.

The Scotsman screamed and tried to pull himself away, but he was tripped, then held down by three archers while the man evidently known throughout the north as the Scarecrow knelt between his legs. Somewhere in the clearing fog a raven cawed. A handful of archers was staring north in case the Scots returned, but most were watching the Scarecrow and his knife. 'You want to keep your shrivelled collops?' Sir Geoffrey asked the Scotsman. 'Then tell me how many there are of you.'

'Fifteen thousand? Sixteen?' The Scotsman was suddenly eager to talk.

'He means ten or eleven thousand,' Sir Geoffrey announced to the listening archers, 'which is more than enough for our few arrows. And is your bastard King here?'

The Scotsman bridled at that, but a touch of the knife blade to his groin reminded him of his predicament. 'David Bruce is here, aye.'

'Who else?'

The desperate Scotsman named his army's other leaders. The King's half-brother and heir to his throne, Lord Robert Stewart, was with the invading army, as were the Earls of Moray, of March, of Wigtown, Fife and Menteith. He named others, clan chiefs and wild men from the wastelands of the far north, but Carr was more interested in two of the earls. 'Fife and Menteith?' he asked. 'They're here?'

'Aye, sir, they are.'

'But they swore fealty to King Edward,' Sir Geoffrey said, evidently disbelieving the man.

'They march with us now,' the Scotsman insisted, 'as does Douglas of Liddesdale.'

'That ripe bastard,' Sir Geoffrey said, 'that shit of hell.' He stared northwards through the fog shredding from the ridge, which was being revealed as a narrow and rocky plateau running north and south. The pasture on the plateau was thin and the ridge's weathered stone protruded through the grass like the ribs of a starving man. Off to the north-east, beyond the valley of mist, the cathedral and castle of Durham reared up on their river-lapped crag, while to the west were hills and woods and stone-walled fields cut with small streams. Two buzzards sailed above the ridge, going towards the Scottish army that was still concealed by the fog which lingered to the north, but Thomas was thinking that it would not be long before troops came to find the men who had run their fellow Scots away from the crossroads.

Sir Geoffrey leaned back and went to return his knife to its scabbard, then seemed to remember something and grinned at the prisoner. 'You were going to take me back to Scotland in a cage, is that right?'

'No!'

'But you were! And why would I want to see Scotland? I can

32

peer down a jakes whenever I want.' He spat at the prisoner then nodded at the archers. 'Hold him.'

'No!' the Scotsman shouted, then the shout turned to a terrible scream as Sir Geoffrey leaned forward with the knife again. The prisoner twitched and heaved as the Scarecrow, the front of his padded gambeson now sheeted with blood, stood up. The prisoner was still screaming, hands clutched to his bloody groin, and the sight brought a smile to the Scarecrow's lips. 'Throw the rest of him into the fire,' he said, then turned to look at the other two Scottish prisoners. 'Who is your master?' he demanded of them.

They hesitated, then one licked his lips. 'We serve Douglas,' he said proudly.

'I hate Douglas. I hate every Douglas that ever dropped out of the devil's backside.' Sir Geoffrey shuddered, then turned to his horse. 'Burn them both,' he ordered.

Thomas, looking away from the sudden blood, had seen a stone cross fallen at the crossroad's centre. He stared at it, not seeing the carved dragon, but hearing the echoes of the noise and then the new screams as the prisoners were hurled into the flames. Eleanor ran to him and held his arm tight.

'Pretty,' Beggar said.

'Here, Beggar, here!' Sir Geoffrey called. 'Hoist me!' The giant made a step with his hands and Sir Geoffrey used it to climb into his saddle, then he kicked the horse towards Thomas and Eleanor. 'I'm always hungry,' Sir Geoffrey said, 'after a gelding.' He turned to watch the fire where one of the Scotsmen, hair flaming, tried to escape, but was prodded back into the inferno by a dozen bowstaves. The man's howl was abruptly cut short as he collapsed. 'I'm in the mood to geld and burn Scotsmen today,' Sir Geoffrey said, 'and you look like a Scot to me, boy.'

'I'm not a boy,' Thomas said, the anger rising in him.

'You look like a bloody boy to me, boy. A Scots boy, maybe?' Sir Geoffrey, plainly amused by Thomas's temper, grinned at his newest victim who did indeed look young, though Thomas was twenty-two summers old and had fought for the last four of them in Brittany, Normandy and Picardy. 'You look Scots, boy,' the Scarecrow said, daring Thomas to defy him again. 'All the Scots are black!' he appealed to the crowd to judge Thomas's complexion, and it was

true that Thomas had a sun-darkened skin and black hair, but so did a score or more of the Scarecrow's own archers. And though Thomas looked young he also looked hard. His hair was cropped close to his skull and four years of war had hollowed his cheeks, but there was still something distinctive in his looks, a handsomeness that attracted the eye and served to spur Sir Geoffrey Carr's jealousy. 'What's on your horse?' Sir Geoffrey jerked his head towards Thomas's mare.

'Nothing of yours,' Thomas said.

'What's mine is mine, boy, and what's yours is mine if I want it. Mine to take or mine to give. Beggar! You want that girl?'

Beggar grinned behind his beard and jerked his head up and down. 'Pretty,' he said. He scratched at the lice in his beard. 'Beggar likes pretty.'

'I reckon you can have the pretty when I'm through with her,' Sir Geoffrey said with a grin and he took the whip from where it hung at his waist and cracked it in the air. Thomas saw that the long leather thong had a small iron claw at its end. Sir Geoffrey grinned at Thomas again, then drew back the whip as a threat. 'Strip her, Beggar,' he said, 'let's give the boys a bit of pleasure,' and he was still grinning as Thomas swung his heavy bowstave hard into the teeth of Sir Geoffrey's horse and the animal reared up, screaming, as Thomas knew it would, and the Scarecrow, unready for the motion, fell backwards, flailing for balance, and his men, who should have protected him, were so intent on the burning Scottish prisoners that not one drew a bow or a blade before Thomas had dragged Sir Geoffrey down from the saddle and had him on the ground with a knife at his throat.

'I've been killing men for four years,' Thomas said, 'and not all of them were Frenchmen.'

'Thomas!' Eleanor screamed.

'Take her, Beggar! Take her!' Sir Geoffrey shouted. He heaved up, but Thomas was an archer and years of drawing his big black bow had given him extraordinary strength in the arms and chest and Sir Geoffrey could not budge him, so he spat at Thomas instead. 'Take her, Beggar!' he yelled again.

The Scarecrow's men ran towards their master, but checked when they saw that Thomas had a knife at his captive's throat.

'Strip her, Beggar! Strip the pretty! We'll all have her!' Sir Geoffrey bawled, apparently oblivious of the blade at his gullet.

'Who reads here? Who reads?' Father Hobbe bellowed. The odd question checked everyone, even Beggar who had already snatched off Eleanor's hat and now had his huge left arm around her neck while his right hand gripped the neckline of her frock. 'Who in this company can read?' Father Hobbe demanded again as he brandished the parchment he had taken from one of the sacks on the back of Thomas's horse. 'This is a letter from my lord the Bishop of Durham who is with our lord the King in France and it is sent to John Fossor, Prior of Durham, and only Englishmen who have fought with our King would carry such a letter. We have brought it from France.'

'It proves nothing!' Sir Geoffrey shouted, then spat at Thomas again as the blade was pressed hard into his throat.

'And in what language is this letter written?' A new horseman had spurred through the Scarecrow's men. He wore no surcoat or jupon, but the badge on his battered shield was a scallop shell on a cross and it proclaimed that he was not one of Sir Geoffrey's followers. 'What language?' he asked once more.

'Latin,' Thomas said, his knife still pressing hard into Sir Geoffrey's neck.

'Let Sir Geoffrey up,' the newcomer commanded Thomas, 'and I shall read the letter.'

'Tell him to let my woman go,' Thomas snarled.

The horseman looked surprised at being given an order by a mere archer, but he did not protest. Instead he urged his horse towards Beggar. 'Let her go,' he said and, when the big man did not obey, he half drew his sword. 'You want me to crop your ears, Beggar? Is that it? Two ears gone? Then your nose, then your cock, is that what you want, Beggar? You want to be shorn like a summer ewe? Trimmed down like an elf?'

'Let her go, Beggar,' Sir Geoffrey said sullenly.

Beggar obeyed and stepped back and the horseman leaned down from his saddle to take the letter from Father Hobbe. 'Let Sir Geoffrey go,' the newcomer ordered Thomas, 'for we shall have peace between Englishmen today, at least for a day.'

The horseman was an old man, at least fifty years old, with a

great shock of white hair that looked as though it had never been close to a brush or comb. He was a large man, tall and big-bellied, on a sturdy horse that had no trapper, but only a tattered saddle cloth. The man's full-length mail coat was sadly rusted in places and torn in others, while over the coat he had a breastplate that had lost two of its straps. A long sword hung at his right thigh. He looked to Thomas like a yeoman farmer who had ridden to war with whatever equipment his neighbours could lend him, but he had been recognized by Sir Geoffrey's archers who had snatched off their hats and helmets when he appeared and who now treated him with deference. Even Sir Geoffrey seemed cowed by the white-haired man who frowned as he read the letter. 'Thesaurus, eh?' He was speaking to himself. 'And a fine kettle of fish that is! A thesaurus indeed!' Thesaurus was Latin, but the rest of his words were spoken in Norman French and he was evidently confident that no archer would understand him.

'Mention of treasure' – Thomas used the same language, which had been taught to him by his father – 'makes men excited. Over-excited.'

'Good Lord above, good Lord indeed, you speak French! Miracles never cease. Thesaurus, it does mean treasure, doesn't it? My Latin is not what it was when I was young. I had it flogged into me by a priest and it seems to have mostly leaked out since. A treasure, eh? And you speak French!' The horseman showed genial surprise that Thomas spoke the language of aristocrats, though Sir Geoffrey, who did not speak French, looked alarmed for it suggested Thomas might be a good deal better born than he had thought. The horse-man gave the letter back to Father Hobbe, then spurred to Sir Geoffrey. 'You were picking a squabble with an Englishman, Sir Geoffrey, a messenger, no less, from our lord the King. How do you explain that?'

'I don't have to explain anything,' Sir Geoffrey said, 'my lord.' The last two words were added reluctantly.

'I should fillet you now,' his lordship said mildly, 'then have you stuffed and mounted on a pole to scare the crows away from my newly born lambs. I could show you at Skipton Fair, Sir Geoffrey, as an example to other sinners.' He seemed to consider that idea for a few heartbeats, then shook his head. 'Just get on your horse,'

36

he said, 'and fight the Scots today instead of quarrelling with your fellow Englishman.' He turned in his saddle and raised his voice so all the archers and men-at-arms could hear him. 'All of you, back down the ridge! And quick, before the Scots come and drive you off! You want to join those rascals in the fire?' He pointed to the three Scottish prisoners who were now nothing but dark shrivelled shapes in the bright flames, then he beckoned Thomas and changed his language to French. 'You've really come from France?'

'Yes, my lord.'

'Then do me the courtesy, my dear fellow, of speaking with me.'

They went south, leaving a broken stone cross, burned men and arrow-struck corpses in a thinning mist, where the army of Scotland had come to Durham.

Bernard de Taillebourg took the crucifix from about his neck and kissed the writhing figure of Christ that was pinned to the small wooden cross. 'God be with you, my brother,' he murmured to the old man lying on the stone bench cushioned by a palliasse of straw and a folded blanket. A second blanket, just as thin, covered the old man whose hair was white and wispy.

'It is cold,' Brother Hugh Collimore said feebly, 'so cold.' He spoke in French, though to de Taillebourg the old monk's accent was barbarous for it was the French of Normandy and of England's Norman rulers.

'Winter comes,' de Taillebourg said. 'You can smell it on the wind.'

'I am dying' – Brother Collimore turned his red-rimmed eyes on his visitor – 'and can smell nothing. Who are you?'

'Take this,' de Taillebourg said and gave his crucifix to the old monk, then he stoked up the wood fire, put two more logs on the revived blaze and sniffed a jug of mulled wine that sat in the hearth. It was not too rank and so he poured some into a horn cup. 'At least you have a fire,' he said, stooping to peer through the small window, no bigger than an arrow slit, that faced west across the encircling Wear. The monk's hospital was on the slope of Durham's

hill, beneath the cathedral, and de Taillebourg could see the Scottish men-at-arms carrying their lances through the straggling remnants of mist on the skyline. Few of the mail-clad men had horses, he noticed, suggesting that the Scots planned to fight on foot.

Brother Collimore, his face pale and his voice frail, gripped the small cross. 'The dying are allowed a fire,' he said, as though he had been accused of indulging himself in luxury. 'Who are you?'

'I come from Cardinal Bessières,' de Taillebourg said, 'in Paris, and he sends you his greetings. Drink this, it will warm you.' He held the mulled wine towards the old man.

Collimore refused the wine. His eyes were cautious. 'Cardinal Bessières?' he asked, his tone implying that the name was new to him.

'The Pope's legate in France.' De Taillebourg was surprised that the monk did not recognize the name, but thought perhaps the dying man's ignorance would be useful. 'And the Cardinal is a man,' the Dominican went on, 'who loves the Church as fiercely as he loves God.'

'If he loves the Church,' Collimore said with a surprising force, 'then he will use his influence to persuade the Holy Father to take the papacy back to Rome.' The statement exhausted him and he closed his eyes. He had never been a big man, but now, beneath his lice-ridden blanket, he seemed to have shrunk to the size of a ten-year-old and his white hair was thin and fine like a small infant's. 'Let him move the papacy to Rome,' he said again, though feebly, 'for all our troubles have worsened since it was moved to Avignon.'

'Cardinal Bessières wants nothing more than to move the Holy Father back to Rome,' de Taillebourg lied, 'and perhaps you, brother, can help us achieve that.'

Brother Collimore appeared not to hear the words. He had opened his eyes again, but just lay gazing up at the whitewashed stones of the arched ceiling. The room was low, chill and white. Sometimes, when the summer sun was high, he could see the flicker of reflected water on the white stones. In heaven, he thought, he would be forever within sight of crystal rivers and under a warm sun. 'I was in Rome once,' he said wistfully. 'I remember going

down some steps into a church where a choir sang. So beautiful.'

'The Cardinal wants your help,' de Taillebourg said.

'There was a saint there.' Collimore was frowning, trying to remember. 'Her bones were yellow.'

'So the Cardinal sent me to see you, brother,' de Taillebourg said softly. His servant, dark-eyed and elegant, watched from the door.

'Cardinal Bessières,' Brother Collimore said in a whisper.

'He sends you his greetings in Christ, brother.'

'What Bessières wants,' Collimore said, still in a whisper, 'he takes with whips and scorpions.'

De Taillebourg half smiled. So Collimore did know of Cardinal Bessières after all, and no wonder, but perhaps fear of Bessières would be sufficient to elicit the truth. The monk had closed his eyes again and his lips were moving silently, suggesting he was praying. De Taillebourg did not disturb the prayers, but just gazed through the small window to where the Scots were making their battle line on the far hill. The invaders faced southwards so that the left end of their line was nearest to the city and de Taillebourg could see men jostling for position as they tried to take the places of honour closest to their lords. The Scots had evidently decided to fight on foot so that the English archers could not destroy their men-at-arms by cutting down their horses. There was no sign of those English yet, though from all de Taillebourg had heard they could not have assembled a great force. Their army was in France, outside Calais, not here, so perhaps it was merely a local lord leading his retainers? Yet plainly there were enough men to persuade the Scots to form a battle line, and de Taillebourg did not expect David's army to be delayed for long. Which meant that if he wanted to hear the old man's story and be away from Durham before the Scots entered the city then he had best make haste. He looked back at the monk, 'Cardinal Bessières wants only the glory of the Church and of God. And he wants to know about Father Ralph Vexille.'

'Dear God,' Collimore said, and his fingers traced the bone figure on the small crucifix as he opened his eyes and turned his head to stare at the priest. The monk's expression suggested it was the first time he had really noticed de Taillebourg and he shuddered, recognizing in his visitor a man who believed suffering gave merit.

A man, Collimore reflected, who would be as implacable as his master in Paris. 'Vexille!' Collimore said, as though he had almost forgotten the name, and then he sighed. 'It is a long tale,' he said tiredly.

'Then I will tell you what I know of it,' de Taillebourg said. The gaunt Dominican was pacing the room now, turning and turning again in the small space under the highest part of the arched ceiling. 'You have heard,' he demanded, 'that a battle was fought in Picardy in the summer? Edward of England fought his cousin of France and a man came from the south to fight for France and on his banner was the device of a yale holding a cup.' Collimore blinked, but said nothing. His eyes were fixed on de Taillebourg who, in turn, stopped his pacing to look at the priest. 'A yale holding a cup,' he repeated.

'I know the beast,' Collimore said sadly. A yale was an heraldic animal, unknown in nature, clawed like a lion, horned like a goat and scaled like a dragon.

'He came from the south,' de Taillebourg said, 'and he thought that by fighting for France he would wash from his family's crest the ancient stains of heresy and of treason.' Brother Collimore was far too sick to see that the priest's servant was now listening intently, almost fiercely, or to notice that the Dominican had raised his voice slightly to make it easier for the servant, who still stood in the doorway, to overhear. 'This man came from the south, riding in pride, believing his soul to be beyond reproof, but no man is beyond God's reach. He thought he would ride in victory into the King's affections, but instead he shared France's defeat. God will sometimes humble us, brother, before raising us to glory.' De Taillebourg spoke to the old monk, but his words were for his servant's ears. 'And after the battle, brother, when France wept, I found this man and he talked of you.'

Brother Collimore looked startled, but said nothing.

'He talked of you,' Father de Taillebourg said, 'to me. And I am an Inquisitor.'

Brother Collimore's fingers fluttered in an attempt to make the sign of the cross. 'The Inquisition,' he said feebly, 'has no authority in England.'

'The Inquisition has authority in heaven and in hell, and you

think little England can stand against us?' The fury in de Taille-bourg's voice echoed in the hospital cell. 'To root out heresy, brother, we will ride to the ends of the earth.'

The Inquisition, like the Dominican order of friars, was dedicated to the eradication of heresy, and to do it they employed fire and pain. They could not shed blood, for that was against the law of the Church, but any pain inflicted without blood-letting was per-mitted, and the Inquisition knew well that fire cauterized bleeding and that the rack did not pierce a heretic's skin and that great weights pressed on a man's chest burst no veins. In cellars reeking of fire, fear, urine and smoke, in a darkness shot through with flamelight and the screams of heretics, the Inquisition hunted down the enemies of God and, by the application of bloodless pain, brought their souls into a blessed unity with Christ.

'A man came from the south,' de Taillebourg said to Collimore again, 'and the crest on his shield was a yale holding a cup.'

'A Vexille,' Collimore said.

'A Vexille,' de Taillebourg said, 'who knew your name. Now why, brother, would a heretic from the southern lands know the name of an English monk in Durham?'

Brother Collimore sighed. 'They all knew,' he said tiredly, 'the whole family knew. They knew because Ralph Vexille was sent to me. The bishop thought I could cure him of madness, but his family feared he would tell me secrets instead. They wanted him dead, but we locked him away in a cell where no one but I could reach him.'

'And what secrets did he tell you?' de Taillebourg asked.

'Madness,' Brother Collimore said, 'just madness.' The servant stood in the doorway and watched him.

'Tell me of the madness,' the Dominican ordered.

'The mad speak of a thousand things,' Brother Collimore said, 'they speak of spirits and phantoms, of snow in summer and dark-ness in the daylight.'

'But Father Ralph spoke to you of the Grail,' de Taillebourg said flatly.

'He spoke of the Grail,' Brother Collimore confirmed.

The Dominican let out a sigh of relief. 'What did he tell you of the Grail?'

Hugh Collimore said nothing for a while. His chest rose and fell so feebly that the motion was scarcely visible, then he shook his head. 'He told me that his family had owned the Grail and that he had stolen and hidden it! But he spoke of a hundred such things. A hundred such things.'

'Where would he have hidden it?' de Taillebourg enquired.

'He was mad. Mad. It was my job, you know, to look after the mad? We starved or beat them to drive the devils out, but it did not always work. In winter we would plunge them into the river, through the ice, and that worked. Devils hate the cold. It worked with Ralph Vexille, or mostly it worked. We released him after a while. The demons were gone, you see.'

'Where did he hide the Grail?' De Taillebourg's voice was harder and louder.

Brother Collimore stared at the flicker of reflected water light on the ceiling. 'He was mad,' he whispered, 'but he was harmless. Harmless. And when he left here he was sent to a parish in the south. In the far south.'

'At Hookton in Dorset?'

'At Hookton in Dorset,' Brother Collimore agreed, 'where he had a son. He was a great sinner, you see, even though he was a priest. He had a son.'

Father de Taillebourg stared at the monk who had, at last, given him some news. A son? 'What do you know of the son?'

'Nothing.' Brother Collimore sounded surprised that he should be asked.

'And what do you know of the Grail?' de Taillebourg probed.

'I know that Ralph Vexille was mad,' Collimore said in a whisper.

De Taillebourg sat on the hard bed. 'How mad?'

Collimore's voice became even softer. 'He said that even if you found the Grail then you would not know it, not unless you were worthy.' He paused and a look of puzzlement, almost amazement, showed briefly on his face. 'You had to be worthy, he said, to know what the Grail was, but if you were worthy then it would shine like the very sun. It would dazzle you.'

De Taillebourg leaned close to the monk. 'You believed him?'

'I believe Ralph Vexille was mad,' Brother Collimore said.

'The mad sometimes speak truth,' de Taillebourg said.

42

'I think,' Brother Collimore went on as though the Inquisitor had not spoken, 'that God gave Ralph Vexille a burden too great for him to bear.'

'The Grail?' de Taillebourg asked.

'Could you bear it? I could not.'

'So where is it?' de Taillebourg persisted. 'Where is it?'

Brother Collimore looked puzzled again. 'How would I know?'

'It was not at Hookton,' de Taillebourg said, 'Guy Vexille searched for it.'

'Guy Vexille?' Brother Collimore asked.

'The man who came from the south, brother, to fight for France and ended in my custody.'

'Poor man,' the monk said.

Father de Taillebourg shook his head. 'I merely showed him the rack, let him feel the pincers and smell the smoke. Then I offered him life and he told me all he knew and he told me the Grail was not at Hookton.'

The old monk's face twitched in a smile. 'You did not hear me, father. If a man is unworthy then the Grail would not reveal itself. Guy Vexille could not have been worthy.'

'But Father Ralph did possess it?' De Taillebourg sought reassurance. 'You think he really possessed it?'

'I did not say as much,' the monk said.

'But you believe he did?' de Taillebourg asked and, when Brother Collimore said nothing, he nodded to himself. 'You do believe he did.' He slipped off the bed, going to his knees and a look of awe came to his face as his linked hands clawed at each other. 'The Grail,' he said in a tone of utter wonder.

'He was mad,' Brother Collimore warned him.

De Taillebourg was not listening. 'The grail,' he said again, '*le Graal*!' He was clutching himself now, rocking back and forth in ecstasy. '*Le Graal*!'

'The mad say things,' Brother Collimore said, 'and they do not know what they say.'

'Or God speaks through them,' de Taillebourg said fiercely.

'Then God sometimes has a terrible tongue,' the old monk replied.

'You must tell me,' de Taillebourg insisted, 'all that Father Ralph told you.'

43

'But it was so long ago!'

'It is *le Graal*!' de Taillebourg shouted and, in his frustration, he shook the old man. 'It is *le Graal*! Don't tell me you have forgotten.' He glanced through the window and saw, raised on the far ridge, the red saltire on the yellow banner of the Scottish King and beneath it a mass of grey-mailed men with their thicket of lances, pikes and spears. No English foe was in sight, but de Taillebourg would not have cared if all the armies of Christendom were come to Durham for he had found his vision, it was the Grail, and though the world should tremble with armies all about him, he would pursue it.

And an old monk talked.

The horseman with the rusted mail, broken-strapped breastplate and scallop-decorated shield named himself as Lord Outhwaite of Witcar. 'Do you know the place?' he asked Thomas.

'Witcar, my lord? I've not heard of it.'

'Not heard of Witcar! Dear me. And it's such a pleasant place, very pleasant. Good soil, sweet water, fine hunting. Ah, there you are!' This last was to a small boy mounted on a large horse and leading a second destrier by the reins. The boy wore a jupon that had the scalloped cross emblazoned in yellow and red and, tugging the warhorse behind him, he spurred towards his master.

'Sorry, my lord,' the boy said, 'but Hereward do haul away, he do.' Hereward was evidently the destrier he led. 'And he hauled me clean away from you!'

'Give him to this young man here,' Lord Outhwaite said. 'You can ride?' he added earnestly to Thomas.

'Yes, my lord.'

'Hereward is a handful though, a rare handful. Kick him hard to let him know who's master.'

A score of men appeared in Lord Outhwaite's livery, all mounted and all with armour in better repair than their master's. Lord Outhwaite turned them back south. 'We were marching on Durham,' he told Thomas, 'just minding our own affairs as good Christians should, and the wretched Scots appeared! We won't

make Durham now. I was married there, you know? In the cathedral. Thirty-two years ago, can you credit it?' He beamed happily at Thomas. 'And my dear Margaret still lives, God be praised. She'd like to hear your tale. You really were at Wadicourt?'

'I was, my lord.'

'Fortunate you, fortunate you!' Lord Outhwaite said, then hailed yet more of his men to turn them about before they blundered into the Scots. Thomas was rapidly coming to realize that Lord Outhwaite, despite his ragged mail and dishevelled appearance, was a great lord, one of the magnates of the north country, and his lordship confirmed this opinion by grumbling that he had been forbidden by the King to fight in France because he and his men might be needed to fend off an invasion by the Scots. 'And he was quite right!' Lord Outhwaite sounded surprised. 'The wretches have come south! Did I tell you my eldest boy was in Picardy? That's why I'm wearing this.' He plucked at a rent in the old mail coat. 'I gave him the best armour we had because I thought we wouldn't need it here! Young David of Scotland always seemed peaceable enough to me, but now England's overrun by his fellows. Is it true that the slaughter at Wadicourt was vast?'

'It was a field of dead, my lord.'

'Theirs, not ours, God and His saints be thanked.' His lordship looked across at some archers straggling southwards. 'Don't dawdle!' he called in English. 'The Scots will be looking for you soon enough.' He looked back to Thomas and grinned. 'So what would you have done if I hadn't come along?' he asked, still using English. 'Cut the Scarecrow's throat?'

'If I had to.'

'And had your own slit by his men,' Lord Outhwaite observed cheerfully. 'He's a poisonous tosspot. God only knows why his mother didn't drown him at birth, but then she was a goddamned turd-hearted witch if ever there was one.' Like many lords who had grown up speaking French, Lord Outhwaite had learned his English from his parents' servants and so spoke it coarsely. 'He deserves a slit throat, the Scarecrow does, but he's a bad enemy to have. He holds a grudge better than any man alive, but he has so many grudges that maybe he don't have room for one more. He hates Sir William Douglas most of all.'

45

'Why?'

'Because Willie had him prisoner. Mind you, Willie Douglas has held most of us prisoner at one time or another and one or two of us have even held him in return, but the ransom near killed Sir Geoffrey. He's down to his last score of retainers and I'd be surprised if he's got more than three halfpennies in a pot. The Scarecrow's a poor man, very poor, but he's proud, and that makes him a bad enemy to have.' Lord Outhwaite paused to raise a genial hand to a group of archers wearing his livery. 'Wonderful fellows, wonderful. So tell me about the battle at Wadicourt. Is it true that the French rode down their own archers?'

'They did, my lord. Genoese crossbowmen.'

'So tell me all that happened.'

Lord Outhwaite had received a letter from his eldest son that told of the battle in Picardy, but he was desperate to hear of the fight from someone who had stood on that long green slope between the villages of Wadicourt and Crécy, and Thomas now told how the enemy had attacked late in the afternoon and how the arrows had flown down the hill to cut the King of France's great army into heaps of screaming men and horses, and how some of the enemy had still come through the line of newly dug pits and past the arrows to hack at the English men-at-arms, and how, by the battle's end, there were no arrows left, just archers with bleeding fingers and a long hill of dying men and animals. The very sky had seemed rinsed with blood.

The telling of the tale took Thomas down off the ridge and out of sight of Durham. Eleanor and Father Hobbe walked behind, leading the mare and sometimes interjecting with their own comments, while a score of Lord Outhwaite's retainers rode on either side to listen to the battle's tale. Thomas told it well and it was plain Lord Outhwaite liked him; Thomas of Hookton had always possessed a charm that had protected and recommended him, even though it sometimes made men like Sir Geoffrey Carr jealous. Sir Geoffrey had ridden ahead and, when Thomas reached the water meadows where the English force gathered, the knight pointed at him as if he were launching a curse and Thomas countered by making the sign of the cross. Sir Geoffrey spat.

Lord Outhwaite scowled at the Scarecrow. 'I have not forgotten

the letter your priest showed me' – he spoke to Thomas in French now – 'but I trust you will not leave us to deliver it to Durham yourself? Not while we have enemies to fight?'

'Can I stand with your lordship's archers?' Thomas asked.

Eleanor hissed her disapproval, but both men ignored her. Lord Outhwaite nodded his acceptance of Thomas's offer, then gestured that the younger man should climb down from the horse. 'One thing does puzzle me, though,' he went on, 'and that is why our lord the King should entrust such an errand to one so young.'

'And so base born?' Thomas asked with a smile, knowing that was the real question Lord Outhwaite had been too fastidious to ask.

His lordship laughed to be found out. 'You speak French, young man, but carry a bow. What are you? Base or well born?'

'Well enough, my lord, but out of wedlock.'

'Ah!'

'And the answer to your question, my lord, is that our lord the King sent me with one of his chaplains and a household knight, but both caught a sickness in London and that is where they remain. I came on with my companions.'

'Because you were eager to speak with this old monk?'

'If he lives, yes, because he can tell me about my father's family. My family.'

'And he can tell you about this treasure, this *thesaurus*. You know of it?'

'I know something of it, my lord,' Thomas said cautiously.

'Which is why the King sent you, eh?' Lord Outhwaite queried, but did not give Thomas time to answer the question. He gathered his reins. 'Fight with my archers, young man, but take care to stay alive, eh? I would like to know more of your *thesaurus*. Is the treasure really as great as the letter says?'

Thomas turned away from the ragged-haired Lord Outhwaite and stared up the ridge where there was nothing to be seen now except the bright-leaved trees and a thinning plume of smoke from the burned-out hovels. 'If it exists, my lord' – he spoke in French – 'then it is the kind of treasure that is guarded by angels and sought by demons.'

47

'And you seek it?' Lord Outhwaite asked with a smile.

Thomas returned the smile. 'I merely seek the Prior of Durham, my lord, to give him the bishop's letter.'

'You want Prior Fossor, eh?' Lord Outhwaite nodded towards a group of monks. 'That's him over there. The one in the saddle.' He had indicated a tall, white-haired monk who was astride a grey mare and surrounded by a score of other monks, all on foot, one of whom carried a strange banner that was nothing but a white scrap of cloth hanging from a painted pole. 'Talk to him,' Lord Outhwaite said, 'then seek my flag. God be with you!' He said the last four words in English.

'And with your lordship,' Thomas and Father Hobbe answered together.

Thomas walked towards the Prior, threading his way through archers who clustered about three wagons to receive spare sheaves of arrows. The small English army had been marching towards Durham on two separate roads and now the men straggled across fields to come together in case the Scots descended from the high ground. Men-at-arms hauled mail coats over their heads and the richer among them buckled on whatever pieces of plate armour they owned. The army's leaders must have had a swift conference for the first standards were being carried northwards, showing that the English wanted to confront the Scots on the higher ground of the ridge rather than be attacked in the water meadows or try to reach Durham by a circuitous route. Thomas had become accustomed to the English banners in Brittany, Normandy and Picardy, but these flags were all strange to him: a silver crescent, a brown cow, a blue lion, the Scarecrow's black axe, a red boar's head, Lord Outhwaite's scallop-emblazoned cross and, gaudiest of all, a great scarlet flag showing a pair of crossed keys thickly embroidered in gold and silver threads. The prior's flag looked shabby and cheap compared to all those other banners for it was nothing but a small square of frayed cloth beneath which the prior was working himself into a frenzy. 'Go and do God's work,' he shouted at some nearby archers, 'for the Scots are animals! Animals! Cut them down! Kill them all! God will reward each death! Go and smite them! Kill them!' He saw Thomas approaching. 'You want a blessing, my son? Then God give strength to your bow and add bite to your arrows!

48

May your arm never tire and your eye never dim. God and the saints bless you while you kill!'

Thomas crossed himself then held out the letter. 'I came to give you this, sir,' he said.

The prior seemed astonished that an archer should address him so familiarly, let alone have a letter for him and at first he did not take the parchment, but one of his monks snatched it from Thomas and, seeing the broken seal, raised his eyebrows. 'My lord the bishop writes to you,' he said.

'They are animals!' the prior repeated, still caught up in his peroration, then he realized what the monk had said. 'My lord bishop writes?'

'To you, brother,' the monk said.

The prior seized the painted pole and dragged the makeshift banner down so it hung near to Thomas's face. 'You may kiss it,' he said grandly.

'Kiss it?' Thomas was quite taken aback. The ragged cloth, now it was close by his nose, smelt musty.

'It is St Cuthbert's corporax cloth,' the prior said excitedly, 'taken from his tomb, my son! The blessed St Cuthbert will fight for us! The very angels of heaven will follow him into the battle.'

Thomas, faced with the saint's relic, went to his knees and drew the cloth to his lips. It was linen, he thought, and now he could see it was embroidered about its edge with an intricate pattern in faded blue thread. In the centre of the cloth, which was used during Mass to hold the wafers, was an elaborate cross, embroidered in silver threads that scarcely showed against the frayed white linen. 'It is really St Cuthbert's cloth?' he asked.

'His alone!' the prior exclaimed. 'We opened his tomb in the cathedral this very morning, and we prayed to him and he will fight for us today!' The prior jerked the flag up and waved it towards some men-at-arms who spurred their horses northwards. 'Perform God's work! Kill them all! Dung the fields with their noxious flesh, water it with their treacherous blood!'

'The bishop wants this young man to speak with Brother Hugh Collimore,' the monk who had read the letter now told the prior, 'and the King wishes it too. His lordship says there is a treasure to be found.'

'The King wishes it?' the prior looked in astonishment at Thomas. 'The King wishes it?' he asked again and then he came to his senses and realized there was great advantage in royal patronage and so he snatched the letter and read it himself, only to find even more advantage than he had anticipated. 'You come in search of a great *thesaurus*?' he asked Thomas suspiciously.

'So the bishop believes, sir,' Thomas responded.

'What treasure?' the prior snapped and all the monks gaped at him as the notion of a treasure momentarily made them forget the proximity of the Scottish army.

'The treasure, sir' – Thomas avoided giving a truthful answer – 'is known to Brother Collimore.'

'But why send you?' the prior asked, and it was a fair question for Thomas looked young and possessed no apparent rank.

'Because I have some knowledge of the matter too,' Thomas said, wondering if he had said too much.

The prior folded the letter, inadvertently tearing off the seal as he did so, and thrust it into a pouch that hung from his knotted belt. 'We shall talk after the battle,' he said, 'and then, and only then, I shall decide whether you may see Brother Collimore. He is sick, you know? Ailing, poor soul. Maybe he is dying. It may not be seemly for you to disturb him. We shall see, we shall see.' He plainly wanted to talk to the old monk himself and so be the sole possessor of whatever knowledge Collimore might have. 'God bless you, my son,' the prior dismissed Thomas, then hoisted his sacred banner and hurried north. Most of the English army was already climbing the ridge, leaving only their wagons and a crowd of women, children and those men too sick to walk. The monks, making a procession behind their corporax cloth, began to sing as they followed the soldiers.

Thomas ran to a cart and took a sheaf of arrows, which he thrust into his belt. He could see that Lord Outhwaite's men-at-arms were riding towards the ridge, followed by a large group of archers. 'Maybe the two of you should stay here,' he said to Father Hobbe.

'No!' Eleanor said. 'And you should not be fighting.'

'Not fight?' Thomas asked.

'It is not your battle!' Eleanor insisted. 'We should go to the city! We should find the monk.'

Thomas paused. He was thinking of the priest who, in the swirl of fog and smoke, had killed the Scotsman and then spoken to him in French. I am a messenger, the priest had said. '*Je suis un avant-coureur*,' had been his exact words and an *avant-coureur* was more than a mere messenger. A herald, perhaps? An angel even? Thomas could not drive away the image of that silent fight, the men so ill matched, a soldier against a priest, yet the priest had won and then had turned his gaunt, bloodied face on Thomas and announced himself: '*Je suis un avant-coureur*.' It was a sign, Thomas thought, and he did not want to believe in signs and visions, he wanted to believe in his bow. He thought perhaps Eleanor was right and that the conflict with its unexpected victor was a sign from heaven that he should follow the *avant-coureur* into the city, but there were also enemies up on the hill and he was an archer and archers did not walk away from a battle. 'We'll go to the city,' he said, 'after the fight.'

'Why?' she demanded fiercely.

But Thomas would not explain. He just started walking, climbing a hill where larks and finches flitted through the hedges and field-fares, brown and grey, called from the empty pastures. The fog was all gone and a drying wind blew across the Wear.

And then, from where the Scots waited on the higher ground, the drums began to beat.

Sir William Douglas, Knight of Liddesdale, prepared himself for battle. He pulled on leather breeches thick enough to thwart a sword cut and over his linen shirt he hung a crucifix that had been blessed by a priest in Santiago de Compostela where St James was buried. Sir William Douglas was not a particularly religious man, but he paid a priest to look after his soul and the priest had assured Sir William that wearing the crucifix of St James, the son of thunder, would ensure he received the last rites safe in his own bed. About his waist he tied a strip of red silk that had been torn from one of the banners captured from the English at Bannockburn. The silk had been dipped in the holy water of the font in the chapel of Sir William's castle at Hermitage and Sir William had been persuaded

that the scrap of silk would ensure victory over the old and much hated enemy.

He wore a haubergeon taken from an Englishman killed in one of Sir William's many raids south of the border. Sir William remembered that killing well. He had seen the quality of the Englishman's haubergeon at the very beginning of the fight and he had bellowed at his men to leave the fellow alone, then he had cut the man down by striking at his ankles and the Englishman, on his knees, had made a mewing sound that had made Sir William's men laugh. The man had surrendered, but Sir William had cut his throat anyway because he thought any man who made a mewing sound was not a real warrior. It had taken the servants at Hermitage two weeks to wash the blood out of the fine mesh of the mail. Most of the Scottish leaders were dressed in hauberks, which covered a man's body from neck to calves, while the haubergeon was much shorter and left the legs unprotected, but Sir William intended to fight on foot and he knew that a hauberk's weight wearied a man quickly and tired men were easily killed. Over the haubergeon he wore a full-length surcoat that showed his badge of the red heart. His helmet was a sallet, lacking any visor or face protection, but in battle Sir William liked to see what his enemies to the left and right were doing. A man in a full helm or in one of the fashionable pig-snouted visors could see nothing except what the slit right in front of his eyes let him see, which was why men in visored helmets spent the battle jerking their heads left and right, left and right, like a chicken among foxes, and they twitched until their necks were sore and even then they rarely saw the blow that crushed their skulls. Sir William, in battle, looked for men whose heads were jerking like hens, back and forth, for he knew they were nervous men who could afford a fine helmet and thus pay a finer ransom. He carried his big shield. It was really too heavy for a man on foot, but he expected the English to loose their archery storm and the shield was thick enough to absorb the crashing impact of yard-long, steel-pointed arrows. He could rest the foot of the shield on the ground and crouch safe behind it and, when the English ran out of arrows, he could always discard it. He carried a spear in case the English horsemen charged, and a sword, which was his favourite killing weapon. The sword's hilt encased a scrap of hair cut from

the corpse of St Andrew, or at least that was what the pardoner who had sold Sir William the scrap had claimed.

Robbie Douglas, Sir William's nephew, wore mail and a sallet, and carried a sword and shield. It had been Robbie who had brought Sir William the news that Jamie Douglas, Robbie's older brother, had been killed, presumably by the Dominican priest's servant. Or perhaps Father de Taillebourg had done the killing? Certainly he must have ordered it. Robbie Douglas, twenty years old, had wept for his brother. 'How could a priest do it?' Robbie had demanded of his uncle.

'You have a strange idea of priests, Robbie,' Sir William had said. 'Most priests are weak men given God's authority and that makes them dangerous. I thank God no Douglas has ever put on a priest's robe. We're all too honest.'

'When this day's done, uncle,' Robbie Douglas said, 'you'll let me go after that priest.'

Sir William smiled. He might not be an overtly religious man, but he did hold one creed sacred and that was that any family member's murder must be avenged and Robbie, he reckoned, would do vengeance well. He was a good young man, hard and handsome, tall and straightforward, and Sir William was proud of his youngest sister's son. 'We'll talk at day's end,' Sir William promised him, 'but till then, Robbie, stay close to me.'

'I will, uncle.'

'We'll kill a good few Englishmen, God willing,' Sir William said, then led his nephew to meet the King and to receive the blessing of the royal chaplains.

Sir William, like most of the Scottish knights and chieftains, was in mail, but the King wore French-made plate, a thing so rare north of the border that men from the wild tribes came to stare at this sun-reflecting creature made of moving metal. The young King seemed just as impressed for he took off his surcoat and walked up and down admiring himself and being admired as his lords came for a blessing and to offer advice. The Earl of Moray, whom Sir William believed was a fool, wanted to fight on horseback and the King was tempted to agree. His father, the great Robert the Bruce, had beaten the English at the Bannockburn on horseback, and not just beaten them, but humiliated them. The flower of Scotland had

ridden down the nobility of England and David, King now of his father's country, wanted to do the same. He wanted blood beneath his hooves and glory attached to his name; he wanted his reputation to spread through Christendom and so he turned and gazed longingly at his red and yellow painted lance propped against the bough of an elm.

Sir William Douglas saw where the King was looking. 'Archers,' he said laconically.

'There were archers at the Bannockburn,' the Earl of Moray insisted.

'Aye, and the fools didn't know how to use them,' Sir William said, 'but you can't depend on the English being fools for ever.'

'And how many archers can they have?' the Earl asked. 'There are said to be thousands of bowmen in France, hundreds more in Brittany and as many again in Gascony, so how many can they have here?'

'They have enough,' Sir William growled curtly, not bothering to hide the contempt he felt for John Randolph, third Earl of Moray. The Earl was just as experienced in war as Sir William, but he had spent too long as a prisoner of the English and the consequent hatred made him impetuous.

The King, young and inexperienced, wanted to side with the Earl whose friend he was, but he saw that his other lords were agreeing with Sir William who, though he held no great title nor position of state, was more battle-hardened than any man in Scotland. The Earl of Moray sensed that he was losing the argument and he urged haste. 'Charge now, sir,' he suggested, 'before they can make a battle line.' He pointed southwards to where the first English troops were appearing in the pastures. 'Cut the bastards down before they're ready.'

'That,' the Earl of Menteith put in quietly, 'was the advice given to Philip of Valois in Picardy. It didn't serve there and it won't serve here.'

'Besides which,' Sir William Douglas remarked caustically, 'we have to contend with stone walls.' He pointed to the walls which bounded the pastures where the English were beginning to form their line. 'Maybe Moray can tell us how armoured knights get past stone walls?' he suggested.

The Earl of Moray bridled. 'You take me for a fool, Douglas?'

'I take you as you show yourself, John Randolph,' Sir William answered.

'Gentlemen!' the King snapped. He had not noticed the stone walls when he formed his battle line beside the burning cottages and the fallen cross. He had only seen the empty green pastures and the wide road and his even wider dream of glory. Now he watched the enemy straggle from the far trees. There were plenty of archers coming, and he had heard how those bowmen could fill the sky with their arrows and how their steel arrow heads drove deep into horses and how the horses then went mad with pain. And he dared not lose this battle. He had promised his nobles that they would celebrate the feast of Christmas in the hall of the English King in London and if he lost then he would lose their respect and encourage some to rebellion. He had to win and, being impatient, he wanted to win quickly. 'If we charge fast enough,' he suggested tentatively, 'before they all reach their lines—'

'Then, you'll break your horse's legs on the stone walls,' Sir William said with scant respect for his royal master. 'If your majesty's horse even gets that far. You can't protect a horse from arrows, sir, but you can weather the storm on foot. Put your pikes up front, but mix them with men-at-arms who can use their shields to protect the pike-holders. Shields up, heads down and hold hard, that's how we win this.'

The King tugged at the espalier which covered his right shoulder and had an annoying habit of riding up on the top edge of the breastplate. Traditionally the defence of Scottish armies was in the hands of pikemen who used their monstrously long weapons to hold off the enemy knights, but pikemen needed both hands to hold their unwieldy blades and so became easy targets for English bowmen who liked to boast that they carried the lives of Scottish pikemen in their arrow bags. So protect the pikemen with the shields of the men-at-arms and let the enemy waste their arrows. It made sense, but it still irked David Bruce that he could not lead his horsemen in an earth-shaking assault while the trumpets screamed at the heavens.

Sir William saw his King's hesitation and pressed his argument. 'We have to stand, sir, and we have to wait, and we have to let

our shields take the arrows, but in the end, sir, they'll tire of wasting shafts and they'll come to the attack and that's when we'll chop them down like dogs.'

A growl of assent greeted this. The Scottish lords, hard men all, armed and armoured, bearded and grim, were confident that they could win this fight because they so outnumbered the enemy, but they also knew there was no short cut to victory, not when archers opposed them, and so they would have to do what Sir William said: endure the arrows, goad the enemy, then give them slaughter.

The King heard his lords agree with Sir William and so, reluctantly, he abandoned his dream of breaking the enemy with mounted knights. That was a disappointment, but he looked about his lords and thought that with such men beside him he could not possibly lose. 'We shall fight on foot,' he decreed, 'and chop them down like dogs. We shall slaughter them like whipped puppies!' And afterwards, he thought, when the survivors were fleeing southwards, the Scottish cavalry could finish the slaughter.

But for now it would be footman against footman and so the war banners of Scotland were carried forward and planted across the ridge. The burning cottages were mere embers now that cradled three shrunken bodies, black and small as children, and the King planted his flags close to those dead. He had his own standard, red saltire on yellow field, and the banner of Scotland's saint, white saltire on blue, in the line's centre and to left and right the flags of the lesser lords flew. The lion of Stewart brandished its blade, the Randolph falcon spread its wings while to east and west the stars and axes and crosses snapped in the wind. The army was arrayed in three divisions, called sheltrons, and the three sheltrons were so large that the men on the far flanks jostled in towards the centre to keep themselves on the flatter ground of the ridge's summit.

The rearmost ranks of the sheltrons were composed of the tribesmen from the islands and the north, men who fought bare-legged, without metal armour, wielding vast swords that could club a man to death as easily as cut him down. They were fearsome fighters, but their lack of armour made them horribly vulnerable to arrows and so they were placed at the rear and the leading ranks of the three sheltrons were filled by men-at-arms and pikemen. The men-at-arms carried swords, axes, maces or war-hammers and, most

important, the shields that could protect the pikemen whose weapons were tipped with a spike, a hook and an axehead. The spike could hold an enemy at bay, the hook could haul an armoured man out of the saddle or off his feet, and the axe could smash through his mail or plate. The line bristled with the pikes that made a steel hedge to greet the English and priests walked along the hedge consecrating the weapons and the men who held them. Soldiers knelt to receive their blessings. A few of the lords, like the King himself, were mounted, but only so that they could see over the heads of their army, and those men stared south to see the last of the English troops come into view. So few of them! Such a small army to beat! To the left of the Scots was Durham, its towers and ramparts thick with folk watching the battle, and in front was this small army of Englishmen who did not possess the sense to retreat south towards York. They would fight on the ridge instead and the Scots had the advantage of position and numbers. 'If you hate them!' Sir William Douglas shouted at his men on the right of the Scottish battle line, 'then let them hear you!'

The Scots bellowed their hatred. They clashed swords and spears against their shields, they shrieked to the sky and, in the line's centre, where the King's sheltron waited under the banners of the cross, a troop of drummers began to beat huge goatskin drums. Each drum was a big ring of oak over which was stretched two goat skins that were tightened with ropes until an acorn, dropped onto a skin, would bounce as high as the hand that had let it go and the drums, beaten with withies, made a sharp, almost metallic sound that filled the sky. They made an assault of pure noise.

'If you hate the English, let them know!' the Earl of March shouted from the left of the Scottish line that lay closest to the city. 'If you hate the English, let them know!' and the roar became louder, the clash of spear stave on shield was stronger, and the noise of Scotland's hate spread across the ridge so that nine thousand men were howling at the three thousand who were foolish enough to confront them.

'We shall cut them down like stalks of barley,' a priest promised, 'we shall soak the fields with their stinking blood and fill all hell with their English souls.'

'Their women are yours!' Sir William told his men. 'Their wives

and their daughters will be your toys tonight!' He grinned at his nephew Robbie. 'You'll have your pick of Durham's women, Robbie.'

'And London's women,' Robbie said, 'before Christmas.'

'Aye, them too,' Sir William promised.

'In the name of the Father, and of the Son, and of the Holy Ghost,' the King's senior chaplain shouted, 'send them all to hell! Each and every foul one of them to hell! For every Englishman you kill today means a thousand less weeks in purgatory!'

'If you hate the English,' Lord Robert Stewart, Steward of Scotland and heir to the throne, called, 'let them hear!' And the noise of that hate was like a thunder that filled the deep valley of the Wear, and the thunder reverberated from the crag where Durham stood and still the noise swelled to tell the whole north country that the Scots had come south.

And David, King of those Scots, was glad that he had come to this place where the dragon cross had fallen and the burning houses smoked and the English waited to be killed. For this day he would bring glory to St Andrew, to the great house of Bruce, and to Scotland.

Thomas, Father Hobbe and Eleanor followed the prior and his monks who were still chanting, though the brothers' voices were now ragged for they were breathless from hurrying. St Cuthbert's corporax cloth swayed to and fro and the banner attracted a straggling procession of women and children who, not wanting to wait out of sight of their men, carried spare sheaves of arrows up the hill. Thomas wanted to go faster, to get past the monks and find Lord Outhwaite's men, but Eleanor deliberately hung back until he turned on her angrily. 'You can walk faster,' he protested in French.

'I can walk faster,' she said, 'and you can ignore a battle!' Father Hobbe, leading the horse, understood the tone even though he did not comprehend the words. He sighed, thus earning himself a savage look from Eleanor. 'You do not need to fight!' she went on.

'I'm an archer,' Thomas said stubbornly, 'and there's an enemy up there.'

'Your King sent you to find the Grail!' Eleanor insisted. 'Not to die! Not to leave me alone! Me and a baby!' She had stopped now, hands clutching her belly and with tears in her eyes. 'I am to be alone here? In England?'

'I won't die here,' Thomas said scathingly.

'You know that?' Eleanor was even more scathing. 'God spoke to you, perhaps? You know what other men do not? You know the day of your dying?'

Thomas was taken aback by the outburst. Eleanor was a strong girl, not given to tantrums, but she was distraught and weeping now. 'Those men,' Thomas said, 'the Scarecrow and Beggar, they won't touch you. I'll be here.'

'It isn't them!' Eleanor wailed. 'I had a dream last night. A dream.'

Thomas put his hands on her shoulders. His hands were huge and strengthened by hauling on the hempen string of the big bow. 'I dreamed of the Grail last night,' he said, knowing that was not quite true. He had not dreamed of the Grail, rather he had woken to a vision which had turned out to be a deception, but he could not tell Eleanor that. 'It was golden and beautiful,' he said, 'like a cup of fire.'

'In my dream,' Eleanor said, gazing up at him, 'you were dead and your body was all black and swollen.'

'What is she saying?' Father Hobbe asked.

'She had a bad dream,' Thomas said in English, 'a nightmare.'

'The devil sends us nightmares,' the priest asserted. 'It is well known. Tell her that.'

Thomas translated that for her, then he stroked a wisp of golden hair away from her forehead and tucked it under her knitted cap. He loved her face, so earnest and narrow, so cat-like, but with big eyes and an expressive mouth. 'It was just a nightmare,' he reassured her, '*un cauchemar.*'

'The Scarecrow,' Eleanor said with a shudder, 'he is the *cauchemar.*'

Thomas drew her into an embrace. 'He won't come near you,' he promised her. He could hear a distant chanting, but nothing like the monks' solemn prayers. This was a jeering, insistent chant, heavy as the drumbeat that gave it rhythm. He could not hear the words, but he did not need to. 'The enemy,' he said to Eleanor, 'are waiting for us.'

'They are not my enemy,' she said fiercely.

'If they get into Durham,' Thomas retorted, 'then they will not know that. They will take you anyway.'

'Everyone hates the English. Do you know that? The French hate you, the Bretons hate you, the Scots hate you, every man in Christendom hates you! And why? Because you love fighting! You do! Everyone knows that about the English. And you? You have no need to fight today, it is not your quarrel, but you can't wait to be there, to kill again!'

Thomas did not know what to say, for there was truth in what Eleanor had said. He shrugged and picked up his heavy bow. 'I

60

fight for my King, and there's an army of enemies on the hill here. They outnumber us. Do you know what will happen if they get into Durham?'

'I know,' Eleanor said firmly, and she did know for she had been in Caen when the English archers, disobeying their King, had swarmed across the bridge and laid the town waste.

'If we don't fight them and stop them here,' Thomas said, 'then their horsemen will hunt us all down. One after the other.'

'You said you would marry me,' Eleanor declared, crying again. 'I don't want my baby to be fatherless, I don't want it to be like me.' She meant illegitimate.

'I will marry you, I promise. When the battle is done we shall be married in Durham. In the cathedral, yes?' He smiled at her. 'We can be married in the cathedral.'

Eleanor was pleased with the promise, but too furious to show her pleasure. 'We should go to the cathedral now,' she snapped. 'We would be safe there. We should pray at the high altar.'

'You can go to the city,' Thomas said. 'Let me fight my King's enemies and you go to the city, you and Father Hobbe, and you find the old monk and you can both talk to him, and afterwards you can go to the cathedral and wait for me there.' He unstrapped one of the big sacks on the mare's back and took out his haubergeon, which he hauled over his head. The leather lining felt stiff and cold, and smelt of mould. He forced his hands down the sleeves, then strapped the sword belt about his waist and hung the weapon on his right side. 'Go to the city,' he told Eleanor, 'and talk to the monk.'

Eleanor was crying. 'You are going to die,' she said, 'I dreamed it.'

'I can't go to the city,' Father Hobbe protested.

'You're a priest,' Thomas barked, 'not a soldier! Take Eleanor to Durham. Find Brother Collimore and talk to him.' The prior had insisted that Thomas wait and suddenly it seemed very sensible to send Father Hobbe to talk to the old monk before the prior poisoned his memories. 'Both of you,' Thomas insisted, 'talk to Brother Collimore. You know what to ask him. And I shall see you there this evening, in the cathedral.' He took his sallet, with its broad rim to deflect the downward stroke of a blade, and tied it onto his head.

He was angry with Eleanor because he sensed she was right. The imminent battle was not his concern except that fighting was his trade and England his country. 'I will not die,' he told Eleanor with an obstinate irrationality, 'and you will see me tonight.' He tossed the horse's reins to Father Hobbe. 'Keep Eleanor safe,' he told the priest. 'The Scarecrow won't risk anything inside the monastery or in the cathedral.'

He wanted to kiss Eleanor goodbye, but she was angry with him and he was angry with her and so he took his bow and his arrow bag and walked away. She said nothing for, like Thomas, she was too proud to back away from the quarrel. Besides, she knew she was right. This clash with the Scots was not Thomas's fight, whereas the Grail was his duty. Father Hobbe, caught between their obstinacy, walked in silence, but did note that Eleanor turned more than once, evidently hoping to catch Thomas looking back, but all she saw was her lover climbing the path with the great bow across his shoulder.

It was a huge bow, taller than most men and as thick about its belly as an archer's wrist. It was made from yew; Thomas was fairly sure it was Italian yew though he could never be certain because the raw stave had drifted ashore from a wrecked ship. He had shaped the stave, leaving the centre thick, and he had steamed the tips to curve them against the way the bow would bend when it was drawn. He had painted the bow black, using wax, oil and soot, then tipped the two ends of the stave with pieces of nocked antler horn to hold the cord. The stave had been cut so that at the belly of the bow, where it faced Thomas when he drew the hempen string, there was hard heartwood which was compressed when the arrow was hauled back while the outer belly was springy sapwood and when he released the cord the heartwood snapped out of its compression and the sapwood pulled it back into shape and between them they sent the arrow hissing with savage force. The belly of the bow, where his left hand gripped the yew, was whipped with hemp and above the hemp, which had been stiffened with hoof glue, he had nailed a scrap of silver cut from a crushed Mass vessel that his father had used in Hookton church, and the piece of silver cup showed the yale with the Grail in its clawed grip. The yale came from Thomas's family's coat of arms, though he had not

known that when he grew up for his father had never told him the tale. He had never told Thomas he was a Vexille from a family that had been lords of the Cathar heretics, a family that had been burned out of their home in southern France and which had fled to hide themselves in the darkest corners of Christendom.

Thomas knew little of the Cathar heresy. He knew his bow and he knew how to select an arrow of slender ash or birch or hornbeam, and he knew how to fledge the shaft with goose feathers and how to tip it with steel. He knew all that, yet he did not know how to drive that arrow through shield, mail and flesh. That was instinct, something he had practised since childhood; practised till his string fingers were bleeding; practised until he no longer thought when he drew the string back to his ear; practised until, like all archers, he was broad across the chest and hugely muscled in his arms. He did not need to know how to use a bow, it was just an instinct like breathing or waking or fighting.

He turned when he reached a stand of hornbeams that guarded the upper path like a rampart. Eleanor was walking stubbornly away and Thomas had an urge to shout to her, but knew she was already too far off and would not hear him. He had quarrelled with her before; men and women, it seemed to Thomas, spent half their lives fighting and half loving and the intensity of the first fed the passion of the second, and he almost smiled for he recognized Eleanor's stubbornness and he even liked it; and then he turned and walked through the trampled drifts of fallen hornbeam leaves along the path between stone-walled pastures where hundreds of saddled stallions were grazing. These were the warhorses of the English knights and men-at-arms and their presence in the pastures told Thomas that the English expected the Scots to attack because a knight was far better able to defend himself on foot. The horses were kept saddled so that the mailed men-at-arms could either retreat swiftly or else mount up and pursue a beaten enemy.

Thomas could still not see the Scottish army, but he could hear their chanting, which was given force by the hellish beat of the big drums. The sound was making some of the pastured stallions nervous and three of them, pursued by pageboys, galloped beside the stone wall with their eyes showing white. More pages were exercising destriers just behind the English line, which was divided into

63

three battles. Each battle had a knot of horsemen at the centre of its rear rank, the mounted men being the commanders beneath their bright banners, while in front of them were four or five rows of men-at-arms carrying swords, axes, spears and shields, and ahead of the men-at-arms, and crowded thick in the spaces between the three battles, were the archers.

The Scots, two arrow shots away from the English, were on slightly higher ground and also divided into three divisions which, like the English battles, were arrayed beneath their clusters of commanders' banners. The tallest flag, the red and yellow royal standard, was in the centre. The Scottish knights and men-at-arms, like the English, were on foot, but each of their sheltrons was much larger than its opposing English battle, three or four times larger, but Thomas, tall enough to look over the English line, could see there were not many archers in the enemy ranks. Here and there along the Scottish line he could see some long bowstaves and there were a few crossbows visible among the thicket of pikes, but there were not nearly so many bowmen as were in the English array, though the English, in turn, were hugely outnumbered by the Scottish army. So the battle, if it ever started, would be between arrows and Scottish pikes and men-at-arms, and if there were not enough arrows then the ridge must become an English graveyard.

Lord Outhwaite's banner of the cross and scallop shell was in the left-hand battle and Thomas crossed to it. The prior, dismounted now, was in the space between the left and centre divisions where one of his monks swung a censer and another brandished the Mass cloth on its painted pole. The prior himself was shouting, though Thomas could not tell whether he called insults at the enemy or prayers to God for the Scottish chanting was so loud. Thomas could not distinguish the enemy's words either, but the sentiment was plain enough and it was sped on its way by the massive drums.

Thomas could see the huge drums now and observe the passion with which the drummers beat the great skins to make a noise as sharp as snapping bone. Loud, rhythmic and reverberating, an assault of ear-piercing thunder, and in front of the drums at the centre of the enemy line some bearded men whirled in a wild dance. They came darting from the rear of the Scottish line and they wore no mail or iron, but were draped in thick folds of cloth

and brandished long-bladed swords about their heads and had small round leather shields, scarce larger than serving platters, strapped to their left forearms. Behind them the Scottish men-at-arms beat the flats of their sword blades against their shields while the pike-men thumped the ground with the butts of their long weapons to add to the noise of the huge drums. The sound was so great that the prior's monks had abandoned their chanting and now just gazed at the enemy.

'What they do' – Lord Outhwaite, on foot like his men, had to raise his voice to make himself heard – 'is try to scare us with noise before they kill us.' His lordship limped, whether through age or some old wound, Thomas did not like to ask; it was plain he wanted somewhere he could pace about and kick the turf and so he had come to talk with the monks, though now he turned his friendly face on Thomas. 'And you want to be most careful of those scoun-drels,' he said, pointing at the dancing men, 'because they're wilder than scalded cats. It's said they skin their captives alive.' Lord Outhwaite made the sign of the cross. 'You don't often see them this far south.'

'Them?' Thomas asked.

'They're tribesmen from the farthest north,' one of the monks explained. He was a tall man with a fringe of grey hair, a scarred face and only one eye. 'Scoundrels, they are,' the monk went on, 'scoundrels! They bow down to idols!' He shook his head sadly. 'I've never journeyed that far north, but I hear their land is shrouded in perpetual fog and that if a man dies with a wound to his back then his woman eats her own young and throws herself off the cliffs for the shame of it.'

'Truly?' Thomas asked.

'It's what I've heard,' the monk said, making the sign of the cross.

'They live on birds' nests, seaweed and raw fish.' Lord Outhwaite took up the tale, then smiled. 'Mind you, some of my people in Witcar do that, but at least they pray to God as well. At least I think they do.'

'But your folk don't have cloven hooves,' the monk said, staring at the enemy.

'The Scots do?' a much younger monk with a face left horribly scarred by smallpox asked anxiously.

65

'The clansmen do,' Lord Outhwaite said. 'They're scarcely human!' He shook his head then held out a hand to the older monk. 'It's Brother Michael, isn't it?'

'Your lordship flatters to remember me,' the monk answered, pleased.

'He was once a man-at-arms to my Lord Percy,' Lord Outhwaite explained to Thomas, 'and a good one!'

'Before I lost this to the Scots,' Brother Michael said, raising his right arm so that the sleeve of his robe fell to reveal a stump at his wrist, 'and this,' he pointed to his empty eye socket, 'so now I pray instead of fight.' He turned and gazed at the Scottish line. 'They are noisy today,' he grumbled.

'They're confident,' Lord Outhwaite said placidly, 'and so they should be. When was the last time a Scottish army outnumbered us?'

'They might outnumber us,' Brother Michael said, 'but they've picked a strange place to do it. They should have gone to the southern end of the ridge.'

'And so they should, brother,' Lord Outhwaite agreed, 'but let us be grateful for small mercies.' What Brother Michael meant was the Scots were sacrificing their advantage of numbers by fighting on the narrow ridge top where the English line, though thinner and with far fewer men, could not be overlapped. If the Scots had gone further south, where the ridge widened as it fell away to the water meadows, they could have outflanked their enemy. Their choice of ground might have been a mistake that helped the English, but that was small consolation when Thomas tried to estimate the size of the enemy army. Other men were doing the same and their guesses ranged from six to sixteen thousand, though Lord Outhwaite reckoned there were no more than eight thousand Scots. 'Which is only three or four times our number,' he said cheerfully, 'and not enough of them are archers. God be thanked for English archers.'

'Amen,' Brother Michael said.

The smallpox-scarred younger monk was staring in fascination at the thick Scottish line. 'I've heard that the Scots paint their faces blue. I can't see any though.'

Lord Outhwaite looked astonished. 'You heard what?'

'That they paint their faces blue, my lord,' the monk said, embarrassed now, 'or maybe they only paint half the face. To scare us.'

'To scare us?' His lordship was amused. 'To make us laugh, more like. I've never seen it.'

'Nor I,' Brother Michael put in.

'It's just what I've heard,' the young monk said.

'They're frightening enough without paint,' Lord Outhwaite pointed to a banner opposite his own part of the line. 'I see Sir William's here.'

'Sir William?' Thomas asked.

'Willie Douglas,' Lord Outhwaite said. 'I was a prisoner of his for two years and I'm still paying the bankers because of it.' He meant that his family had borrowed money to pay the ransom. 'I liked him, though. He's a rogue. And he's fighting with Moray?'

'Moray?' Brother Michael asked.

'John Randolph, Earl of Moray.' Lord Outhwaite nodded at another banner close to the red-heart flag of Douglas. 'They hate each other. God knows why they're together in the line.' He stared again at the Scottish drummers who leaned far back to balance the big instruments against their bellies. 'I hate those drums,' he said mildly. 'Paint their faces blue! I never heard such nonsense!' he chuckled.

The prior was haranguing the nearest troops now, telling them that the Scots had destroyed the great religious house at Hexham. 'They defiled God's holy church! They killed the brethren! They have stolen from Christ Himself and put tears onto the cheeks of God! Wreak His vengeance! Show no mercy!' The nearest archers flexed their fingers, licked lips and stared at the enemy who were showing no sign of advancing. 'You will kill them,' the prior shrieked, 'and God will bless you for it! He will shower blessings on you!'

'They want us to attack them,' Brother Michael remarked drily. He seemed embarrassed by his prior's passion.

'Aye,' Lord Outhwaite said, 'and they think we'll attack on horseback. See the pikes?'

'They're good against men on foot too, my lord,' Brother Michael said.

'That they are, that they are,' Lord Outhwaite agreed. 'Nasty things, pikes.' He fidgeted with some of the loose rings of his mail coat and looked surprised when one of them came away in his fingers. 'I do like Willie Douglas,' he said. 'We used to hunt together when I was his prisoner. We caught some very fine boar in Liddes- dale, I remember.' He frowned. 'Such noisy drums.'

'Will we attack them?' the young monk summoned up the cour- age to enquire.

'Dear me no, I do hope not,' Lord Outhwaite said. 'We're out- numbered! Much better to hold our ground and let them come to us.'

'And if they don't come?' Thomas asked.

'Then they'll slink off home with empty pockets,' Lord Outhwaite said, 'and they won't like that, they won't like it at all. They're only here for plunder! That's why they dislike us so much.'

'Dislike us? Because they're here for plunder?' Thomas had not understood his lordship's thinking.

'They're envious, young man! Plain envious. We have riches, they don't, and there are few things more calculated to provoke hatred than such an imbalance. I had a neighbour in Witcar who seemed a reasonable fellow, but then he and his men tried to take advantage of my absence when I was Douglas's prisoner. They tried to ambush the coin for my ransom, if you can believe it! It was just envy, it seems, for he was poor.'

'And now he's dead, my lord?' Thomas asked, amused.

'Dear me, no,' his lordship said reprovingly, 'he's in a very deep hole in the bottom of my keep. Deep down with the rats. I throw him coins every now and then to remind him why he's there.' He stood on tiptoe and gazed westwards where the hills were higher. He was looking for Scottish men-at-arms riding to make an assault from the south, but he saw none. 'His father,' he said, meaning Robert the Bruce, 'wouldn't be waiting there. He'd have men riding around our flanks to put the fear of God up our arses, but this young pup doesn't know his trade, does he? He's in the wrong place altogether!'

'He's put his faith in numbers,' Brother Michael said.

'And perhaps their numbers will suffice,' Lord Outhwaite replied gloomily and made the sign of the cross.

Thomas, now that he had a chance to see the ground between the armies, could understand why Lord Outhwaite was so scornful of the Scottish King who had drawn up his army just south of the burned cottages where the dragon cross had fallen. It was not just that the narrowness of the ridge confined the Scots, denying them a chance to outflank the numerically inferior English, but that the ill-chosen battlefield was obstructed by thick blackthorn hedges and at least one stone wall. No army could advance across those obstacles and hope to hold its line intact, but the Scottish King seemed confident that the English would attack him for he did not move. His men shouted insults in the hope of provoking an attack, but the English stayed stubbornly in their ranks.

The Scots jeered even louder when a tall man on a great horse rode out from the centre of the English line. His stallion had purple ribbons twisted into its black mane and a purple trapper embroidered with golden keys that was so long that it swept the ground behind the horse's rear hooves. The stallion's head was protected by a leather face plate on which was mounted a silver horn, twisted like a unicorn's weapon. The rider wore plate armour that was polished bright and had a sleeveless surcoat of purple and gold, the same colours displayed by his page, standard-bearer and the dozen knights who followed him. The tall rider had no sword, but instead was armed with a great spiked morningstar like the one Beggar carried. The Scottish drummers redoubled their efforts, the Scots soldiers shouted insults and the English cheered until the tall man raised a mailed hand for silence.

'We're to get a homily from his grace,' Lord Outhwaite said gloomily. 'Very fond of the sound of his own voice is his grace.'

The tall man was evidently the Archbishop of York and, when the English ranks were silent, he again raised his mailed right hand high above his purple plumed helmet and made an extravagant sign of the cross. '*Dominus vobiscum*,' he called. '*Dominus vobiscum*.' He rode down the line, repeating the invocation. 'You will kill God's enemy today,' he called after each promise that God would be with the English. He had to shout to make himself heard over the din of the enemy. 'God is with you, and you will do His work by making many widows and orphans. You will fill Scotland with grief as a just punishment for their godless impiety. The Lord of Hosts is with

69

you; God's vengeance is your task!' The Archbishop's horse stepped high, its head tossing up and down as his grace carried his encouragement out to the flanks of his army. The last wisps of mist had long burned away and, though there was still a chill in the air, the sun had warmth and its light glinted off thousands of Scottish blades. A pair of one-horse wagons had come from the city and a dozen women were distributing dried herrings, bread and skins of ale.

Lord Outhwaite's squire brought an empty herring barrel so his lordship could sit. A man played a reed pipe nearby and Brother Michael sang an old country song about the badger and the pardoner and Lord Outhwaite laughed at the words, then nodded his head towards the ground between the armies where two horsemen, one from each army, were meeting. 'I see we're being courteous today,' he remarked. An English herald in a gaudy tabard had ridden towards the Scots and a priest, hastily appointed as Scotland's herald, had come to greet him. The two men bowed from their saddles, talked a while, then returned to their respective armies. The Englishman, coming near the line, spread his hands in a gesture that said the Scots were being stubborn.

'They come this far south and won't fight?' the prior demanded angrily.

'They want us to start the battle,' Lord Outhwaite said mildly, 'and we want them to do the same.' The heralds had met to discuss how the battle should be fought and each had plainly demanded that the other side begin by making an assault, and both sides had refused the invitation, so now the Scots tried again to provoke the English by insult. Some of the enemy advanced to within bowshot and shouted that the English were pigs and their mothers were sows, and when an archer raised his bow to reward the insults an English captain shouted at him. 'Don't waste arrows on words,' he called.

'Cowards!' A Scotsman dared to come even closer to the English line, well within half a bowshot. 'You bastard cowards! Your mothers are whores who suckled you on goat piss! Your wives are sows! Whores and sows! You hear me? You bastards! English bastards! You're the devil's turds!' The fury of his hatred made him shake. He had a bristling beard, a ragged jupon and a coat of mail

70

with a great rent in its backside so that when he turned round and bent over he presented his naked arse to the English. It was meant as an insult, but was greeted by a roar of laughter.

'They'll have to attack us sooner or later,' Lord Outhwaite stated calmly. 'Either that or go home with nothing, and I can't see them doing that. You don't raise an army of that size without hope of profit.'

'They sacked Hexham,' the prior observed gloomily.

'And got nothing but baubles,' Lord Outhwaite said dismissively. 'The real treasures of Hexham were taken away for safekeeping long ago. I hear Carlisle paid them well enough to be left alone, but well enough to make eight or nine thousand men rich?' He shook his head. 'Those soldiers don't get paid,' he told Thomas, 'they're not like our men. The King of Scotland doesn't have the cash to pay his soldiers. No, they want to take some rich prisoners today, then sack Durham and York, and if they're not to go home poor and empty-handed then they'd best hitch up their shields and come at us.'

But still the Scots would not move and the English were too few to make an attack, though a straggle of men were constantly arriving to reinforce the Archbishop's army. They were mostly local men and few had any armour or any weapons other than farm implements like axes and mattocks. It was close to midday now and the sun had chased the chill off the land so that Thomas was sweating under his leather and mail. Two of the prior's lay servants had arrived with a horse-drawn cart loaded with casks of small beer, sacks of bread, a box of apples and a great cheese, and a dozen of the younger monks carried the provisions along the English line. Most of the army was sitting now, some were even sleeping and many of the Scots were doing the same. Even their drummers had given up, laying their great instruments on the pasture. A dozen ravens circled overhead and Thomas, thinking their presence presaged death, made the sign of the cross, then was relieved when the dark birds flew north across the Scottish troops.

A group of archers had come from the city and were cramming arrows into their quivers, a sure sign that they had never fought with the bow for a quiver was a poor instrument in battle. Quivers were likely to spill arrows when a man ran, and few held more

than a score of points. Archers like Thomas preferred a big bag made of linen stretched about a withy frame in which the arrows stood upright, their feathers kept from being crushed by the frame and their steel heads projecting through the bag's neck, which was secured by a lace. Thomas had selected his arrows carefully, rejecting any with warped shafts or kinked feathers. In France, where many of the enemy knights possessed expensive plate armour, the English would use bodkin arrows with long, narrow and heavy heads that lacked barbs and so were more likely to pierce breast-plates or helmets, but here they were still using the hunting arrows with their wicked barbs that made them impossible to pull out of a wound. They were called flesh arrows, but even a flesh arrow could pierce mail at two hundred paces.

Thomas slept for a time in the early afternoon, only waking when Lord Outhwaite's horse almost stepped on him. His lordship, along with the other English commanders, had been summoned to the Archbishop and so he had called for his horse and, accompanied by his squire, rode to the army's centre. One of the Archbishop's chaplains carried a silver crucifix along the line. The crucifix had a leather bag hanging just below the feet of Christ and in the bag, the chaplain claimed, were the knuckle bones of the martyred St Oswald. 'Kiss the bag and God will preserve you,' the chaplain promised, and archers and men-at-arms jostled for a chance to obey. Thomas could not get close enough to kiss the bag, but he did manage to reach out and touch it. Many men had amulets or strips of cloth given them by their wives, lovers or daughters when they left their farms or houses to march against the invaders. They touched those talismans now as the Scots, sensing that something was about to happen at last, climbed to their feet. One of their great drums began its awful noise.

Thomas glanced to his right where he could just see the tops of the cathedral's twin towers and the banner flying from the castle's ramparts. Eleanor and Father Hobbe should be in the city by now and Thomas felt a pang of regret that he had parted from his woman in such anger, then he gripped his bow so that the touch of its wood might keep her from evil. He consoled himself with the knowledge that Eleanor would be safe in the city and tonight, when the battle was won, they could make up their quarrel. Then, he

supposed, they would marry. He was not sure he really wanted to marry, it seemed too early in his life to have a wife even if it was Eleanor, whom he was sure he loved, but he was equally sure she would want him to abandon the yew bow and settle in a house and that was the very last thing Thomas wanted. What he wanted was to be a leader of archers, to be a man like Will Skeat. He wanted to have his own band of bowmen that he could hire out to great lords. There was no shortage of opportunity. Rumour said that the Italian states would pay a fortune for English archers and Thomas wanted a part of it, but Eleanor must be looked after and he did not want their child to be a bastard. There were enough bastards in the world without adding another.

The English lords talked for a while. There were a dozen of them and they glanced constantly at the enemy and Thomas was close enough to see the anxiety on their faces. Was it worry that the enemy was too many? Or that the Scots were refusing battle and, in the next morning's mist, might vanish northwards?

Brother Michael came and rested his old bones on the herring barrel that had served Lord Outhwaite as a seat. 'They'll send you archers forward. That's what I'd do. Send you archers forward to provoke the bastards. Either that or drive them off, but you don't drive Scotsmen off that easily. They're brave bastards.'

'Brave? Then why aren't they attacking?'

'Because they're not fools. They can see these.' Brother Michael touched the black stave of Thomas's bow. 'They've learned what archers can do. You've heard of Halidon Hill?' He raised his eyebrows in surprise when Thomas shook his head. 'Of course, you're from the south. Christ could come again in the north and you southerners would never hear about it, or believe it if you did. But it was thirteen years ago now and they attacked us by Berwick and we cut them down in droves. Or our archers did, and they won't be enthusiastic about suffering the same fate here.' Brother Michael frowned as a small click sounded. 'What was that?'

Something had touched Thomas's helmet and he turned to see the Scarecrow, Sir Geoffrey Carr, who had cracked his whip, just glancing the metal claw at its tip off the crest of Thomas's sallet. Sir Geoffrey coiled his whip as he jeered at Thomas. 'Sheltering behind monks' skirts, are we?'

73

Brother Michael restrained Thomas. 'Go, Sir Geoffrey,' the monk ordered, 'before I call down a curse onto your black soul.'

Sir Geoffrey put a finger into a nostril and pulled out something slimy that he flicked towards the monk. 'You think you frighten me, you one-eyed bastard? You who lost your balls when your hand was chopped off?' He laughed, then looked back to Thomas. 'You picked a fight with me, boy, and you didn't give me a chance to finish it.'

'Not now!' Brother Michael snapped.

Sir Geoffrey ignored the monk. 'Fighting your betters, boy? You can hang for that. No' – he shuddered, then pointed a long bony finger at Thomas – 'you *will* hang for that! You hear me? You will hang for it.' He spat at Thomas, then turned his roan horse and spurred it back down the line.

'How come you know the Scarecrow?' Brother Michael asked.

'We just met.'

'An evil creature,' Brother Michael said, making the sign of the cross, 'born under a waning moon when a storm was blowing.' He was still watching the Scarecrow. 'Men say that Sir Geoffrey owes money to the devil himself. He had to pay a ransom to Douglas of Liddesdale and he borrowed deep from the bankers to do it. His manor, his fields, everything he owns is in danger if he can't pay, and even if he makes a fortune today he'll just throw it away at dice. The Scarecrow's a fool, but a dangerous one.' He turned his one eye on Thomas. 'Did you really pick a fight with him?'

'He wanted to rape my woman.'

'Aye, that's our Scarecrow. So be careful, young man, because he doesn't forget slights and he never forgives them.'

The English lords must have come to some agreement for they reached out their mailed fists and touched metal knuckle on metal knuckle, then Lord Outhwaite turned his horse back towards his men. 'John! John!' he called to the captain of his archers. 'We'll not wait for them to make up their minds,' he said as he dismounted, 'but be provocative.' It seemed Brother Michael's prognostication was right; the archers would be sent forward to annoy the Scots. The plan was to enrage them with arrows and so spur them into a hasty attack.

A squire rode Lord Outhwaite's horse back to the walled pasture

as the Archbishop of York rode his destrier out in front of the army. 'God will help you!' he called to the men of the central division that he commanded. 'The Scots fear us!' he shouted. 'They know that with God's help we will make many children fatherless in their blighted land! They stand and watch us because they fear us. So we must go to them.' That sentiment brought a cheer. The Archbishop raised a hand to silence his men. 'I want the archers to go forward,' he called, 'only the archers! Sting them! Kill them! And God bless you all. God bless you mightily!'

So the archers would begin the battle. The Scots were stubbornly refusing to move in hope that the English would make the attack, for it was much easier to defend ground than assault a formed enemy, but now the English archers would go forward to goad, sting and harass the enemy until they either ran away or, more likely, advanced to take revenge.

Thomas had already selected his best arrow. It was new, so new that the green-tinted glue that was pasted about the thread holding the feathers in place was still tacky, but it had a breasted shaft, one that was slightly wider behind the head and then tapered away towards the feathers. Such a shaft would hit hard and it was a lovely straight piece of ash, a third as long again as Thomas's arm, and Thomas would not waste it even though his opening shot would be at very long range.

It would be a long shot for the Scottish King was at the rear of the big central sheltron of his army, but it would not be an impossible shot for the black bow was huge and Thomas was young, strong and accurate.

'God be with you,' Brother Michael said.

'Aim true!' Lord Outhwaite called.

'God speed your arrows!' the Archbishop of York shouted.

The drummers beat louder, the Scots jeered and the archers of England advanced.

Bernard de Taillebourg already knew much of what the old monk told him, but now that the story was flowing he did not interrupt. It was the tale of a family that had been lords of an obscure county

in southern France. The county was called Astarac and it lay close to the Cathar lands and, in time, became infected with the heresy. 'The false teaching spread,' Brother Collimore had said, 'like a murrain. From the inland sea to the ocean, and northwards into Burgundy.' Father de Taillebourg knew all this, but he had said nothing, just let the old man go on describing how, when the Cathars were burned out of the land and the fires of their deaths had sent the smoke pouring to heaven to tell God and His angels that the true religion had been restored to the lands between France and Aragon, the Vexilles, among the last of the nobility to be contaminated by the Cathar evil, had fled to the farthest corners of Christendom. 'But before they left,' Brother Collimore said, gazing up at the white painted arch of the ceiling, 'they took the treasures of the heretics for safekeeping.'

'And the Grail was among them?'

'So they said, but who knows?' Brother Collimore turned his head and frowned at the Dominican. 'If they possessed the Grail, why did it not help them? I have never understood that.' He closed his eyes. Sometimes, when the old man was pausing to draw breath and almost seemed asleep, de Taillebourg would look through the window to see the two armies on the far hill. They did not move, though the noise they made was like the crackling and roaring of a great fire. The roaring was the noise of men's voices and the crackling was the drums and the twin sounds rose and fell with the vagaries of the wind gusting in the rocky defile above the River Wear. Father de Taillebourg's servant still stood in the doorway where he was half hidden by one of many piles of undressed stone that were stacked in the open space between the castle and the cathedral. Scaffolding hid the cathedral's nearest tower and small boys, eager to get a glimpse of the fighting, were scrambling up the web of lashed poles. The masons had abandoned their work to watch the two armies.

Now, after questioning why the Grail had not helped the Vexilles, Brother Collimore did fall into a brief sleep and de Taillebourg crossed to his black-dressed servant. 'Do you believe him?'

The servant shrugged and said nothing.

'Has anything surprised you?' de Taillebourg asked.

'That Father Ralph has a son,' the servant answered. 'That was new to me.'

'We must speak with that son,' the Dominican said grimly, then turned back because the old monk had woken.

'Where was I?' Brother Collimore asked. A small trickle of spittle ran from a corner of his lips.

'You were wondering why the Grail did not help the Vexilles,' Bernard de Taillebourg reminded him.

'It should have done,' the old monk said. 'If they possessed the Grail why did they not become powerful?'

Father de Taillebourg smiled. 'Suppose,' he said to the old monk, 'that the infidel Muslims were to gain possession of the Grail, do you think God would grant them its power? The Grail is a great treasure, brother, the greatest of all the treasures upon the earth, but it is not greater than God.'

'No,' Brother Collimore agreed.

'And if God does not approve of the Grail-keeper then the Grail will be powerless.'

'Yes,' Brother Collimore acknowledged.

'You say the Vexilles fled?'

'They fled the Inquisitors,' Brother Collimore said with a sly glance at de Taillebourg, 'and one branch of the family came here to England where they did some service to the King. Not our present King, of course,' the old monk made clear, 'but his great-grandfather, the last Henry.'

'What service?' de Taillebourg asked.

'They gave the King a hoof from St George's horse.' The monk spoke as though such things were commonplace. 'A hoof set in gold and capable of working miracles. At least the King believed it did for his son was cured of a fever by being touched with the hoof. I am told the hoof is still in Westminster Abbey.'

The family had been rewarded with land in Cheshire, Collimore went on, and if they were heretics they did not show it, but lived like any other noble family. Their downfall, he said, had come at the beginning of the present reign when the young King's mother, aided by the Mortimer family, had tried to keep her son from taking power. The Vexilles had sided with the Queen and when she lost they had fled back to the continent. 'All of them except one son,' Brother Collimore said, 'the eldest son, and that was Ralph, of course. Poor Ralph.'

'But if his family had fled back to France, why did you treat him?' de Taillebourg asked, puzzlement marring the face that had blood scabs on the abrasions where he had beaten himself against the stone that morning. 'Why not just execute him as a traitor?'

'He had taken holy orders,' Collimore protested, 'he could not be executed! Besides, it was known he hated his father and he had declared himself for the King.'

'So he was not all mad,' de Taillebourg put in drily.

'He also possessed money,' Collimore went on, 'he was noble and he claimed to know the secret of the Vexilles.'

'The Cathar treasures?'

'But the demon was in him even then! He declared himself a bishop and preached wild sermons in the London streets. He said he would lead a new crusade to drive the infidel from Jerusalem and promised that the Grail would ensure success.'

'So you locked him up?'

'He was sent to me,' Brother Collimore said reprovingly, 'because it was known that I could defeat the demons.' He paused, remembering. 'In my time I scourged hundreds of them! Hundreds!'

'But you did not fully cure Ralph Vexille?'

The monk shook his head. 'He was like a man spurred and whipped by God so that he wept and screamed and beat himself till the blood ran.' Brother Collimore, unaware that he could have been describing de Taillebourg, shuddered. 'And he was haunted by women too. I think we never cured him of that, but if we did not drive the demons clean out of him we did manage to make them hide so deep that they rarely dared show themselves.'

'Was the Grail a dream given to him by demons?' the Dominican asked.

'That was what we wanted to know,' Brother Collimore replied.

'And what answer did you find?'

'I told my masters that Father Ralph lied. That he had invented the Grail. That there was no truth in his madness. And then, when his demons no longer made him a nuisance, he was sent to a parish in the far south where he could preach to the gulls and to the seals. He no longer called himself a lord, he was simply Father Ralph, and we sent him away to be forgotten.'

'To be forgotten?' de Taillebourg repeated. 'Yet you had news of him. You discovered he had a son.'

The old monk nodded. 'We had a brother house near Dorchester and they sent me news. They told me that Father Ralph had found himself a woman, a housekeeper, but what country priest doesn't? And he had a son and he hung an old spear in his church and said it was St George's lance.'

De Taillebourg peered at the western hill for the noise had become much louder. It looked as though the English, who were by far the smaller army, were advancing and that meant they would lose the battle and that meant Father de Taillebourg had to be out of this monastery, indeed out of this city, before Sir William Douglas arrived seeking vengeance. 'You told your masters that Father Ralph lied. Did he?'

The old monk paused and to de Taillebourg it seemed as if the firmament itself held its breath. 'I don't think he lied,' Collimore whispered.

'So why did you tell them he did?'

'Because I liked him,' Brother Collimore said, 'and I did not think we could whip the truth out of him, or starve it from him, or pull it out by trying to drown him in cold water. I thought he was harmless and should be left to God.'

De Taillebourg gazed through the window. The Grail, he thought, the Grail. The hounds of God were on the scent. He would find it! 'One of the family came back from France,' the Dominican said, 'and stole the lance and killed Father Ralph.'

'I heard.'

'But they did not find the Grail.'

'God be thanked for that,' Brother Collimore said faintly.

De Taillebourg heard a movement and saw that his servant, who had been listening intently, was now watching the courtyard. The servant must have heard someone approaching and de Taillebourg, leaning closer to Brother Collimore, lowered his voice so he would not be overheard. 'How many people know of Father Ralph and the Grail?'

Brother Collimore thought for a few heartbeats. 'No one has spoken of it for years,' he said, 'until the new bishop came. He must have heard rumours for he asked me about it. I told him that Ralph Vexille was mad.'

'He believed you?'

'He was disappointed. He wanted the Grail for the cathedral.'

Of course he did, de Taillebourg thought, for any cathedral that possessed the Grail would become the richest church in Christendom. Even Genoa, which had its gaudy piece of green glass that they claimed was the Grail, took money from thousands of pilgrims. But put the real Grail in a church and folk would come to it in their hundreds of thousands and they would bring coins and jewels by the wagonload. Kings, queens, princes and dukes would throng the aisle and compete to offer their wealth.

The servant had vanished, slipping soundlessly behind one of the piles of building stone, and de Taillebourg waited, watching the door and wondering what trouble would show there. Then, instead of trouble, a young priest appeared. He wore a rough cloth gown, had unruly hair and a broad, guileless, sunburned face. A young woman, pale and frail, was with him. She seemed nervous, but the priest greeted de Taillebourg cheerfully. 'A good day to you, father.'

'And to you, father,' de Taillebourg responded politely. His servant had reappeared behind the strangers, preventing them from leaving unless de Taillebourg gave his permission. 'I am taking Brother Collimore's confession,' de Taillebourg said.

'A good one, I hope,' Father Hobbe said, then smiled. 'You don't sound English, father?'

'I am French,' de Taillebourg said.

'As am I,' Eleanor said in that language, 'and we have come to talk with Brother Collimore.'

'Talk with him?' de Taillebourg asked pleasantly.

'The bishop sent us,' Eleanor said proudly, 'and the King did too.'

'Which King, child?'

'*Edouard d'Angleterre*,' Eleanor boasted. Father Hobbe, who spoke no French, was looking from Eleanor to the Dominican.

'Why would Edward send you?' de Taillebourg asked and, when Eleanor looked flustered, he repeated the question. 'Why would Edward send you?'

'I don't know, father,' Eleanor said.

'I think you do, my child, I think you do.' He stood and Father Hobbe, sensing trouble, took Eleanor's wrist and tried to pull her from the room, but de Taillebourg nodded at his servant and

gestured towards Father Hobbe and the English priest was still trying to understand why he was suspicious of the Dominican when the knife slid between his ribs. He made a choking noise, then coughed and the breath rattled in his throat as he slid down to the flagstones. Eleanor tried to run, but she was not nearly fast enough and de Taillebourg caught her by the wrist and jerked her roughly back. She screamed and the Dominican silenced her by clapping a hand over her mouth.

'What's happening?' Brother Collimore asked.

'We are doing God's work,' de Taillebourg said soothingly, 'God's work.'

And on the ridge the arrows flew.

Thomas advanced with the archers of the left-hand battle and they had not gone more than twenty yards when, just beyond a ditch, a bank and some newly planted blackthorn saplings, they were forced to their right because a great scoop had been taken out of the ridge's flank to leave a hollow of ground with sides too steep for the plough. The hollow was filled with bracken that had turned yellow and at its far side was a lichen-covered stone wall and Thomas's arrow bag caught and tore on a rough piece of the coping as he clambered across. Only one arrow fell out, but it dropped into a mushroom fairy ring and he tried to work out whether that was a good or a bad omen, but the noise of the Scottish drums distracted him. He picked up the arrow and hurried on. All the enemy drummers were working now, rattling their skins in a frenzy so that the air itself seemed to vibrate. The Scottish men-at-arms were hefting their shields, making sure they protected the pikemen, and a crossbowman was working the ratchet that dragged back his cord and lodged it on the trigger's hook. The man glanced up anxiously at the advancing English bowmen, then discarded the ratchet handles and laid a metal quarrel in the crossbow's firing trough. The enemy had begun to shout and Thomas could distinguish some words now. 'If you hate the English,' he heard, then a crossbow bolt hummed past him and he forgot about the enemy chant. Hundreds of English archers were advancing through the fields, most of them running.

The Scots only had a few crossbows, but those weapons outranged the longer war bows of the English who were hurrying to close that range. An arrow slithered across the grass in front of Thomas. Not a crossbow bolt, but an arrow from one of the few Scottish yew bows and the sight of the arrow told him he was almost in range. The first of the English archers had stopped and drawn back their cords and then their arrows flickered into the sky. A bowman in a padded leather jerkin fell backwards with a crossbow bolt embedded in his forehead. Blood spurted skywards where his last arrow, shot almost vertically, soared uselessly.

'Aim at the archers!' a man in a rusted breastplate bellowed. 'Kill their archers first!'

Thomas stopped and looked for the royal standard. It was off to his right, a long way off, but he had shot at further targets in his time and so he turned and braced himself and then, in the name of God and St George, he put his chosen arrow onto the string and drew the white goose feathers back to his ear. He was staring at King David II of Scotland, saw the sun glint gold off the royal helmet, saw too that the King's visor was open and he aimed for the chest, nudged the bow right to compensate for the wind, and loosed. The arrow went true, not vibrating as a badly made arrow would, and Thomas watched it climb and saw it fall and saw the King jerk backwards and then the courtiers closed about him and Thomas laid his second arrow across his left hand and sought another target. A Scottish archer was limping from the line, an arrow in his leg. The men-at-arms closed about the wounded man, sealing their line with heavy shields. Thomas could hear hounds baying deep among the enemy formation, or perhaps he was hearing the war howl of the tribesmen. The King had turned away and men were leaning towards him. The sky was filled with the whisper of flying arrows and the noise of the bows was a steady, deep music. The French called it the devil's harp music. There were no Scottish archers left that Thomas could see. They had all been made targets by the English bowmen and the arrows had ripped the enemy archers into bloody misery, so now the English turned their missiles on the men with pikes, swords, axes and spears. The tribesmen, all hair and beard and fury, were beyond the men-at-arms who were arrayed six or eight men deep, so the arrows rattled and clanged

82

on armour and shields. The Scottish knights and men-at-arms and pike-carriers were sheltering as best they could, crouching under the bitter steel rain, but some arrows always found the gaps between the shields while others drove clean through the leather-covered willow boards. The thudding sound of the arrows hitting shields was rivalling the sharper noise of the drums.

'Forward, boys! Forward!' One of the archers' leaders encouraged his men to go twenty paces nearer the enemy so that their arrows could bite harder into the Scottish ranks. 'Kill them, lads!' Two of his men were lying on the grass, proof that the Scottish archers had done some damage before they were overwhelmed with English arrows. Another Englishman was staggering as though he were drunk, weaving back towards his own side and clutching his belly from which blood trickled down his leggings. A bow's cord broke, squirting the arrow sideways as the archer swore and reached under his tunic to find a spare.

The Scots could do nothing now. They had no archers left and the English edged closer and closer until they were driving their arrows in a flat trajectory that whipped the steel heads through shields, mail and even the rare suit of plate armour. Thomas was scarce seventy yards from the enemy line and choosing his targets with cold deliberation. He could see a man's leg showing under a shield and he put an arrow through the thigh. The drummers had fled and two of their instruments, their skins split like rotten fruit, lay discarded on the turf. A nobleman's horse was close behind the dismounted ranks and Thomas put a missile deep into the destrier's chest and, when he next looked, the animal was down and there was a flurry of panicking men trying to escape its thrashing hooves and all of those men, exposing themselves by letting their shields waver, went down under the sting of the arrows and then a moment later a pack of a dozen hunting dogs, long-haired, yellow-fanged and howling, burst out of the cowering ranks and were tumbled down by the slicing arrows.

'Is it always this easy?' a boy, evidently at his first battle, asked a nearby archer.

'If the other side don't have archers,' the older man answered, 'and so long as our arrows last, then it's easy. After that it's shit hard.'

Thomas drew and released, shooting at an angle across the Scottish front to whip a long shaft behind a shield and into a bearded man's face. The Scottish King was still on his horse, but protected now by four shields that were all bristling with arrows and Thomas remembered the French horses labouring up the Picardy slope with the feather-tipped shafts sticking from their necks, legs and bodies. He rummaged in his torn arrow bag, found another missile and shot it at the King's horse. The enemy was under the flail now and they would either run from the arrow storm or else, enraged, charge the smaller English army and, judging by the shouts coming from the men behind the arrow-stuck shields, Thomas suspected they would attack.

He was right. He had time to shoot one last arrow and then there was a sudden terrifying roar and the whole Scottish line, seemingly without anyone giving an order, charged. They ran howling and screaming, stung into the attack by the arrows, and the English archers fled. Thousands of enraged Scotsmen were charging and the archers, even if they shot every arrow they possessed into the advancing horde, would be overwhelmed in a heartbeat and so they ran to find shelter behind their own men-at-arms. Thomas tripped as he climbed the stone wall, but he picked himself up and ran on, then saw that other archers had stopped and were shooting at their pursuers. The stone wall was holding up the Scots and he turned round himself and put two arrows into defenceless men before the enemy surged across the barrier and forced him back again. He was running towards the small gap in the English line where St Cuthbert's Mass cloth waved, but the space was choked with archers trying to get behind the armoured line and so Thomas went to his right, aiming for the sliver of open ground that lay between the army's flank and the ridge's steep side.

'Shields forward!' a grizzled warrior, his helmet visor pushed up, shouted at the English men-at-arms. 'Brace hard! Brace hard!' The English line, only four or five ranks deep, steadied to meet the wild attack with their shields thrust forward and right legs braced back. 'St George! St George!' a man called. 'Hold hard now! Thrust hard and hold hard!'

Thomas was on the flank of the army now and he turned to see that the Scots, in their precipitate charge, had widened their line.

They had been arrayed shoulder to shoulder in their first position, but now, running, they had spread out and that meant their westernmost sheltron had been pushed down the ridge's slope and into the deep hollow that so unexpectedly narrowed the battle ground. They were down in the hollow's bottom, staring up at the skyline, doomed.

'Archers!' Thomas shouted, thinking himself back in France and responsible for a troop of Will Skeat's bowmen. 'Archers!' he bellowed, advancing to the hollow's lip. 'Now kill them!' Men came to his side, yelped in triumph and drew back their cords.

Now was the killing time, the archers' time. The Scottish right wing was down in the sunken ground and the archers were above them and could not miss. Two monks were bringing spare sheaves of arrows, each sheaf holding twenty-four shafts evenly spaced about two leather discs that kept the arrows apart and so protected their feathers from being crushed. The monks cut the twine holding the arrows and spilt the missiles on the ground beside the archers who drew again and again and killed again and again as they shot down into the pit of death. Thomas heard the deafening crash as the men-at-arms collided in the field's centre, but here, on the English left, the Scots would never come to their enemy's shields because they had spilled into the low yellow bracken of death's kingdom.

Thomas's childhood had been spent in Hookton, a village on England's south coast where a stream, coming to the sea, had carved a deep channel in the shingle beach. The channel curved to leave a hook of land that protected the fishing boats and once a year, when the rats became too thick in the holds and bilges of the boats, the fishermen would strand their craft at the bottom of the stream, fill their bilges with stones and let the incoming tide flood the stinking hulls. It was a holiday for the village children who, standing on the top of the Hook, waited for the rats to flee the boats and then, with cheers and screams of delight, they would stone the animals. The rats would panic and that would only increase the children's glee as the adults stood around and laughed, applauded and encouraged.

It was like that now. The Scots were in the low ground, the archers were on the lip of the hill and death was their dominion.

The arrows were flashing straight down the slope, scarce any arc in their flight, and striking home with the sound of cleavers hitting flesh. The Scots writhed and died in the hollow and the yellow autumn bracken turned red. Some of the enemy tried to climb towards their tormentors, but they became the easiest targets. Some attempted to escape up the far side and were struck in the back, while some fled down the hill in ragged disarray. Sir Thomas Rokeby, Sheriff of Yorkshire and commander of the English left, saw their escape and ordered two score of his men to mount their horses and scour the valley. The mailed riders swung their swords and morningstars to finish the archers' bloody work.

The base of the hollow was a writhing, bloody mass. A man in plate armour, a plumed helmet on his head, tried to climb out of the carnage and two arrows whipped through his breastplate and a third found a slit in his visor and he fell back, twitching. A thicket of arrows jutted from the falcon on his shield. The arrows became fewer now, for there were not many Scotsmen left to kill and then the first archers scrambled down the slope with drawn knives to pillage the dead and kill the wounded.

'Who hates the English now?' one of the archers jeered. 'Come on, you bastards, let's hear you? Who hates the English now?'

Then a shout sounded from the centre. 'Archers! To the right! To the right!' The voice had a note of sheer panic. 'To the right! For God's sake, now!'

The men-at-arms of the English left were scarcely engaged in the fight because the archers were slaughtering the Scots in the low bracken. The English centre was holding firm for the Archbishop's men were arrayed behind a stone wall which, though only waist high, was a more than adequate barrier against the Scottish assault. The invaders could stab, lunge and hack over the wall's coping, and they could try to climb it and they could even try to pull it down stone by stone, but they could not push it over and so they were checked by it and the English, though far fewer, were able to hold even though the Scots were lunging at them with their heavy pikes. Some English knights called for their horses and, once mounted

86

and armed with lances, pressed up close behind their beleaguered comrades and rammed the lances at Scottish eyes. Other men-at-arms ducked under the unwieldy pikes and hacked with swords and axes at the enemy and all the while the long arrows drove in from the left. The noise in the centre was the shouting of men in the rearward ranks, the screaming of the wounded, the clangour of blade on blade, the crack of blade on shield and the clatter of lance on pike, but the wall meant that neither side could press the other back and so, crammed against the stones and encumbered by the dead, they just lunged, hacked, suffered, bled and died.

But on the English right, where Lord Neville and Lord Percy commanded, the wall was unfinished, nothing more than a pile of stones that offered no obstacle to the assault of the Scottish left wing that was commanded by the Earl of March and by the King's nephew, Lord Robert Stewart. Their sheltron, closest to the city, was the largest of the three Scottish divisions and it came at the English like a pack of wolves who had not fed in a month. The attackers wanted blood and the archers fled from their howling charge like sheep scattering before fangs and then the Scots struck the English right and the sheer momentum of their assault drove the defenders back twenty paces before, somehow, the men-at-arms managed to hold the Scots who were now stumbling over the bodies of the men they had wounded or killed. The English, cramming themselves shoulder to shoulder, crouched behind their shields and shoved back, stabbing swords at ankles and faces, and grunting with the effort of holding the vast pressure of the Scottish horde.

It was hard to fight in the front ranks. Men shoved from behind so that Englishmen and Scotsmen were close as lovers, too close to wield a sword in anything except a rudimentary stab. The ranks behind had more room and a Scotsman chopped down with a pike that he wielded like a giant axe, its blade crunching down into an enemy's head to split helmet, leather liner, scalp and skull as easily as an unboiled egg. Blood fountained across a dozen men as the dead soldier fell and other Scots pushed into the gap his death had caused, and a clansman tripped on the body and screamed as an Englishman sawed at his exposed neck with a blunt knife. The pike dropped again, killing a second man, and this time, when it was

lifted up, the dead man's crumpled visor was caught on the pike's bloody spike.

The drums, those that were still whole, had begun their noise again, and the Scots heaved to their rhythm. 'The Bruce! The Bruce!' some chanted while others called on their patron, 'St Andrew! St Andrew!' Lord Robert Stewart, gaudy in his blue and yellow colours and with a thin fillet of gold about the brow of his helmet, used a two-handed sword to chop at the English men-at-arms who cowered from the rampant Scots. Lord Robert, safe from arrows at last, had lifted his visor so he could see the enemy. 'Come on!' he screamed at his men. 'Come on! Hard into them! Kill them! Kill them!' The King had promised that the Christmas feast would be in London and there seemed only a small screen of frightened men to break before that promise could come true. The riches of Durham, York and London were just a few sword strokes away; all the wealth of Norwich and Oxford, of Bristol and Southampton was only a handful of deaths from Scottish purses. 'Scotland! Scotland! Scotland!' Lord Robert called. 'Scotland!' And the pikeman, because the trapped visor was obstructing his blade, was beating on a man's helmet with the hook side of his weapon's head, not chopping through the metal, but smashing it, hammering the broken helmet into the dying man's brain so that blood and jelly oozed from the visor's slits. An Englishman screamed as a Scottish pike struck through his mail into his groin. A boy, perhaps a page, reeled back with his eyes bloodied from a sword slash. 'Scotland!' Lord Robert could smell the victory now. So close! He shoved on, felt the English line jar and move back, saw how thin it was, fended off a lunge with his shield, stabbed with his sword to kill a fallen and wounded enemy, shouted at his squires to keep a watch for any rich English nobleman whose ransom could enrich the house of Stewart. Men grunted as they stabbed and hacked. A tribesman reeled from the fight, gasping for breath, trying to hold his guts inside his slashed belly. A drummer was beating the Scots on. 'Bring my horse!' Lord Robert called to a squire. He knew that the beaten English line had to break in a moment and then he would mount, take his lance, and pursue the beaten enemy. 'On! On!' he shouted. 'On!' And the man wielding the long-hafted pike, the huge Scotsman who had driven a gap into the English front

rank and who seemed to be carving a bloody path south all by himself, suddenly made a mewing noise. His pike, high in the air where it was still fouled with the bent visor, faltered. The man jerked and his mouth opened and closed, opened and closed again, but he could not speak because an arrow, its white feathers bloodied, jutted from his head.

An arrow, Lord Robert saw, and suddenly the air was thick with them and he pulled down the visor of his helmet so that the day went dark.

The damned English archers were back.

Sir William Douglas had not realized how deep and steep-sided was the bracken-covered saddle in the ridge's flank until he reached its base and there, under the flail of the archers, found he could neither go forward nor back. The front two ranks of Scottish men-at-arms were all either dead or wounded and their bodies made a heap over which he could not climb in his heavy mail. Robbie was screaming defiance and trying to scramble over that heap, but Sir William unceremoniously dragged his nephew back and thrust him down into the bracken. 'This isn't a place to die, Robbie!'

'Bastards!'

'They may be bastards, but we're the fools!' Sir William crouched beside his nephew, covering them both with his huge shield. To go back was unthinkable, for that would be running from the enemy, yet he could not advance and so he just marvelled at the force of the arrows as they thumped into the shield's face. A rush of bearded tribesmen, more nimble than the men-at-arms because they refused to wear metal armour, seethed past him, howling their wild defiance as they scrambled bare-legged across the heap of dying Scots, but then the English arrows began to strike and hurl the clansmen back. The arrows made sounds like bladders rupturing as they struck and the clansmen mewed and groaned, twitching as more arrows thumped home. Each missile provoked a spurt of blood so that Sir William and Robbie Douglas, unscathed beneath their heavy shield, were spattered with gore.

A sudden tumult among the nearby men-at-arms provoked more arrows and Sir William bellowed angrily at the soldiers to lie down, hoping that stillness would persuade the English archers that no

Scotsmen lived, but the men-at-arms called back that the Earl of Moray had been hit. 'Not before time,' Sir William growled to Robbie. He hated the Earl more than he hated the English, and he grinned when a man shouted that his lordship was not just hit, but dead, and then another hail of arrows silenced the Earl's retainers and Sir William heard the missiles clanging on metal, thumping into flesh and striking the willow boards of shields, and when the rattle of arrows was done there was just the moaning and weeping, the hissing of breath, and the creak of leather as men died or tried to extricate themselves from under the piles of dying.

'What happened?' Robbie asked.

'We didn't scout the land properly,' Sir William answered. 'We outnumber the bastards and that made us confident.' Ominously, in the arrowless quiet, he heard laughter and the thump of boots. A scream sounded and Sir William, who was old in war, knew that the English troops were coming down into the bowl to finish off the injured. 'We're going to run back soon,' he told Robbie, 'there's no choice in it. Cover your arse with your shield and run like the devil.'

'We're running away?' Robbie asked, appalled.

Sir William sighed. 'Robbie, you damned fool, you can run forward and you can die and I'll tell your mother you died like a brave man and a halfwit, or you can get the hell back up the hill with me and try to win this battle.'

Robbie did not argue, but just looked back up the Scottish side of the hollow where the bracken was flecked with white-feathered arrows. 'Tell me when to run,' he said.

A dozen archers and as many English men-at-arms were using knives to cut Scottish throats. They would pause before finishing off a man-at-arms to discover whether he had any value as a source of ransom, but few men had such value and the clansmen had none. The latter, hated above all the Scots because they were so different, were treated as vermin. Sir William cautiously raised his head and decided this was the moment to retreat. It was better to scramble out of this bloody trap than be captured and so, ignoring the indignant shouts of the English, he and his nephew scrambled back up the slope. To Sir William's surprise no arrows came. He had expected the grass and bracken to be thrashed with arrows as

he clambered out of the hollow, but he and Robbie were left alone. He turned halfway up the slope and saw that the English bowmen had vanished, leaving only men-at-arms on this flank of the field. At their head, watching him from the hollow's farther lip, was Lord Outhwaite, who had once been Sir William's prisoner. Outhwaite, who was lame, was using a spear as a stave and, seeing Sir William, he raised the weapon in greeting.

'Get yourself some proper armour, Willie!' Sir William shouted. Lord Outhwaite, like the Knight of Liddesdale, had been christened William. 'We're not done with you yet.'

'I fear not, Sir William, I do indeed fear not,' Lord Outhwaite called back. He steadied himself with his spear. 'I trust you're well?'

'Of course I'm not well, you bloody fool! Half my men are down there.'

'My dear fellow,' Outhwaite said with a grimace, and then waved genially as Sir William pushed Robbie on up the hill and followed him to safety.

Sir William, once back on the high ground, took stock. He could see that the Scots had been beaten here on their right, but that had been their own fault for charging headlong into the low ground where the archers had been able to kill with impunity. Those archers had mysteriously vanished, but Sir William guessed they had been pulled clear across the field to the Scottish left flank that had advanced a long way ahead of the centre. He could tell that because Lord Robert Stewart's blue and yellow banner of the lion was so far ahead of the King's red and yellow flag. So the battle was going well on the left, but Sir William could see it was going nowhere in the centre because of the stone wall that obstructed the Scottish advance.

'We'll achieve nothing here,' he told Robbie, 'so let's be useful.' He turned and raised his bloody sword. 'Douglas!' he shouted. 'Douglas!' His standard-bearer had disappeared and Sir William supposed that the man, with his red-hearted flag, was dead in the low ground. 'Douglas!' he called again and, when sufficient of his men had come to him, he led them to the embattled central sheltron. 'We fight here,' he told them, then pushed his way to the King who was on horseback in the second or third rank, fighting beneath his banner that was thick stuck with arrows. He was also fighting

with his visor raised and Sir William saw that the King's face was half obscured with blood. 'Put your visor down!' he roared.

The King was trying to stab a long lance across the stone wall, but the press of men made his efforts futile. His blue and yellow surcoat had been torn to reveal the bright plate metal beneath. An arrow thudded into his right espalier that had again ridden up on the breastplate and he tugged it down just as another arrow ripped open the left ear of his stallion. He saw Sir William and grinned as though this was fine sport. 'Pull your visor down!' Sir William bellowed and he saw that the King was not grinning, but rather a whole flap of his cheek had been torn away and the blood was still welling from the wound and spilling from the helmet's lower rim to soak the torn surcoat. 'Have your cheek bandaged!' Sir William shouted over the din of fighting.

The King let his frightened horse back away from the wall. 'What happened on the right?' His voice was made indistinct by his wound.

'They killed us,' Sir William said curtly, inadvertently jerking his long sword so that drops of blood sprayed from its tip. 'No, they murdered us,' he growled. 'There was a break in the ground and it snared us.'

'Our left is winning! We'll break them there!' The King's mouth kept filling with blood, which he spat out, but despite the copious bleeding he did not seem over-concerned with the wound. It had been inflicted at the very beginning of the battle when an arrow had hissed over the heads of his army to rip a gouge in his cheek before spending itself in his helmet's liner. 'We'll hold them here,' he told Sir William.

'John Randolph's dead,' Sir William told him. 'The Earl of Moray,' he added when he saw that the King had not understood his first words.

'Dead?' King David blinked, then spat more blood. 'He's dead? Not a prisoner?' Another arrow slapped at his flag, but the King was oblivious of the danger. He turned and stared at his enemy's flags. 'We'll have the Archbishop say a prayer over his grave, then the bastard can say grace over our supper.' He saw a gap in the front Scottish rank and spurred his horse to fill it, then lunged with his lance at an English defender. The King's blow broke the man's shoulder, mangling the bloody wound with the debris of torn mail.

'Bastards!' the King spat. 'We're winning!' he called to his men, then a rush of Douglas's followers pushed between him and the wall. The newcomers struck the stone wall like a great wave, but the wall proved stronger and the wave broke on its stones. Swords and axes clashed over the coping and men from both sides dragged the dead out of their paths to clear a passage to the slaughter. 'We'll hold the bastards here,' the King assured Sir William, 'and turn their right.'

But Sir William, his ears ever attuned to the noise of battle, had heard something new. For the last few minutes he had been listening to shouts, clangour, screams and drums, but one sound had been missing and that was the devil's harp music, the deep-toned pluck of bowstrings, but he heard it again now and he knew that though scores of the enemy might have been killed, few of those dead were archers. And now the bows of England had begun their awful work again. 'You want advice, sire?'

'Of course.' The King looked bright-eyed. His destrier, wounded by several arrows, took small nervous steps away from the thickest fighting that raged just paces away.

'Put your visor down,' Sir William said, 'and then pull back.'

'Pull back?' The King wondered if he had misheard.

'Pull back!' Sir William said again, and he sounded hard and sure, yet he was not certain why he had given the advice. It was another damn premonition like the one he had experienced in the fog at dawn, yet he knew the advice was good. Pull back now, pull all the way back to Scotland where there were great castles that could withstand a storm of arrows, yet he knew he could not explain the advice. He could find no reason for it. A dread had seized his heart and filled him with foreboding. From any other man the advice would have been reckoned cowardice, but no one would ever accuse Sir William Douglas, the Knight of Liddesdale, of cowardice.

The King thought the advice was a bad jest and he gave a snorting laugh. 'We're winning!' he told Sir William as more blood spilt from his helmet and slopped down to his saddle. 'Is there any danger on the right?' he asked.

'None,' Sir William said. The hollow in the ground would be as effective at stopping an English advance as it had been at foiling the Scottish attack.

94

'Then we'll win this battle on our left,' the King declared, then hauled on his reins to turn away. 'Pull back indeed!' The King laughed, then took a piece of linen from one of his chaplains and pushed it between his cheek and his helmet. 'We're winning!' he said to Sir William again, then spurred to the east. He was riding to bring Scotland victory and to show that he was a worthy son of the great Bruce. 'St Andrew!' he shouted through thick blood. 'St Andrew!'

'You think we should pull back, uncle?' Robbie Douglas asked. He was as confused as the King. 'But we're winning!'

'Are we?' Sir William listened to the music of the bows. 'Best say your prayers, Robbie,' he said, 'best say your bloody prayers and ask God to let the devil take the bloody archers.'

And pray that God or the devil was listening.

Sir Geoffrey Carr was stationed on the English left where the Scots had been so decisively rebuffed by the terrain and his few men-at-arms were now down in the blood-reeking hollow in search of prisoners. The Scarecrow had watched the Scots trapped in the low ground and he had grinned with feral delight as the arrows had slashed down into the attackers. One enraged tribesman, his thick folds of swathing plaid stuck with arrows as thick as a hedgehog's spines, had tried to fight up the slope. He had been swearing and cursing, repeatedly struck by arrows, one was even sticking from his skull, which was smothered in tangled hair, and another was caught in the thicket of his beard, yet still he had come, bleeding and ranting, so filled with hate that he did not even know he should be dead, and he managed to struggle within five paces of the bowmen before Sir Geoffrey had flicked his whip to take the man's left eye from its socket clean as a hazel from its shell and then an archer had stepped forward and casually split the man's arrow-spitted skull with an axe. The Scarecrow coiled the whip and fingered the damp on the tip's iron claw. 'I do enjoy a battle,' he had said to no one in particular. Once the attack was stalled he had seen that one of the Scottish lords, all gaudy in blue and silver, was lying dead among the heap of corpses and that was a pity. That

was a real pity. There was a fortune gone with that death and Sir Geoffrey, remembering his debts, had ordered his men down into the pit to cut throats, pillage corpses and find any prisoner worth a half-decent ransom. His archers had been taken off to the other side of the field, but his men-at-arms were left to find some cash. 'Hurry, Beggar!' Sir Geoffrey shouted, 'Hurry! Prisoners and plunder! Look for gentlemen and lords! Not that there are any gentlemen in Scotland!' This last observation, made only to himself, amused the Scarecrow so that he laughed aloud. The joke seemed to improve as he thought about it and he almost doubled over in merriment. 'Gentlemen in Scotland!' he repeated and then he saw a young monk staring worriedly at him.

The monk was one of the prior's men, distributing food and ale to the troops, but he had been alarmed by Sir Geoffrey's wild cackle. The Scarecrow, going abruptly silent, stared wide-eyed at the monk and then, silently, let the coils of the whip fall from his hand. The soft leather made no sound as it rippled down, then Sir Geoffrey moved his right arm at lightning speed and the whip struck to loop itself about the young monk's neck. Sir Geoffrey jerked the lash. 'Come here, boy,' he ordered.

The jerk made the monk stumble so that he dropped the bread and apples he had been carrying, then he was standing close beside Sir Geoffrey's horse and the Scarecrow was leaning down from the saddle so that the monk could smell his fetid breath. 'Listen, you pious little turd,' Sir Geoffrey hissed, 'if you don't tell me the truth I'll cut off what you don't need and what you don't use except to piss through and feed it to my swine, do you understand me, boy?'

The monk, terrified, just nodded.

Sir Geoffrey looped the whip one more time round the young man's neck and gave it a good tug just to let the monk know who was in charge. 'An archer, fellow with a black bow, had a letter for your prior.'

'He did, sir, yes, sir.'

'And did the prior read it?'

'Yes, sir, he did, sir.'

'And did he tell you what was in it?'

The monk instinctively shook his head, then saw the rage in the Scarecrow's eye and in his panic he blurted out the word he had

first overheard when the letter was opened. '*Thesaurus*, sir, that's what's in it, *thesaurus*.'

'*Thesaurus*?' Sir Geoffrey said, stumbling over the foreign word. 'And what, you gelded piece of weasel shit, what, in the name of a thousand virgins, is a *thesaurus*?'

'Treasure, sir, treasure. Latin, sir. *Thesaurus*, sir, is Latin for . . .' the monk's voice trailed away. '. . . treasure,' he finished lamely.

'Treasure.' Sir Geoffrey repeated the word flatly.

The monk, half choking, was suddenly eager to repeat the gossip that had circulated amongst the brethren since Thomas of Hookton had encountered the prior. 'The King sent him, sir, his majesty himself, and my lord the bishop too, sir, from France, and they're looking for a treasure, sir, but no one knows what it is.'

'The King?'

'Or where it is, sir, yes, sir, the King himself, sir. He sent him, sir.'

Sir Geoffrey looked into the monk's eyes, saw no guile and so unlooped the whip. 'You dropped some apples, boy.'

'I did, sir, I did, sir, yes.'

'Feed one to my horse.' He watched the monk retrieve an apple, then his face suddenly contorted with anger. 'Wipe the mud off it first, you toadspawn! Clean it!' He shuddered, then stared northwards, but he was not seeing the surviving Scots of the enemy's right wing scramble out of the low ground and he did not even notice the escape of his hated enemy, Sir William Douglas, who had impoverished him. He saw none of these things because the Scarecrow was thinking of treasure. Of gold. Of heaps of gold. Of his heart's desire. Of money and jewels and coins and plate and women and everything a heart could ever want.

The sheltron on the Scottish left, rampant and savage, forced the English right so far back that a great gap appeared between the English centre, behind its stone wall, and the retreating division on its right. That retreat meant that the right flank of the central division was now exposed to Scottish attack, indeed the rear of the Archbishop's battle was exposed to the Scots, but then, from all across the ridge, the archers came to the rescue.

They came to make a new line that protected the Archbishop's flank, a line that faced sideways onto the triumphant Scottish assault and the swarm of archers drove their arrows into Lord Robert Stewart's sheltron. They could not miss. These were bowmen who started their archery practice at a hundred paces and finished over two hundred paces from the straw-filled targets, and now they were shooting at twenty paces and the arrows flew with such force that some pierced through mail, body and mail again. Men in armour were being spitted by the arrows and the right-hand side of the Scottish advance crumpled in blood and pain, and every man who fell exposed another victim to the bowmen who were shooting as fast as they could lay their arrows on the cords. The Scots were dying by the score. They were dying and they were screaming. Some men instinctively tried to charge the archers, but were immediately cut down; no troops could stand that assault of feathered steel and suddenly the Scots were pulling back, tripping over the dead left by their charge, stumbling back across the pasture to where they had begun their charge and they were pursued every step of the way by the hissing arrows until, at last, an English voice ordered the archers to rest their bows. 'But stay here!' the man ordered, wanting the archers who had come from the left wing to stay on the beleaguered right.

Thomas was among the archers. He counted his arrows, finding only seven left in his bag and so he began hunting in the grass for shot arrows that were not badly damaged, but then a man nudged him and pointed to a cart that was trundling across the field with spare sheaves. Thomas was astonished. 'In France we were ever running out of arrows.'

'Not here.' The man had a hare lip, which made him hard to understand. 'They keep 'em in Durham. In the castle. Three counties send 'em here.' He scooped up two new sheaves.

The arrows were made all across England and Wales. Some folk cut and trimmed the shafts, others collected the feathers, women span the cords and men boiled the hide, hoof and verdigris glue while smiths forged the heads, and then the separate parts were carried to towns where the arrows were assembled, bundled and sent on to London, York, Chester or Durham where they awaited an emergency. Thomas broke the twine on two sheaves and put

the new arrows in a bag he had taken from a dead archer. He had found the man lying behind the Archbishop's troops and Thomas had left his old torn bag beside the man's body and now had a new bag filled with fresh arrows. He flexed the fingers of his right hand. They were sore, proof he had not shot enough arrows since the battle in Picardy. His back ached as it always did after he had shot the bow twenty or more times. Each draw was the equivalent of lifting a man one-handed and the effort of it dug the ache deep into his spine, but the arrows had driven the Scottish left wing clean back to where it had started and where, like their English enemies, they now drew breath. The ground between the two armies was littered with spent arrows, dead men and wounded, some of whom moved slowly as they tried to drag themselves back to their comrades. Two dogs sniffed at a corpse, but skittered away when a monk shied a stone at them.

Thomas unlooped the string of his bow so that the stave straightened. Some archers liked to leave their weapons permanently strung until the stave had taken on the curve of a tensioned bow, and were said to have followed the string; the curve was supposed to show that the bow was well used and thus that its owner was an experienced soldier, but Thomas reckoned a bow that had followed the string was weakened and so he unstrung his as often as he could. That also helped to preserve the cord. It was difficult to fashion a cord of exactly the right length, and inevitably it stretched, but a good hempen string, soaked with glue, could last the best part of a year if it was kept dry and not subjected to constant tension. Like many archers, Thomas liked to reinforce his bowcords with women's hair because that was meant to protect the strings from snapping in a fight. That and praying to St Sebastian. Thomas let the string hang from the top of the bow, then squatted in the grass where he took the arrows from his bag one by one and span them between his fingers to detect any warping in their shafts.

'The bastards will be back!' A man with a silver crescent on his surcoat strode down the line. 'They'll be back for more! But you've done well!' The silver crescent was half obscured by blood. An archer spat and another impulsively stroked his unstrung bow. Thomas thought that if he lay down he would probably sleep, but he was assailed by the ridiculous fear that the other archers would

retreat and leave him there, sleeping, and the Scots would find and kill him. The Scots, though, were resting like the English. Some men were bent over as if they caught their breath, others were sitting on the grass while a few clustered round a barrel of water or ale. The big drums were silent, but Thomas could hear the scrape of stone on steel as men sharpened blades blunted by the battle's first clash. No insults were being shouted on either side now, men just eyed each other warily. Priests knelt beside dying men, praying their souls into heaven, while women shrieked because their husbands, lovers or sons were dead. The English right wing, its numbers thinned by the ferocity of the Scottish attack, had moved back to its original place and behind them were scores of dead and dying men. The Scottish casualties left behind by the precipitate retreat were being stripped and searched and a fight broke out between two men squabbling over a handful of tarnished coins. Two monks carried water to the wounded. A small child played with broken rings from a mail coat while his mother attempted to prise a broken visor off a pike that she reckoned would make a good axe. A Scotsman, thought dead, suddenly groaned and turned over and a man-at-arms stepped to him and stabbed down with his sword. The enemy stiffened, relaxed and did not move again. 'Ain't resurrection day yet, you bastard,' the man-at-arms said as he dragged his sword free. 'Goddamn son of a whore,' he grumbled, wiping his sword on the dead man's ragged surcoat, 'waking up like that! Gave me a turn!' He was not speaking to anyone in particular, but just crouched beside the man he had killed and began searching his clothes.

The cathedral towers and castle walls were thick with spectators. A heron flew beneath the ramparts, following the looping river that sparkled prettily under the autumn sun. Thomas could hear corncrakes down the slope. Butterflies, surely the last of the year, flew above the blood-slicked grass. The Scots were standing, stretching, pulling on helmets, pushing their forearms into their shield loops and hefting newly sharpened swords, pikes and spears. Some glanced over to the city and imagined the treasures stored in the cathedral crypt and castle cellars. They dreamed of chests crammed with gold, vats overflowing with coin, rooms heaped with silver, taverns running with ale and streets filled with women. 'In the

name of the Father and of the Son,' a priest called, 'and of the Holy Ghost. St Andrew is with you. You fight for your King! The enemy are godless imps of Satan! God is with us!'

'Up, boys, up!' an archer called on the English side. Men stood, strung their bows and took the first arrow from the bag. Some crossed themselves, oblivious that the Scots did the same.

Lord Robert Stewart, mounted on a fresh grey stallion, pushed his way towards the front of the Scottish left wing. 'They'll have few arrows left,' he promised his men, 'few arrows. We can break them!' His men had so nearly broken the damned English last time. So nearly, and surely another howling rush would obliterate the small defiant army and open the road to the opulent riches of the south.

'For St Andrew!' Lord Robert called and the drummers began their beating, 'for our King! For Scotland!'

And the howling began again.

Bernard de Taillebourg went to the cathedral when his business in the monastery's small hospital was finished. His servant was readying the horses as the Dominican strode down the great nave between the vast pillars painted in jagged stripes of red, yellow, green and blue. He went to the tomb of St Cuthbert to say a prayer. He was not certain that Cuthbert was an important saint – he was certainly not one of the blessed souls who commanded the ear of God in heaven – but he was much revered locally, and his tomb, thickly decorated with jewels, gold and silver, testified to that devotion.

At least a hundred women were gathered about the grave, most of them crying, and de Taillebourg pushed some out of his way so he could get close enough to touch the embroidered pall that shrouded the tomb. One woman snarled at him, then realized he was a priest and, seeing his bloodied, bruised face, begged his forgiveness. Bernard de Taillebourg ignored her, stooping instead to the tomb. The pall was tasselled and the women had tied little shreds of cloth to the tassels, each scrap a prayer. Most prayers were for health, for the restoration of a limb, for the gift of sight,

or to save a child's life, but today they were begging Cuthbert to bring their menfolk safely down from the hill.

Bernard de Taillebourg added his own prayer. Go to St Denis, he beseeched Cuthbert, and ask him to speak to God. Cuthbert, even if he could not hold God's attention, could certainly find St Denis who, being French, was bound to be closer to God than Cuthbert. Beg Denis to pray that God's speed attend my errand and that God's blessing be upon the search and that God's grace give it success. And pray God to forgive us our sins, but know that our sins, grievous though they be, are committed only in God's service. He moaned at the thought of this day's sins, then he kissed the pall and took a coin from the purse under his robe. He dropped the coin in the great metal jar where pilgrims gave what they could to the shrine and then he hurried back down the cathedral's nave. A crude building, he thought, its coloured pillars so fat and gross and its carvings as clumsy as a child's scratchings, so unlike the new and graceful abbeys and churches that were rising in France. He dipped his fingers in the holy water, made the sign of the cross and went out into the sunlight where his servant was waiting with their mounts.

'You could have left without me,' he said to the servant.

'It would be easier,' the servant said, 'to kill you on the road and then go on without you.'

'But you won't do that,' de Taillebourg said, 'because the grace of God has come into your soul.'

'Thanks be to God,' the servant said.

The man was not a servant by birth, but a knight and gently born. Now, at de Taillebourg's pleasure, he was being punished for his sins and for the sins of his family. There were those, and Cardinal Bessières was among them, who thought the man should have been stretched on the rack, that he should have been pressed by great weights, that the burning irons should have seared into his flesh so that his back arched as he screamed repentance at the ceiling, but de Taillebourg had persuaded the Cardinal to do nothing except show this man the instruments of the Inquisition's torture. 'Then give him to me,' de Taillebourg had said, 'and let him lead me to the Grail.'

'Kill him afterwards,' the Cardinal had instructed the Inquisitor.

'All will be different when we have the Grail,' de Taillebourg had said evasively. He still did not know whether he would have to kill this thin young man with the sun-dark skin and the black eyes and the narrow face who had once called himself the Harlequin. He had adopted the name out of pride because harlequins were lost souls, but de Taillebourg believed he might well have saved this harlequin's soul. The Harlequin's real name was Guy Vexille, Count of Astarac, and it had been Guy Vexille whom de Taillebourg had been describing when he spoke to Brother Collimore about the man who had come from the south to fight for France in Picardy. Vexille had been seized after the battle when the French King had been looking for scapegoats and a man who dared display the crest of a family declared heretic and rebel had made a good scapegoat.

Vexille had been given to the Inquisition in the expectation that they would torture the heresy out of him, but de Taillebourg had liked the Harlequin. He had recognized a fellow soul, a hard man, a dedicated man, a man who knew that this life meant nothing because all that counted was the next, and so de Taillebourg had spared Vexille the agonies. He had merely shown him the chamber where men and women screamed their apologies to God, and then he had questioned him gently and Vexille had revealed how he had once sailed to England to find the Grail and, though he had killed his uncle, Thomas's father, he had not found it. Now, with de Taillebourg, he had listened to Eleanor tell Thomas's story. 'Did you believe her?' the Dominican now asked.

'I believed her,' Vexille said.

'But was she deceived?' The Inquisitor wondered. Eleanor had told them that Thomas had been charged to seek the Grail, but that his faith was weak and his search half-hearted. 'We shall still have to kill him,' de Taillebourg added.

'Of course.'

De Taillebourg frowned. 'You do not mind?'

'Killing?' Guy Vexille sounded surprised that de Taillebourg should even ask. 'Killing is my job, father,' the Harlequin said. Cardinal Bessières had decreed that everyone who sought the Grail should be killed, all except those who sought it on the Cardinal's own behalf, and Guy Vexille had willingly become God's murderer. He certainly had no qualms about slitting his cousin Thomas's

throat. 'You want to wait here for him?' he asked the Inquisitor. 'The girl said he would be in the cathedral after the battle.'

De Taillebourg looked across to the hill. The Scots would win, he was sure, and that made it doubtful that Thomas of Hookton would come to the city. More likely he would flee southwards in panic. 'We shall go to Hookton.'

'I searched Hookton once,' Guy Vexille said.

'Then you will search it again,' de Taillebourg snapped.

'Yes, father.' Guy Vexille humbly lowered his head. He was a sinner; it was required of him that he show penitence and so he did not argue. He just did de Taillebourg's bidding and his reward, he had been promised, would be reinstatement. He would be given back his pride, allowed to lead men to war again and forgiven by the Church.

'We shall leave now,' de Taillebourg said. He wanted to go before William Douglas came in search of them and, even more urgently, before anyone discovered the three bodies in the hospital cell. The Dominican had closed the door on the corpses and doubtless the monks would believe Collimore was sleeping and so would not disturb him, but de Taillebourg still wanted to be free of the city when the bodies were found and so he pulled himself into the saddle of one of the horses they had stolen from Jamie Douglas that morning. It seemed a long time ago now. He pushed his shoes into the stirrups, then kicked a beggar away. The man had been clawing at de Taillebourg's leg, whining that he was hungry, but now reeled away from the priest's savage thrust.

The noise of battle swelled. The Dominican looked at the ridge again, but the fight was none of his business. If the English and the Scots wished to maul each other then let them. He had greater matters on his mind, matters of God and the Grail and of heaven and hell. He had sins on his conscience too, but they would be shriven by the Holy Father and even heaven would understand those sins once he had found the Grail.

The gates of the city, though strongly guarded, were open so that the wounded could be brought inside and food and drink carried to the ridge. The guards were older men and had been ordered to make certain that no Scottish raiders tried to enter the city, but they had not been charged to stop anyone leaving and so they took

104

no notice of the haggard priest with the bruised face mounted on a warhorse, nor of his elegant servant. So de Taillebourg and the Harlequin rode out of Durham, turned towards the York road, put back their heels and, as the sound of battle echoed from the city's crag, rode away southwards.

It was mid-afternoon when the Scots attacked a second time, but this assault, unlike the first, did not come hard on the heels of fleeing archers. Instead the archers were drawn up ready to receive the charge and this time the arrows flew thick as starlings. Those on the Scottish left who had so nearly broken the English line were now faced by twice as many archers, and their charge, which had begun so confidently, slowed to a crawl and then stopped altogether as men crouched behind shields. The Scottish right never advanced at all, while the King's central sheltron was checked fifty paces from the stone wall behind which a crowd of archers sent an incessant shower of arrows. The Scots would not retreat, they could not advance, and for a time the long-shafted arrows thumped onto shields and into carelessly exposed bodies, then Lord Robert Stewart's men edged back out of range and the King's sheltron followed and so another pause came over the red-earthed battle-field. The drums were silent and no more insults were being shouted across the littered pastureland. The Scottish lords, those who still lived, gathered under their King's saltire banner and the Archbishop of York, seeing his enemies in council, called his own lords together. The Englishmen were gloomy. The enemy, they reasoned, would never expose themselves to what the Archbishop described as a third baptism of arrows. 'The bastards will slink off northwards,' the Archbishop predicted, 'God damn their bloody souls.'

'Then we follow them,' Lord Percy said.

'They move faster than us,' the Archbishop said. He had taken off his helmet and its leather liner had left an indentation in his hair, circling his skull.

'We'll slaughter their foot,' another lord said wolfishly.

'Damn their infantry,' the Archbishop snapped, impatient with such foolery. He wanted to capture the Scottish lords, the men

mounted on the swiftest and most expensive horses, for it was their ransoms that would make him rich, and he especially wanted to capture those Scottish nobles like the Earl of Menteith who had sworn fealty to Edward of England and whose presence in the enemy army proved their treachery. Such men would not be ransomed, but would be executed as an example to other men who broke their oaths, but if the Archbishop was victorious today then he could lead this small army into Scotland and take the traitors' estates. He would take everything from them: the timber from their parks, the sheets from their beds, the beds themselves, the slates off their roofs, their pots, their pans, their cattle, even the rushes from their streambeds. 'But they won't attack again,' the Archbishop said.

'Then we shall have to be clever,' Lord Outhwaite put in cheerfully.

The other lords looked suspiciously at Outhwaite. Cleverness was not a quality they prized for it hunted no boars, killed no stags, enjoyed no women and took no prisoners. Churchmen could be clever, and doubtless there were clever fools at Oxford, and even women could be clever so long as they did not flaunt it, but on a battlefield? Cleverness?

'Clever?' Lord Neville asked pointedly.

'They fear our archers,' Lord Outhwaite said, 'but if our archers are seen to have few arrows, then that fear will go and they might well attack again.'

'Indeed, indeed . . .' the Archbishop began and then stopped, for he was quite as clever as Lord Outhwaite, clever enough, indeed, to hide how clever he was. 'But how would we convince them?' he asked.

Lord Outhwaite obliged the Archbishop by explaining what he suspected the Archbishop had already grasped. 'I think, your grace, that if our archers are seen scavenging the field for arrows then the enemy will draw the correct conclusion.'

'Or, in this case,' the Archbishop laid it on broadly for the benefit of the other lords, 'the incorrect conclusion.'

'Oh, that's good,' one of those other lords said warmly.

'It could be made even better, your grace,' Lord Outhwaite suggested diffidently, 'if our horses were brought forward? The

enemy might then assume we were readying ourselves to flee?'

The Archbishop did not hesitate. 'Bring all the horses up,' he said.

'But . . .' A lord was frowning.

'Archers to scavenge for arrows, squires and pages to bring up the horses for the men-at-arms,' the Archbishop snapped, understanding completely what Lord Outhwaite had in mind and eager to put it into effect before the enemy decided to withdraw northwards.

Lord Outhwaite gave the orders to the bowmen himself and, within a few moments, scores of archers were out in the space between the armies where they gathered spent arrows. Some of the archers grumbled, calling it tomfoolery because they felt exposed to the Scottish troops who once again began to jeer them. One archer, farther forward than most, was struck in the chest by a crossbow quarrel and he fell to his knees, a look of astonishment on his face, and choked up blood into his cupped palm. Then he began weeping and that only made the choking worse and then a second man, going to help the first, was hit in the thigh by the same crossbow. The Scots were howling their derision at the wounded men, then cowered as a dozen English archers loosed arrows at the lone crossbowman. 'Save your arrows! Save your arrows!' Lord Outhwaite, mounted on his horse, roared at the bowmen. He galloped closer to them. 'Save your arrows! For God's sake! Save them!' He was bellowing loud enough for the enemy to hear him, then a group of Scotsmen, tired of sheltering from the archers, ran forward in an evident attempt to cut off Lord Outhwaite's retreat and all the English scampered for their own line. Lord Outhwaite put back his spurs and easily evaded the rush of men who contented themselves with butchering the two wounded archers. The rest of the Scots, seeing the English run, laughed and jeered. Lord Outhwaite turned and gazed at the two dead bowmen. 'We should have brought those lads in,' he chided himself.

No one answered. Some of the archers were looking resentfully at the men-at-arms, supposing that their horses had been brought up to aid their flight, but then Lord Outhwaite barked at groups of archers to get behind the men-at-arms. 'Line up at the back! Not all of you. We're trying to make them believe we're short of arrows and if you didn't have arrows you wouldn't be standing out in

front, now would you? Hold the horses where they are!' He shouted this last order to the squires, pages and servants who had brought up the destriers. The men-at-arms were not to mount yet, the horses were simply being held at the back of the line, just behind the place where half the archers now formed. The enemy, seeing the horses, must conclude that the English, short of arrows, were contemplating flight.

And so the simple trap was baited.

A silence fell on the battlefield, except that the wounded were moaning, ravens calling and some women crying. The monks began to chant again, but they were still on the English left and to Thomas, now on the right, the sound was faint. A bell rang in the city. 'I do fear we're being too clever,' Outhwaite remarked to Thomas. His lordship was not a man who could keep silent and there was no one else in the right-hand division convenient for conversation and so he selected Thomas. He sighed. 'It doesn't always work, being clever.'

'It worked for us in Brittany, my lord.'

'You were in Brittany as well as Picardy?' Lord Outhwaite asked. He was still mounted and was gazing over the men-at-arms towards the Scots.

'I served a clever man there, my lord.'

'And who was that?' Lord Outhwaite was pretending to be interested, perhaps regretting that he had even begun the conversation.

'Will Skeat, my lord, only he's Sir William now. The King knighted him at the battle.'

'Will Skeat?' Lord Outhwaite was engaged now. 'You served Will? By the good Lord, you did? Dear William. I haven't heard that name in many a year. How is he?'

'Not well, my lord,' Thomas said, and he told how Will Skeat, a commoner who had become the leader of a band of archers and men-at-arms who were feared wherever men spoke French, had been grievously wounded at the battle in Picardy. 'He was taken to Caen, my lord.'

Lord Outhwaite frowned. 'That's back in French hands, surely?'

'A Frenchman took him there, my lord,' Thomas explained, 'a friend, because there's a doctor in the city who can work miracles.' At the end of the battle, when men could at last think they had

lived through the horror, Skeat's skull had been opened to the sky and when Thomas had last seen him Skeat had been dumb, blind and powerless.

'I don't know why the French make better physicians,' Lord Outhwaite said in mild annoyance, 'but it seems they do. My father always said they did, and he had much trouble with his phlegm.'

'This man's Jewish, my lord.'

'And with his shoulders. Jewish! Did you say Jewish?' Lord Outhwaite sounded alarmed. 'I have nothing against Jews,' he went on, though without conviction, 'but I can think of a dozen good reasons why one should never resort to a Jewish physician.'

'Truly, my lord?'

'My dear fellow, how can they harness the power of the saints? Or the healing properties of relics? Or the efficacy of holy water? Even prayer is a mystery to them. My mother, rest her soul, had great pain in her knees. Too much praying, I always thought, but her physician ordered her to wrap her legs in cloths that had been placed on the grave of St Cuthbert and to pray thrice a day to St Gregory of Nazianzus and it worked! It worked! But no Jew could prescribe such a cure, could he? And if he did it would be blasphemous and bound to fail. I must say I think it most ill advised to have placed poor Will into a Jew's hands. He deserves better, indeed he does.' He shook his head reprovingly. 'Will served my father for a time, but was too smart a fellow to stay cooped up on the Scottish border. Not enough plunder, you see? Went off on his own, he did. Poor Will.'

'The Jewish doctor,' Thomas said stubbornly, 'cured me.'

'We can only pray.' Lord Outhwaite ignored Thomas's claim and spoke in a tone which suggested that prayer, though needful, would almost certainly prove useless. Then he cheered up suddenly. 'Ah! I think our friends are stirring!' The Scottish drums had begun to beat and all along the enemy's line men were hitching up shields, dropping visors or hefting swords. They could see that the English had brought their horses closer, presumably to aid their retreat, and that the enemy line was apparently stripped of half its archers, so they must have believed that those bowmen were perilously short of missiles, yet the Scots still chose to advance on foot, knowing that even a handful of arrows could madden their horses and throw

a mounted charge into chaos. They shouted as they advanced, as much to hearten themselves as put fear in the English, but they became more confident when they reached the place where the bodies lay from their last charge and still no arrows flew.

'Not yet, lads, not yet.' Lord Outhwaite had taken command of the archers on the right wing. The Lords Percy and Neville commanded here, yet both were content to allow the older man give orders to the bowmen while they waited with their men-at-arms. Lord Outhwaite glanced constantly across the field to where the Scots advanced on the English left wing, where his own men were, but he was satisfied that the hollow of ground would go on protecting them just as the stone wall shielded the centre. It was here on the side of the ridge closest to Durham where the Scots were strongest and the English most vulnerable. 'Let them get closer,' he warned the archers. 'We want to finish them off once and for all, poor fellows.' He began tapping his fingers on his saddle's pommel, keeping time with the few remaining big Scottish drums and waiting until the front rank of Scots was only a hundred paces away. 'Foremost archers,' he called when he judged the enemy was close enough, 'that's you fellows in front of the line! Start shooting!'

About half the archers were in plain sight in the army's front and they now drew their bows, cocked the arrows up into the air and loosed. The Scots, seeing the volley coming, began to run, hoping to close the range quickly so that only a handful of the arrows would hurt.

'All archers!' Lord Outhwaite boomed, fearing he had waited too long, and the archers who had been concealed behind the men-at-arms began to shoot over the heads of the troops in front. The Scots were close now, close enough so that even the worst archer could not fail to hit his mark, so close that the arrows were again piercing through mail and bodies, and strewing the ground with more wounded and dying men. Thomas could hear the arrows striking home. Some clanged off armour, some thumped into shields, but many made a sound like a butcher's axe when it slaughtered cattle at winter's coming. He aimed at a big man whose visor was raised and sent an arrow down his throat. Another arrow into a tribesman whose face was contorted with hate. Then an arrow's nock split on him, spinning the broken missile away when he released the string.

He plucked the feathered scraps from the string, took a new arrow and drove it into another bearded tribesman who was all fury and hair. A mounted Scotsman was encouraging his men forward and then he was flailing in the saddle, struck by three arrows and Thomas loosed another shaft, striking a man-at-arms clean in the chest so that the point ripped through mail, leather, bone and flesh. His next arrow sank into a shield. The Scots were floundering, trying to force themselves into the rain of death. 'Steady, boys, steady!' an archer called to his fellows, fearing they were snatching at the strings and thus not using the full force of their bows.

'Keep shooting!' Lord Outhwaite called. His fingers still tapped the pommel of his saddle, though the Scottish drums were faltering. 'Lovely work! Lovely work!'

'Horses!' Lord Percy ordered. He could see that the Scots were on the edge of despair for the English archers were not after all short of arrows. 'Horses!' he bellowed again, and his men-at-arms ran back to haul themselves into saddles. Pages and squires handed up the big heavy lances as men fiddled armoured feet into stirrups, glanced at the suffering enemy and then snapped down their visors.

'Shoot! Shoot!' Lord Outhwaite called. 'That's the way, lads!' The arrows were pitiless. The Scottish wounded cried to God, called for their mothers and still the feathered death hammered home. One man, wearing the lion of Stewart, spewed a pink mist of blood and spittle. He was on his knees, but managed to stand, took a step, fell to his knees again, shuffled forward, blew more blood-stained bubbles and then an arrow buried itself in his eye and went through his brain to scrape against the back of his skull and he went backwards as though hit by a thunderbolt.

Then the great horses came.

'For England, Edward and St George!' Lord Percy called and a trumpeter took up the challenge as the great destriers charged. They unceremoniously thrust the archers aside as the lances dropped.

The turf shook. Only a few horsemen were attacking, but the shock of their charge struck the enemy with stunning force and the Scots reeled back. Lances were relinquished in men's bodies as the knights drew swords and hacked down at frightened, cowering men who could not run because the press of bodies was too great. More horsemen were mounting up and those men-at-arms who

did not want to wait for their stallions were running forward to join the carnage. The archers joined them, drawing swords or swinging axes. The drums were at last silent and the slaughter had begun.

Thomas had seen it happen before. He had seen how, in an eyeblink, a battle could change. The Scots had been pressing all day, they had so nearly shattered the English, they were rampant and winning, yet now they were beaten and the men of the Scottish left, who had come so close to giving their King his victory, were the ones who broke. The English warhorses galloped into their ranks to make bloody lanes and the riders swung swords, axes, clubs and morningstars at panicked men. The English archers joined in, mobbing the slower Scots like packs of hounds leaping onto deer. 'Prisoners!' Lord Percy shouted at his retainers. 'I want prisoners!' A Scotsman swung an axe at his horse, missed and was chopped down by his lordship's sword, an archer finished the job with a knife and then slit the man's padded jerkin to search for coins. Two carpenters from Durham hacked with woodworker's adzes at a struggling man-at-arms, bludgeoning his skull, killing him slowly. An archer reeled back, gasping, his belly cut open and a Scot followed him, screaming in rage, but then was tripped by a bowstave and went down under a swarm of men. The trappers of the English horses were dripping with blood as their riders turned to cut their way back through the Scottish host. They had ridden clean through and now spurred back to meet the next wave of English men-at-arms who fought with visors open for the panicking enemy was not offering any real resistance.

Yet the Scottish right and centre were intact.

The right had again been pushed into the low ground, but now, instead of archers fighting them from the rim, they faced the English men-at-arms who were foolish enough to go down into the hollow to meet the Scottish charge. Mailed men clashed over the bodies of the Scottish dead, clambering awkwardly in their metal suits to swing swords and axes against shields and skulls. Men grunted as they killed. They snarled, attacked and died in the muddy bracken, yet the fight was futile for if either side gained an advantage they only pressed their enemy back up the slope and immediately the losing side had the ground as their ally and they would press back downhill and more dead joined the corpses in the hollow's bottom and so the fight surged forward and back, each great swing leaving men

weeping and dying, calling on Jesus, cursing their enemy, bleeding.

Beggar was there, a great rock of a man who stood astride the corpse of the Earl of Moray, mocking the Scots and inviting them to fight, and half a dozen came and were killed before a pack of Highland clansmen came screaming to kill him and he roared at them, swinging his huge spiked mace, and to the Scarecrow, watching from above, he looked like a great shaggy bear assailed by mastiffs. Sir William Douglas, too canny to be caught a second time in the low ground, also watched from the opposing rim and was amazed that men would go willingly down to the slaughter. Then, knowing that the battle would neither be won nor lost in that pit of death, he turned back to the centre where the King's sheltron still had a chance of gaining a great victory despite the disaster on the Scottish left.

For the King's men had got past the stone wall. In places they had pulled it down and in others it had at last collapsed before the press of men, and though the fallen stones still presented a formidable obstacle to soldiers cumbered by heavy shields and coats of mail they were clambering across and thrusting back the English centre. The Scots had charged into the arrows, endured them and even trapped a score of archers whom they slaughtered gleefully and now they hacked and stabbed their way towards the Archbishop's great banner. The King, his visor sticky with blood from his wounded cheek, was in the forefront of the sheltron. The King's chaplain was beside his master, wielding a spiked club, and Sir William and his nephew joined the attack. Sir William was suddenly ashamed of the premonition that had made him advise a retreat. This was how Scotsmen fought! With passion and savagery. The English centre was reeling back, scarce holding its ranks. Sir William saw that the enemy had fetched their horses close up to the battle line and he surmised they were readying themselves to flee and so he redoubled his efforts. 'Kill them!' he roared. If the Scots could break the line then the English would be in chaos, unable to reach their horses, and mere meat for the butchers.

'Kill! Kill!' the King, conspicuous on horseback, shouted at his men.

'Prisoners!' the Earl of Menteith, more sensible, called. 'Take prisoners!'

'Break them! Break them now!' Sir William roared. He slammed his shield forward to receive a sword stroke, stabbed beneath it and felt his blade pierce a mail coat. He turned the sword and jerked it free before the flesh could grip the steel. He pushed with his shield, unable to see over its top rim, felt the enemy stagger back, lowered the shield in anticipation of a lunge underneath, then rammed it forward again, throwing the enemy back. He stumbled forward, almost losing his footing by tripping on the man he had wounded, but he caught his weight by dropping the bottom edge of the shield on the ground, pushed himself upright and thrust the sword into a bearded face. The blade glanced off the cheekbone, taking an eye, and that man fell backwards, mouth agape, abandoning the fight. Sir William half ducked to avoid an axe blow, caught another sword on his shield and stabbed wildly towards the two men attacking him. Robbie, swearing and cursing, killed the axeman, then kicked a fallen man-at-arms in the face. Sir William lunged underhand and felt his sword scrape on broken mail and he twisted to stop the blade being trapped and yanked it back so that a gush of blood spilled through the metal rings of the wounded man's armour. That man fell, gasping and twitching, and more Englishmen came from the right, desperate to stop the Scottish attack that threatened to pierce clean through the Archbishop's line. 'Douglas!' Sir William roared. 'Douglas!' He was calling on his followers to come and support him, to shove and to gouge and to hack the last enemy down. He and his nephew had carved a bloody path deep into the Archbishop's ranks and it would take only a moment's fierce fighting to break the English centre and then the real slaughter could begin. Sir William ducked as another axe flailed at him. Robbie killed that man, driving his sword through the axeman's throat, but Robbie immediately had to parry a spear thrust and in doing it he staggered back against his uncle. Sir William shoved his nephew upright and hammered his shield into an enemy's face. Where the hell were his men? 'Douglas!' Sir William thundered again. 'Douglas!'

And just then a sword or spear tangled his feet and he fell and instinctively he covered himself with the shield. Men pounded past him and he prayed that they were his followers who were breaking the last English resistance and he waited for the enemy's screaming to begin, but instead there was an insistent tap on his helmet. The

tapping stopped, then started again. 'Sir William?' a gentle voice enquired.

The screaming had begun so Sir William could scarcely hear, but the gentle tapping on the crown of his helmet persuaded him it was safe to lower his shield. It took him a moment to see what was happening for his helmet had been wrenched askew when he fell and he had to pull it round. 'God's teeth,' he said when the world came into view.

'Dear Sir William,' the kindly voice said, 'I assume you yield? Of course you do. And is that young Robbie? My, how you've grown, young man! I remember you as a pup.'

'Oh, God's teeth,' Sir William said again, looking up at Lord Outhwaite.

'Can I give you a hand?' Lord Outhwaite asked solicitously, reaching down from his saddle. 'And then we can talk ransoms.'

'Jesus,' Sir William said, 'God damn it!' for he understood now that the feet pounding past had been English feet and that the screaming was coming from the Scots.

The English centre had held after all, and for the Scots the battle had turned to utter disaster.

It was the archers again. The Scots had lost men all day and still they outnumbered their enemy, but they had no answer to the arrows and when the Scottish centre broke down the wall and surged across its remains, so the Scottish left had retreated and exposed the flank of the King's sheltron to the English arrows.

It took a few moments for the bowmen to realize their advantage. They had joined the pursuit of the broken Scottish left and were unaware how close to victory was the Scottish centre, but then one of Lord Neville's men understood the danger. 'Archers!' His roar could be heard clear across the Wear in Durham. 'Archers!' Men broke off their plundering and pulled arrows from the bags.

The bows began sounding again, each deep harp note driving an arrow into the flank of the rampaging Scots. David's sheltron had forced the central English battle back across a pasture, they had stretched it thin and they were closing on the Archbishop's great

banner, and then the arrows began to bite and after the arrows came the men-at-arms from the English right wing, the retainers of Lord Percy and of Lord Neville, and some were already mounted on their big horses that were trained to bite, rear and kick with their iron-shod hooves. The archers, discarding their bows yet again, followed the horsemen with axes and swords, and this time their women came as well with knives unsheathed.

The Scottish King hacked at an Englishman, saw him fall, then heard his standard-bearer shout in terror and he turned to see the great banner falling. The standard-bearer's horse had been hamstrung; it screamed as it collapsed and a rabble of archers and men-at-arms clawed at man and beast, snatched at the banner and hauled the standard-bearer down to a ghastly death, but then the royal chaplain seized the reins of the King's horse and dragged David Bruce out of the mêlée. More Scotsmen gathered about their King, escorting him away, and behind them the English were hacking down from saddles, chopping with their swords, cursing as they killed, and the King tried to turn back and continue the fight, but the chaplain forced his horse away. 'Ride, sir! Ride!' the chaplain shouted. Frightened men blundered into the King's horse that trampled on a clansman then stumbled on a corpse. There were Englishmen in the Scottish rear now and the King, seeing his danger, put back his spurs. An enemy knight took a swing at him, but the King parried the blow and galloped past the danger. His army had disintegrated into groups of desperate fugitives. He saw the Earl of Menteith try to mount a horse, but an archer seized his lordship's leg and hauled him back, then sat on him and put a knife to his throat. The Earl shouted that he yielded. The Earl of Fife was a prisoner, the Earl of Strathearn was dead, the Earl of Wigtown was being assailed by two English knights whose swords rang on his plate armour like blacksmiths' hammers. One of the big Scottish drums, its skins split and tattered, rolled down the hill, going faster and faster as the slope steepened, thumping hollow on the rocks until at last it fell sideways and slid to a halt.

The King's great banner was in English hands now as were the standards of a dozen Scottish lords. A few Scots galloped north. Lord Robert Stewart, who had so nearly won the day, was free and clear on the eastern side of the ridge while the King plunged down

the western side, going into shadow because the sun was now lower than the hills towards which he rode in desperate need of refuge. He thought of his wife. Was she pregnant? He had been told that Lord Robert had hired a witch to lay a spell on her womb so that the throne would pass from Bruce to Stewart. 'Sir! Sir!' One of his men was screaming at him and the King came out of his reverie to see a group of English archers already down in the valley. How had they headed him off? He pulled on the reins, leaned right to help the horse round and felt the arrow thump into the stallion's chest. Another of his men was down, tumbling along the stony ground that was tearing his mail into bright shreds. A horse screamed, blood fanned across the dusk and another arrow slammed into the King's shield that was slung on his back. A third arrow was caught in his horse's mane and the stallion was slowing, plunging up and down as it laboured for breath.

The King struck back with his spurs, but the horse could not go faster. He grimaced and the gesture opened the crusted wound on his cheek so that blood spilled from his open visor down his ripped surcoat. The horse stumbled again. There was a stream ahead and a small stone bridge and the King marvelled that anyone should make a masonry bridge over so slight a watercourse, and then the horse's front legs just collapsed and the King was rolling on the ground, miraculously free of his dying mount and without any broken bones and he scrambled up and ran to the bridge where three of his men waited on horseback, one with a riderless stallion. But even before the King could reach the three men the arrows flickered and hammered home, each one making the horses stagger sideways from the shock of its impact. The stallion screamed, tore itself free of the man's grasp and galloped eastwards with blood dripping from its belly. Another horse collapsed with an arrow deep in its rump, two in its belly and another in its jugular. 'Under the bridge!' the King shouted. There would be shelter under the arch, a place to hide, and when he had a dozen men he would make a break for it. Dusk could not be far off and if they waited for nightfall and then walked all night they might be in Scotland by dawn.

So four Scotsmen, one of them a King, huddled under the stone bridge and caught their breath. The arrows had stopped flying, their horses were all dead and the King dared to hope that the English

archers had gone in search of other prey. 'We wait here,' he whispered. He could hear screams from the high ground, he could hear hooves on the slope, but none sounded close to the little low bridge. He shuddered, realizing the magnitude of the disaster. His army was gone, his great hopes were nothing, the Christmas feast would not be in London and Scotland lay open to its enemies. He peered northwards. A group of clansmen splashed through the stream and suddenly six English horsemen appeared and drove their destriers off the high bank and the big swords hacked down and there was blood swirling downstream to run around the King's mailed feet and he shrank back into the shadows as the men-at-arms spurred westwards to find more fugitives. Horses clattered over the bridge and the four Scotsmen said nothing, dared not even look at each other until the sound of the hooves had faded. A trumpet was calling from the ridge and its note was hateful: triumphant and scornful. The King closed his eyes because he feared he would shed tears.

'You must see a physician, sir,' a man said and the King opened his eyes to see it was one of his servants who had spoken.

'This can't be cured,' the King said, meaning Scotland.

'The cheek will mend, sir,' the servant said reassuringly.

The King stared at his retainer as though the man had spoken in some strange foreign tongue and then, terribly and suddenly, his badly wounded cheek began to hurt. There had been no pain all day, but now it was agony and the King felt tears well from his eyes. Not from pain, but shame, and then, as he tried to blink the tears away there were shouts, falling shadows and the splash of boots as men jumped from the bridge. The attackers had swords and spears and they plunged under the bridge's arch like otter-hunters come to the kill and the King roared his defiance and leaped at the man who was in front and his rage was such that he forgot to draw his sword and instead punched the man with his armoured fist and he felt the Englishman's teeth crunch under the blow, saw the blood spurt and he drove the man down into the stream, hammering him, and then he could not move because other men were pinioning him. The man beneath him, half drowned with broken teeth and bloodied lips, began to laugh.

For he had taken a prisoner. And he would be rich.

He had captured the King.

PART TWO

England and Normandy, 1346–7

The Winter Siege

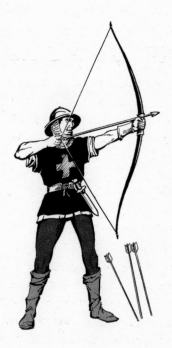

It was dark in the cathedral. So dark that the bright colours painted on the pillars and walls had faded into blackness. The only light came from the candles on the side altars and from beyond the rood screen where flames shivered in the choir and black-robed monks chanted. Their voices wove a spell in the dark, twining and falling, surging and rising, a sound that would have brought tears to Thomas's eyes if he had possessed any tears left to shed. '*Libera me, Domine, de morte aeterna*,' the monks intoned as the candle smoke twisted up to the cathedral's roof. Deliver me, Lord, from everlasting death, and on the flagstones of the choir lay the coffin in which Brother Hugh Collimore lay undelivered, his hands crossed on his tunic, his eyes closed and, unknown to the prior, a pagan coin placed beneath his tongue by one of the other monks who feared the devil would take Collimore's soul if the ferryman who carried the souls of the departed across the river of the afterworld was not paid.

'*Requiem aeternam dona eis, Domine*,' the monks chanted, requesting the Lord to give Brother Collimore eternal rest, and in the city beneath the cathedral, in the small houses that clung to the side of the rock, there was weeping for so many Durham men had been killed in the battle, but the weeping was as nothing to the tears that would be shed when the news of the disaster returned to Scotland. The King was taken prisoner, and so was Sir William Douglas and the Earls of Fife and of Menteith and of Wigtown, and the Earl of Moray was dead as was the Constable of Scotland and the King's Marshal and the King's Chamberlain, all of them butchered, their bodies stripped naked and mocked by their enemies, and with them were hundreds of their countrymen, their white flesh

laced bloody and food now for foxes and wolves and dogs and ravens. The gorestained Scottish standards were on the altar of Durham's cathedral and the remnants of David's great army were fleeing through the night and on their heels were the vengeful English going to ravage and plunder the lowlands, to take back what had been stolen and then to steal some more. '*Et lux perpetua luceat eis,*' the monks chanted, praying that eternal light would shine upon the dead monk, while on the ridge the other dead lay beneath the dark where the white owls shrieked.

'You must confide in me,' the prior hissed at Thomas at the back of the cathedral. Small candles flickered on the scores of side altars where priests, many of them refugees from nearby villages sacked by the Scots, said Masses for the dead. The Latin of those rural priests was often execrable, a source of amusement to the cathedral's own clergy and to the prior who sat beside Thomas on a stone ledge. 'I am your superior in God,' the prior insisted, but still Thomas stayed silent and the prior became angry. 'The King has commanded you! The bishop's letter says so! So tell me what you seek.'

'I want my woman back,' Thomas said, and he was glad it was dark in the cathedral for his eyes were red from crying. Eleanor was dead and Father Hobbe was dead and Brother Collimore was dead, all of them knifed and no one knew by whom, though one of the monks spoke of a dark man, a servant who had come with the foreign priest, and Thomas was remembering the messenger he had seen in the dawn, and Eleanor had been alive then and they had not quarrelled and now she was dead and it was his fault. His fault. The sorrow came to him, overwhelmed him and he howled his misery at the cathedral's nave.

'Be quiet!' said the prior, shocked at the noise.

'I loved her!'

'There are other women, hundreds of them.' Disgusted, he made the sign of the cross. 'What did the King send you to find? I order you to tell me.'

'She was pregnant,' Thomas said, gazing up into the roof, 'and I was going to marry her.' His soul felt as empty and dark as the space above him.

'I order you to tell me!' the Prior repeated. 'In the name of God, I order you!'

'If the King wishes you to know what I seek,' Thomas spoke in French though the prior had been using English, 'then the King will be pleased to tell you.'

The prior stared angrily towards the rood screen. The French language, tongue of aristocrats, had silenced him, making him wonder who this archer was. Two men-at-arms, their mail clinking slightly, walked across the flagstones on their way to thank St Cuthbert for their survival. Most of the English army was far to the north, resting through the dark hours before resuming their pursuit of the beaten enemy, but some knights and men-at-arms had come to the city where they guarded the valuable prisoners who had been placed in the bishop's residence in the castle. Perhaps, the prior thought, the treasure that Thomas of Hookton sought was no longer important; after all, a king had been captured along with half the earls of Scotland and their ransoms would wring that wretched country dry, yet he could not rid himself of the word *thesaurus*. A treasure, and the Church was ever in need of money. He stood. 'You forget,' he said coldly, 'that you are my guest.'

'I do not forget,' Thomas said. He had been given space in the monks' guest quarters, or rather in their stables for there were greater men who needed the warmer rooms. 'I do not forget,' he said again, tiredly.

The prior now gazed up into the roof's high darkness. 'Perhaps,' he suggested, 'you know more of Brother Collimore's murder than you pretend?' Thomas did not answer; the prior's words were nonsense and the prior knew it, for he and Thomas had both been on the battlefield when the old monk had been killed, and Thomas's grief over Eleanor's murder was heartfelt, but the prior was angry and frustrated and he spoke unthinkingly. Hopes of treasure did that to a man. 'You will stay in Durham,' the prior commanded, 'until I give you permission to leave. I have given instructions that your horse is to be kept in my stables. You understand me?'

'I understand you,' Thomas said tiredly, then he watched the prior walk away. More men-at-arms were entering the cathedral, their heavy swords clattering against pillars and tombs. In the shadows, behind one of the side altars, the Scarecrow, Beggar and Dickon watched Thomas. They had been shadowing him since the battle's end. Sir Geoffrey was wearing a fine coat of mail now,

which he had taken from a dead Scotsman, and he had debated whether to join the pursuit, but instead had sent a sergeant and a half-dozen men with orders to take whatever they could when the pillage of Scotland began. Sir Geoffrey himself was gambling that Thomas's treasure, because it had interested a king, would be worthy of his own interest and so he had decided to follow the archer.

Thomas, oblivious of the Scarecrow's gaze, bent forward, eyes tight shut, thinking he would never be whole again. His back and arm muscles burned from a day of drawing a bow and the fingers of his right hand were scraped raw by the cord. If he closed his eyes he saw nothing but Scotsmen coming towards him and the bow making a dark line down memory's picture and the white of the arrows' feathers dwindling in their flight, and then that picture would vanish and he would see Eleanor writhing under the knife that had tortured her. They had made her speak. Yet what did she know? That Thomas had doubted the Grail, that he was a reluctant searcher, that he only wanted to be a leader of archers, and that he had let his woman and his friend go to their deaths.

A hand touched the back of his head and Thomas almost hurled himself aside in the expectation of something worse, a blade, perhaps, but then a voice spoke and it was Lord Outhwaite. 'Come outside, young man,' he ordered Thomas, 'somewhere that the Scarecrow can't overhear us.' He said that loudly and in English, then softened his tone and used French. 'I've been looking for you.' He touched Thomas's arm, encouraging him. 'I heard about your girl and I was sorry. She was a pretty thing.'

'She was, my lord.'

'Her voice suggested she was well born,' Lord Outhwaite said, 'so her family will doubtless help you exact revenge?'

'Her father is titled, my lord, but she was his bastard.'

'Ah!' Lord Outhwaite stumped along, helping his limping gait with the spear he had carried for most of the day. 'Then he probably won't help, will he? But you can do it on your own. You seem capable enough.' His lordship had taken Thomas into a cold, fresh night. A high moon flirted with silver-edged clouds while on the western ridge great fires burned to plume a veil of red-touched smoke above the city. The fires lit the battlefield for the men and

124

women of Durham who searched the dead for plunder and knifed the Scottish wounded to make them dead so they could also be plundered. 'I'm too old to join a pursuit,' Lord Outhwaite said, staring at the distant fires, 'too old and too stiff in the joints. It's a young man's hunt, and they'll pursue them all the way to Edinburgh. Have you ever seen Edinburgh Castle?'

'No, my lord.' Thomas spoke dully, not caring if he ever saw Edinburgh or its castle.

'Oh, it's fine! Very fine!' Lord Outhwaite said enthusiastically. 'Sir William Douglas captured it from us. He smuggled men past the gate inside barrels. Great big barrels. A clever man, eh? And now he's my prisoner.' Lord Outhwaite peered at the castle as though he expected to see Sir William Douglas and the other high-born Scottish captives shinning down from the battlements. Two torches in slanting metal cressets lit the entrance where a dozen men-at-arms stood guard. 'A rogue, our William, a rogue. Why is the Scarecrow following you?'

'I've no idea, my lord.'

'I think you do.' His lordship rested against a pile of stone. The area by the cathedral was heaped with stone and timber for the builders were repairing one of the great towers. 'He knows you seek a treasure so he now seeks it too.'

Thomas paid attention to that, looking sharply at his lordship, then looking back at the cathedral. Sir Geoffrey and his two men had come to the door, but they evidently dared not venture any closer for fear of Lord Outhwaite's displeasure. 'How can he know?' Thomas asked.

'How can he not know?' Lord Outhwaite asked. 'The monks know about it, and that's as good as asking a herald to announce it. Monks gossip like market wives! So the Scarecrow knows you might be the source of great wealth and he wants it. What is this treasure?'

'Just treasure, my lord, though I doubt it has great intrinsic worth.'

Lord Outhwaite smiled. He said nothing for a while, but just stared across the dark gulf above the river. 'You told me, did you not,' he said finally, 'that the King sent you in the company of a household knight and a chaplain from the royal household?'

'Yes, my lord.'

'And they fell ill in London?'

'They did.'

'A sickly place. I was there twice, and twice is more than enough! Noxious! My pigs live in cleaner conditions! But a royal chaplain, eh? No doubt a clever fellow, not a country priest, eh? Not some ignorant peasant tricked out with a phrase or two of Latin, but a rising man, a fellow who'll be a bishop before long if he survives his fever. Now why would the King send such a man?'

'You must ask him, my lord.'

'A royal chaplain, no less,' Lord Outhwaite went on as though Thomas had not spoken, then he fell silent. A scatter of stars showed between the clouds and he gazed up at them, then sighed. 'Once,' he said, 'a long time ago, I saw a crystal vial of our Lord's blood. It was in Flanders and it liquefied in answer to prayer! There's another vial in Gloucestershire, I'm told, but I've not seen that one. I did once stroke the beard of St Jerome in Nantes; I've held a hair from the tail of Balaam's ass; I've kissed a feather from the wing of St Gabriel and brandished the very jawbone with which Samson slew so many Philistines! I have seen a sandal of St Paul, a fingernail from Mary Magdalene and six fragments of the true cross, one of them stained by the very same holy blood that I saw in Flanders. I have glimpsed the bones of the fishes with which our Lord fed the five thousand, I have felt the sharpness of one of the arrow heads that felled St Sebastian and smelt a leaf from the apple tree of the Garden of Eden. In my own chapel, young man, I have a knuckle bone of St Thomas and a hinge from the box in which the frankincense was given to the Christ child. That hinge cost me a great deal of money, a great deal. So tell me, Thomas, what relic is more precious than all those I have seen and all those I hope to see in the great churches of Christendom?'

Thomas stared at the fires on the ridge where so many dead lay. Was Eleanor in heaven already? Or was she doomed to spend thousands of years in purgatory? That thought reminded him that he had to pay for Masses to be said for her soul.

'You stay silent,' Lord Outhwaite observed. 'But tell me, young man, do you think I really possess a hinge from the Christ child's toy box of frankincense?'

126

'I wouldn't know, my lord.'

'I sometimes doubt it,' Lord Outhwaite said genially, 'but my wife believes! And that's what matters: belief. If you believe a thing possesses God's power then it will work its power for you.' He paused, his great shaggy head raised to the darkness as if he smelt for enemies. 'I think you search for a thing of God's power, a great thing, and I believe that the devil is trying to stop you. Satan himself is stirring his creatures to thwart you.' Lord Outhwaite turned an anxious face on Thomas. 'This strange priest and his dark servant are the devil's minions and so is Sir Geoffrey! He is an imp of Satan if ever there was one.' He threw a glance towards the cathedral's porch where the Scarecrow and his two henchmen had retreated into the shadows as a procession of cowled monks came into the night. 'Satan is working mischief,' Lord Outhwaite said, 'and you must fight it. Do you have sufficient funds?'

After the talk of the devil the commonplace question about funds surprised Thomas. 'Do I have funds, my lord?'

'If the devil fights you, young man, then I would help you and few things in this world are more helpful than money. You have a search to make, you have journeys to finish and you will need funds. So, do you have enough?'

'No, my lord,' Thomas said.

'Then permit me to help you.' Lord Outhwaite placed a bag of coins on the pile of stones. 'And perhaps you would take a companion on your search?'

'A companion?' Thomas asked, still bemused.

'Not me! Not me! I'm much too old.' Lord Outhwaite chuckled. 'No, but I confess I am fond of Willie Douglas. The priest who I think killed your woman also killed Douglas's nephew, and Douglas wants revenge. He asks, no, he begs that the dead man's brother be permitted to travel with you.'

'He's a prisoner, surely?'

'I suppose he is, but young Robbie's hardly worth ransoming. I suppose I might fetch a few pounds for him, but nothing like the fortune I intend to exact for his uncle. No, I'd rather Robbie travelled with you. He wants to find the priest and his servant and I think he could help you.' Lord Outhwaite paused and when Thomas did not answer, he pressed his request. 'He's a good young man, Robbie.

I know him, I like him, and he's capable. A good soldier too, I'm told.'

Thomas shrugged. At this moment he did not care if half Scotland travelled with him. 'He can come with me, my lord,' he said, 'if I'm allowed to go anywhere.'

'What do you mean? Allowed?'

'I'm not permitted to travel.' Thomas sounded bitter. 'The prior has forbidden me to leave the city and he's taken my horse.' Thomas had found the horse, brought into Durham by Father Hobbe, tied at the monastery's gate.

Lord Outhwaite laughed. 'And you will obey the prior?'

'I can't afford to lose a good horse, my lord,' Thomas said.

'I have horses,' Lord Outhwaite said dismissively, 'including two good Scottish horses that I took today, and at dawn tomorrow the Archbishop's messengers will ride south to take news of this day to London and three of my men will accompany them. I suggest you and Robbie go with them. That will get the two of you safe to London and after that? Where will you go after that?'

'I'm going home, my lord,' Thomas said, 'to Hookton, to the village where my father lived.'

'And will that murderous priest expect you to go there?'

'I can't say.'

'He will search for you. Doubtless he considered waiting for you here, but that was too dangerous. Yet he'll want your knowledge, Thomas, and he'll torment you to find it. Sir Geoffrey will do the same. That wretched Scarecrow will do anything for money, but I suspect the priest is the more dangerous.'

'So I keep my eyes open and my arrows sharp?'

'I would be cleverer than that,' Lord Outhwaite said. 'I have always found that if a man is hunting you then it's best that he finds you in a place of your own choosing. Don't be ambushed, but be ready to ambush him.'

Thomas accepted the wisdom of the advice, but sounded dubious all the same. 'And how will they know where I go?'

'Because I will tell them,' Lord Outhwaite said, 'or rather, when the prior complains that you have disobeyed him by leaving the city, I shall tell him and his monks will then inform anyone whose ears they can reach. Monks are garrulous creatures. So where

would you like to face your enemies, young man? At your home?'

'No, my lord,' Thomas said hastily, then thought for a few heart-beats. 'At La Roche-Derrien,' he went on.

'In Brittany?' Lord Outhwaite sounded surprised. 'Is what you seek in Brittany?'

'I don't know where it is, my lord, but I have friends in Brittany.'

'Ah, and I trust you will also see me as a friend.' He pushed the bag of coins towards Thomas. 'Take it.'

'I shall repay you, my lord.'

'You will repay me,' his lordship said, standing, 'by bringing me the treasure and letting me touch it just once before it goes to the King.' He glanced at the cathedral where Sir Geoffrey lurked. 'I think you had better sleep in the castle tonight. I have men there who can keep that wretched Scarecrow at bay. Come.'

Sir Geoffrey Carr watched the two men go. He could not attack Thomas while Lord Outhwaite was with him, for Lord Outhwaite was too powerful; but power, the Scarecrow knew, came from money and it seemed there was treasure adrift in the world, treasure that interested the King and now interested Lord Outhwaite too.

So the Scarecrow, come hell or the devil to oppose him, intended to find it first.

Thomas was not going to La Roche-Derrien. He had lied, naming the town because he knew it and because he did not mind if his pursuers went there, but he planned to be elsewhere. He would go to Hookton to see if his father had hidden the Grail there and afterwards, for he did not expect to find it, he would go to France for it was there that the English army laid siege to Calais and it was there that his friends were, and there that an archer could find proper employment. Will Skeat's men were in the siege lines and Will's archers had wanted Thomas to be their leader and he knew he could do the job. He could lead his own band of men, be as feared as Will Skeat was feared. He thought about it as he rode southwards, though he did not think consistently or well. He was too obsessed with the deaths of Eleanor and Father Hobbe, and

torturing himself with the memory of his last look back at Eleanor and his remembrance of that glance meant that he saw the country through which he rode distorted by tears.

Thomas was supposed to ride south with the men carrying the news of the English victory to London, but he got no further than York. He was supposed to leave York at dawn, but Robbie Douglas had vanished. The Scotsman's horse was still in the Archbishop's stables and his baggage was where he had dropped it in the yard, but Robbie was gone. For a moment Thomas was tempted to leave the Scot behind, but some vague sense of resented duty made him stay. Or perhaps it was that he did not much care for the company of the men-at-arms who rode with their triumphant news and so he let them go and went to look for his companion.

He found the Scot gaping up at the gilded bosses of the Minster's ceiling. 'We're supposed to be riding south,' Thomas said.

'Aye,' Robbie answered curtly, otherwise ignoring Thomas.

Thomas waited. After a short while: 'I said that we're supposed to be riding south.'

'So we are,' Robbie agreed, 'and I'm not stopping you.' He waved a magnanimous arm. 'Ride on!'

'You're giving up the hunt for de Taillebourg?' Thomas asked. He had learned the priest's name from Robbie.

'No.' Robbie still had his head back as he stared at the magnificence of the transept's ceiling. 'I'll find him and then I'll gralloch the bastard.'

Thomas did not know what gralloch meant, but decided the word was bad news for de Taillebourg. 'So why the hell are you here?'

Robbie frowned. He had a shock of curling brown hair and a snub face that, at first glance, made him look boyish, though a second look would detect the strength in his jawline and the hardness of his eyes. He at last turned those eyes on Thomas. 'What I can't stand,' he said, 'are those damned laddies! Those bastards!'

It took a couple of heartbeats before Thomas realized he meant the men-at-arms who had been their companions on the ride from Durham to York, the men who were now two hours south on the road to London. 'What was wrong with them?'

'Did you hear them last night? Did you?' Robbie's indignation flared, attracting the attention of two men who were on a high

trestle where they were painting the feeding of the five thousand on the nave's wall. 'And the night before?' Robbie went on.

'They got drunk,' Thomas said, 'but so did we.'

'Telling how they fought the battle!' Robbie said. 'And to hear the bastards you'd think we ran away!'

'You did,' Thomas said.

Robbie had not heard him. 'You'd think we didn't fight at all! Boasting, they were, and we nearly won. You hear that?' He poked an aggressive finger into Thomas's chest. 'We damn nearly won, and those bastards made us sound like cowards!'

'You lost,' Thomas said.

Robbie stared at Thomas as though he could not believe his ears. 'We drove you back halfway to bloody London! Had you running, we did! Pissing in your breeks! We damn nearly won, we did, and those bastards are gloating. Just gloating! I wanted to murder the pack of them!' A score of folk were listening. Two pilgrims, making their way on their knees to the shrine behind the high altar, were staring open-mouthed at Robbie. A priest was frowning nervously, while a child sucked its thumb and gazed aghast at the shock-headed man who was shouting so loudly. 'You hear me?' Robbie yelled. 'We damn nearly won!'

Thomas walked away.

'Where are you off to?' Robbie demanded.

'South,' Thomas said. He understood Robbie's embarrassment. The messengers, carrying news of the battle, could not resist embellishing the story of the fight when they were entertained in castle or monastery and so a hard-fought, savage piece of carnage had become an easy victory. No wonder Robbie was offended, but Thomas had small sympathy. He turned and pointed at the Scotsman. 'You should have stayed at home.'

Robbie spat in disgust, then became aware of his audience. 'Had you running,' he said hotly, then leaped over to catch up with Thomas. He grinned and there was a sudden and appealing charm in his face. 'I didn't mean to shout at you,' he said, 'I was just angry.'

'Me too,' Thomas said, but his anger was at himself and it was mingled with guilt and grief that did not lessen as the two rode south. They took to the road in mornings heavy with dew, rode

through autumn mists, hunched under the lash of rain, and for almost every step of the journey Thomas thought of Eleanor. Lord Outhwaite had promised to bury her and have Masses said for her soul and Thomas sometimes wished he was sharing her grave.

'So why is de Taillebourg chasing you?' Robbie asked on the day they rode away from York. They spoke in English for, though Robbie was from the noble house of Douglas, he spoke no French.

For a time Thomas said nothing, and just when Robbie thought he would not answer at all he gave a snort of derision. 'Because,' he said, 'the bastard believes that my father possessed the Grail.'

'The Grail!' Robbie crossed himself. 'I heard it was in Scotland.'

'In Scotland?' Thomas asked, astonished. 'I know Genoa claims to have it, but Scotland?'

'And why not?' Robbie bristled. 'Mind you,' he relented, 'I've heard there's one in Spain, too.'

'Spain?'

'And if the Spanish have one,' Robbie said, 'then the French will have to have one as well, and for all I know the Portuguese too.' He shrugged, then looked back to Thomas. 'So did your father have another?'

Thomas did not know what to answer. His father had been wayward, mad, brilliant, difficult and tortured. He had been a great sinner and, for all that, he might well have been a saint as well. Father Ralph had laughed at the wider reaches of superstition, he had mocked the pig bones sold by pardoners as relics of the saints, yet he had hung an old, blackened and bent spear in his church's rafters and claimed it was the lance of St George. He had never mentioned the Grail to Thomas, but since his death Thomas had learned that the history of his family was entwined with the Grail. In the end he elected to tell Robbie the truth. 'I don't know,' he said, 'I simply don't know.'

Robbie ducked under a branch that grew low across the road. 'Are you telling me this is the real Grail?'

'If it exists,' Thomas said and he wondered again if it did. He supposed it was possible, but wished it was not. Yet he had been charged with the duty of finding out and so he would seek his father's one friend and he would ask that man about the Grail and when he received the expected answer he would go back to France

and join Skeat's archers. Will Skeat himself, his one-time commander and friend, was stranded in Caen, and Thomas had no knowledge whether Will still lived or, if he did, whether he could speak or understand or even walk. He could find out by sending a letter to Sir Guillaume d'Evecque, Eleanor's father, and Will could be given safe passage in return for the release of some minor French nobleman. Thomas would repay Lord Outhwaite with money plundered from the enemy and then, he told himself, he would find his consolation in the practice of his skill, in archery, in the killing of the King's enemies. Perhaps de Taillebourg would come and find him and Thomas would kill him like he would put down a rat. As for Robbie? Thomas had decided he liked the Scotsman, but he did not care whether he stayed or went.

Robbie only understood that de Taillebourg would seek Thomas and so he would stay at the archer's side until he could kill the Dominican. He had no other ambition, just to avenge his brother: that was a family duty. 'You touch a Douglas,' he told Thomas, 'and we'll fillet you. We'll skin you alive. It's a blood feud, see?'

'Even if the killer is the priest?'

'It's either him or his servant,' Robbie said, 'and the servant obeys the master: either way the priest's responsible, so he dies. I'll slit his bloody throat.' He rode for a while in silence, then grinned. 'And then I'll go to hell, but at least there'll be plenty of Douglases keeping the devil company.' He laughed.

It took ten days to reach London and, once there, Robbie pretended to be unimpressed, as though Scotland had cities of this size in every other valley, but after a while he dropped the pretence and just stared in awe at the great buildings, crowded streets and serried market stalls. Thomas used Lord Outhwaite's coins so they could lodge in a tavern just outside the city walls beside the horse pond in Smithfield and close to the green where more than three hundred traders had their stalls. 'And it's not even market day?' Robbie exclaimed, then snatched at Thomas's sleeve. 'Look!' A juggler was spinning half a dozen balls in the air – that was nothing unusual for any county fair would show the same – but this man was standing on two swords, using them as stilts, with his bare feet poised on the swords' points. 'How does he do it?' Robbie asked. 'And look!' A dancing bear was shuffling to the tune of a flute just

beneath the gibbet where two bodies hung. This was the place where London's felons were brought to be sent on their swift way to hell. Both corpses were encased in chains to hold the rotting flesh to their bones and the stench of the decaying corpses mingled with the smell of smoke and the reek of the frightened cattle who were bought and sold on the green, which stretched between London's wall and the Priory of St Bartholomew where Thomas paid a priest to say Masses for the souls of Eleanor and Father Hobbe.

Thomas, pretending to Robbie that he was far more familiar with London than was the truth, had chosen the tavern in Smithfield for no other reason than its sign was two crossed arrows. This was only his second visit to the city and he was as impressed, confused, dazzled and surprised as Robbie. They wandered the streets, gaping at churches and noblemen's houses, and Thomas used Lord Outhwaite's money to buy himself some new boots, calfskin leggings, an oxhide coat and a fine woollen cloak. He was tempted by a sleek French razor in an ivory case, but, not knowing the razor's value, feared he was being cheated; he reckoned he could steal himself a razor from a Frenchman's corpse when he reached Calais. Instead he paid a barber to shave him and then, dressed in his new finery, spent the cost of the unbought razor on one of the tavern's women and afterwards lay with tears in his eyes because he was thinking of Eleanor.

'Is there a reason we're in London?' Robbie asked him that night.

Thomas drained his ale and beckoned the girl to bring more. 'It's on our way to Dorset.'

'That's as good a reason as any.'

London was not really on the way from Durham to Dorchester, but the roads to the capital were so much better than those that wandered across the country and so it was quicker to travel through the great city. However, after three days, Thomas knew they must move on and so he and Robbie rode westwards. They skirted Westminster and Thomas thought for an idle heartbeat of visiting John Pryke, the royal chaplain sent to accompany him to Durham who had fallen ill in London and now either lived or died in the abbey's hospital, but Thomas had no stomach to talk of the Grail and so he rode on.

The air became cleaner as they went deeper into the country. It was not reckoned safe to travel these roads, but Thomas's face was so grim that other travellers reckoned he was the danger rather than the prey. He was unshaven and he dressed, as he always had, in black, and the misery of the last days had put deep lines on his thin face. With Robbie's mass of unkempt hair, the two of them looked like any other vagabonds who wandered the roads, except these two were fearsomely armed. Thomas carried his sword, bow and arrow bag, while Robbie had his uncle's sword with the scrap of St Andrew's hair encased in its hilt. Sir William had reckoned he would have small use for the sword in the next few years while his family attempted to find the vast ransom, and so he had lent it to Robbie with the encouragement to use it well.

'You think de Taillebourg will be in Dorset?' Robbie asked Thomas as they rode through a stinging rain shower.

'I doubt it.'

'So why are we going?'

'Because he may go there eventually,' Thomas said, 'him and his damn servant.' He knew nothing about the servant except what Robbie had told him: that the man was fastidious, elegant, dark in looks and mysterious, but Robbie had never heard his name. Thomas, finding it hard to believe that a priest would have killed Eleanor, had persuaded himself that the servant was the killer and so planned to make the man suffer in agony.

It was late afternoon when they ducked under the arch of Dorchester's east gate. A guard there, alarmed by their weapons, challenged them, but backed down when Thomas answered in French. It suggested he was an aristocrat and the guard sullenly let the two horsemen pass, then watched as they climbed East Street past All Saints' church and the county jail. The houses grew more prosperous as they neared the town's centre and, close to St Peter's church, the wool-merchants' homes might not have been out of place in London. Thomas could smell the shambles behind the houses where the butchers worked their trade, then he led Robbie into Cornhill, past the shop of the pewterer who had a stammer and a wall eye, then past the blacksmith where he had once bought some arrow heads. He knew most of these folk. The Dogman, a legless beggar who had come by his nickname because he lapped water from the

River Cerne like a dog, was heaving down South Street on the wooden bricks strapped to his hands. Dick Adyn, brother of the town's jailer, was driving three sheep up the hill and paused to deliver a genial insult to Willie Palmer who was closing up his hosiery shop. A young priest hurried into an alley with a book wrapped in his arms and averted his eyes from a woman squatting in the gutter. A gust of wind blew woodsmoke low into the street. Dorcas Galton, brown hair drawn up into a bun, shook a rug out of an upstairs window and laughed aloud at something Dick Adyn said. They all spoke in the local accent, soft and broad and buzzing like Thomas's own, and he almost curbed the horse to speak with them, but Dick Adyn glanced at him and then looked swiftly away and Dorcas slammed the window shut. Robbie looked formidable, but Thomas's gaunt looks were even more frightening and none of the townsfolk recognized him as the bastard son of Hookton's last priest. They would know him if he introduced himself, but war had changed Thomas. It had given him a hardness that repelled strangers. He had left Dorset a boy, but come back as one of Edward of England's prized killers and when he left the town by the south gate a constable gave both him and Robbie good riddance and told them to stay away. 'Be lucky the pair of you ain't in jail!' the man called, emboldened by his municipal coat of mail and ancient spear. Thomas stopped his horse, turned in the saddle and just stared at the man who suddenly found reason to duck back into the alley beside the gate. Thomas spat and rode on.

'Your home town?' Robbie asked caustically.

'Not now,' Thomas said and he wondered where home was these days, and for some odd reason La Roche-Derrien came unbidden to his thoughts and he found himself remembering Jeanette Chenier in her great house beside the River Jaudy, and that recollection of an old love made him feel guilty yet again for Eleanor. 'Where's your home town?' he asked Robbie rather than dwell on memories.

'I grew up close to Langholm.'

'Where's that?'

'On the River Esk,' Robbie said, 'not far north of the border. It's a hard country, so it is. Not like this.'

'This is a good countryside,' Thomas said mildly. He looked up at the high green walls of Maiden Castle where the devil played on

All Hallow's Eve and where the corncrakes now made their harsh song. There were ripe blackberries in the hedgerows and, as the shadows lengthened, fox cubs skittering at the edge of the fields. A few miles on and the evening had almost shaded to night, but he could smell the sea now and he imagined that he could hear it, sucking and surging on the Dorset shingle. This was the ghost time of day when the souls of the dead flickered at the edges of men's sight and when good folk hurried home to their fire and to their thatch and to their bolted doors. A dog howled in one of the villages.

Thomas had thought to ride to Down Mapperley where Sir Giles Marriott, the squire of Hookton among other villages, had his hall, but it was late and he did not think it wise to arrive at the hall after dark. Besides, Thomas wanted to see Hookton before he spoke with Sir Giles and so he turned his tired horse towards the sea and led Robbie under the high dark loom of Lipp Hill. 'I killed my first men up on that hill,' he boasted.

'With the bow?'

'Four of them,' Thomas said, 'with four arrows.' That was not entirely true for he must have shot seven or eight arrows, maybe more, but he had still killed four of the raiders who had come across the Channel to pillage Hookton. And now he was deep in the twilight shadow of Hookton's sea valley and he could see the fret of breaking waves flashing white in the late dusk as he rode down beside the stream to the place where his father had preached and died.

No one lived there now. The raiders had left the village dead. The houses had been burned, the church roof had fallen and the villagers were buried in a graveyard choked by nettles, thorn and thistles. It was four and a half years since that raiding party had landed at Hookton led by Thomas's cousin, Guy Vexille, the Count of Astarac, and by Eleanor's father, Sir Guillaume d'Evecque. Thomas had killed four of the crossbowmen and that had been the beginning of his life as an archer. He had abandoned his studies at Oxford and, until this moment, had never returned to Hookton. 'This was home,' he told Robbie.

'What happened?'

'The French happened,' Thomas said and gestured at the darkling sea. 'They sailed from Normandy.'

'Jesus.' Robbie, for some reason, was surprised. He knew that the borderlands of England and Scotland were places where buildings were burned, cattle stolen, women raped and men killed, but he had never thought it happened this far south. He slid down from his horse and walked to a heap of nettles that had been a cottage. 'There was a village here?'

'A fishing village,' Thomas said and he strode down what was once the street to where the nets had been mended and the women had smoked fish. His father's house was a heap of burned-out timbers, choked with bindweed now. The other cottages were the same, their thatch and wattle reduced to ash and soil. Only the church to the west of the stream was recognizable, its gaunt walls open to the sky. Thomas and Robbie tied their horses to hazel saplings in the graveyard, then took their baggage into the ruined church. It was already too dark to explore, yet Thomas could not sleep and so he went down to the beach and he remembered that Easter morning when the Norman ships had grounded on the shingle and the men had come shrieking in the dawn with swords and crossbows, axes and fire. They had come for the Grail. Guy Vexille believed it to be in his uncle's possession and so the Harlequin had put the village of Hookton to the sword. He had burned it, destroyed it and gone from it without the Grail.

The stream made its little noise as it twisted inside the shingle Hook on its way to meet the great sound of the sea. Thomas sat down on the Hook, swathed in his new cloak, with the great black bow beside him. The chaplain, John Pryke, had talked of the Grail in the same awed tones that Father Hobbe had used when he spoke of the relic. The Grail, Father Pryke said, was not just the cup from which Christ had drunk wine at the Last Supper, but the vessel into which Christ's dying blood had poured from the cross. 'Longinus,' Father Pryke had said in his excitable manner, 'was the centurion beneath the cross and, when the spear struck the dolorous blow, he raised the dish to catch the blood!'

How, Thomas wondered, did the cup go from the upper room where Christ had eaten his last meal into the possession of a Roman centurion? And, stranger still, how had it reached Ralph Vexille? He closed his eyes, swaying back and forwards, ashamed of his disbelief. Father Hobbe had always called him Doubting Thomas.

'You mustn't seek explanations,' Father Hobbe had said again and again, 'because the Grail is a miracle. It transcends explanations.'

'*C'est une tasse magique*,' Eleanor had added, implicitly adding her reproof to Father Hobbe's.

Thomas so wanted to believe it was a magic cup. He wanted to believe that the Grail existed just beyond human sight, behind a veil of disbelief, a thing half visible, shimmering, wonderful, poised in light and glowing like pale fire. He wanted to believe that one day it would take on substance and that from its bowl, which had held the wine and the blood of Christ, would flow peace and healing. Yet if God wanted the world to be at peace and if He wanted sickness defeated, why did He hide the Grail? Father Hobbe's answer had been that mankind was not worthy to hold the cup, and Thomas wondered if that was true. Was anyone worthy? And perhaps, Thomas thought, if the Grail had any magic then it was to exaggerate the faults and virtues of those who sought it. Father Hobbe had become more saintlike in his pursuit and the strange priest and his dark servant more malevolent. It was like one of those crystal lenses that jewellers used to magnify their work, only the Grail was a crystal that magnified character. What, Thomas wondered, did it reveal of his own? He remembered his unease at the thought of marrying Eleanor, and suddenly he began to weep, to heave with sobs, to cry more than he had already cried since her murder. He rocked to and fro, his grief as deep as the sea that beat on the shingle, and it was made worse by the knowledge that he was a sinner, unshriven, his soul doomed to hell.

He missed his woman, he hated himself, he felt empty, alone and doomed, and so, in his father's dead village, he wept.

It began to rain later, a steady rain that soaked through the new cloak and chilled Thomas and Robbie to the bone. They had lit a fire that flickered feebly in the old church, hissing under the rain and giving them a small illusion of warmth. 'Are there wolves here?' Robbie asked.

'Supposed to be,' Thomas said, 'though I never saw one.'

139

'We have wolves in Eskdale,' Robbie said, 'and at night their eyes glow red. Like fire.'

'There are monsters in the sea here,' Thomas said. 'Their bodies wash ashore sometimes and you can find their bones in the cliffs. Sometimes, even on calm days, men wouldn't come back from fishing and you'd know the monsters had taken them.' He shivered and crossed himself.

'When my grandfather died,' Robbie said, 'the wolves circled the house and howled.'

'Is it a big house?'

Robbie seemed surprised by the question. He considered it for a moment, then nodded. 'Aye,' he said. 'My father's a laird.'

'A lord?'

'Like a lord,' Robbie said.

'He wasn't at the battle?'

'He lost a leg and an arm at Berwick. So we boys have to fight for him.' He said he was the youngest of four sons. 'Three now,' he said, crossing himself and thinking of Jamie.

They half slept, woke, shivered, and in the dawn Thomas walked back to the Hook to watch the new day seep grey along the sea's ragged edge. The rain had stopped, though a cold wind shredded the wave-tops. The grey turned a leprous white, then silvery as the gulls called over the long shingle where, at the top of the Hook's bank, he found the weathered remnants of four posts. They had not been there when he left, but beneath one of them, half buried in stones, was a yellowish scrap of skull and he guessed this was one of the crossbowmen he had killed with his tall black bow on that Easter day. Four posts, four dead men and Thomas supposed that the four heads had been placed on the poles to gaze out to sea till the gulls pecked out their eyes and flensed the flesh back to the bare skulls.

He stared into the ruined village, but could see no one. Robbie was still inside the church from which a tiny wisp of smoke drifted, but otherwise Thomas was alone with the gulls. There were not even sheep, cattle or goats on Lipp Hill. He walked back inland, his feet crunching on the shingle, then realized he still held the broken curve of skull and he hurled it into the stream where the fishing boats had been flooded to rid them of rats and then, feeling hungry,

140

he went and took the piece of hard cheese and dark bread from the saddlebag that he had dumped beside the church door. The walls of the church, now he could see them properly in the daylight, appeared lower than he remembered, probably because local folk had come with carts and taken the stones away for barns or sties or house walls. Inside the church there was only a tangle of thorns, nettles and a few gnarled lengths of charred timber that had long been overgrown by grass. 'I was almost killed in here,' he told Robbie, and he described how the raiders had beaten on the church door as he had kicked out the horn panes of the east window and jumped down into the graveyard. He remembered how his foot had crushed the silver Mass cup as he scrambled over the altar.

Had that silver cup been the Grail? He laughed aloud at the thought. The Mass cup had been a silver goblet on which was incised the badge of the Vexilles, and that badge, cut from the crushed cup, was now pinned to Thomas's bow. It was all that was left of the old goblet, but it had not been the Grail. The Grail was much older, much more mysterious and much more frightening.

The altar was long gone, but there was a shallow clay bowl in the nettles where it had stood. Thomas kicked the plants aside and picked up the bowl, remembering how his father would fill it with wafers before the Mass and cover it with a piece of linen cloth and then hurry it to the church, getting angry if any of the villagers did not take off their hats and bow to the sacrament as he passed. Thomas had kicked the bowl as he climbed onto the altar to escape the Frenchmen, and here it still was. He smiled ruefully, thought about keeping the bowl, but tossed it back into the nettles. Archers should travel light.

'Someone's coming,' Robbie warned him, running to fetch his uncle's sword. Thomas picked up the bow and took an arrow from his bag, and just then he heard the thump of hooves and the baying of hounds. He went to the ruins of the door and saw a dozen great deerhounds splashing through the stream with tongues lolling between their fangs; he had no time to run from them, only to flatten himself against the wall as the hounds streaked for him.

'Argos! Maera! Back off now! Mind your goddamn manners!' the horseman bellowed at his hounds, reinforcing his commands with

the crack of a whip over their heads, but the beasts surrounded Thomas and leaped up at him. Yet it was not in threat: they were licking his face and wagging their tails. 'Orthos!' the huntsman snapped at one dog, then he stared hard at Thomas. He did not recognize him, but the hounds obviously knew him and that gave the huntsman pause.

'Jake,' Thomas said.

'Sweet Jesus Christ!' Jake said. 'Sweet Jesus! Look what the tide brought in. Orthos! Argos! Off and away, you bastards, off and away!' The whip cracked loud and the hounds, still excited, backed away. Jake shook his head. 'It's Thomas, isn't it?'

'How are you, Jake?'

'Older,' Jake Churchill said gruffly, then climbed down from the saddle, pushed through the hounds and greeted Thomas with an embrace. 'It was your damned father who named these dogs. He thought it was a joke. It's good to see you, boy.' Jake was grey-bearded, his face dark as a nut from the weather and his skin scarred from countless brushes with thorns. He was Sir Giles Marriott's chief huntsman and he had taught Thomas how to shoot a bow and how to stalk a deer and how to go hidden and silent through country. 'Good Christ Almighty, boy,' he said, 'but you've fair grown up. Look at the size of you!'

'Boys do grow up, Jake,' Thomas said, then gestured at Robbie. 'He's a friend.'

Jake nodded at the Scotsman, then hauled two of the hounds away from Thomas. The dogs, named for hounds from Greek and Latin myth, whined excitedly. 'And what the hell are you two doing down here?' Jake wanted to know. 'You should have come up to the hall like Christians!'

'We got here late,' Thomas explained, 'and I wanted to see the place.'

'Nothing to see here,' Jake said scornfully. 'Nothing but hares here now.'

'You're hunting hare now?'

'I don't bring ten brace of hounds to snaffle hares, boy. No, Lally Gooden's boy saw the pair of you sneaking in here last night and so Sir Giles sent me down to see what evil was brewing. We had a pair of vagabonds trying to set up home here in the spring and

they had to be whipped on their way. And last week there was a pair of foreigners creeping about.'

'Foreigners?' Thomas asked, knowing that Jake could well mean nothing more than that the strangers had come from the next parish.

'A priest and his man,' Jake said, 'and if he hadn't been a priest I'd have loosed the dogs on him. I don't like foreigners, don't see no point to them. Those horses of yours looks hungry. So do the two of you. You want breakfast? Or are you going to stand there and spoil those damned hounds by patting them half to death?'

They rode back to Down Mapperley, following the hounds through the tiny village. Thomas remembered the place as big, twice the size of Hookton, and as a child he had thought it almost a town, but now he saw how small it was. Small and low, so that on horseback he towered above the thatched cottages that had seemed so palatial when he was a child. The dungheaps beside each cottage were as high as the thatch. Sir Giles Marriott's hall, just beyond the village, was also thatched, the moss-thick roof sweeping almost to the ground. 'He'll be pleased to see you,' Jake promised.

And so Sir Giles was. He was an old man now, a widower who had once been wary of Thomas's wildness, but now greeted him like a lost son. 'You're thin, boy, too thin. Ain't good for a man to be thin. You'll have breakfast, the two of you? Pease pudding and small ale is what we've got. There was bread yesterday, but not today. When do we bake more bread, Gooden?' This was demanded of a servant.

'Today's Wednesday, sir,' the servant said reprovingly.

'Tomorrow then,' Sir Giles told Thomas. 'Bread tomorrow, no bread today. It's bad luck to bake bread on Wednesday. It poisons you, Wednesday's bread. I must have eaten Monday's. You say you're Scottish?' This was to Robbie.

'I am, sir.'

'I thought all Scotsmen had beards,' Sir Giles said. 'There was a Scotsman in Dorchester, wasn't there Gooden? You remember him? He had a beard. He played the gittern and danced well. You must remember him.'

'He was from the Scilly Isles,' the servant said.

'That's what I just said. But he had a beard, didn't he?'

143

'He did, Sir Giles. A big one.'

'There you are then,' Sir Giles spooned some pease pudding into a mouth that only had two teeth left. He was fat, white-haired and red-faced and at least fifty years old. 'Can't ride a horse these days, Thomas,' he admitted. 'Ain't good for anything now except sitting about the place and watching the weather. Did Jake tell you there be foreigners scuttling about?'

'He did, sir.'

'A priest! Black and white robes like a magpie. He wanted to talk about your father and I said there was nothing to talk about. Father Ralph's dead, I said, and God rest his poor soul.'

'Did the priest ask for me, sir?' Thomas asked.

Sir Giles grinned. 'I said I hadn't seen you in years and hoped never to see you again, and then his servant asked me where he might look for you and I told him not to talk to his betters without permission. He didn't like that!' he chuckled. 'So then the magpie asked about your father and I said I hardly knew him. That was a lie, of course, but he believed me and took himself off. Put some logs on that fire, Gooden. A man could freeze to death in his own hall if it was left to you.'

'So the priest left, sir?' Robbie asked. It seemed unlike de Taille-bourg just to accept a denial and meekly go away.

'He was frightened of dogs,' Sir Giles said, still amused. 'I had some of the hounds in here and if he hadn't been dressed like a magpie I'd have let them loose, but it don't do to kill priests. There's always trouble afterwards. The devil comes and plays his games if you kill a priest. But I didn't like him and I told him I wasn't sure how long I could keep the dogs heeled. There's some ham in the kitchen. Would you like some ham, Thomas?'

'No, sir.'

'I do hate winter.' Sir Giles stared into the fire, which now blazed huge in his wide hearth. The hall had smoke blackened beams supporting the huge expanse of thatch. At one end a carved timber screen hid the kitchens while the private rooms were at the other end, though since his wife had died Sir Giles no longer used the small chambers, but lived, ate and slept beside the hall fire. 'I reckon this'll be my last winter, Thomas.'

'I hope not, sir.'

'Hope what you damned well like, but I won't last it through. Not when the ice comes. A man can't keep warm these days, Thomas. It bites into you, the cold does, bites into your marrow and I don't like it. Your father never liked it either.' He was staring at Thomas now. 'Your father always said you'd go away. Not to Oxford. He knew you didn't like that. Like whipping a destrier between the shafts, he used to say. He knew you'd run off and be a soldier. He always said you had wild blood in you.' Sir Giles smiled, remembering. 'But he also said you'd come home one day. He said you'd come back to show him what a fine fellow you'd become.'

Thomas blinked back tears. Had his father really said that? 'I came back this time,' he said, 'to ask you a question, sir. The same question, I think, that the French priest wanted to ask you.'

'Questions!' Sir Giles grumbled. 'I never did like questions. They need answers, see? Of course you want some ham! What do you mean, no? Gooden? Ask your daughter to unwrap that ham, will you?'

Sir Giles heaved himself to his feet and shuffled across the hall to a great chest of dark, polished oak. He raised the lid and, groaning with the effort of bending over, began to rummage through the clothes and boots that were jumbled inside. 'I find now, Thomas,' he went on, 'that I don't need questions. I sit in the manor court every second week and I know whether they're guilty or innocent the moment they're fetched into the hall! Mind you, we have to pretend otherwise, don't we? Now, where is it? Ah!' He found whatever he sought and brought it back to the table. 'There, Thomas, damn your question and that's your answer.' He pushed the bundle across the table.

It was a small object wrapped in ancient sacking. Thomas had an absurd premonition that this was the Grail itself and was ridiculously disappointed when he discovered the bundle contained a book. The book's front cover was a soft leather flap, four or five times larger than the pages, which could be used to wrap the volume that, when Thomas opened it, proved to be written in his father's hand. However, being by his father, nothing in it was straightforward. Thomas leafed through the pages swiftly, discovering notes written in Latin, Greek and a strange script which he thought must be Hebrew. He turned back to the first page where only three words

were written and, reading them, felt his blood run cold. *'Calix meus inebrians.'*

'Is it your answer?' Sir Giles asked.

'Yes, sir.'

Sir Giles peered at the first page. 'It's Latin that, isn't it?'

'Yes, sir.'

'Thought it was. I looked, of course, but couldn't make head nor tail of it and I didn't like to ask Sir John,' – Sir John was the priest of St Peter's in Dorchester – 'or that lawyer fellow, what's his name? The one who dribbles when he gets excited. He speaks Latin, or he says he does. What does it mean?'

'"My cup makes me drunk",' Thomas said.

'"My cup makes me drunk"!' Sir Giles thought that was splendidly funny. 'Aye, your father's wits were well off the wind. A good man, a good man, but dear me! "My cup makes me drunk"!'

'It's from one of the psalms,' Thomas said, turning to the second page, which was written in the script he thought was Hebrew, though there was something odd about it. One of the recurrent symbols looked like a human eye and Thomas had never seen that in a Hebrew script before though, in all honesty, he had seen little Hebrew. 'It's from the psalm, sir,' he went on, 'that begins by saying God is our shepherd.'

'He's not my shepherd,' Sir Giles grumbled. 'I'm not some damned sheep.'

'Nor me, sir,' Robbie declared.

'I did hear' – Sir Giles looked at Robbie – 'that the King of Scotland was taken prisoner.'

'He was, sir?' Robbie asked innocently.

'Probably nonsense,' Sir Giles replied, then he began telling a long tale about meeting a bearded Scotsman in London, and Thomas ignored the story to look through the pages of his father's book. He felt a kind of strange disappointment because the book suggested that the search for the Grail was justified. He wanted someone to tell him it was nonsense, to release him from the cup's thrall, but his father had taken it seriously enough to write this book. But his father, Thomas reminded himself, had been mad.

Mary, Gooden's daughter, brought in the ham. Thomas had known Mary since they were both children playing in puddles and

he smiled a greeting at her, then saw that Robbie was gazing at her as though she was an apparition from heaven. She had dark long hair and a full mouth and Thomas was sure Robbie would be discovering more than a few rivals in Down Mapperley. He waited until Mary had gone, then held up the book. 'Did my father ever talk to you about this, sir?'

'He talked of everything,' Sir Giles said. 'Talked like a woman, he did. Never stopped! I was your father's friend, Thomas, but I was never much of a man for religion. If he talked of it too much, I fell asleep. He liked that.' Sir Giles paused to cut a slice of ham. 'But your father was mad.'

'You think this is madness, sir?' Thomas held up the book again.

'Your father was mad for God, but he was no fool. I never knew a man with so much common sense and I miss it. I miss the advice.'

'Does that girl work here?' Robbie asked, gesturing at the screen behind which Mary had disappeared.

'All her life,' Sir Giles said. 'You remember Mary, Thomas?'

'I tried to drown her when we were both children,' Thomas said. He turned the pages of his father's book again though he had no time now to tease any meanings from the tangled words. 'You do know what this is, sir, don't you?'

Sir Giles paused, then nodded. 'I know, Thomas, that many men want what your father claims to have possessed.'

'So he did make that claim?'

Another pause. 'He hinted at it,' Sir Giles said heavily, 'and I don't envy you.'

'Me?'

'Because he gave me that book, Thomas, and he said that if anything happened to him I was to keep it until you were old enough and man enough to take up the task. That's what he said.' Sir Giles stared at Thomas and saw his old friend's son flinch. 'But if the two of you want to stay for a while,' he said, 'then you'd be welcome. Jake Churchill needs help. He tells me he's never seen so many fox cubs and if we don't kill some of the bastards then there'll be some rare massacres among the lambs next year.'

Thomas glanced at Robbie. Their task was to find de Taillebourg and avenge the deaths of Eleanor, Father Hobbe and Robbie's brother, but it was unlikely, he thought, that the Dominican would

147

come back here. Robbie, however, plainly wanted to stay: Mary Gooden had seen to that. And Thomas was tired. He did not know where to seek the priest and so the chance to stay in this hall was welcome. It would be an opportunity to study the book and thus follow his father down the long, tortuous path of the Grail.

'We'll stay, sir,' Thomas said.

For a while.

It was the first time that Thomas had ever lived like a lord. Not a great lord, perhaps, not as an earl or a duke with scores of men to command, but still in privilege, ensconced in the manor – even if the manor was a thatched timber hall with a beaten earth floor – the days his to wile away as other people did life's hard work of cutting firewood, drawing water, milking cows, churning butter, pounding dough and washing clothes. Robbie was more used to it, but reckoned life was much easier in Dorset. 'Back home,' he said, 'there's always some damn English raiders coming over the hill to steal your cattle or take your grain.'

'Whereas you,' Thomas said, 'would never dream of riding south and stealing from the English.'

'Why would I even think of such a thing?' Robbie asked, grinning.

So, as winter closed down on the land, they hunted Sir Giles Marriott's acres to make the fields safe for the lambing season and to bring back venison to Sir Giles's table; they drank in the Dorchester taverns and laughed at the mummers who came for the winter fair. Thomas found old friends and told them stories of Brittany, Normandy and Picardy, some of which were true, and he won the golden arrow at the fair's archery competition and he presented it to Sir Giles who hung it in the hall and declared it the finest trophy he had ever seen. 'My son could shoot a good arrow. A very good arrow. I'd like to think he could have won this trophy himself.'

Sir Giles's only son had died of a fever and his only daughter was married to a knight who held land in Devon and Sir Giles liked neither son-in-law nor daughter. 'They'll inherit the property when

149

I die,' he told Thomas, 'so you and Robbie may as well enjoy it now.'

Thomas persuaded himself that he was not ignoring the search for the Grail because of the hours he spent poring over his father's book. The pages were thick vellum, expensive and rare, which showed how important these notes had been to Father Ralph, but even so they made small sense to Thomas. Much of the book was stories. One told how a blind man, caressing the cup, had received his sight but then, disappointed in the Grail's appearance, lost it again. Another told how a Moorish warrior had tried to steal the Grail and been turned into a serpent for his impiety. The longest tale in the book was about Perceval, a knight of antiquity who went on crusade and discovered the Grail in Christ's tomb. This time the Latin word used to describe the grail was *crater*, meaning bowl, whereas on other pages it was *calix*, a cup, and Thomas wondered if there was any significance in the distinction. If his father had possessed the Grail, would he not have known whether it was a cup or a bowl? Or perhaps there was no real difference. Whatever, the long tale told how the bowl had sat on a shelf of Christ's tomb in plain view of all who entered the sepulchre, both Christian pilgrims and their pagan enemies, yet not till Sir Perceval entered the grotto on his knees was the Grail actually seen by anyone, for Sir Perceval was a man of righteousness and thus worthy of having his eyes opened. Sir Perceval removed the bowl, bringing it back to Christendom where he planned to build a shrine worthy of the treasure, but, the tale laconically recorded, 'he died'. Thomas's father had written beneath this abrupt conclusion: 'Sir Perceval was Count of Astarac and was known by another name. He married a Vexille.'

'Sir Perceval!' Sir Giles was impressed. 'He was a member of your family, eh? Your father never mentioned that to me. At least I don't think he did. I did sleep through a lot of his tales.'

'He usually scoffed at stories like this,' Thomas said.

'We often mock what we fear,' Sir Giles observed sententiously. Suddenly he grinned. 'Jake tells me you caught that old dog fox by the Five Marys.' The Five Marys were ancient grave mounds that the locals claimed were dug by giants and Thomas had never understood why there were six of them.

'It wasn't there,' Thomas said, 'but back of the White Nothe.'

'Back of White Nothe? Up on the cliffs?' Sir Giles stared at Thomas, then laughed. 'You were on Holgate's land! You rascals!' Sir Giles, who had always complained mightily when Thomas had poached from his land, now found this predation on a neighbour hugely amusing. 'He's an old woman, Holgate. So are you making head or tail of that book?'

'I wish I knew,' Thomas said, staring at the name Astarac. All he knew was that Astarac was a fief or county in southern France and the home of the Vexille family before they were declared rebel and heretic. He had also learned that Astarac was close to the Cathar heartlands, close enough for the contagion to catch the Vexilles, and when, a hundred years before, the French King and the true Church had burned the heretics out of the land they had also forced the Vexilles to flee. Now it seemed that the legendary Sir Perceval was a Vexille? It seemed to Thomas that the further he penetrated the mystery the greater the entanglement. 'Did my father ever talk to you of Astarac, sir?' He asked Sir Giles.

'Astarac? What's that?'

'Where his family came from.'

'No, no, he grew up in Cheshire. That's what he always said.'

But Cheshire had merely been a refuge, a place to hide from the Inquisition: was that where the Grail was now hidden? Thomas turned a page to find a long passage describing how a raiding column had tried to attack the tower of Astarac and had been repulsed by the sight of the Grail. 'It dazzled them,' Father Ralph had written, 'so that 364 of them were cut down.' Another page recorded that it was impossible for a man to tell a lie while he held his hand on the Grail, 'or else he will be stricken dead'. A barren woman would be granted the gift of children by stroking the Grail and if a man were to drink from it on Good Friday he would be vouchsafed a glimpse of 'she whom he will take to wife in heaven'. Another story related how a knight, carrying the Grail across a wilderness, was pursued by heathens and, when it seemed he must be caught, God sent a vast eagle that caught him, his horse and the precious Grail up into the sky, leaving the pagan warriors howling in frustrated rage.

One phrase was copied over and over in the pages of the book:

151

'*Transfer calicem istem a me*', and Thomas could feel his father's misery and frustration reaching through the repeated phrase. 'Take this cup from me,' the words meant and they were the same words Christ had spoken in the Garden of Gethsemane as he pleaded with God the Father to spare him the pain of hanging on the tree. The phrase was sometimes written in Greek, a language Thomas had studied but never mastered fully; he managed to decipher most of the Greek text, but the Hebrew remained a mystery.

Sir John, the ancient vicar of St Peter's, agreed that it was a strange kind of Hebrew. 'I've forgotten all the Hebrew I ever learned,' he told Thomas, 'but I don't remember seeing a letter like that!' He pointed to the symbol that looked like a human eye. 'Very odd, Thomas, very odd. It's almost Hebrew.' He paused a while, then said plaintively, 'If only poor Nathan was still here.'

'Nathan?'

'He was before your time, Thomas. Nathan collected leeches and sent them to London. Physicians there prized Dorset leeches, did you know that? But, of course, Nathan was a Jew and he left with the others.' The Jews had been expelled from England almost fifty years before, an event still green in the priest's memory. 'No one has ever discovered where he found his leeches,' Sir John went on, 'and I sometimes wonder if he put a curse on them.' He frowned at the book. 'This belonged to your father?'

'It did.'

'Poor Father Ralph,' Sir John said, intimating that the book must have been the product of madness. He closed the volume and carefully wrapped the soft leather cover about the pages.

There was no sign of de Taillebourg, nor any news of Thomas's friends in Normandy. He wrote a difficult letter to Sir Guillaume which told how his daughter had died and begging for any news of Will Skeat whom Sir Guillaume had taken to Caen to be treated by Mordecai, the Jewish doctor. The letter went to Southampton and from there to Guernsey and Thomas was assured it would be sent on to Normandy, but no reply had come by Christmas and Thomas assumed the letter was lost. Thomas also wrote to Lord Outhwaite, assuring his lordship that he was being assiduous in his search and recounting some of the stories from his father's book.

Lord Outhwaite sent a reply that congratulated Thomas on what

he had discovered, then revealed that Sir Geoffrey Carr had left for Brittany with half a dozen men. Rumour, Lord Outhwaite reported, claimed that the Scarecrow's debts were larger than ever, 'which, perhaps, is why he has gone to Brittany'. It would not just be hope of plunder that had taken the Scarecrow to La Roche-Derrien, but the law which said a debtor was not required to make repayments while he served the King abroad. 'Will you follow the Scarecrow?' Lord Outhwaite enquired, and Thomas sent an answer saying he would be in La Roche-Derrien by the time Lord Outhwaite read these words, and then did nothing about leaving Dorset. It was Christmas, he told himself, and he had always enjoyed Christmas.

Sir Giles celebrated the twelve days of the feast in high style. He ate no meat from Advent Sunday, which was not a particular hardship for he loved eels and fish, but on Christmas Eve he ate nothing but bread, readying himself for the first feast of the season. Twelve empty hives were brought into the hall and decorated with sprigs of ivy and holly; a great candle, big enough to burn through the whole season, was placed on the high table and a vast log set to burn in the hearth, and Sir Giles's neighbours were invited to drink wine and ale, and eat beef, wild boar, venison, goose and brawn. The wassail cup, filled with mulled and spiced claret, was passed about the hall and Sir Giles, as he did every night of Christmas, wept for his dead wife and was drunkenly asleep by the time the candles burned out. On the fourth night of Christmas, Thomas and Robbie joined the hogglers as, disguised as ghosts and green men and wild men, they pranced about the parish extorting funds for the Church. They went as far as Dorchester, encroaching on two other parishes as they did, and got into a fight with the hogglers from All Saints' and they ended the night in the Dorchester jail from which they were released by an amused George Adyn who brought them a morning pot of ale and one of his wife's famous hog's puddings. The Twelfth Night feast was a boar that Robbie had speared, and after it was eaten, and when the guests were lying half drunk and satiated on the hall rushes, it began to snow. Thomas stood in the doorway and watched the flakes whirling in the light of a flickering torch.

'We must be away soon,' Robbie had come to join him.

'Away?'

'We have work to do,' the Scot said.

Thomas knew that was true, but he did not want to leave. 'I thought you were happy enough here?'

'So I am,' Robbie said, 'and Sir Giles is more generous than I deserve.'

'So?'

'It's Mary,' Robbie said. He was embarrassed and did not finish.

'Pregnant?' Thomas guessed.

Robbie crossed himself. 'It seems so.'

Thomas stared at the snow. 'If you give her enough money to make a dowry,' he said, 'she'll thrive.'

'I've only got three pounds left,' Robbie said. He had been given a purse by his uncle, Sir William, supposedly with enough money to last a year.

'That should be enough,' Thomas said. The snow whirled in a gust of wind.

'It'll leave me with nothing!' Robbie protested.

'You should have thought of that before you ploughed the field,' Thomas said, remembering how he had been in just this predicament with a girl in Hookton. He turned back to the hall where a harpist and flautist made music to the drunks. 'We should go,' he said, 'but I don't know where.'

'You said you wanted to go to Calais?'

Thomas shrugged. 'You think de Taillebourg will seek us there?'

'I think,' Robbie said, 'that once he knows you have that book he'll follow you into hell itself.'

Thomas knew Robbie was right, but the book was not proving to be of any great help. It never specifically said that Father Ralph had possessed the Grail, nor described a place where a searcher might look for it. Thomas and Robbie had been looking. They had combed the sea caves in the cliffs near Hookton where they had found driftwood, limpets and seaweed. There had been no golden cup half hidden in the shingle. So where to go now? Where to look? If Thomas went to Calais then he could join the army, but he doubted de Taillebourg would seek him out in the heart of England's soldiery. Maybe, Thomas thought, he should go back to Brittany and he knew that it was not the Grail or the necessity to face de Taillebourg that attracted him to La Roche-Derrien, but

154

the thought that Jeanette Chenier might have returned home. He thought of her often, thought of her black hair, of her fierce spirit and defiance, and every time he thought of her he suffered guilt because of Eleanor.

The snow did not last. It thawed and a hard rain came from the west to lash the Dorset coast. A big English ship was wrecked on the Chesil shingle and Thomas and Robbie took one of Sir Giles's wagons down to the beach and with the aid of Jake Churchill and two of his sons fought off a score of other men to rescue six packs of wool that they carried back to Down Mapperley and presented to Sir Giles who thereby made a year's income in one day.

And next morning the French priest came to Dorchester.

The news was brought by George Adyn. 'I know as you said we should be watching for foreigners,' he told Thomas, 'and this one be real foreign. Dressed like a priest, he is, but who knows? Looks like a vagabond, he does. You say the word' – he winked at Thomas – 'and we'll give the bugger a proper whipping and send him on up to Shaftesbury.'

'What will they do with him there?' Robbie asked.

'Give him another whipping and send him back,' George said.

'Is he a Dominican?' Thomas asked.

'How would I know? He's talking gibberish, he is. He don't talk proper, not like a Christian.'

'What colour is his gown?'

'Black, of course.'

'I'll come and talk to him,' Thomas said.

'He only jabbers away, he does. Your honour!' This was in greeting to Sir Giles, and Thomas then had to wait while the two men discussed the health of various cousins and nephews and other relatives, and it was close to midday by the time he and Robbie rode into Dorchester and Thomas thought, for the thousandth time, what a good town this was and how it would be a pleasure to live here.

The priest was brought out into the small jail yard. It was a fine day. Two blackbirds hopped along the top wall and an aconite was

blooming in the yard corner. The priest proved to be a young man, very short, with a squashed nose, protuberant eyes and bristling black hair. He wore a gown so shabby, torn and stained that it was little wonder the constables had thought the man a vagrant; a misconception that made the little priest indignant. 'Is this how the English treat God's servants? Hell is too good for you English! I shall tell the bishop and he will tell the Archbishop and he will inform the Holy Father and you will all be declared anathema! You will all be excommunicated!'

'See what I mean?' George Adyn asked. 'Yaps away like a dog fox, but he don't make sense.'

'He's speaking French,' Thomas told him, then turned to the priest. 'What's your name?'

'I want to see the bishop now. Here!'

'What's your name?'

'Bring me the local priest!'

'I'll punch your bloody ears out first,' Thomas said. 'Now what's your name?'

He was called Father Pascal, and he had just endured a journey of exquisite discomfort, crossing the winter seas from Normandy, from a place south of Caen. He had travelled first to Guernsey and then on to Southampton from where he had walked, and he had done it all without any knowledge of English. It was a miracle to Thomas that Father Pascal had come this far. And it seemed even more of a miracle because Father Pascal had been sent to Hookton from Evecque, with a message for Thomas.

Sir Guillaume d'Evecque had sent him, or rather Father Pascal had volunteered to make the journey, and it was urgent for he was bringing a plea for help. Evecque was under siege. 'It is terrible!' Father Pascal said. By now, calmed and placated, he was by the fire in the Three Cocks where he was eating goose and drinking bragget, a mixture of warmed mead and dark ale. 'It is the Count of Coutances who is besieging him. The Count!'

'Why is that terrible?' Thomas enquired.

'Because the Count is his liege lord!' the priest exclaimed, and Thomas understood why Father Pascal said it was terrible. Sir Guillaume held his lands in fief to the Count and by making war on his own tenant the Count was declaring Sir Guillaume an outlaw.

'But why?' Thomas asked.

Father Pascal shrugged. 'The Count says it is because of what happened at the battle. Do you know what happened at the battle?'

'I know,' Thomas said, and because he was translating for Robbie he had to explain anyway. The priest referred to the battle that had been fought the previous summer by the forest at Crécy. Sir Guillaume had been in the French army, but in the middle of the fight he had seen his enemy, Guy Vexille, and had turned his men-at-arms against Vexille's troops.

'The Count says that is treason,' the priest explained, 'and the King has given his blessing.'

Thomas said nothing for a while. 'How did you know I was here?' he finally asked.

'You sent a letter to Sir Guillaume.'

'I didn't think it reached him.'

'Of course it did. Last year. Before this trouble started.'

Sir Guillaume was in trouble, but his manor of Evecque, Father Pascal said, was built of stone and blessed with a moat and so far the Count of Coutances had found it impossible to break the wall or cross the moat, but the Count had scores of men while Sir Guillaume had a garrison of only nine. 'There are some women too' – Father Pascal tore at a goose leg with his teeth – 'but they don't count.'

'Does he have food?'

'Plenty, and the well is good.'

'So he can hold for a time?'

The priest shrugged. 'Maybe? Maybe not? He thinks so, but what do I know? And the Count has a machine, a . . .' He frowned, trying to find the word.

'A trebuchet?'

'No, no, a springald!' A springald was like a massive crossbow that shot a huge dart. Father Pascal stripped the last morsel off the bone. 'It is very slow and it broke once. But they mended it. It batters at the wall. Oh, and your friend is there,' he mumbled, his mouth full.

'My friend?'

'Skeat, is that the name? He's there with the doctor. He can talk

157

now, and he walks. He is much better, yes? But he cannot recognize people, not unless they speak.'

'Unless they speak?' Thomas asked, puzzled.

'If he sees you,' the priest explained, 'he does not know you. Then you speak and he knows you.' He shrugged again. 'Strange, eh?' He drained his pot. 'So what will you do, monsieur?'

'What does Sir Guillaume want me to do?'

'He wants you close by in case he needs to escape, but he's written a letter to the King explaining what happened in the battle. I sent the letter to Paris. Sir Guillaume thinks the King may relent so he waits for an answer, but me? I think Sir Guillaume is like this goose. Plucked and cooked.'

'Did he say anything about his daughter?'

'His daughter?' Father Pascal was puzzled. 'Oh! The bastard daughter? He said you would kill whoever killed her.'

'I will, too.'

'And that he wants your help.'

'He can have it,' Thomas said, 'and we'll leave tomorrow.' He looked at Robbie. 'We're going back to war.'

'Who am I fighting for?'

Thomas grinned. 'Me.'

Thomas, Robbie and the priest left next morning. Thomas took a change of clothes, a full arrow bag, his bow, sword and mail coat and, wrapped in a piece of deerskin, his father's book that seemed like a heavy piece of baggage. In truth it was lighter than a sheaf of arrows, yet the duty its possession implied weighed on Thomas's conscience. He told himself he was merely riding to help Sir Guillaume, yet he knew he was continuing the quest for his father's secret.

Two of Sir Giles's tenants rode with them to bring back the mare that Father Pascal rode and the two stallions which Sir Giles had purchased from Thomas and Robbie. 'You don't want to take them on a boat,' Sir Giles said, 'horses and boats don't mix.'

'He paid us too much,' Robbie remarked as they rode away.

'He doesn't want his son-in-law to get it,' Thomas said. 'Besides,

he's a generous man. He gave Mary Gooden another three pounds as well. For her dowry. He's a lucky man.'

Something in Thomas's tone caught Robbie's attention. '"He" is? You mean she's found a husband?'

'A nice fellow. A thatcher in Tolpuddle. They'll be wed next week.'

'Next week!' Robbie sounded aggrieved that his girl was marrying. It did not matter that he was abandoning her, it still cut his pride. 'But why would he marry her?' he asked after a while. 'Or doesn't he know she's pregnant?'

'He thinks the child is his,' Thomas said, keeping a straight face, 'and well it might be, I hear.'

'Jesus!' Robbie swore when that made sense, then he turned to look back along the road and he smiled, remembering the good times. 'He's a kind man,' he said of Sir Giles.

'A lonely one,' Thomas said. Sir Giles had not wanted them to leave, but accepted they could not stay.

Robbie sniffed the air. 'There's more snow coming.'

'Never!' It was a morning of gentle sunlight. Crocus and aconite were showing in sheltered spots and the hedgerows were noisy with chaffinches and robins. But Robbie had indeed smelt snow. As the day wore on, the skies became low and grey, the wind went into the east and hit their faces with a new bite and the snow followed. They found shelter in a verderer's house in the woods, crowding in with the man, his wife, five daughters and three sons. Two cows had a byre at one end of the house and four goats were tethered at the other. Father Pascal confided to Thomas that this was very like the house in which he had grown up, but he wondered if conventions in England were the same as in the Limousin. 'Conventions?' Thomas asked.

'In our house,' Father Pascal said, blushing, 'the women pissed with the cows and the men with the goats. I would not want to do the wrong thing.'

'It's the same here,' Thomas assured him.

Father Pascal had proved a good companion. He had a fine singing voice and once they had shared their food with the verderer and his family the priest sang some French songs. Afterwards, as the snow still fell and the smoke from the fire swirled thick under the

159

thatch, he sat and talked with Thomas. He had been the village priest at Evecque and, when the Count of Coutances attacked, he had found refuge in the manor. 'But I do not like being cooped up,' he said, and so he had offered to carry Sir Guillaume's message to England. He had escaped from Evecque, he said, by first throwing his clothes across the moat and then swimming after them. 'It was cold,' he said, 'I have never been so cold! I told myself it is better to be cold than to be in hell, but I don't know. It was terrible.'

'What does Sir Guillaume want us to do?' Thomas asked him.

'He did not say. Perhaps, if the besiegers can be discouraged . . . ?' He shrugged. 'The winter is not a good time for a siege, I think. Inside Evecque they are comfortable, they are warm, they have the harvest stored, and the besiegers? They are wet and cold. If you can make them more uncomfortable, who knows? Perhaps they will abandon the siege?'

'And you? What will you do?'

'I have no work left at Evecque,' the priest said. Sir Guillaume had been declared a traitor and his goods pronounced forfeited so his serfs had been taken off to the Count of Coutances's estates, while his tenants, pillaged and raped by the besiegers, had mostly fled. 'So perhaps I go to Paris? I cannot go to the Bishop of Caen.'

'Why not?'

'Because he has sent men to help the Count of Coutances.' Father Pascal shook his head in sad wonderment. 'The bishop was impoverished by the English in the summer,' he explained, 'so he needs money, land and goods, and he hopes to get some from Evecque. Greed is a great provoker of war.'

'Yet you're on Sir Guillaume's side?'

Father Pascal shrugged. 'He is a good man. But now? Now I must look to Paris for preferment. Or maybe Dijon. I have a cousin there.'

They struggled east for the next two days, riding across the dead heaths of the New Forest, which lay under a soft whiteness. At night the small lights of the forest villages glittered hard in the cold. Thomas feared if they would reach Normandy too late to help Sir Guillaume, but that doubt was not reason enough to abandon the effort and so they struggled on. Their last few miles to Southampton were through a melting slush of mud and snow, and Thomas wondered how they were to reach Normandy, which was an enemy

160

province. He doubted that any shipping would go there from South-ampton because any English boat going close to the Normandy coast was liable to be snapped up by pirates. He knew plenty of boats would be going to Brittany, but that was a long walk from Caen. 'We go through the islands, of course,' Father Pascal said.

They spent one night in a tavern and next morning found space on the *Ursula*, a cog bound for Guernsey and carrying barrels of salt pork, kegs of nails, barrel staves, iron ingots, pots packed in sawdust, bolts of wool, sheaves of arrows and three crates of cattle horns. It was also carrying a dozen bowmen who were travelling to the garrison of the castle which guarded the anchorage at St Peter Port. Come a bad west wind, the *Ursula*'s captain told them, and dozens of ships carrying wine from Gascony to England could be blown up-channel and St Peter Port was one of their last harbours of refuge, though the French sailors knew it too and in bad weather their ships would swarm off the island trying to pick up a prize or two. 'Does that mean they'll be waiting for us?' Thomas asked. The Isle of Wight was slipping astern and the ship was plunging into a winter-grey sea.

'Not waiting for us, they won't be, not us. They know the *Ursula*, they do,' the captain, a toothless man with a face horribly scarred from the pox, grinned, 'they do know her and they do love her.' Which meant, presumably, that he had paid his dues to the men of Cherbourg and Carteret. However, he had paid no dues to Neptune or whatever spirit governed the winter sea for, though he claimed some special foreknowledge of winds and waves and asserted that both would be calm, the *Ursula* rolled like a bell swung on a beam: up and down, pitching hard over so that the cargo slid in the hold with a noise like thunder; and the evening sky was grey as death and then sleet began to seethe on the torn water. The captain, clinging to the steering oar with a grin, said it was nothing but a little blow that should not worry any good Christian, but others in his crew either touched the crucifix nailed to the single mast or else bowed their heads to a small shrine on the afterdeck where a crude wooden image was wrapped in bright ribbons. The image was supposed to be St Ursula, the patron of ships, and Thomas said a prayer to her himself as he crouched in a small space under the foredeck, ostensibly sheltering there with the other passengers,

but the overhead deck seams gaped and a mixture of rainwater and seawater continually slopped through. Three of the archers were sick and even Thomas, who had crossed the channel twice before and had been raised among fishermen and spent days aboard their small boats, was feeling ill. Robbie, who had never been to sea, looked cheerful and interested in everything that was happening aboard.

'It's these round ships,' he yelled over the noise, 'they roll!'

'You know about ships, do you?' Thomas asked.

'It seems obvious,' Robbie said.

Thomas tried to sleep. He wrapped himself in his damp cloak, curled up and lay as still as the pitching boat would let him and, astonishingly, he did fall asleep. He woke a dozen times that night and each time he wondered where he was and when he remembered he wondered whether the night would ever end or whether he would ever be warm again.

Dawn was sickly grey and the cold bit into Thomas's bones, but the crew was altogether more cheerful for the wind had dropped and the sea was merely sullen, the long foam-streaked waves rising and falling sluggishly about a wicked group of rocks that appeared to be home for a myriad seabirds. It was the only land in sight.

The captain stumped across the deck to stand beside Thomas. 'The Casquets,' he said, nodding at the rocks. 'A lot of widows have been made on those old stones.' He made the sign of the cross, spat over the gunwales for luck and then looked up to a widening rift in the clouds. 'We're making good time,' he said, 'thanks be to God and to Ursula.' He looked askance at Thomas. 'So what takes you to the islands?'

Thomas thought of inventing some excuse, family perhaps, then thought the truth might elicit something more interesting. 'We want to go on to Normandy,' he said.

'They don't like Englishmen much in Normandy, not since our King paid them a visit last year.'

'I was there.'

'Then you'll know why they don't like us.'

Thomas knew the captain was right. The English had killed thousands in Caen, then burned farms, mills and villages in a great swathe east and north. It was a cruel way to wage war, but it could

162

persuade the enemy to come out of his strongholds and give battle. Doubtless that was why the Count of Coutances was laying Evecque's lands waste, in hope that Sir Guillaume would be enticed out of his stone walls to defend them. Except Sir Guillaume had only nine men and could not hope to face the Count in open battle. 'We've business in Caen,' Thomas admitted, 'if we can ever reach the place.'

The captain picked at a nostril, then flicked something into the sea. 'Look for the troy frairs,' he said.

'The what?'

'*Troy Frairs*,' he said again. 'It's a boat and that's her name. It's French. She ain't big, no larger than that little tub.' He pointed to a small fishing boat, her hull tarred black, from which two men cast weighted nets into the broken sea about the Casquets. 'A man called Ugly Peter runs the *Troy Frairs*. He might carry you to Caen, or maybe to Carteret or Cherbourg. Not that I told you that.'

'Of course not,' Thomas said. He supposed the captain meant that Ugly Peter commanded a boat called *Les Trois Frères*. He stared at the fishing boat and wondered what kind of life it was to drag sustenance from this hard sea. It was easier, no doubt, to smuggle wool into Normandy and wine back to the islands.

All morning they ran southwards until at last they made landfall. A small island lay off to the east and a larger, Guernsey, to the west, and from both rose pillars of smoke from cooking fires that promised shelter and warm food, but though that promise fluttered in the sky, the wind backed and the tide turned and it took the rest of the day for the *Ursula* to beat down to the harbour where she anchored under the loom of the castle built on its rocky island. Thomas, Robbie and Father Pascal were rowed ashore and found respite from the cold wind in a tavern with a fire burning in a wide hearth beside which they ate fish stew and black bread washed down with a watery ale. They slept on straw-filled sacks that were home to lice.

It was four days before Ugly Peter, whose real name was Pierre Savon, put into the harbour, and another two before he was ready to leave again with a cargo of wool on which no duty would be paid. He was happy to take passengers, though only at a price which left Robbie and Thomas feeling robbed. Father Pascal was carried

163

free on the grounds that he was a Norman and a priest which meant, according to Pierre the Ugly, that God loved him twice over and so was unlikely to sink *Les Trois Frères* so long as Father Pascal was aboard.

God must have loved the priest for he sent a gentle west wind, clear skies and calm seas so that *Les Trois Frères* seemed to fly her way to the River Orne. They went up to Caen on the tide, arriving in the morning, and once they were ashore Father Pascal offered Thomas and Robbie a blessing, then hitched up his shabby robe and began walking east to Paris. Thomas and Robbie, carrying heavy bundles of mail, weapons, arrows and spare clothing, went south through the city.

Caen looked no better than when Thomas had left it the previous year after it had been laid waste by English archers who, disregarding their King's orders to discontinue their attack, had swarmed over the river and hacked to death hundreds of men and women inside the city. Robbie stared in awe at the destruction on Île St Jean, the newest part of Caen, which had suffered most from the English sack. Few of the burned houses had been rebuilt and there were ribs, skulls and long bones showing in the rivers' mud at the falling tide's margin. The shops were half bare, though a few countryfolk were in town selling food from carts and Thomas bought dried fish, bread and rock-hard cheese. Some looked askance at his bowstave, but he assured them he was a Scotsman and thus an ally of France. 'They do have proper bows in Scotland, don't they?' he asked Robbie.

'Of course we do.'

'Then why didn't you use them at Durham?'

'We just don't have enough,' Robbie said, 'and besides, we'd rather kill you bastards up close. Make sure you're dead, see?' He stared open-mouthed at a girl carrying a pail of milk. 'I'm in love.'

'If it's got tits you fall in love,' Thomas said. 'Now come on.' He led Robbie to Sir Guillaume's town house, the place where he had met Eleanor, and though Sir Guillaume's crest of three hawks was still carved in stone above the door there was now a new banner flying over the house: a flag showing a hump-backed boar with great tusks. 'Whose flag is that?' Thomas had crossed the small

square to talk with a cooper who was hammering an iron ring down the flanks of a new barrel.

'It's the Count of Coutances,' the cooper said, 'and the bastard's already raised our rents. And I don't care if you do serve him.' He straightened and frowned at the bowstave. 'Are you English?'

'*Écossais*,' Thomas said.

'Ah!' The cooper was intrigued and leaned closer to Thomas. 'Is it true, monsieur,' he asked, 'that you paint your faces blue in battle?'

'Always,' Thomas said, 'and our arses.'

'*Formidable*!' the cooper said, impressed.

'What's he saying?' Robbie asked.

'Nothing.' Thomas pointed at the oak which grew at the centre of the small square. A few shrivelled leaves still clung to the twigs. 'I was hanged from that tree,' he told Robbie.

'Aye, and I'm the Pope of Avignon.' Robbie heaved up his bundle. 'Did you ask him where we could buy horses?'

'Expensive things, horses,' Thomas said, 'and I thought we might save ourselves the bother of buying.'

'We're footpads now?'

'Indeed,' Thomas said. He led Robbie off the island across the bridge where so many archers had died in the frenzied attack, and then through the old city. That had been less damaged than the Île St Jean because no one had tried to defend the narrow streets, while the castle, which had never fallen to the English, had only suffered from cannon balls that had done little except chip the stones about the gate. A red and yellow banner flew from the castle rampart and men-at-arms, wearing the same coloured livery, challenged Thomas and Robbie as they were leaving the old city. Thomas answered by saying they were Scottish soldiers seeking employment from the Count of Coutances. 'I thought he'd be here,' Thomas lied, 'but we hear he's at Evecque.'

'And getting nowhere,' the guard commander said. He was a bearded man whose helmet had a great split that suggested he had taken it from a corpse. 'He's been pissing at those walls for two months now and got nowhere, but if you want to die at Evecque, boys, then good luck to you.'

They walked past the walls of the Abbaye aux Dames and Thomas

had a sudden vision of Jeanette again. She had been his lover, but then had met Edward Woodstock, the Prince of Wales, and what chance did Thomas have after that? It had been here, in the Abbaye aux Dames, that Jeanette and the Prince had lived during the brief siege of Caen. Where was Jeanette now? Thomas wondered. Back in Brittany? Still seeking her infant son? Did she ever think of him? Or did she regret fleeing from the Prince of Wales in the belief that the Picardy battle would be lost? Perhaps, by now, she would be married again. Thomas suspected she had taken a small fortune in jewels when she had fled the English army, and a rich widow, scarce more than twenty years old, made an attractive bride.

'What happens' – Robbie interrupted his thoughts – 'if they find out you're not Scottish?'

Thomas held up the two fingers of his right hand that drew the bowcord. 'They cut those off.'

'Is that all?'

'Those are the first things they cut off.'

They walked on south through a country of small steep hills, tight fields, thick woods and deep lanes. Thomas had never been to Evecque and, though it was not far from Caen, some of the peasants they asked had never heard of it, but when Thomas asked which way the soldiers had been going during the winter they pointed on southwards. They spent their first night in a roofless hovel, a place that had evidently been abandoned when the English came in the summer and swept through Normandy.

They woke at dawn and Thomas put two arrows into a tree, just to keep in practice. He was cutting the steel heads out of the trunk when Robbie picked up the bow. 'Can you teach me to use it?' he asked.

'What I can teach you,' Thomas said, 'will take ten minutes. But the rest will need a lifetime. I began shooting arrows when I was seven and after ten years I was beginning to get good at it.'

'It can't be that difficult,' Robbie protested, 'I've killed a stag with a bow.'

'That was a hunting bow,' Thomas said. He gave Robbie one of the arrows and pointed to a willow that had stubbornly kept its leaves. 'Hit the trunk.'

Robbie laughed. 'I can't miss!' The willow was scarcely thirty paces away.

'Go on, then.'

Robbie drew the bow, glancing once at Thomas as he realized just how much strength was needed to bend the great yew stave. It was twice as stiff as the shorter hunting bows he had used in Scotland. 'Jesus,' he said softly as he hauled the string back to his nose and realized his left arm was trembling slightly with the tension of the weapon, but he peered down the arrow to check his aim and was about to loose when Thomas held up a hand. 'You're not ready yet.'

'I damn well am,' Robbie said, though the words came out as grunts for the bow needed immense force to hold in the drawn position.

'You're not ready,' Thomas said, 'because there's four inches of the arrow sticking out in front of the bow. You have to pull it back until the arrow head touches your left hand.'

'Oh, sweet Jesus,' Robbie said and took a breath, nerved himself and pulled until the string was past his nose, past his eye and close by his right ear. The steel arrow head touched his left hand, but now he could no longer aim by looking down the arrow's shaft. He frowned as he realized the difficulty that implied, then compensated by edging the bow to the right. His left arm was shaking with the tension and, unable to keep the arrow drawn, he released, then twitched as the hemp string whipped along his inner left forearm. The arrow's feathers flashed white as they passed a foot from the willow's trunk. Robbie swore in amazement, then handed the bow to Thomas. 'So the trick of it,' he said, 'is learning how to aim it?'

'The trick,' Thomas said, 'is not aiming at all. It's something that just happens. You look at the target and you let the arrow fly.' Some archers, the lazy ones, only drew to the eye and that made them accurate, but their arrows lacked force. The good archers, the archers who drove down armies or brought down kings in shining armour, pulled the string all the way back. 'I taught a woman to shoot last summer,' Thomas said, taking back the bow, 'and she became good. Really good. She hit a hare at seventy paces.'

'A woman!'

'I let her use a longer string,' Thomas said, 'so the bow didn't

need as much strength, but she was still good.' He remembered Jeanette's delight when the hare tumbled in the grass, squealing, the arrow pinned through its haunches. Jeanette. Why was he thinking of her so much?

They walked on through a world edged white with frost. The puddles had frozen and the leafless hedgerows were outlined with a sharp white rime that faded as the sun climbed. They crossed two streams, then climbed through beechwoods towards a plateau which, when they reached it, proved to be a wild place of thin turf that had never been cut with a plough. A few gorse bushes broke the grass, but otherwise the road ran across a featureless plain beneath an empty sky. Thomas had thought that the heathland would be nothing but a narrow belt of high country and that they must soon drop into the wooded valleys again, but the road stretched on and he felt ever more like a hare on a chalk upland under the gaze of a buzzard. Robbie felt the same and the two of them left the road to walk where the gorse provided some intermittent cover.

Thomas kept looking ahead and behind. This was horse country, a firm-turfed upland where riders could go full gallop and where there were no woods or gullies in which two men on foot could hide. And the high ground seemed to extend for ever.

At midday they reached a circle of standing stones, each about the height of a man and heavily encrusted with lichen. The circle was twenty yards across and one of the stones had fallen and they rested their backs against it while they took a meal of bread and cheese. 'The devil's wedding party, eh?' Robbie said.

'The stones, you mean?'

'We have them in Scotland.' Robbie twisted round and brushed fragments of snail shell from the fallen stone. 'They're people who were turned into rocks by the devil.'

'In Dorset,' Thomas said, 'folk say that God turned them into stone.'

Robbie wrinkled his face at that idea. 'Why would God do that?'

'For dancing on the sabbath.'

'They'd just go to hell for that,' Robbie said, then idly scratched at the turf with his heel. 'We dig the stones up when we have the time. Look for gold, see?'

'You ever find any?'

'We do in the mounds sometimes. Pots anyway, and beads. Rubbish really. We throw it away as often as not. And we find elf stones, of course.' He meant the mysterious stone arrow heads that were supposedly shot from elfin bowstrings. He stretched out, enjoying the feeble warmth of the sun that was now as high as it would climb in the midwinter sky. 'I miss Scotland.'

'I've never been.'

'God's own country,' Robbie said forcefully, and he was still talking about Scotland's wonders when Thomas fell gently asleep. He dozed, then was woken because Robbie had kicked him.

The Scot was standing on the fallen stone. 'What is it?' Thomas asked.

'Company.'

Thomas stood beside him and saw four horsemen a mile or more to the north. He dropped back to the turf, pulled upon his bundle and took out a single sheaf of arrows, then hooked the bowstring over the nocked tips of the stave. 'Maybe they haven't seen us,' he said optimistically.

'They have,' Robbie commented, and Thomas climbed onto the stone again to see that the horsemen had left the road; they had stopped now and one of them stood in his stirrups to get a better look at the two strangers at the stone circle. Thomas could see they were wearing mail coats under their cloaks. 'I can take three of them,' he said, patting the bow, 'if you manage the fourth.'

'Ah, be kind to a poor Scotsman,' Robbie said, drawing his uncle's sword, 'leave me two. I have to make money, remember.' He might have been facing a fight with four horsemen in Normandy, but he was still a prisoner of Lord Outhwaite and so bound to pay his ransom that had been set at a mere two hundred pounds. His uncle's was ten thousand and in Scotland the Douglas clan would be worrying how to raise it.

The horsemen still watched Thomas and Robbie, doubtless wondering who and what they were. The riders would not be fearful; after all they were mailed and armed and the two strangers were on foot and men on foot were almost certainly peasants and peasants were no threat to horsemen in armour. 'A patrol from Evecque?' Robbie wondered aloud.

'Probably.' The Count of Coutances would have men roaming the country looking for food. Or perhaps the horsemen were reinforcements riding to the Count's aid, but whoever they were they would regard any stranger in this countryside as prey for their weapons.

'They're coming,' Robbie said as the four men spread into a line. The riders must have assumed the two strangers would try to escape and so were making the line to snare them. 'The four horsemen, eh?' Robbie said. 'I can never remember what the fourth one is.'

'Death, war, pestilence and famine,' Thomas said, putting the first arrow on the string.

'It's famine I always forget,' Robbie said. The four riders were a half-mile away, swords drawn, cantering on the fine solid turf. Thomas was holding the bow low so they would not be ready for the arrows. He could hear the hoofbeats now and he thought of the four horsemen of the apocalypse, the dreadful quartet of riders whose appearance would presage the end of time and the last great struggle between heaven and hell. War would appear on a horse the colour of blood, famine would be on a black stallion, pestilence would ravage the world on a white mount while death would ride the pale horse. Thomas had a sudden memory of his father sitting bolt upright, head back, intoning the Latin: '*et ecce equus pallidus*'. Father Ralph used to say the words to annoy his housekeeper and lover, Thomas's mother, who, though she knew no Latin, understood that the words were about death and hell and she thought, rightly as it turned out, that her priest lover was inviting hell and death to Hookton.

'Behold a pale horse,' Thomas said. Robbie gave him a puzzled look. '"I saw a pale horse,"' Thomas quoted, '"and the name of its rider was Death, and Hell followed him."'

'Is hell another of the riders?' Robbie asked.

'Hell is what these bastards are about to get,' Thomas said and he brought up the bow and dragged back the cord and felt a sudden anger and hate in his heart for the four men, and then the bow sounded, the cord's note hard and deep, and before the sound had died he was already plucking a second arrow from where he had stuck a dozen point-down in the turf. He hauled the cord back and the four horsemen were still riding straight for them as Thomas

aimed at the left-hand rider. He loosed, took a third arrow, and now the sound of the hooves on the frost-hardened turf was as loud as the Scottish drums at Durham and the second man from the right was thrashing left and right, falling back, an arrow jutting from his chest and the rider on the left was lying back on his saddle's cantle, and the other two, at last understanding their danger, were swerving to throw off Thomas's aim. Gobbets of earth and grass were thrown up from the horses' hooves as they slewed away. If the two unwounded riders had any sense, Thomas thought, they would ride away as though Hell and Death were on their heels, ride back the way they had come in a desperate bid to escape the arrows, but instead, with the rage of men who had been challenged by what they believed to be an inferior enemy, they curved back towards their prey and Thomas let the third arrow fly. The first two men were both out of it, one fallen from his saddle and the other lolling on his horse that just cropped the winter-pale turf; and the third arrow flew hard and straight at its victim, but his galloping horse tossed up its head and the arrow slid down the side of its skull, blood bright on the black hide: the horse twisted away from the pain and the rider, unready for the turn, was flailing for balance, but Thomas had no time to watch him for the fourth rider was inside the stone circle and closing on him. The man had a vast black cloak that billowed behind as he turned the pale grey horse and he shouted his defiance as he stretched out the sword to whip the point like a lance head into Thomas's chest, but Thomas had his fourth arrow on the cord and the man suddenly understood that he was a split second too late. 'Non!' he shouted, and Thomas did not even draw the bow fully back, but let it fly off the half-string and the arrow still had enough force to bury itself in the man's head, splitting the bridge of his nose and driving deep into his skull. He twitched, his sword arm dropped, Thomas felt the wind as the man's horse thundered past him and then the rider fell back over the stallion's rump.

The third man, the one unseated from the black horse, had fallen in the stone circle's centre and now approached Robbie. Thomas plucked an arrow from the turf. 'No!' Robbie called. 'He's mine.'

Thomas relaxed the string.

'*Chien bâtard*,' the man said to Robbie. He was much older than

171

the Scotsman and must have taken Robbie for a mere boy for he half smiled as he came fast forward to lunge his sword and Robbie stepped back, parried, and the blades rang like bells in the clear air. '*Bâtard*!' the man spat and attacked again.

Robbie stepped back once more, yielding ground until he had almost reached the stone ring, and his retreat worried Thomas who had stretched his string again, but then Robbie parried so fast and riposted so quickly that the Frenchman was going backwards in a sudden and desperate hurry. 'You English bastard,' Robbie said. He swung his blade low and the man dropped his own blade to parry and Robbie just kicked it aside and lunged so that his uncle's blade sank into the man's neck. 'Bastard English bastard,' Robbie snarled, ripping the blade free in a spray of bright blood. 'Bloody English pig!' He freed the sword and swung it back to bury its edge in what was left of the man's neck.

Thomas watched the man fall. Blood was bright on the grass. 'He wasn't English,' Thomas said.

'It's just a habit when I fight,' Robbie said. 'It's the way my uncle trained me.' He stepped towards his victim. 'Is he dead?'

'You half cut off his head,' Thomas said, 'what do you think?'

'I think I'll take his money,' Robbie said and knelt beside the dead man.

One of the first two men to be struck by Thomas's arrows was still alive. The breath bubbled in his throat and showed pink and frothy at his lips. He was the man lolling in his saddle and he moaned as Thomas spilled him down to the ground.

'Is he going to live?' Robbie had crossed to see what Thomas was doing.

'Christ, no,' Thomas said and took out his knife.

'Jesus!' Robbie stepped back as the man's throat was cut. 'Did you have to?'

'I don't want the Count of Coutances to know there are only two of us,' Thomas said. 'I want the Count of Coutances to be as scared as hell of us. I want him to think the devil's own horsemen are hunting his men.'

They searched the four corpses and, after a lumbering chase, managed to collect the four horses. From the bodies and the saddle-bags they took close to eighteen pounds of bad French silver

coinage, two rings, three good daggers, four swords, a fine mail coat that Robbie claimed to replace his own, and a gold chain that they hacked in half with one of the captured swords. Then Thomas used the two worst swords to picket a pair of the horses beside the road and on the horses' backs he tied two of the corpses so that they hung in the saddle, bending sideways with vacant eyes and white skin laced with blood. The other two corpses, stripped of their mail, were placed on the road and in each of their dead mouths Thomas put sprigs of gorse. That gesture meant nothing, but to whoever found the bodies it would suggest something strange, even Satanic. 'It'll worry the bastards,' Thomas explained.

'Four dead men should give them a twitch,' Robbie said.

'They'll be scared to hell if they think the devil's loose,' Thomas said. The Count of Coutances would scoff if he knew there were only two young men come as reinforcements for Sir Guillaume d'Evecque, but he could not ignore four corpses and hints of weird ritual. And he could not ignore death.

To which end, when the corpses were arranged, Thomas took the big black cloak, the money and the weapons, the best of the stallions and the pale horse.

For the pale horse belonged to Death.

And with it Thomas could make nightmares.

A single short burst of thunder sounded as Thomas and Robbie neared Evecque. They did not know how close they were, but they were riding through country where all the farms and cottages had been destroyed which told Thomas that they must be within the manor's boundaries. Robbie, on hearing the rumble, looked puzzled for the sky immediately above them was clear, although there were dark clouds to the south. 'It's too cold for thunder,' he said.

'Maybe it's different in France?'

They left the road and followed a farm track that twisted through woods and petered out beside a burned building that still smoked gently. It made little sense to burn such steadings and Thomas doubted that the Count of Coutances had initially ordered the destruction, but Sir Guillaume's long defiance and the bloody-mindedness of most soldiers would ensure that the pillage and burning would happen anyway. Thomas had done the same in Brittany. He had listened to the screams and protests of families who had to watch their home being burned and then he had touched the fire to the thatch. It was war. The Scots did it to the English, the English to the Scots, and here the Count of Coutances was doing it to his own tenant.

A second clap of thunder sounded and just after its echo had died Thomas saw a great veil of smoke in the eastern sky. He pointed to it and Robbie, recognizing the smear of campfires and realizing the need for silence, just nodded. They left their horses in a thicket of hazel saplings and then climbed a long wooded hill. The setting sun was behind them, throwing their shadows long on the dead leaves. A woodpecker, red-headed and wings barred white, whirred

174

loud and low above their heads as they crossed the ridge line to see the village and manor of Evecque beneath them.

Thomas had never seen Sir Guillaume's manor before. He had imagined it would be like Sir Giles Marriott's hall with one great barn-like room and a few thatched outbuildings, but Evecque was much more like a small castle. At the corner closest to Thomas it even had a tower: a square and not very tall tower, but properly crenellated and flying its banner of three stooping hawks to show that Sir Guillaume was not yet beaten. The manor's saving feature, though, was its moat, which was wide and thickly covered with a vivid green scum. The manor's high walls rose sheer from the water and had few windows, and those were nothing but arrow slits. The roof was thatched and sloped inwards to a small courtyard. The besiegers, whose tents and shelters lay in the village to the north of the manor, had succeeded in setting fire to the roof at some point, but Sir Guillaume's few defenders must have managed to extinguish the flames for only one small portion of the thatch was missing or blackened. None of those defenders was visible now, though some of them must have been peering though the arrow slits that showed as small black specks against the grey stone. The only visible damage to the manor was some broken stones at one corner of the tower where it looked as though a giant beast had nibbled at the masonry, and that was probably the work of the springald that Father Pascal had mentioned, but the oversized cross-bow had obviously broken again and irremediably for Thomas could see it lying in two gigantic pieces in the field beside the tiny stone village church. It had done very little damage before its main beam broke and Thomas wondered if the eastern, hidden, side of the building had been hurt more. The manor's entrance must be on that far side and Thomas suspected the main siege works would also be there.

Only a score of besiegers were in sight, most doing nothing more threatening than sitting outside the village houses, though a half-dozen men were gathered around what looked like a small table in the churchyard. None of the Count's men was closer to the manor than a hundred and fifty paces, which suggested that the defenders had succeeded in killing some of their enemies with cross-bows and the rest had learned to give the garrison a wide berth.

175

The village itself was small, not much bigger than Down Mapperley, and, like the Dorset village, had a watermill. There were a dozen tents to the south of the houses and twice as many little turf shelters and Thomas tried to work out how many men could be sheltered in the village, tents and turf huts and decided the Count must now have about 120 men.

'What do we do?' Robbie asked.

'Nothing for now. Just watch.'

It was a tedious vigil for there was little activity beneath them. Some women carried pails of water from the watermill's race, others were cooking on open fires or collecting clothes that had been spread out to dry over some bushes at the edge of the fields. The Count of Coutances's banner, showing the black boar on a white field spangled with blue flowers, flew on a makeshift staff outside the largest house in the village. Six other banners hung above the thatched rooftops, showing that other lords had come to share the plunder. A half-dozen squires or pages exercised some warhorses in the meadow behind the encampment, but otherwise Evecque's attackers were doing little except wait. Siege work was boring work. Thomas remembered the idle days outside La Roche-Derrien, though those long hours had been broken by the terror and excitement of the occasional assault. These men, unable to assault Evecque's walls because of the moat, could only wait and hope to starve the garrison into surrender or else tempt it into a sally by burning farms. Or perhaps they were waiting for a long piece of seasoned wood to repair the broken arm of the abandoned springald.

Then, just as Thomas was deciding that he had seen enough, the group of men who had been gathered about what he had thought was a low table beside the churchyard hedge suddenly ran back towards the church.

'What in God's name is that?' Robbie asked, and Thomas saw that it had not been a table they were crowding round, but a vast pot cradled in a heavy wooden frame.

'It's a cannon,' Thomas said, unable to hide his awe, and just then the gun fired and the great metal pot and its huge wooden cradle both vanished inside a swelling burst of dirty smoke and, out of the corner of his eye, he saw a piece of stone fly away from the damaged corner of the manor. A thousand birds flew up from

hedgerows, thatch and trees as the gun's booming thunder rolled up the hill and washed past him. That vast clap of sound was the thunder they had heard earlier in the afternoon. The Count of Coutances had managed to find a gun and was using it to nibble away at the manor. The English had used guns at Caen last summer, though not all the guns in their army, nor all the best efforts of the Italian gunners, had hurt Caen's castle. Indeed, as the smoke slowly cleared from the encampment, Thomas saw that this shot had made little impact on the manor. The noise seemed more violent than the missile itself, yet he supposed that if the Count's gunners could fire enough stones then eventually the masonry must give way and the tower collapse into the moat to make a rubble causeway across the water. Stone by stone, fragment by fragment, maybe three or four shots a day, and thus the besiegers would undermine the tower and make their rough path into Evecque.

A man rolled a small barrel out of the church, but another man waved him back and the barrel was taken back inside. The church had to be their powder store, Thomas thought, and the man had been sent back because the gunners had shot their last missile for the day and would not reload until morning. And that suggested an idea, but he pushed it away as impractical and stupid.

'Have you seen enough?' he asked Robbie.

'I've never seen a gun before,' Robbie said, staring down at the distant pot as if hoping that it would be fired again, but Thomas knew it was unlikely that the gunners would discharge it again this evening. It took a long time to charge a cannon and, once the black powder was packed into its belly and the missile put into the neck, the gun had to be sealed with damp loam. The loam would confine the explosion that propelled the missile and it needed time to dry before the gun was fired, so it was unlikely that there would be another shot before morning. 'It sounds more trouble than it's worth,' Robbie said sourly when Thomas had explained it. 'So you reckon they'll not fire again?'

'They'll wait till morning.'

'I've seen enough then,' Robbie said and they crawled back through the beeches until they were over the ridge, then went down to their picketed horses and rode into the falling night. There was a half-moon, cold and high, and the night was bitter, so bitter

they decided they must risk a fire, though they did their best to hide it by taking refuge in a deep gully with rock walls where they made a crude roof of boughs covered in hastily cut turfs. The fire flickered through the holes in the roof to light the rock walls red, but Thomas doubted that any of the besiegers would patrol the woods in the dark. No one willingly went into deep trees at night for all kinds of beasts and monsters and ghosts stalked the woodlands, and that thought reminded Thomas of the summer journey he had made with Jeanette when they had slept night after night in the woods. It had been a happy time and the remembrance of it made him feel sorry for himself and then, as ever, guilty for Eleanor's sake and he held his hands to the small fire. 'Are there green men in Scotland?' he asked Robbie.

'In the woods, you mean? There are goblins. Evil little bastards, they are.' Robbie made the sign of the cross and, in case that was not sufficient, leaned over and touched the iron hilt of his uncle's sword.

Thomas was thinking of goblins and other creatures, things that waited in the night woods. Did he really want to go back to Evecque tonight? 'Did you notice,' he said to Robbie, 'that no one in Coutances's camp seemed very disturbed that four of their horsemen hadn't returned? We didn't see anyone going looking for them, did we?'

Robbie thought about it, then shrugged. 'Maybe the horsemen didn't come from the camp?'

'They did,' Thomas said with a confidence he did not entirely feel and for a moment he guiltily wondered if the four horsemen had nothing to do with Evecque, then reminded himself that the riders had initiated the fight. 'They must have come from Evecque,' he said, 'and they'll be worried there by now.'

'So?'

'So will they have put more sentries on their camp tonight?'

Robbie shrugged. 'Does it matter?'

'I'm thinking,' Thomas said, 'that I have to tell Sir Guillaume that we're here, and I don't know how to do that except by making a big noise.'

'You could write a message,' Robbie suggested, 'and put it round an arrow?'

Thomas stared at him. 'I don't have parchment,' he said patiently, 'and I don't have ink, and have you ever tried shooting an arrow wrapped up in parchment? It would probably fly like a dead bird. I'd have to stand by the moat and it would be easier to throw the arrow from there.'

Robbie shrugged. 'So what do we do?'

'Make a noise. Announce ourselves.' Thomas paused. 'And I'm thinking that the cannon will break the tower down eventually if we don't do something.'

'The cannon?' Robbie asked, then stared at Thomas. 'Sweet Jesus,' he said after a while as he thought of the difficulties. 'Tonight?'

'Once Coutances and his men know we're here,' Thomas said, 'they'll double their sentries, but I'll bet the bastards are half asleep tonight.'

'Aye, and wrapped up warm if they've any damn sense,' Robbie said. He frowned. 'But that gun looked like a rare great pot. How the hell do you break it?'

'I was thinking of the black powder in the church,' Thomas said. 'Set fire to it?'

'There're plenty of campfires in the village,' Thomas said and he wondered what would happen if they were captured in the enemy encampment, but it was pointless to worry about that. If the gun was to be made useless then it was best to strike before the Count of Coutances knew an enemy had come to harass him, and that made this night the ideal opportunity. 'You don't have to come,' Thomas told Robbie. 'It's not as if your friends are inside the manor.'

'Hold your breath,' Robbie said scornfully. He frowned again. 'What's going to happen afterwards?'

'Afterwards?' Thomas thought. 'It depends on Sir Guillaume. If he gets no answer from the King then he'll want to break out. So he has to know we're here.'

'Why?'

'In case he needs our help. He did send for us, didn't he? Sent for me, anyway. So we go on making a noise. We make ourselves a nuisance. We give the Count of Coutances some nightmares.'

'The two of us?'

'You and me,' Thomas said, and the saying of it made him realize

that Robbie had become a friend. 'I think you and I can make trouble,' he added with a smile. And they would begin this night. In this bitter and cold night, beneath a hard-edged moon, they would conjure the first of their nightmares.

They went on foot and despite the bright half-moon it was dark under the trees and Thomas began to worry about whatever demons, goblins and spectres haunted these Norman woods. Jeanette had told him that in Brittany there were *nains* and *gorics* that stalked the dark, while in Dorset it was the Green Man who stamped and growled in the trees behind Lipp Hill, and the fisher-men spoke of the souls of the drowned men who would sometimes drag themselves on shore and moan for the wives they had left behind. On All Soul's Eve the devil and the dead danced on Maiden Castle, and on other nights there were lesser ghosts in and about the village and up on the hill and in the church tower and wherever a man looked, which was why no one left his house at night without a scrap of iron or a piece of mistletoe or, at the very least, a piece of cloth that had been touched by a holy wafer. Thomas's father had hated that superstition, but when his people had lifted their hands for the sacrament and he saw a scrap of cloth tied about their palms he had not refused them.

And Thomas had his own superstitions. He would only ever pick up the bow with his left hand; the first arrow to be shot from a newly strung bow had to be tapped three times against the stave, once for the Father, once for the Son and a third time for the Holy Spirit; he would not wear white clothes and he put his left boot on before his right. For a long time he had worn a dog's paw about his neck, then had thrown it away in the conviction it brought ill luck, but now, after Eleanor's death, he wondered if he should have kept it. Thinking of Eleanor, his mind slid back to the darker beauty of Jeanette. Did she remember him? Then he tried not to think of her, because thinking of an old love might bring ill luck and he touched the bole of a tree as he passed to cleanse away the thought.

Thomas was looking for the red glow of dying campfires beyond the trees that would tell him that they were close to Evecque, but

the only light was the silver of the moon tangled in the high branches. *Nains* and *gorics*: what were they? Jeanette had never told him, except to say they were spirits that haunted the country. They must have something similar here in Normandy. Or perhaps they had witches? He touched another tree. His mother had firmly believed in witches and his father had instructed Thomas to say his paternoster if he ever got lost. Witches, Father Ralph had believed, preyed upon lost children, and later, much later, Thomas's father had told him that witches began their invocation of the devil by saying the paternoster backwards and Thomas, of course, had tried it though he had never dared finish the whole prayer. *Olam a son arebil des*, the backward Paternoster began, and he could say it still, even managing the difficult reversals of *temptationem* and *supersubstantialem*, though he was careful never to finish the whole prayer in case there was a stench of brimstone, a crack of flame and the terror of the devil descending on black wings with eyes of fire.

'What are you muttering?' Robbie asked.

'I'm trying to say *supersubstantialem* backwards,' Thomas said.

Robbie chuckled. 'You're a strange one, Thomas.'

'*Melait nats bus repus*,' Thomas said.

'Is that French?' Robbie said. 'Because I have to learn it.'

'You will,' Thomas promised him, then at last he glimpsed fires between the trees and they both went silent as they climbed the long slope to the crest among the beeches that overlooked Evecque.

No lights showed from the manor. A clean and cold moonlight glistened on the green-scummed moat that looked smooth as ice – perhaps it was ice? – and the white moon threw a black shadow into the damaged corner of the tower, while a glow of firelight showed on the manor's farther side, confirming Thomas's suspicion that there was a siege work opposite the building's entrance. He guessed that the Count's men had dug trenches from which they could douse the gateway with crossbow bolts as other men tried to bridge the moat where the drawbridge would be missing. Thomas remembered the crossbow bolts spitting from the walls of La Roche-Derrien and he shivered. It was bitter cold. Soon, Thomas thought, the dew would turn to frost, silvering the world. Like Robbie he was wearing a wool shirt beneath a leather jerkin and a coat of mail over which he had a cloak, yet still he was shivering and he

wished he was back in the shelter of their gully where the fire burned.

'I can't see anyone,' Robbie said.

Nor could Thomas, but he went on looking for the sentries. Maybe the cold was keeping everyone under a roof? He searched the shadows near the guttering campfires, watched for any movement in the darkness about the church and still saw no one. Doubtless there were sentinels in the siege works opposite the manor entrance, but surely they would be watching for any defender trying to sneak out of the back of the manor? Except who would swim a moat on a night this cold? And the besiegers were surely bored by now and their watchfulness would be low. He saw a silver-edged cloud sailing closer to the moon. 'When the cloud covers the moon,' he told Robbie, 'we go.'

'And God bless us both,' Robbie said fervently, making the sign of the cross. The cloud seemed to move so slowly, then at last it veiled the moon and the glimmering landscape faded into grey and black. There was still a wan, faint light, but Thomas doubted the night would get any blacker and so he stood, brushed the twigs off his cloak and started towards the village along a track that had been beaten across the eastern slope of the ridge. He guessed the path had been made by pigs being taken to get fat on the beechmast in the woods and he remembered how Hookton's pigs had roamed the shingle eating fish heads and how his mother had always claimed it tainted the taste of their bacon. Fishy bacon, she had called it, and compared it unfavourably with the bacon of her native Weald in Kent. That, she had always said, had been proper bacon, nourished on beechmast and acorn, the best. Thomas stumbled on a tussock of grass. It was difficult to follow the track because the night suddenly seemed much darker, perhaps because they were on lower ground.

He was thinking of bacon and all the time they were getting closer to the village and Thomas was suddenly scared. He had seen no sentries, but what about dogs? One barking bitch in the night and he and Robbie could be dead men. He had not brought the bow, but suddenly wished he had – though what could he do with it? Shoot a dog? At least the path was easily visible now for it was lit by the campfires and the two of them walked confidently as

though they belonged in the village. 'You must do this all the time,' Thomas said to Robbie softly.

'This?'

'When you raid across the border.'

'Hell, we stay in the open country. Go after cattle and horses.'

They were among the shelters now and stopped talking. A sound of deep snoring came from one small turf hut and an unseen dog whined, but did not bark. A man was sitting in a chair outside a tent, presumably guarding whoever slept inside, but the guard himself was asleep. A small wind stirred the branches in an orchard by the church and the stream made a splashing noise as it plunged over the little weir beside the mill. A woman laughed softly in one of the houses where some men began to sing. The tune was new to Thomas and the deep voices smothered the sound of the churchyard gate, which squealed as he pushed it open. The church had a small wooden belfry and Thomas could hear the wind sighing on the bell. 'Is that you, Georges?' a man called from the porch.

'*Non.*' Thomas spoke more curtly than he intended, and the tone brought the man out from the black shadows of the porch's arch and Thomas, thinking he had initiated trouble, put his hand behind his back to grasp the hilt of his dagger.

'Sorry, sir.' The man had mistaken Thomas for an officer, maybe even a lord. 'I've been expecting a relief, sir.'

'He's probably still sleeping,' Thomas said.

The man stretched, yawning hugely. 'The bastard never wakes up.' The sentry was little more than a shadow in the dark, but Thomas sensed he was a big man. 'And it's cold here,' the man went on, 'God, but it's cold. Did Guy and his men come back?'

'One of their horses threw a shoe,' Thomas said.

'That's what it was! And I thought they'd found that ale shop in Saint-Germain. Christ and his angels, but that girl with the one eye! Have you seen her?'

'Not yet,' Thomas said. He was still holding his dagger, one of the weapons that the archers called a misericord because it was used to put unhorsed and wounded men-at-arms out of their misery. The blade was slender and sufficiently flexible to slide between the joints of armour and seek out the life beneath, but he was reluctant to draw it. This sentry suspected nothing and his only offence was to

want a long conversation. 'Is the church open?' Thomas asked the sentry.

'Of course. Why not?'

'We have to pray,' Thomas said.

'Must be a guilty conscience that makes men pray at night, eh?' The sentry was affable.

'Too many one-eyed girls,' Thomas said. Robbie, not speaking French, stood to one side and stared at the great black shadow of the gun.

'A sin worth repenting,' the man chuckled, then he drew himself up. 'Would you wait here while I wake Georges? It won't take a moment.'

'Take as long as you like,' Thomas said grandly, 'we shall be here till dawn. You can let Georges sleep if you want. The two of us will keep watch.'

'You're a living saint,' the man said, then he fetched his blanket from the porch before walking away with a cheerful goodnight. Thomas, when the man was gone, walked into the porch where he immediately kicked an empty barrel that rolled over with a great clatter. He swore and went still, but no one called from the village to demand an explanation for the noise.

Robbie crouched beside him. The dark was impenetrable in the porch, but they groped with their hands to discover a half-dozen empty barrels. They stank of rotten eggs and Thomas guessed they had once held black powder. He whispered to Robbie the gist of the conversation he had held with the sentry. 'But what I don't know,' he went on, 'is whether he's going to wake Georges or not. I don't think so, but I couldn't tell.'

'Who does he think we are?'

'Two men-at-arms probably,' Thomas said. He pushed the empty barrels aside, then stood and groped for the rope that lifted the latch of the church door. He found it, then winced as the hinges squealed. Thomas could still see nothing, but the church had the same sour stench as the empty barrels. 'We need some light,' he whispered. His eyes slowly became accustomed to the gloom and he saw the faintest glimmer of light showing from the big eastern window over the altar. There was not even a small flame burning above the sanctuary where the wafers were kept, presumably

because it was too dangerous with the gunpowder being stored in the nave. Thomas found the powder easily enough by bumping into the stack of barrels that were just inside the door. There were at least two score of them each about the size of a water pail, and Thomas guessed the cannon used one or maybe two barrels for each shot. Say three or four shots a day? So maybe there was two weeks' supply of powder here. 'We need some light,' he said again, turning, but Robbie made no response. 'Where are you?' Thomas hissed the question, but again there was no answer and then he heard a boot thump hollow against one of the empty barrels in the porch and he saw Robbie's shadow flicker in the clouded moonlight of the graveyard.

Thomas waited. A campfire smouldered not far beyond the thorn hedge that kept cattle out of the village's graves and he saw a shadow crouch beside the dying flames and then there was a sudden flare of brightness, like summer lightning, and Robbie reeled back and then Thomas, dazzled and alarmed by the flare, could see nothing. He had gone to the church door and he expected to hear a shout from one of the men in the village, but instead he heard only the squeal of the gate and the Scotsman's footsteps. 'I used an empty barrel,' Robbie said, 'except it wasn't as empty as I thought. Or else the powder gets into the wood.'

He was standing in the porch and the barrel was in his hands; he had used it to scoop up some embers. The powder residue had flared, burning his eyebrows, and now fire leaped up the barrel's inside. 'What do I do with it?' he asked.

'Christ!' Thomas imagined the church exploding. 'Give it to me,' he said, and he took the barrel, which was hot to the touch, and he ran with it into the church, his way lit by the flames, and he thrust the burning wood deep between two stacks of full barrels. 'Now we get out,' he said to Robbie.

'Did you look for the poor box?' Robbie said. 'Only if we're going to smash the church, we might as well take the poor box.'

'Come on!' Thomas snatched Robbie's arm and dragged him through the porch.

'It's a waste to leave it,' Robbie said.

'There's no bloody poor box,' Thomas said, 'the village is full of soldiers, you idiot!'

185

They ran, dodging between graves and pounding past the bulbous cannon, which lay in its wooden firing cradle. They climbed a fence that filled a gap in the thorn hedge, then sprinted past the gaunt shape of the broken springald and the turf-roofed shelters, not caring if they made a noise, and two dogs began to bark, then a third howled at them and a man jumped up from beside the entrance of one of the big tents. '*Qui va là?*' he called, and began to wind his crossbow, but Thomas and Robbie were already past him and out in the open field where they stumbled on the uneven turf. The moon came from behind the cloud and Thomas could see his breath like a mist.

'*Halte!*' the man shouted.

Thomas and Robbie stopped. Not because the man had given them the order, but because a red light was filling the world. They turned and stared, and the sentry who had challenged them now forgot them as the night became scarlet.

Thomas was not sure what he had expected. A lance of flame to pierce the heavens? A great noise like thunder? Instead the noise was almost soft, like a giant's inrush of breath, and a soft blossoming flame spilled from the church windows as though the gates of hell had just been opened and the fires of death were filling the nave, but that great red glow only lasted an instant before the roof of the church lifted off and Thomas distinctly saw the black rafters splaying apart like butchered ribs. 'Sweet Jesus Christ,' he blasphemed.

'God in His heaven,' Robbie said, wide-eyed.

Now the flames and smoke and air were boiling above the cauldron of the unroofed church, and still new barrels exploded, one after the other, each one pulsing a wave of fire and fumes into the sky. Neither Thomas nor Robbie knew it, but the powder had needed stirring because the heavier saltpetre found its way to the bottom of the barrels and the lighter charcoal was left at the top and that meant much of the powder was slow to catch the fire, but the explosions were serving to mix the remaining powder that pulsed bright and scarlet to spew a red cloud over the village.

Every dog in Evecque was barking or howling, and men, women and children were crawling from their beds to stare at the hellish glow. The noise of the explosions rolled across the meadows and echoed from the manor walls and startled hundreds of birds up

from their roosts in the woodlands. Debris splashed in the moat, throwing up sharp-edged shards of thin ice that mirrored the fire so it seemed the manor was surrounded by a lake of sparkling flame.

'Jesus,' Robbie said in awe, then the two of them ran on towards the beech trees at the high eastern side of the pastureland.

Thomas began to laugh as he stumbled up the path to the trees. 'I'll go to hell for that,' he said, stopping among the beeches and making the sign of the cross.

'For burning a church?' Robbie was grinning, his eyes reflecting the brightness of the fires. 'You should see what we did to the Black Canons at Hexham! Christ, half Scotland will be in hell for that one.'

They watched the fire for a few moments, then turned into the darkness of the woods. Dawn was not far off. There was a lightness in the east where a wan grey, pale as death, edged the sky. 'We have to go deeper into the forest,' Thomas said, 'we have to hide.'

Because the hunt for the saboteurs was about to start and in the first light, as the smoke still made a great pall above Evecques, the Count of Coutances sent twenty horsemen and a pack of hounds to find the men who had destroyed his store of powder, but the day was cold, the ground hard with frost and the quarry's small scent faded early. Next day, in his petulance, the Count ordered his forces to make an attack. They had been readying gabions – great basketwork tubes woven from willow that were filled with earth and stones – and the plan was to fill the moat with the gabions and then swarm over the resultant bridge to assault the gatehouse. The gateway lacked its drawbridge which had been taken down early in the siege to leave an open and inviting archway which was blocked by nothing more than a low stone barricade.

The Count's advisers told him there were not enough gabions, that the moat was deeper than he thought, that the time was not propitious, that Venus was in the ascendant and Mars in the decline, and that he should, in brief, wait until the stars smiled on him and the garrison was hungrier and more desperate, but the Count had lost face and he ordered the assault anyway and his men did their best. They were protected so long as they held the gabions, for the earth-filled baskets were proof against any crossbow bolt, but once

the gabions were thrown into the moat the attackers were exposed to Sir Guillaume's six crossbowmen who were sheltering behind the low stone wall that had been built across the manor's entrance arch where the drawbridge had once been. The Count had crossbowmen of his own and they were protected by pavises, full-length shields carried by a second man to protect the archer while he laboriously wound the cord of the crossbow, but the men throwing the gabions had no protection once their burdens were thrown and eight of them died before the rest realized that the moat really was too deep and that there were not nearly enough gabions. Two pavise-holders and a crossbowman were badly wounded before the Count accepted he was wasting his time and called the attackers back. Then he cursed Sir Guillaume on the fourteen hump-backed devils of St Candace before getting drunk.

Thomas and Robbie survived. On the day after they had burned the Count's powder Thomas shot a deer, and next day Robbie discovered a rotting hare in a gap in a hedge and when he pulled the body out discovered a snare that must have been set by one of Sir Guillaume's tenants who had either been killed or chased off by the Count's men. Robbie washed the snare in a stream and set it in another hedge and next morning found a hare choking in the tightening noose.

They dared not sleep in the same place two nights running, but there was plenty of shelter in the deserted and burned-out farms. They spent most of the next weeks in the country south of Evecque where the valleys were deeper, the hills steeper and the woods thicker. Here there were plenty of hiding places and it was in that tangled landscape that they made the Count's nightmare worse. Tales began to be told in the besiegers' encampment of a tall man in black on a pale horse and whenever the man on the pale horse appeared, someone would die. The death would be caused by a long arrow, an English arrow, yet the man on the horse had no bow, only a staff topped by a deer's skull, and everyone knew what creature rode the pale horse and what a skull on a pole denoted. The men who had seen the apparition told their womenfolk in the Count's encampment and the womenfolk cried to the Count's chaplain and the Count said they were dreaming, but the corpses were real enough. Four brothers, come from distant Lyons to earn

188

money by serving in the siege, packed their belongings and went. Others threatened to follow. Death stalked Evecque.

The Count's chaplain said folk were touched by the moon and he rode into the dangerous south country, loudly chanting prayers and scattering holy water, and when the chaplain survived unscathed the Count told his men they had been fools, that there was no Death riding a pale horse, and next day two men died only this time they were in the east. The tales grew in the telling. The horseman was now accompanied by giant hounds whose eyes glowed, and the horseman did not even need to appear to explain any misfortune. If a horse tripped, if a man broke a bone, if a woman spilled food, if a crossbow string snapped, then it was blamed on the mysterious man who rode the pale horse.

The confidence of the besiegers plunged. There were mutterings of doom and six men-at-arms went south to seek employment in Gascony. Those who remained grumbled that they did the devil's work and nothing the Count of Coutances did seemed to restore his men's spirits. He tried cutting back trees to stop the mysterious archer shooting into the camp, but there were too many trees and not enough axes, and the arrows still came. He sent to the Bishop of Caen who wrote a blessing on a piece of vellum and sent it back, but that had no effect on the black-cloaked rider whose appearance presaged death, and so the Count, who fervently believed he did God's work and feared to fail in case he incurred God's wrath, now appealed to God for help.

He wrote to Paris.

Louis Bessières, Cardinal Archbishop of Livorno, a city he had only seen once when he travelled to Rome (on his return, he had made a detour so he would not be forced to see Livorno a second time), walked slowly down the Quai des Orfèvres on the Île de la Cité in Paris. Two servants went ahead of him, using staves to clear the way for the Cardinal who appeared not to be paying attention to the lean, hollow-cheeked priest who spoke to him so urgently. The Cardinal, instead, examined the wares on offer in the goldsmiths' shops lining the quai that was named for their trade: Goldsmith's

Quay. He admired a necklace of rubies and even considered buying it, but then discovered a flaw in one of the stones. 'So sad,' he murmured, then moved to the next shop. 'Exquisite!' he exclaimed of a salt cellar made in silver and emblazoned with four panels on which pictures of country life were enamelled in blue, red, yellow and black. A man ploughed on one panel and broadcast seed on the next, a woman cut the harvest on the third while on the last panel the two sat at table admiring a glowing loaf of bread. 'Quite exquisite,' the Cardinal enthused, 'don't you think it beautiful?'

Bernard de Taillebourg scarcely gave the salt cellar a glance. 'The devil is at work against us, your eminence,' he said angrily.

'The devil is always at work against us, Bernard,' the Cardinal said reprovingly, 'that is the devil's job. There would be something desperately amiss in the world if the devil were not at work against us.' He caressed the salt cellar, running his fingers over the delicate curves of the panels, then decided the shape of the base was not quite right. Something crude there, he thought, a clumsiness in the design and, with a smile for the shopkeeper, he put it back on the table and strolled on. The sun shone; there was even some warmth in the winter air and a sparkle on the Seine. A legless man with wooden blocks on his stumps swung on short crutches across the road and held out a dirty hand towards the Cardinal whose servants rushed at the man with their staves. 'No, no!' the Cardinal called and felt in his purse for some coins. 'God's blessing on you, my son,' he said. Cardinal Bessières liked giving alms, he liked the melting gratitude on the faces of the poor, and he especially liked their look of relief when he called off his servants a heartbeat before they used their staves. Sometimes the Cardinal paused just a fraction too long and he liked that too. But today was a warm, sunlit day stolen from a grey winter and so he was in a kindly mood.

Once past the Sabot d'Or, a tavern for scriveners, he turned away from the river into the tangle of alleys that twisted about the labyrinthine buildings of the royal palace. Parliament, such as it was, met here, and the lawyers scuttled the dark passages like rats, yet here and there, piercing the gloom, gorgeous buildings reared up to the sun. The Cardinal loved these alleys and had a fancy that shops magically disappeared overnight to be replaced by others. Had that laundry always been there? And why had he never noticed

the bakery? And surely there had been a lute-makers' business beside the public privy? A furrier hung bear coats from a rack and the Cardinal paused to feel the pelts. De Taillebourg still yapped at him, but he scarcely listened.

Just past the furrier's was an archway guarded by men in blue and gold livery. They wore polished breastplates, plumed helmets and carried pikes with brightly polished blades. Few folk got past them, but the guards hastily stepped back and bowed as the Cardinal passed. He gave them a benevolent wave suggestive of a blessing, then followed a damp passage into a courtyard. This was all royal land now and the courtiers offered the Cardinal respectful bows for he was more than a cardinal, he was also Papal Legate to the throne of France. He was God's ambassador and Bessières looked the part for he was a tall man, strongly built and burly enough to overawe most men without his scarlet robes. He was good-looking and knew it, and vain, which he pretended he did not know, and he was ambitious, which he hid from the world but not from himself. After all, a cardinal archbishop had only one more throne to mount before he came to the crystal steps of the greatest throne of all and Bernard de Taillebourg seemed the unlikely instrument that might give Louis Bessières the triple crown for which he yearned.

And so the Cardinal wearily turned his attention to the Dominican as the two left the courtyard and climbed the stairs into the Sainte-Chapelle. 'Tell me' – Bessières broke into whatever de Taillebourg had been saying – 'about your servant. Did he obey you?'

De Taillebourg, so rudely interrupted, took a few seconds to adjust his thoughts, then he nodded. 'He obeyed me in all things.'

'He showed humility?'

'He did his best to show humility.'

'Ah! So he still has pride?'

'It is ingrained in him,' de Taillebourg said, 'but he fought it.'

'And he did not desert you?'

'No, your eminence.'

'So he is back here in Paris?'

'Of course,' de Taillebourg said curtly, then realized what tone he had used. 'He is at the friary, your eminence,' he added humbly.

'I wonder whether we should show him the undercroft again?' the Cardinal suggested as he walked slowly towards the altar. He

loved the Sainte-Chapelle, loved the light that flooded between the high slender pillars. This was, he thought, as close to heaven as man came on earth: a place of supple beauty, overwhelming brightness and enchanting grace. He wished he had thought to order some singing, for the sound of eunuchs' voices piercing the high fanwork of the chapel's stones could take a man very close to ecstasy. Priests were running to the high altar, knowing what it was that the Cardinal had come to see. 'I do find,' he went on, 'that a few moments in the undercroft compel a man to seek God's grace.'

De Taillebourg shook his head. 'He has been there already, your eminence.'

'Take him again.' There was a hardness in the Cardinal's voice now. 'Show him the instruments. Show him a soul on the rack or under the fire. Let him know that hell is not confined to Satan's realm. But do it today. We may have to send you both away.'

'Send us away?' De Taillebourg sounded surprised.

The Cardinal did not enlighten him. Instead he knelt before the high altar and took off his scarlet hat. He rarely, and only reluctantly, removed the hat in public for he was uncomfortably aware that he was going bald, but it was necessary now. Necessary and awe-inspiring, for one of the priests had opened the reliquary beneath the altar and brought out the purple cushion with its lace fringe and golden tassels, which he now presented to the Cardinal. And on the cushion lay the crown. It was so old, so fragile, so black and so very brittle that the Cardinal held his breath as he reached for it. The very earth seemed to stop in its motion, all sounds went silent, even heaven was still as he reached and then touched and then lifted the crown that was so light it seemed to have scarce any weight at all.

It was the crown of thorns.

It was the very crown that had been crammed onto Christ's head where it became imbued with his sweat and blood, and the Cardinal's eyes filled with tears as he raised it to his lips and kissed it gently. The twigs, woven into the spiky circlet, were spindly. They were frail as a wren's leg bones, yet the thorns were sharp still, as sharp as the day when they had been raked over the Saviour's head to pour blood down His precious face, and the Cardinal lifted the

crown high, using two hands, and he marvelled at its lightness as he lowered it onto his thinning scalp to let it rest there. Then, hands clasped, he stared up at the golden cross on the altar.

He knew the clergy of Sainte-Chapelle disliked his coming here and wearing the crown of thorns. They had complained of it to the Archbishop of Paris and the Archbishop had whined to the King, but Bessières still came because he had the power to come. He had the Pope's delegated power and France needed the Pope's support. England was besieging Calais and Flanders was warring in the north and all of Gascony was now again swearing allegiance to Edward of England and Brittany was in revolt against its rightful French Duke and seethed with English bowmen. France was assailed and only the Pope could persuade the powers of Christendom to come to its aid.

And the Pope would probably do that for the Holy Father was himself French. Clement had been born in the Limousin and had been Chancellor of France before being elected to the throne of St Peter and installed in the great papal palace at Avignon. And there, in Avignon, Clement listened to the Romans who tried to persuade him to move the papacy back to their eternal city. They whispered and plotted, bribed and whispered again, and Bessières feared that Clement might one day give in to those wheedling voices.

But if Louis Bessières became Pope then there would be no more talk of Rome. Rome was a ruin, a pestilent sewer surrounded by petty states forever at war with each other, and God's Vicar on earth could never be safe there. But while Avignon was a good refuge for the papacy, it was not perfect because the city and its county of Venaissin both belonged to the kingdom of Naples and the Pope, in Louis Bessières's view, should not be a tenant.

Nor should the Pope live in some provincial city. Rome had once ruled the world so the Pope had belonged in Rome, but in Avignon? The Cardinal, the thorns resting so lightly on his brow, stared up at the great blue and scarlet of the passion window above the altar; he knew which city deserved the papacy. Only one. And Louis Bessières was certain that, once he was Pope, he could persuade the King of France to yield the Île de la Cité to the Holy Father and so Cardinal Bessières would bring the papacy north and give it a new

and glorious refuge. The palace would be his home, the Cathedral of Notre Dame would be his new St Peter's and this glorious Sainte-Chapelle his private shrine where the crown of thorns would be his own relic. Perhaps, he thought, the thorns should be incorporated into the Pope's triple crown. He liked that idea, and he imagined praying here on his private island. The goldsmiths and the beggars, the lawyers and the whores, the laundries and the lute-makers would be sent across the bridges to the rest of Paris and the Île de la Cité would become a holy place. And then the Vicar of Christ would have the power of France always at his side and so the kingdom of God would spread and the infidel would be slain and there would be peace on earth.

But how to become Pope? There were a dozen men who wanted to succeed Clement, yet Bessières alone of those rivals knew of the Vexilles, and he alone knew that they had once owned the Holy Grail and might, perhaps, own it still.

Which was why Bessières had sent de Taillebourg to Scotland. The Dominican had returned empty-handed, but he had learned some things. 'So you do not think the Grail is in England?' Bessières now asked him, keeping his voice low so that Sainte-Chapelle's priests could not overhear their conversation.

'It may be hidden there,' de Taillebourg sounded gloomy, 'but it is not in Hookton. Guy Vexille searched the place when he raided it. We looked again and it is nothing but ruin.'

'You still think Sir Guillaume took it to Evecque?'

'I think it possible, your eminence,' de Taillebourg said. Then: 'Not likely,' he qualified the answer, 'but possible.'

'The siege goes badly. I was wrong about Coutances. I offered him a thousand fewer years in purgatory if he captured Evecque by St Timothy's Day, but he does not have the vigour to press a siege. Tell me about this bastard son.'

De Taillebourg made a dismissive gesture. 'He is nothing. He doubts the Grail even exists. All he wants is to be a soldier.'

'An archer, you tell me?'

'An archer,' de Taillebourg confirmed.

'I think you are wrong about him. Coutances writes to say that their work is being impeded by an archer. One archer who shoots long arrows of the English type.'

De Taillebourg said nothing.

'One archer,' the Cardinal pressed on, 'who probably destroyed Coutances's whole stock of black powder. It was the only supply in Normandy! If we want more it will have to be brought from Paris.'

The Cardinal lifted the crown from his head and placed it on the cushion. Then, slowly, reverently, he pressed his forefinger against one of the thorns and the watching priests leaned forward. They feared he was trying to steal one of the thorns, but the Cardinal was only drawing blood. He winced as the thorn broke his skin, then he lifted his finger to his mouth and sucked. There was a heavy gold ring on the finger and hidden beneath the ruby, which was cunningly hinged, was a thorn he had stolen eight months before. Sometimes, in the privacy of his bed chamber, he scratched his forehead with the thorn and imagined being God's deputy on earth. And Guy Vexille was the key to that ambition. 'What you will do,' he ordered de Taillebourg when the taste of the blood was gone, 'is show Guy Vexille the undercroft again to remind him what hell awaits him if he fails us. Then go with him to Evecque.'

'You'd send Vexille to Evecque?' De Taillebourg could not hide his surprise.

'He is ruthless and he is cruel,' the Cardinal said as he stood and put on his hat, 'and you tell me he is ours. So we shall spend money and we shall give him black powder and enough men to crush Evecque and bring Sir Guillaume to the undercroft.' He watched as the crown of thorns was taken back to its reliquary. And soon, he thought, in this chapel, in this place of light and glory, he would have a greater prize. He would have a treasure to bring all Christendom and its riches to his throne of gold. He would have the Grail.

Thomas and Robbie were both filthy; their clothes were caked with dirt; their mail coats were snagged with twigs, dead leaves and earth; and their hair was uncut, greasy and matted. At night they shivered, the cold seeping into the marrow of their souls, but by day they had never felt so alive for they played a game of life and

death in the small valleys and tangled woods about Evecque. Robbie, clad in a swathing black cloak and carrying the skull on its pole, rode the white horse to lead Coutances's men into ambush where Thomas killed. Sometimes Thomas merely wounded, but he rarely missed for he was shooting at close range, forced to it by the thickness of the woods, and the game reminded him of the songs the archers liked to sing and the tales their women told about the army's campfires. They were the songs and tales of the common folk, ones never sung by the troubadours, and they told of an outlaw called Robin Hood. It was either Hood or Hude, Thomas was not sure for he had never seen it written down, but he knew Hood was an English hero who had lived a couple of hundred years before and his enemies had been England's French-speaking nobility. Hood had fought them with an English weapon, the war bow, and today's nobility doubtless thought the stories were subversive which was why no troubadour sung them in the great halls. Thomas had some-times thought he might write them down himself, except no one ever wrote in English. Every book Thomas had ever seen was in Latin or French. But why should the Hood songs not be put between covers? Some nights he told the Hood tales to Robbie as the two of them shivered in whatever poor shelter they had found, but the Scotsman thought the stories dull things. 'I prefer the tales of King Arthur,' he said.

'You have those in Scotland?' Thomas asked, surprised.

'Of course we do!' Robbie said. 'Arthur was Scots.'

'Don't be so bloody daft!' Thomas said, offended.

'He was a Scotsman,' Robbie insisted, 'and he killed the bloody English.'

'He was English,' Thomas said, 'and he'd probably never heard of the bloody Scots.'

'Go to hell,' Robbie snarled.

'I'll see you there first,' Thomas spat and thought that if he ever did write the Hood tales he would have the legendary bowman go north and spit a few Scots on some honest English arrows.

They were both ashamed of their tempers next morning. 'It's because I'm hungry,' Robbie said, 'I'm always short-tempered when I'm hungry.'

'And you're always hungry,' Thomas said.

Robbie laughed, then heaved the saddle onto his white horse. The beast shivered. Neither horse had eaten well and they were both weak so Thomas and Robbie were being cautious, not wanting to be trapped in open country where the Count's better horses could outrun their two tired destriers. At least the weather had turned less cold, but then great bands of rain swept in from the western ocean and for a week it poured down and no English bow could be drawn in such weather. The Count of Coutances would doubtless be beginning to believe that his chaplain's holy water had driven the pale horse from Evecque and so spared his men, but his enemies were also spared for no more powder had come for the cannon and now the meadows about the moated house were so waterlogged that trenches flooded and the besiegers were wading through mud. Horses developed hoof rot and men stayed in their shelters shivering with fever.

At every dawn Thomas and Robbie rode first to the woods south of Evecque and there, on the side of the manor where the Count had no entrenchments and only a small sentry post, they stood at the edge of the trees and waved. They had received an answering wave on the third morning that they signalled the garrison, but after that there was nothing until the week of the rain. Then, on the morning after they had argued about King Arthur, Thomas and Robbie waved to the manor and this time they saw a man appear on the roof. He raised a crossbow and shot high into the air. The quarrel was not aimed at the sentry post and if the men on guard there even saw its flight they did nothing, but Thomas watched it fall into the pasture where it splashed in a puddle and skidded through the wet grass.

They did not ride out that day. Instead they waited until evening, until the darkness had fallen, and then Thomas and Robbie crept to the pasture and, on hands and knees, searched the thick wet grass and old cowdung. It seemed to take them hours, but at last Robbie found the bolt and discovered there was a waxed packet wrapped about the short shaft. 'You see?' Robbie said when they were back in their shelter and shivering beside a feeble fire. 'It can be done.' He gestured at the message wrapped about the quarrel. To make the bolt fly the message had been whipped to the shaft with cotton cord that had shrunk and Thomas had to cut it free,

then he unwrapped the waxed parchment and held it close to the fire so he could read the message, which had been written with charcoal. 'It's from Sir Guillaume,' Thomas said, 'and he wants us to go to Caen.'

'Caen?'

'And we're to find a' – Thomas frowned and held the letter with its crabbed handwriting even closer to the flames – 'we're to find a shipmaster called Pierre Villeroy.'

'I wonder if that's Ugly Peter,' Robbie put in.

'No,' Thomas said, peering close at the parchment, 'this man's ship is called the *Pentecost*, and if he's not there we're to look for Jean Lapoullier or Guy Vergon.' Thomas was holding the message so close to the fire that it began to brown and curl as he read the last words aloud. 'Tell Villeroy I want the *Pentecost* ready by St Clement's Day and he must provision for ten passengers going to Dunkirk. Wait with him, and we shall meet you in Caen. Set a fire in the woods tonight to show you have received this.'

That night they did set a fire in the woods. It blazed briefly, then rain came and the fire died, but Thomas was sure the garrison would have seen the flames.

And by dawn, wet, tired and filthy, they were back in Caen.

Thomas and Robbie searched the city's quays but there was no sign of Pierre Villeroy or of his ship, the *Pentecost*, but a tavern-keeper reckoned Villeroy was not far away. 'He carried a cargo of stone to Cabourg,' the man told Thomas, 'and he reckoned he should be back today or tomorrow, and the weather won't have held him up.' He looked askance at the bowstave. 'Is that a goddamn bow?' He meant an English bow.

'Hunting bow from Argentan,' Thomas said carelessly and the lie satisfied the tavern-keeper for there were some men in every French community who could use the long hunting bow, but they were very few and never enough to coalesce into the kind of army that turned hillsides red with noble blood.

'If Villeroy's back today,' the man said, 'he'll be drinking in my tavern tonight.'

'You'll point him out to me?' Thomas asked.

'You can't miss Pierre,' the man laughed, 'he's a giant! A giant with a bald head, a beard you could breed mice in and a poxed skin. You'll recognize Pierre without me.'

Thomas reckoned that Sir Guillaume would be in a hurry when he reached Caen and would not want to waste time coaxing horses onto the *Pentecost*, therefore he spent the day haggling about prices for the two stallions and that night, flush with money, he and Robbie returned to the tavern. There was no sign of a big-bearded giant with a bald head, but it was raining, they were both chilled and reckoned they might as well wait and so they ordered eel stew, bread and mulled wine. A blind man played a harp in the tavern's corner, then began singing about sailors and seals and the strange sea beasts that rose from the ocean floor to howl at the waning moon. Then the food arrived and just as Thomas was about to taste it a stocky man with a broken nose crossed the tavern floor and planted himself belligerently in front of Thomas. He pointed at the bow. 'That's an English bow,' the man said flatly.

'It's a hunting bow from Argentan,' Thomas said. He knew it was dangerous to carry such a distinctive weapon and last summer, when he and Jeanette had walked from Brittany to Normandy, he had disguised the bowstave as a pilgrim's staff, but he had been more careless on this visit. 'It's just a hunting bow,' he repeated casually, then flinched because the eel stew was so hot.

'What does the bastard want?' Robbie asked.

The man heard him. 'You're English.'

'Do I sound English?' Thomas asked.

'So how does he sound?' The man pointed to Robbie. 'Or has he lost his tongue now?'

'He's Scottish.'

'Oh, I'm sure, and I'm the goddamn Duke of Normandy.'

'What you are,' Thomas said mildly, 'is a goddamn nuisance,' and he heaved the bowl of soup into the man's face and kicked the table into his groin. 'Get out!' he told Robbie.

'Christ, I love a fight!' Robbie said. A half-dozen of the scalded man's friends were charging across the floor and Thomas hurled a bench at their legs, tripping two, and Robbie swung his sword at another man.

'They're English!' the scalded man shouted from the floor. 'They're Goddamns!' The English were hated in Caen.

'He's calling you English,' Thomas told Robbie.

'I'll piss down his throat,' Robbie snarled, kicking the scalded man in the head, then he punched another man with the hilt of his sword and was screaming his Scottish war cry as he advanced on the survivors.

Thomas had snatched up their baggage and his bowstave and pulled open a door. 'Come on!' he shouted.

'Call me English, you tosspots!' Robbie challenged. His sword was holding the attackers at bay, but Thomas knew they would summon their courage and charge home and Robbie would almost certainly have to kill one to escape and then there would be a hue and cry and they would be lucky not to end dangling at rope ends from the castle battlements, so he just dragged Robbie backwards through the tavern door. 'Run!'

'I was enjoying that,' Robbie insisted and tried to head back into the tavern, but Thomas pulled him hard away and then shoulder-charged a man coming into the alley.

'Run!' Thomas shouted again and pushed Robbie towards the Île's centre. They dodged into an alley, sprinted across a small square and finally went to ground in the shadows of the porch of St Jean's church. Their pursuers searched for a few minutes, but the night was cold and the patience of the hunters limited.

'There were six of them,' Thomas said.

'We were winning!' Robbie said truculently.

'And tomorrow,' Thomas said, 'when we're supposed to be finding Pierre Villeroy or one of the others, you'd rather be in Caen's jail?'

'I haven't punched a man since the fight at Durham,' Robbie said, 'not properly.'

'What about the hoggling fight in Dorchester?'

'We were too drunk. Doesn't count.' He started to laugh. 'Anyway, you started it.'

'I did?'

'Aye,' Robbie said, 'you chucked the eel stew right in his face! All that stew.'

'I was only trying to save your life,' Thomas pointed out.

'Christ! You were talking English in Caen! They hate the English!'

'So they should,' Robbie said, 'so they should, but what am I supposed to do here? Keep my mouth shut? Hell! It's my language too. God knows why it's called English.'

'Because it is English,' Thomas said, 'and King Arthur spoke it.'

'Sweet Jesus!' Robbie said, then laughed again. 'Hell, I hit that one fellow so hard he won't know what day it is when he wakes up.'

They found shelter in one of the many houses that were still abandoned after the savagery of the English assault in the summer. The house's owners were either far away, or more likely their bones were in the big common grave in the churchyard or mired in the river's bed.

Next morning they went down to the quays again. Thomas remembered wading through the strong current as the cross-bowmen fired from the moored ships. The quarrels had spat up small fountains of water and, because he dared not get his bowstring wet, he had not been able to shoot back. Now he and Robbie walked down the quays to discover the *Pentecost* had magically appeared in the night. She was as big a ship as any that made it upriver, a ship capable of crossing to England with a score of men and horses aboard, but she was high and dry now as the falling tide stranded her on the mud. Thomas and Robbie gingerly crossed the narrow gangplank to hear a monstrous snoring coming from a small fetid cabin in the stern. Thomas fancied the deck itself vibrated every time the man drew breath and he wondered how any creature who made such a sound would react to being woken, but just then a waif of a girl, pale as a dawn mist and thin as an arrow, climbed from the cabin hatch and put some clothes on the deck and a finger to her lips. She looked very fragile and, as she pulled up her robe to tug on stockings, showed legs like twigs. Thomas doubted she could have been more than thirteen years old.

'He's sleeping,' she whispered.

'So I hear,' Thomas said.

'Sh!' She touched her finger to her lips again then hauled a thick woollen shirt over her night-gown, put her thin feet into huge boots and wrapped herself in a big leather coat. She pulled a greasy woollen hat over her fair hair and picked up a bag that appeared

to be made of ancient frayed sailcloth. 'I'm going to buy food,' she said quietly, 'and there's a fire to be made in the forepeak. You'll find a flint and steel on the shelf. Don't wake him!'

With that warning she tiptoed off the ship, swathed in her great coat and boots, and Thomas, appalled at the depth and loudness of the snoring, decided discretion was the best course. He went to the forepeak where he found an iron brazier standing on a stone slab. A fire was already laid in the brazier and, after opening the hatch above to serve as a chimney, he struck sparks from the flint. The kindling was damp, but after a while the fire caught and he fed it scraps of wood so that by the time the girl came back there was a respectable blaze. 'I'm Yvette,' she said, apparently incurious as to who Thomas and Robbie were, 'Pierre's wife,' she explained, then fetched out a huge blackened pan onto which she broke twelve eggs. 'Do you want to eat too?' she asked Thomas.

'We'd like to.'

'You can buy some eggs from me,' she said, nodding at her sail-cloth bag, 'and there's some ham and bread in there. He likes his ham.'

Thomas looked at the eggs whitening on the fire. 'Those are all for Pierre?'

'He's hungry in the morning,' she explained, 'so why don't you cut the ham? He likes it thick.' The ship suddenly creaked and rolled slightly on the mud. 'He's awake,' Yvette said, taking a pewter plate from the shelf. There was a groan from the deck, then footsteps and Thomas backed out of the forepeak and turned to find the biggest man he had ever seen.

Pierre Villeroy was a foot taller than Thomas's bow. He had a chest like a hogshead, a smoothly bald pate, a face terribly scarred by the childhood pox and a beard in which a hare could have become lost. He blinked at Thomas. 'You've come to work,' he grunted.

'No, I brought you a message.'

'Only we've got to start soon,' Villeroy said in a voice that seemed to rumble from some deep cavern.

'A message from Sir Guillaume d'Evecque,' Thomas explained.

'Have to use the low tide, see?' Villeroy said. 'I've three tubs of moss in the hold. I've always used moss. My father did. Others use

shredded hemp, but I don't like it, don't like it at all. Nothing works half as well as fresh moss. It holds, see? And mixes better with the pitch.' His ferocious face suddenly creased into a gap-toothed smile. '*Mon caneton!*' he declared as Yvette brought out his plate heaped with food.

Yvette, his duckling, provided Thomas and Robbie with two eggs apiece, then produced two hammers and a pair of strange iron instruments that looked like blunt chisels. 'We're caulking the seams,' Villeroy explained, 'so I'll heat the pitch and you two can ram moss between the planks.' He scooped a mess of egg yolk into his mouth with his fingers. 'Have to do it while the ship's high and dry between tides.'

'But we've brought you a message,' Thomas insisted.

'I know you have. From Sir Guillaume. Which means he wants the *Pentecost* for a voyage and what Sir Guillaume wants he gets because he's been good to me, he has, but the *Pentecost* ain't no good to him if she sinks, is she? Ain't no good down on the seabed with all the drowned mariners, is she? She has to be caulked. My darling and I almost drowned ourselves yesterday, didn't we, my duckling?'

'She was taking on water,' Yvette agreed.

'Gurgling away, it was,' Villeroy declared loudly, 'all the way from Cabourg to here, so if Sir Guillaume wants to go somewhere then you two had better start work!' He beamed at them above his vast beard, which was now streaked with egg yolk.

'He wants to go to Dunkirk,' Thomas said.

'Planning on making a run for it, is he?' Villeroy mused aloud. 'He'll be over that moat and on his horses and up and away before the Count of Coutances knows what year it is.'

'Why Dunkirk?' Yvette wondered.

'He's joining the English, of course,' Villeroy said without a trace of any resentment for that presumed betrayal by Sir Guillaume. 'His lord has turned against him, the bishops is pissing down his gullet and they do say the King has a finger in the pie, so he might as well change sides now. Dunkirk? He'll be joining the siege of Calais.' He scooped more eggs and ham into his mouth. 'So when does Sir Guillaume want to sail?'

'St Clement's Day,' Thomas said.

'When's that?'

None of them knew. Thomas knew which day of the month was the feast of St Clement, but he did not know how many days away that was, and that ignorance gave him an excuse to avoid what he was certain would be a disgustingly messy, cold and wet job. 'I'll find out,' he said, 'and be back to help you.'

'I'll come with you,' Robbie volunteered.

'You stay here,' Thomas said sternly, 'Monsieur Villeroy has a job for you.'

'A job?' Robbie had not understood the earlier conversation.

'It's nothing much,' Thomas reassured him, 'you'll enjoy it!'

Robbie was suspicious. 'So where are you going?'

'To church, Robbie Douglas,' Thomas said, 'I'm going to church.'

The English had captured Caen the previous summer, then occupied the city just long enough to rape its women and plunder its wealth. They had left Caen battered, bleeding and shocked, but Thomas had stayed when the army marched away. He had been sick and Dr Mordecai had treated him in Sir Guillaume's house and later, when Thomas had been well enough to walk, Sir Guillaume had taken him to the Abbaye aux Hommes to meet Brother Germain, the head of the monastery's scriptorium and as wise a man as any Thomas had ever met. Brother Germain would certainly know when St Clement's Day was, but that was not the only reason Thomas was going to the abbey. He had realized that if any man could understand the strange script in his father's notebook it was the old monk, and the thought that perhaps this morning he would find an answer to the Grail's mystery gave Thomas a pang of excitement. That surprised him. He often doubted the Grail's existence and even more frequently wished the cup would pass from him, but now, suddenly, he felt the thrill of the hunt. More, he was suddenly overwhelmed with the solemnity of the quest, so much so that he stopped walking and stared into the shimmering light reflected from the river and tried to recall his vision of fire and gold in the northern English night. How stupid to doubt, he thought suddenly. Of course the Grail existed! It was just waiting to be found and so bring happiness to a broken world.

'Mind out!' Thomas was startled from his reverie by a man pushing a barrow of oyster shells who barged past him. A small dog was tied to the barrow and it lunged at Thomas, snapping ineffectually at his ankles before yelping as the rope dragged it onwards. Thomas

was hardly aware of man or dog. Instead he was thinking that the Grail must hide itself from the unworthy by giving them doubts. To find it, then, all he had to do was believe in it and, perhaps, to request a little help from Brother Germain.

A porter accosted Thomas in the abbey's gateway, then immediately suffered a coughing fit. The man doubled over, gasped for breath, then straightened slowly and blew his nose onto his fingers, 'I've caught my death,' he wheezed, 'that's what it is, I've caught my death.' He hawked up a gob of mucus and spat it towards the beggars by the gate. 'The scriptorium's that way,' he said, 'past the cloister.'

Thomas made his way to the sunlit room where a score of monks stood at tall, sloping desks. A small fire burned in a central hearth, ostensibly to keep the ink from freezing, but the high room was still cold enough for the monks' breath to mist above their parchments. They were all copying books and the stone chamber clicked and scratched with the sound of the quills. Two novice monks were pounding powder for paints at a side table, another was scraping a lambskin and a fourth was sharpening goose quills, all of them nervous of Brother Germain who sat on a dais where he worked at his own manuscript. Germain was old and small, fragile and bent, with wispy white hair, milky myopic eyes and a bad-tempered expression. His face had been just three inches from his work until he heard Thomas's footsteps, then he abruptly looked up and, though he could not see well, he did at least observe that his unannounced visitor had a sword at his side. 'What business does a soldier have in God's house?' Brother Germain snarled. 'Come to finish what the English started last summer?'

'I have business with you, brother,' Thomas said. The scratching of the quills had abruptly ceased as the monks tried to overhear the conversation.

'Work!' Brother Germain snapped at the monks. 'Work! You are not translated to heaven yet! You have duties, attend to them!' Quills rattled in ink pots and the scratching and pounding and scraping began again. Brother Germain looked alarmed as Thomas stepped up onto the dais. 'Do I know you?' he snarled.

'We met last summer. Sir Guillaume brought me to see you.'

'Sir Guillaume!' Brother Germain, startled, laid his quill down.

'Sir Guillaume? I doubt we'll see him again! Ha! Mewed up by Coutances, that's what I hear, and a good thing. You know what he did?'

'Coutances?'

'Sir Guillaume, you fool! He turned against the King in Picardy! Turned against the King. He made himself a traitor. He was always a fool, always risking his neck, but now he'll be lucky to keep his head. What's that?'

Thomas had unwrapped the book and now placed it on the desk. 'I was hoping, brother,' he said humbly, 'that you could make some sense of—'

'You want me to read it, eh? Never learned yourself and now you think I have nothing better to do than read some nonsense so you can determine its value?' Folk who could not read sometimes came into possession of books and brought them to the monastery to have them valued, hoping against hope that some collection of pious advice might turn out to be a rare book of theology, astrology or philosophy. 'What did you say your name was?' Brother Germain demanded.

'I didn't,' Thomas said, 'but I'm called Thomas.'

The name held no apparent memories for Brother Germain, but nor was he interested any longer for he was immersed in the book, mouthing words under his breath, turning pages with long white fingers, lost in wonder, and then he leafed back to the first page and read the Latin aloud. '"*Calix meus inebrians*".' He breathed the words as if they were sacred, then made the sign of the cross and turned to the next page which was in the strange Hebrew script and he became even more excited. '"To my son,"' he said aloud, evidently translating, '"who is the son of the Tirshatha and the grandson of Hachaliah."' He turned his short-sighted eyes on Thomas. 'Is that you?'

'Me?'

'Are you the grandson of Hachaliah?' Germain asked and, despite his bad eyesight, he must have detected the puzzlement on Thomas's face. 'Oh, never mind!' he said impatiently. 'Do you know what this is?'

'Stories,' Thomas said. 'Stories of the Grail.'

'Stories! Stories! You're like children, you soldiers. Mindless,

cruel, uneducated and greedy for stories. You know what this script is?' He poked a long finger at the strange letters which were dotted with the eye-like symbols. 'You know what it is?'

'It's Hebrew, isn't it?'

'"It's Hebrew, isn't it?"' Brother Germain mocked Thomas with mimicry. 'Of course it's Hebrew, even a fool educated at the university in Paris would know that, but it's their magical script. It's the lettering the Jews use to work their charms, their dark magic.' He peered close at one of the pages. 'There, you see? The devil's name, Abracadabra!' He frowned for a few seconds. 'The writer claims Abracadabra can be raised to this world by invoking his name above the Grail. That seems plausible.' Brother Germain made the sign of the cross again to ward off evil, then peered up at Thomas. 'Where did you get this?' He asked the question sharply, but did not wait for an answer. 'You're him, aren't you?'

'Him?'

'The Vexille that Sir Guillaume brought to me,' Brother Germain said accusingly and made the sign of the cross again. 'You're English!' He made that sound even worse. 'Who will you take this book to?'

'I want to understand it first,' Thomas said, confused by the question.

'Understand it! You?' Brother Germain scoffed. 'No, no. You must leave it with me, young man, so I can make a copy of it and then the book itself must go to Paris, to the Dominicans there. They sent a man to ask about you.'

'About me?' Thomas was even more confused now.

'About the Vexille family. It seems one of your foul brood fought at the King's side this summer, and now he has submitted to the Church. The Inquisition have had . . .' Brother German paused, evidently seeking the right word, '. . . conversations with him.'

'With Guy?' Thomas asked. He knew Guy was his cousin, knew Guy had fought on the French side in Picardy and he knew Guy had killed his father in search of the Grail, but he knew little more.

'Who else? And now, they do say, Guy Vexille is reconciled to the Church,' Brother Germain said as he turned the pages. 'Reconciled to the Church indeed! Can a wolf lay down with lambs? Who wrote this?'

'My father.'

'So you are Hachaliah's grandson,' Brother Germain said with reverence, then he closed his thin hands over the book. 'Thank you for bringing it to me,' he said.

'Can you tell me what the Hebrew passages say?' Thomas asked, baffled by Brother Germain's last words.

'Tell you? Of course I can tell you, but it will mean nothing. You know who Hachaliah was? You are familiar with the Tirshatha? Of course not. The answers would be wasted on you! But I thank you for bringing me the book.' He drew a scrap of parchment towards him, took up his quill and dipped it in the ink. 'If you take this note to the sacristan he will give you a reward. Now I have work.' He signed the note and held it towards Thomas.

Thomas reached for the book. 'I can't leave it here,' he said.

'Can't leave it here! Of course you can! Such a thing belongs to the Church. Besides, I must make a copy.' Brother Germain folded his hands over the book and hunched over it. 'You will leave it,' he hissed.

Thomas had thought of Brother Germain as a friend, or at least not as an enemy, and even the old monk's harsh words about Sir Guillaume's treachery had not altered that opinion, Germain had said that the book must go to Paris, to the Dominicans, but Thomas now understood that Germain was allied with those men of the Inquisition who, in turn, had Guy Vexille on their side. And Thomas understood too that those formidable men were seeking the Grail with an avidity he had not appreciated until this moment, and their path to the Grail lay through him and this book. Those men were his enemies, and that meant that Brother Germain was also his foe and it had been a terrible mistake to bring the book to the abbey. He felt a sudden fear as he reached for the book. 'I have to leave,' he insisted.

Brother Germain tried to hold onto the book, but his twig-like arms could not compete with Thomas's bow-given strength. He nevertheless clutched it stubbornly, threatening to tear its soft leather cover. 'Where will you go?' Brother Germain demanded, then tried to trick Thomas with a false promise. 'If you leave it,' he said, 'I shall make a copy and send the book to you when it is finished.'

Thomas was going north to Dunkirk so he named a place in the other direction. 'I'm going to La Roche-Derrien,' he lied.

'An English garrison?' Brother Germain still tried to pull the book away, then yelped as Thomas slapped his hands. 'You can't take that to the English!'

'I am taking it to La Roche-Derrien,' Thomas said, finally retrieving the book. He folded the soft leather cover over the pages, then half drew his sword because several of the younger monks had slipped from their high stools and looked as though they wanted to stop him, but the sight of the blade dissuaded them from any violence. They just watched as he walked away.

The porter was coughing still, then leaned against the arch and fought for breath while tears streamed from his eyes. 'At least it ain't leprosy,' he managed to say to Thomas, 'I know it ain't leprosy. My brother had leprosy and he didn't cough. Not much anyway.'

'When is St Clement's Day?' Thomas remembered to ask.

'Day after tomorrow, and God love me if I live to see it.'

No one followed Thomas, but that afternoon, while he and Robbie were standing up to their crotches in flooding cold river water and pounding thick moss into the *Pentecost*'s planking, a patrol of soldiers in red and yellow livery asked Pierre Villeroy if he had seen an Englishman dressed in mail and a black cloak.

'That's him down there,' Villeroy said, pointing to Thomas, then laughed. 'If I see an Englishman,' he went on, 'I'll piss down the bastard's throat till he drowns.'

'Bring him to the castle instead,' the patrol's leader said, then led his men to question the crew on the next boat.

Villeroy waited till the soldiers were out of earshot. 'For that,' he said to Thomas, 'you owe me two more rows of caulking.'

'Jesus Christ!' Thomas swore.

'Now He was a properly skilled carpenter,' Villeroy observed through a mouthful of Yvette's apple pie, 'but He was also the Son of God, wasn't he? So he didn't have to do menial jobs like caulking, so it's no damn good asking for His help. Just bang the moss in hard, boy, bang it in hard.'

*   *   *

Sir Guillaume had held the manor from its attackers for close on three months and did not doubt he could hold it indefinitely so long as the Count of Coutances did not bring more gunpowder to the village, but Sir Guillaume knew that his time in Normandy was ended. The Count of Coutances was his liege lord, Sir Guillaume held land of him as the Count held land of the King, and if a man was declared a traitor by his liege lord, and if the King supported the declaration, then a man had no future unless he was to find another lord who owed fealty to a different King. Sir Guillaume had written to the King and he had appealed to friends who had influence at court, but no reply had come. The siege had continued, and so Sir Guillaume must leave the manor. That saddened him for Evecque was his home. He knew every inch of its pastures, knew where to find the shed deer antlers, knew where the young hares lay trembling in the long grass, and knew where the pike brooded like demons in the deeper streams. It was home, but a man declared a traitor had no home and so, on the eve of St Clement's, when his besiegers were sunk in a damp winter gloom, he made his escape.

He had never doubted his ability to escape. The Count of Coutances was a dull, unimaginative, middle-aged man whose experience of war had always been in the service of greater lords. The Count was averse to risk and given to a blustery temper whenever the world escaped his understanding, which happened frequently. The Count certainly did not understand why great men in Paris were encouraging him to besiege Evecque, but he saw the chance of enriching himself and so he obeyed them, even though he was wary of Sir Guillaume. Sir Guillaume was in his thirties and had spent half his life fighting, usually on his own account, and in Normandy he was called the lord of the sea and of the land because he fought on both with enthusiasm and effectiveness. He had been handsome once, hard-faced and golden-haired, but Guy Vexille, Count of Astarac, had taken one eye and had left scars that made Sir Guillaume's face even harder. He was a formidable man, a fighter, but in the hierarchy of kings, princes, dukes and counts he was a lesser being and his lands made it tempting to declare him a traitor.

There were twelve men, three women and eight horses inside the manor, which meant every horse but one had to carry two

riders. After nightfall, when rain was softly falling across Evecque's waterlogged fields, Sir Guillaume ordered planks, put across the gap where the drawbridge should have been, and then the horses, blindfolded, were led one by one across the perilous bridge. The besiegers, huddled from the cold and rain, saw and heard nothing, even though the sentries in the forwardmost works had been placed to guard against just such an attempt to escape.

The horses' blindfolds were taken off, the fugitives mounted and then rode northwards. They were challenged just once by a sentry who demanded to know who they were. 'Who the hell do you think we are?' Sir Guillaume retorted, and the savagery in his voice persuaded the sentry not to ask any more questions. By dawn they were in Caen and the Count of Coutances was still none the wiser. It was only when one of the sentries saw the planks spanning the moat that the besiegers realized their enemy was gone, and even then the Count wasted time by searching the manor. He found furniture, straw and cooking pots, but no treasures.

An hour later a hundred black-cloaked men arrived at Evecque. Their leader carried no banner and their shields had no badges. They looked battle-hardened, like men who earned their living by renting their lances and swords to whoever paid the most, and they curbed their horses beside the makeshift bridge over Evecque's moat and two of them, one a priest, crossed into the courtyard. 'What's been taken?' the priest demanded curtly.

The Count of Coutances turned angrily on the man who wore Dominican robes. 'Who are you?'

'What have your men plundered here?' the priest, gaunt and angry, asked again.

'Nothing,' the Count assured him.

'Then where's the garrison?'

'The garrison? Escaped.'

Bernard de Taillebourg spat in his rage. Guy Vexille, next to him, gazed up at the tower which now flew the Count's banner. 'When did they escape?' he asked. 'And where did they go?'

The Count bridled at the tone. 'Who are you?' he demanded, for Vexille wore no badge on his black surcoat.

'Your equal,' Vexille said coldly, 'and my lord the King will want to know where they have gone.'

No one knew, though a few questions eventually elicited that some of the besiegers had been aware of horsemen going northwards in the cold night and that surely meant that Sir Guillaume and his men had ridden to Caen. And if the Grail had been hidden in Evecque then that would have gone north as well and so de Taillebourg ordered his men to remount their tired horses.

They reached Caen in the early afternoon, but by then the *Pentecost* was halfway down the river to the sea, blown northwards by a fitful wind that barely gave headway against the last of the flooding tide. Pierre Villeroy grumbled at the futility of trying to stem the tide, but Sir Guillaume insisted for he expected his enemies to appear at any moment. He had only two men-at-arms with him now, for the rest had not wanted to follow their lord to a new allegiance. Even Sir Guillaume had little enthusiasm for that enforced loyalty. 'You think I want to fight for Edward of England?' he grumbled to Thomas. 'But what choice do I have? My own lord turned against me. So I'll swear fealty to your Edward and at least I'll live.' That was why he was going to Dunkirk, so that he could make the small journey to the English siege lines about Calais and make his obeisance to King Edward.

The horses had to be abandoned on the quay, so all Sir Guillaume brought aboard the *Pentecost* was his armour, some clothes and three leather bags of money that he dumped on the deck before offering Thomas an embrace. And then Thomas had turned to his old friend, Will Skeat, who had glanced at him without recognition and then looked away. Thomas, about to speak, checked himself. Skeat was wearing a sallet and his hair, white as snow now, hung lank beneath its battered metal brim. His face was thinner than ever, deep-lined, and with a vague look as though he had just woken and did not know where he was. He also looked old. He could not have been more than forty-five, yet he looked sixty, though at least he was alive. When Thomas had last seen him he had been dreadfully wounded with a sword cut through the scalp which had laid his brain open and it had been a miracle he had lived long enough to reach Normandy and the skilled attentions of Mordecai, the Jewish doctor who was now being helped across the precarious gangplank.

Thomas took another step towards his old friend who again

glanced at him without recognition. 'Will?' Thomas said, puzzled. 'Will?'

And at the sound of Thomas's voice light came into Skeat's eyes. 'Thomas!' he exclaimed. 'By God, it is you!' He stepped towards Thomas, stumbling slightly, and the two men embraced. 'By God, Thomas, it's grand to hear an English voice. I've heard nowt but foreign jabber all winter. Good God, boy, you look older.'

'I am older,' Thomas said. 'But how are you, Will?'

'I'm alive, Tom, I'm alive, though I sometimes wonder if it wouldn't have been better to die. Weak as a kitten, I am.' His speech was slightly slurred, as if he had drunk too much, but he was plainly sober.

'I shouldn't call you plain Will now, should I,' Thomas asked, 'for you're Sir William now.'

'Sir William! Me?' Skeat laughed. 'You're full of crap, boy, just like you always were. Always too clever for your own good, eh, Tom?' Skeat did not remember the battle in Picardy, did not remember the King knighting him before the first French charge. Thomas had sometimes wondered whether that act had been pure desperation to raise the archers' spirits for the King had surely seen how hugely his little, sick army was outnumbered and he could not have believed his men would survive. But survive they did, and win, though the cost to Skeat had been terrible. He took off his sallet to scratch his pate and one side of his scalp was revealed as a wrinkled horror of lumpy scar, pink and white. 'Weak as a kitten,' Skeat said again, 'and I haven't pulled a bow in weeks.'

Mordecai insisted that Skeat had to rest. Then he greeted Thomas as Villeroy let go the mooring lines and used a sweep to shove the *Pentecost* into the river's current. Mordecai grumbled about the cold, about the privations of the siege and about the horrors of being aboard a ship, then he smiled his wise old smile. 'You look good, Thomas. For a man who was once hanged you look indecently good. How's your urine?'

'Clear and sweet.'

'Your friend Sir William, now—' Mordecai jerked his head towards the forecabin where Skeat had been bedded down in a pile of skeepskins – 'his urine is very murky. I fear you did me no favours by sending him to me.'

'He's alive.'

'I don't know why.'

'And I sent him to you because you're the best.'

'You flatter me.' Mordecai staggered slightly because the ship had rocked in a small river wave that no one else had noticed, yet he looked alarmed; had he been a Christian he would doubtless have warded off imminent danger by the sign of the cross. Instead he looked worriedly at the ragged sail as though he feared it might collapse and smother him. 'I do detest ships,' he said plaintively. 'Unnatural things. Poor Skeat. He seems to be recovering, I admit, but I cannot boast that I did anything except wash the wound and stop people putting charms of mouldy bread and holy water on his scalp. I find religion and medicine mix uneasily. Skeat lives, I think, because poor Eleanor did the right thing when he was wounded.' Eleanor had put the broken piece of skull on the exposed brain, made a poultice of moss and spider web, then bandaged the wound. 'I was sorry about Eleanor.'

'Me too,' Thomas said. 'She was pregnant. We were going to marry.'

'She was a dear thing, a dear thing.'

'Sir Guillaume must be angry?'

Mordecai rocked his head from side to side. 'When he received your letter? That was before the siege, of course.' He frowned, trying to remember. 'Angry? I don't think so. He grunted, that was all. He was fond of Eleanor, of course, but she was a servant's child, not . . .' He paused. 'Well, it's sad. But as you say, your friend Sir William lived. The brain is a strange thing, Thomas. He understands, I think, though he cannot remember. His speech is slurred, and that might have been expected, but strangest of all is that he does not recognize anyone with his eyes. I will walk into a room and he'll ignore me, then I speak and he knows me. We have all got into the habit of speaking as we get near him. You'll get used to it.' Mordecai smiled. 'But it is good to see you.'

'So you travel to Calais with us?' Thomas asked.

'Dear me, no! Calais?' He shuddered. 'But I couldn't stay in Normandy. I suspect that the Count of Coutances, cheated of Sir Guillaume, would love to make an example of a Jew, so from Dunkirk I shall travel south again. To Montpellier first, I think. My son

is studying medicine there. And from Montpellier? I might go to Avignon.'

'Avignon?'

'The Pope is very hospitable to Jews,' Mordecai said, reaching out for the gunwale as the *Pentecost* shivered under a small wind gust, 'and we need hospitality.'

Mordecai had intimated that Sir Guillaume's reaction to Eleanor's death was callous, but that was not evident when Sir Guillaume spoke of his lost daughter with Thomas as the *Pentecost* cleared the river's mouth and the cold waves stretched to the grey horizon. Sir Guillaume, his ravaged face hard and grim, looked close to tears as he heard how Eleanor had died. 'Do you know anything more about the men who killed her?' he asked when Thomas had finished his tale. Thomas could only repeat what Lord Outhwaite had told him after the battle, about the French priest called de Taillebourg and his strange servant.

'De Taillebourg,' Sir Guillaume said flatly, 'another man to kill, eh?' He made the sign of the cross. 'She was illegitimate' – he spoke of Eleanor, not to Thomas, but to the wind, instead – 'but she was a sweet girl. All of my children are dead now.' He gazed at the ocean, his dirty long yellow hair stirring in the breeze. 'We have so many men to kill, you and I' – he spoke to Thomas now – 'and the Grail to find.'

'Others are looking for it,' Thomas said.

'Then we must find it before them,' Sir Guillaume growled. 'But we go to Calais first, I make my allegiance to Edward and then we fight. By God, Thomas, we fight.' He turned and scowled at his two men-at-arms as if reflecting on how his fortunes and following had been shrunk by fate, then he saw Robbie and grinned. 'I like your Scotsman.'

'He can fight,' Thomas said.

'That's why I like him. And he wants to kill de Taillebourg too?'

'Three of us want to kill him.'

'Then God help the bastard because we'll serve his tripes to the dogs,' Sir Guillaume growled. 'But he'll have to be told you're in the Calais siege lines, eh? If he's to come looking for us he has to know where you are.'

To reach Calais the *Pentecost* needed to go east and north, but

once clear of the land she merely wallowed instead of sailing. A small south-west wind had taken her clear of the river mouth, but then, long before she was out of sight of the Norman shore, the breeze faded and the big ragged sail flapped and slatted and banged on the yard. The ship rolled like a barrel in a long dull swell that came from the west where dark clouds heaped like some gloom-laden range of hills. The winter day faded early, the last of its cold light a sullen glint beneath the clouds. A few spots of fire showed on the darkening land. 'The tide will take us up the sleeve,' Villeroy said gloomily, 'then float us down again. Then up and down and up and down till God or St Nicholas sends us wind.'

The tide took them up the English Channel as Villeroy had predicted, then drifted them down again. Thomas, Robbie and Sir Guillaume's two men-at-arms took it in turns to go down into the stone-filled bilge and hand up pails of water. 'Of course she leaks,' Villeroy told a worried Mordecai, 'all ships leak. She'd leak like a sieve if I didn't caulk her every few months. Bang in the moss and pray to St Nick. It keeps us all from drowning.'

The night was black. The few lights ashore flickered in a damp haze. The sea broke feebly against the hull, and the sail hung uselessly. For a time a fishing boat lay close, a lantern burning on its deck, and Thomas listened to the low chant as the men hauled a net, then they unshipped oars and rowed eastwards until their tiny glimmering light vanished in the haze. 'A west wind will come,' Villeroy said, 'it always does. West from the lost lands.'

'The lost lands?' Thomas asked.

'Out there,' Villeroy said, pointing into the black west. 'If you go as far as a man can sail you'll find the lost lands and you'll see a mountain taller than the sky where Arthur sleeps with his knights.' Villeroy made the sign of the cross. 'And on the clifftops under the mountain you can see the souls of the drowned sailors calling for their womenfolk. It's cold there, always cold, cold and fog-smothered.'

'My father saw those lands once,' Yvette put in.

'He said he did,' Villeroy commented, 'but he was a rare drinker.'

'He said the sea was full of fish,' Yvette went on as if her husband had not spoken, 'and the trees were very small.'

'Cider, he drank,' Villeroy offered. 'Whole orchards went down

his gullet, but he could sail a boat, your father. Drunk or sober, he was a seaman.'

Thomas was staring into the western darkness, imagining a voyage to the land where King Arthur and his knights slept under the fog and where the souls of the drowned called for their lost lovers. 'Time to bail ship,' Villeroy said to him, and Thomas went down into the bilge and scooped the water into buckets until his arms were aching with tiredness, and then he went to the forepeak and slept in the cocoon of sheepskins that Villeroy kept there because, he said, it was colder at sea than on land and a man should drown warm.

Dawn came slow, seeping into the east like a grey stain. The steering oar creaked in its ropes, doing nothing as the ship rocked on the windless swell. The Norman coast was still in sight, a grey-green slash to the south, and as the winter light grew Thomas saw three small ships rowing out from the coast. The three headed up channel until they were east of the *Pentecost*; Thomas assumed they were fishermen and he wished that Villeroy's boat had oars and so could make some progress in this frustrating stillness. There was a pair of great sweeps lashed to the deck, but Yvette said they were only useful in port. 'She's too heavy to row for long,' she said, 'especially when she's full.'

'Full?'

'We carry cargo,' Yvette said. Her man was sleeping in the stern cabin, his snores seeming to vibrate the whole ship. 'Up and down the coast we go,' Yvette said, 'with wool and wine, bronze and iron, building stone and hides.'

'You like it?'

'I love it.' She smiled at him and her young face, which was strangely wedgelike, took on a beauty as she did so. 'My mother now,' she went on, 'she was going to have me put into the bishop's service. Cleaning and washing, cooking and cleaning till your hands are fair worn away by work, but Pierre told me I could live free as a bird on his boat and so we do, so we do.'

'Just the two of you?' The *Pentecost* seemed a large ship for just two, even if one of them was a giant.

'No one else will sail with us,' Yvette said. 'It's bad luck to have a woman on a boat. My father always said that.'

'He was a fisherman?'

'A good one,' Yvette said, 'but he drowned all the same. He was caught on the Casquets on a bad night.' She looked up at Thomas earnestly. 'He did see the lost lands, you know.'

'I believe you.'

'He sailed ever so far north and then west, and he said the men from the north lands know the fishing grounds of the lost lands well and there's fish as far as you can see. He said you could walk on the sea it was so thick with fish, and one day he was creeping through the fog and he saw the land and he saw the trees like bushes and he saw the dead souls on shore. They were dark, he said, like they'd been scorched by hell's fires, and he took fright and he turned and sailed away. It took him two months to get there and a month and a half to come home and all his fish had gone bad because he wouldn't go ashore and smoke them.'

'I believe you,' Thomas said again, though he was not really sure that he did.

'And I think if I drown,' Yvette said, 'then me and Pierre will go to the lost lands together and he won't have to sit on the cliffs and call for me.' She spoke very matter-of-factly, then went to ready some breakfast for her man whose snoring had just ceased.

Sir Guillaume emerged from the forecabin. He blinked at the winter daylight, then strolled aft and pissed across the stern rail while he stared at the three boats which had rowed out from the river and were now a mile or so east of the *Pentecost*. 'So you saw Brother Germain?' he asked Thomas.

'I wish I hadn't.'

'He's a scholar,' Sir Guillaume said, pulling up his trews and tying the waist knot, 'which means he doesn't have balls. Doesn't need to. He's clever, mind you, clever, but he was never on our side, Thomas.'

'I thought he was your friend.'

'When I had power and money, Thomas,' Sir Guillaume said, 'I had many friends, but Brother Germain was never one of them. He's always been a good son of the Church and I should never have introduced you to him.'

'Why not?'

'Once he learned you were a Vexille he reported our conversation

to the bishop and the bishop told the Archbishop and the Archbishop told the Cardinal and the Cardinal spoke to whoever gives him his crumbs, and suddenly the Church got excited about the Vexilles and the fact that your family had once owned the Grail. And it was just about then that Guy Vexille reappeared so the Inquisition took hold of him.' He paused, gazing at the horizon, then made the sign of the cross. 'That's who your de Taillebourg is, I'd wager my life on it. He's a Dominican and most Inquisitors are hounds of God.' He turned his one eye on Thomas. 'Why do they call them the hounds of God?'

'It's a joke,' Thomas said, 'from the Latin. *Domini canis*: the hound of God.'

'Doesn't make me laugh,' Sir Guillaume said gloomily. 'If one of those bastards gets hold of you it's red-hot pokers in the eyes and screams in the night. And I hear they got hold of Guy Vexille and I hope they hurt him.'

'So Guy Vexille is a prisoner?' Thomas was surprised. Brother Germain had said his cousin was reconciled with the Church.

'That's what I heard. I heard he was singing psalms on the Inquisition's rack. And doubtless he told them that your father had possessed the Grail, and how he sailed to Hookton to find it and how he failed. But who else went to Hookton? Me, that's who, so I think Coutances was told to find me, arrest me and haul me to Paris. And meanwhile they sent men to England to find out what they could.'

'And to kill Eleanor,' Thomas said bleakly.

'Which they'll pay for,' Sir Guillaume said.

'And now,' Thomas said, 'they've sent men here.'

'What?' Sir Guillaume asked, startled.

Thomas pointed at the three fishing boats which now were rowing directly towards the *Pentecost*. They were too far away for him to see who or what was on board, but something about their deliberate approach alarmed him. Yvette, coming aft with bread, ham and cheese, saw Thomas and Sir Guillaume staring and she joined them, then uttered a curse that only a fisherman's daughter would ever have learned and ran to the stern cabin and shouted for her man to get on deck.

Yvette's eyes were accustomed to the sea and she knew these

were no fishing boats. They had too many men aboard for a start and after a while Thomas could see those men for himself and his eyes, which were more used to looking for enemies among the green leaves, saw that some of them wore mail and he knew that no man went to sea in mail unless he was intent on killing.

'They'll have crossbows.' Villeroy was on deck now, tying the neck cords of a swathing leather cloak and looking from the approaching boats up to the clouds as if he might see a breath of wind coming from the heavens. The sea was still heaving in great swells, but the water was smooth as beaten brass and there were no wind-driven ripples streaking the swells' long flanks. 'Crossbows,' Villeroy repeated gloomily.

'You want me to surrender?' Sir Guillaume asked Villeroy. His voice was sour, suggesting the question was nothing but sarcasm.

'Ain't for me to tell your lordship what to do' – Villeroy sounded just as sarcastic – 'but your men could fetch some of the bigger stones out of the bilge.'

'What will that achieve?' Sir Guillaume asked.

'I'll drop 'em on the bastards when they try to board. Those little boats? A stone'll go straight through their bottoms and then yon bastards will be trying to swim with mail strapped to their chests.' Villeroy grinned. 'Hard to swim when you're wrapped in iron.'

The stones were fetched, and Thomas readied his arrows and bow. Robbie had donned his mail coat and had his uncle's sword at his side. Sir Guillaume's two men-at-arms were with him in the waist of the boat, the place where any boarding attempt would be made for there the gunwale was closest to the sea. Thomas went to the higher stern where Will Skeat joined him and though he did not recognize Thomas he did see the bow and held out a hand.

'It's me, Will,' Thomas said.

'I know it's you,' Skeat said. He lied and was embarrassed. 'Let me try the bow, boy.'

Thomas gave him the great black stave and watched in sadness as Skeat failed to draw it even halfway. Skeat thrust the weapon back to Thomas with a look of embarrassment. 'I'm not what I was,' he muttered.

'You'll be back, Will.'

Skeat spat over the gunwale. 'Did the King really knight me?'

'He did.'

'Sometimes I think I can remember the battle, Tom, then it fades. Like a fog.' Skeat stared at the three approaching boats, which had spread into a line. Their oarsmen were pulling hard and Thomas could see crossbowmen standing in the bows and stern of each craft. 'Have you ever shot an arrow from a boat?' Skeat asked.

'Never.'

'You're moving and they're moving. It makes it hard. But take it slow, lad, take it slow.'

A man shouted from the closest boat, but the pursuers were still too far away and whatever the man said was lost in the air. 'St Nicholas, St Ursula,' Villeroy prayed, 'send us wind, and send us plenty of it.'

'He's having a go at us,' Skeat said because a crossbowman in the bows of the central boat had raised his weapon. He seemed to cock it high in the air, then he shot and the bolt banged with astonishing force low into the *Pentecost*'s stern. Sir Guillaume, ignoring the threat, climbed onto the rail and took hold of the backstay to keep his balance. 'They're Coutances's men,' he told Thomas, and Thomas saw that some of the men in the nearest boat were wearing the green and black livery that had been the uniform of Evecque's besiegers. More crossbows twanged and two of the bolts thudded into the stern planks and two others whipped past Sir Guillaume to slap into the impotent sail, but most splashed into the sea. It might have been calm, but the crossbowmen were still having a hard time aiming their weapons from the small boats.

And the three attacking boats were small. Each held eight or ten oarsmen and about the same number of archers or men-at-arms. The three craft had plainly been chosen for their speed under oars, but they were dwarfed by the *Pentecost* which would make any attempt to board the bigger vessel very perilous, though one of the three boats seemed determined to come alongside Villeroy's ship. 'What they're going to do,' Sir Guillaume said, 'is let those two boats shower us with quarrels while this bastard' – he gestured at the boat that was pulling hard to close on the *Pentecost* – 'puts her men on board.'

More crossbow bolts thumped into the hull. Two more quarrels pierced the sail and another hit the mast just above a weathered

crucifix that was nailed to the tarred timber. The figure of Christ, white as bone, had lost its left arm and Thomas wondered if that was a bad omen, then tried to forget it as he drew the big bow and shot off an arrow. He only had thirty-four shafts left, but this was not the time to stint on them and so, while the first was still in the air, he loosed a second and the crossbowmen had not finished winding their cords back as the first arrow slashed a rower's arm and the second drove a splinter up from the boat's bow, then a third arrow hissed above the oarsmen's heads to splash into the sea. The rowers ducked, then one gasped and fell forward with an arrow in his back, and the next instant a man-at-arms was struck in the thigh and fell onto two of the oarsmen and there was sudden chaos aboard the boat which slewed sharply away with its oars clattering against each other. Thomas lowered the big bow.

'Taught you well,' Will Skeat said fervently. 'Ah, Tom, you always were a lethal bastard.'

The boat pulled away. Thomas's arrows had been far more accurate than the crossbow bolts for he had been shooting from a much larger and more stable ship than the narrow and overburdened rowboats. Only one of the men aboard those smaller ships had been killed, but the frequency of Thomas's first arrows had put the fear of God into the rowers who could not see where the missiles came from, but only hear the hiss of feathers and the cries of the wounded. Now the other two boats overtook the third and the crossbowmen levelled their weapons.

Thomas took an arrow from the bag and worried what would happen when he had no more shafts, but just then a swirl of ripples showed that a wind was coming across the water. An east wind, of all things, the most unlikely of all winds in this sea, but it came from the east nonetheless and the *Pentecost*'s big brown sail filled and slackened, then filled again, and suddenly she was turning away from her pursuers and the water was gurgling down her flanks. Coutances's men pulled hard on their oars. 'Down!' Sir Guillaume shouted and Thomas dropped behind the rail as a volley of crossbow bolts punched into the *Pentecost*'s hull or flew high to tear the ragged sail. Villeroy shouted at Yvette to man the steering oar, then he sheeted down the mainsail before diving into the stern cabin to fetch a huge and evidently ancient crossbow that he cocked

with a long iron lever. He loaded a rusty bolt into the groove, then shot it at the nearest pursuer. 'Bastards,' he roared. 'Your mothers were goats! They were whoring goats! Poxed whoring goats! Bastards!' He cocked the weapon again, loaded another corroded missile and shot it away, but the bolt plunged into the sea. The *Pentecost* was gathering speed and already out of crossbow range.

The wind filled and the *Pentecost* drew further away from her pursuers. The three rowboats had first gone up channel in the expectation that the flooding tide and a possible western wind would bring the *Pentecost* to them, but with the wind coming from the east the oarsmen could not keep up with their quarry and so the three boats fell astern and finally abandoned the chase. But just as they gave up, so two new pursuers appeared in the mouth of the River Orne. Two ships, both of them large and equipped with big square sails like the *Pentecost*'s mainsail, were coming out to sea. 'The one in front is the *Saint-Esprit*,' Villeroy said. Even at this distance from the river mouth he could distinguish the two boats, 'and the other is the *Marie*. She sails like a pregnant pig, but the *Saint-Esprit* will catch us.'

'The *Saint-Esprit*?' Sir Guillaume sounded appalled. 'Jean Lapoullier?'

'Who else?'

'I thought he was a friend!'

'He was your friend,' Villeroy said, 'so long as you had land and money, but what do you have now?'

Sir Guillaume brooded on the truth of that question for a while. 'So why are you helping me?'

'Because I'm a fool,' Villeroy said cheerfully, 'and because you'll pay me damn well.'

Sir Guillaume grunted at that truism. 'Not if we sail in the wrong direction,' he added after a while.

'The right direction,' Villeroy pointed out, 'is away from the *Saint-Esprit* and downwind, so we'll stand on west.'

They stood on westwards all day. They made good speed, but still the big *Saint-Esprit* slowly closed the gap. In the morning she had been a blur on the horizon; by midday Thomas could see the little platform at her masthead where, Villeroy told him, crossbowmen

224

would be stationed; and by mid-afternoon he could see the black and white eyes painted on her bows. The east wind had increased all through the day until it was blowing strong and cold, whipping the wavetops into white streamers. Sir Guillaume suggested going north, maybe as far as the English shore, but Villeroy claimed not to know that coastline and said he was unsure where he could find shelter there if the weather turned bad. 'And this time of year it can turn fast as a woman's temper,' Villeroy added, and as if to prove him right they ran into violent sleet squalls that hissed on the sea and buffeted the ship and cut visibility down to a few yards. Sir Guillaume again urged a northward course, suggesting they turn while the ship was hidden inside the squall, but Villeroy stubbornly refused and Thomas guessed that the huge man feared being accosted by English ships that loved nothing better than capturing French vessels.

Another squall crashed past them, the rain bouncing up a hand's breadth from the deck and the sleet making a slushy white coating on the eastern flank of every halyard and sheet. Villeroy feared that his sail would split, but dared not shorten the canvas because whenever the squalls passed, leaving the sea white and frantic, the *Saint-Esprit* was always in sight and always a little closer. 'She's a quick one,' Villeroy said grudgingly, 'and Lapoullier knows how to sail her.'

Yet the short winter day was passing and night would offer a chance for the *Pentecost* to escape. The pursuers knew that and they must have been praying that their ship would be given a little extra speed; as dusk fell, she was closing the gap inch by inch, yet still the *Pentecost* kept her lead. They were out of sight of land now, two ships on a seething and darkening ocean, and then, when the night was almost complete, the first flame arrow streaked out from the *Saint-Esprit*'s bow.

It was shot from a crossbow. The flames seared the night, arcing up and then plunging to fall in the *Pentecost*'s wake. 'Send him an arrow back,' Sir Guillaume growled.

'Too far,' Thomas said. A good crossbow would always outrange a yew stave, though in the time it took to reload the crossbow the English archer would have run within range and loosed half a dozen arrows. But Thomas could not do that in this gathering darkness,

nor did he dare waste arrows. He could only wait and watch as a second fire bolt slashed up against the clouds. It too fell behind.

'They don't fly as well,' Will Skeat said.

'What's that, Will?' Thomas had not heard clearly.

'They wrap the shaft in cloth and it slows them down. You ever shot a fire arrow, Tom?'

'Never.'

'Takes fifty paces off the range,' Skeat said, watching a third arrow plunge into the sea, 'and plays hell with accuracy.'

'That one was closer,' Sir Guillaume said.

Villeroy had put a barrel on the deck and he was filling it with seawater. Yvette, meanwhile, had nimbly climbed the rigging to perch herself on the crosstrees where the one yard hung from the masthead and now she hauled up canvas pails of water which she used to soak the sail.

'Can we use fire arrows?' Sir Guillaume asked. 'That thing must have the range.' He nodded at Villeroy's monstrous crossbow. Thomas translated the question for Will Skeat whose French was still rudimentary.

'Fire arrows?' Skeat's face wrinkled as he thought. 'You have to have pitch, Tom,' he said dubiously, 'and you must soak it into the wool and then bind the woollen cloth onto the arrow real hard, but fray the edges a little to get the fire burning nicely. Fire has to be deep in the cloth, not just on the edge because that won't last, and when it's burning hard and deep you send the arrow off before it eats through the shaft.'

'No,' Thomas translated for Sir Guillaume, 'we can't.'

Sir Guillaume cursed, then turned away as the first fire arrow thumped into the *Pentecost*, but the bolt struck low on the stern, so low that the next heave of a wave extinguished the flames with an audible hiss. 'We must be able to do something!' Sir Guillaume raged.

'We can be patient,' Villeroy said. He was standing at the stern oar.

'I can use your bow?' Sir Guillaume asked the big sailor and, when Villeroy nodded, Sir Guillaume cocked the huge crossbow and sent a quarrel back towards the *Saint-Esprit*. He grunted as he pulled on the lever to cock the weapon again, astonished at the

strength needed. A crossbow drawn by a lever was usually much weaker than the bows armed with a wormscrew and ratchet, but Villeroy's bow was massive. Sir Guillaume's bolts must have struck the pursuing ship, but it was too dark to tell if any damage had been done. Thomas doubted it for the *Saint-Esprit*'s bows were high and her gunwales stout. Sir Guillaume was merely driving metal into planks, but the *Saint-Esprit*'s fiery missiles were beginning to threaten the *Pentecost*. Three or four enemy crossbows were firing now and Thomas and Robbie were busy dousing the burning bolts with water, then a flaming quarrel hit the sail and creeping fire began to glow on the canvas, but Yvette succeeded in extinguishing it just as Villeroy pushed the steering oar hard over. Thomas heard the oar's long shank creak under the strain and felt the ship lurch as she turned southwards. 'The *Saint-Esprit* was never quite as quick off the wind,' Villeroy said, 'and she wallows in a cross sea.'

'And we're quicker?' Thomas asked.

'We'll find out,' Villeroy said.

'Why didn't we try to find out earlier?' Sir Guillaume snarled the question.

'Because we didn't have sea room,' Villeroy answered placidly as a flaming bolt seared over the stern deck like a meteor. 'But we're well clear of the cape now.' He meant they were safely to the west of the Norman peninsula and south of them now were the rock-studded sea reaches between Normandy and Brittany. The turn meant that the range suddenly shortened as the *Saint-Esprit* held on westwards and Thomas shot a clutch of arrows at the dim figures of armoured men in the pursuing ship's waist. Yvette had come down to the deck and was hauling on ropes and, when she was satisfied with the new set of the sail, she clambered back up to her eyrie just as two more fire bolts thumped into the canvas and Thomas saw the flames leap up the sail as Yvette dragged up buckets. Thomas sent another arrow high into the night so that it plunged down onto the enemy deck and Sir Guillaume was shooting the heavier crossbow bolts as fast as he could, but neither man was rewarded with a cry of pain. Then the range opened again and Thomas unstrung his bow. The *Saint-Esprit* was turning to follow the *Pentecost* south and, for a few heartbeats, she seemed to disappear

in the dark, but then another fire arrow climbed from her deck and in its sudden light Thomas saw she had made the turn and was again in the *Pentecost*'s wake. Villeroy's sail was still burning, giving the *Saint-Esprit* a mark she could not fail to follow and the pursuing bowmen sent three arrows together, their flames flickering hungrily in the night, and Yvette heaved desperately on the buckets, but the sail was ablaze now and the ship was slowing as the canvas lost its force and then, blessedly, there was a seething hiss and a squall came lashing in from the east.

The sleet pelted down with an extraordinary violence, rattling on the charred sail and drumming on the deck, and Thomas thought it would last forever, but it stopped as suddenly as it had begun and all on board the *Pentecost* stared astern, waiting for the next fire bolt to climb from the *Saint-Esprit*'s deck, but when the flame finally seared into the sky it was a long way off, much too far away for its light to illuminate the *Pentecost* and Villeroy grunted. 'They reckoned we'd turn back west in that squall,' he said with amusement, 'but they were being too clever for their own good.' The *Saint-Esprit* had tried to head off the *Pentecost*, thinking Villeroy would put his ship straight downwind again, but the pursuers had made the wrong guess and they were now a long way to the north and west of their quarry.

More fire arrows burned in the dark, but now they were being shot in all directions in hope that the small light of one would glint a dull reflection from the *Pentecost*'s hull, but Villeroy's ship was drawing ever farther away, pulled by the remnants of her scorched sail. If it had not been for the squall, Thomas thought, they would surely have been overhauled and captured, and he wondered whether the hand of God was somehow sheltering him because he possessed the book of the Grail. Then guilt assailed him; the guilt of doubting the Grail's existence; of wasting Lord Outhwaite's money instead of spending it on the pursuit of the Grail; then the greater guilt and pity of Eleanor and Father Hobbe's wasteful deaths, and so he dropped to his knees on the deck and stared up at the one-armed crucifix. Forgive me, Lord, he prayed, forgive me.

'Sails cost money,' Villeroy said.

'You shall have a new sail, Pierre,' Sir Guillaume promised.

'And let's pray that what's left of this one will get us somewhere,'

Villeroy said sourly. Off to the north a last fire arrow etched red across the black, and then there was no more light, just the endless dark of a broken sea in which the *Pentecost* survived under her tattered sail.

Dawn found them in a mist and with a fitful breeze that fluttered a sail so weakened that Villeroy and Yvette doubled it on itself so that the wind would have more than charred holes to blow upon, and when they reset it the *Pentecost* limped south and west and everyone on board thanked God for the mist because it hid them from the pirates that haunted the gulf between Normandy and Brittany. Villeroy was not sure where they were, though he was certain enough that the Norman coast was to the east and that all the land in that direction was in fealty to the Count of Coutances and so they held on south and west with Yvette perched in the bows to keep a lookout for the frequent reefs. 'They breed rocks, these waters,' Villeroy grumbled.

'Then go into deeper water,' Sir Guillaume suggested.

The big man spat overboard. 'Deeper water breeds English pirates out of the isles.'

They pushed on south, the wind dying and the sea calming. It was still cold, but there was no more sleet and, when a feeble sun began to burn off the shredding mists, Thomas sat beside Mordecai in the bow. 'I have a question for you,' he said.

'My father told me never to get on board a ship,' Mordecai responded. His long face was pale and his beard, which he usually brushed so carefully, was tangled. He was shivering despite a makeshift cloak of sheepskins. 'Did you know,' he went on, 'that Flemish sailors claim that you can calm a storm by throwing a Jew overboard?'

'Do they really?'

'So I'm told,' Mordecai said, 'and if I was on board a Flemish ship I might welcome drowning as an alternative to this existence. What is that?'

Thomas had unwrapped the book that his father had bequeathed him. 'My question,' he said, ignoring Mordecai's question, 'is who is Hachaliah.'

'Hachaliah?' Mordecai repeated the name, then shook his head. 'Do you think the Flemings carry Jews aboard their ships as a

precaution? It would seem a sensible, if cruel, thing to do. Why die when a Jew can die?'

Thomas opened the book to the first page of Hebrew script where Brother Germain had deciphered the name Hachaliah. 'There,' he said, giving the book to the doctor, 'Hachaliah.'

Mordecai peered at the page. 'Grandson of Hachaliah,' he translated aloud, 'and son of the Tirshatha. Of course! It's a confusion about Jonah and the great fish.'

'Hachaliah is?' Thomas asked, staring at the page of strange script.

'No, dear boy!' Mordecai said. 'The superstition about Jews and storms is a confusion about Jonah, a mere ignorant confusion.' He looked back at the page. 'Are you the son of the Tirshatha?'

'I'm the bastard son of a priest,' Thomas said.

'And did your father write this?'

'Yes.'

'For you?'

Thomas nodded. 'I think so.'

'Then you are the son of the Tirshatha and the grandson of Hachaliah,' Mordecai said, then smiled. 'Ah! Of course! Nehemiah. My memory is almost as bad as poor Skeat's, eh? Fancy forgetting that Hachaliah was the father of Nehemiah.'

Thomas was still none the wiser. 'Nehemiah?'

'And he was the Tirshatha, of course he was. Extraordinary, isn't it, how we Jews prosper in foreign states and then they tire of us and we get blamed for every little accident. Then time passes and we are restored to our offices. The Tirshatha, Thomas, was the Governor of Judaea under the Persians. Nehemiah was the Tirshatha, not the King, of course, just Governor for a time under the rule of Artaxerxes.' Mordecai's erudition was impressive, but hardly enlightening. Why would Father Ralph identify himself with Nehemiah who must have lived hundreds of years before Christ, before the Grail? The only answer that Thomas could conjure up was the usual one of his father's madness. Mordecai was turning the parchment pages and winced when one cracked. 'How people do yearn,' he said, 'for miracles.' He prodded a page with a finger stained by all the medicines he had pounded and stirred. '"A golden cup in the Lord's hand that made all the earth drunk", now what on earth does that mean?'

'He's talking about the Grail,' Thomas said.

'I had understood that, Thomas,' Mordecai chided him gently, 'but those words were not written about the Grail. It refers to Babylon. Part of the lamentations of Jeremiah.' He turned another page. 'People like mystery. They want nothing explained, because when things are explained then there is no hope left. I have seen folk dying and known there is nothing to be done, and I am asked to go because the priest will soon arrive with his dish covered by a cloth, and everyone prays for a miracle. It never happens. And the person dies and I get blamed, not God or the priest, but I!' He let the book fall on his lap where the pages stirred in the small wind. 'These are just stories of the Grail, and some odd scriptures that might refer to it. A book, really, of meditations.' He frowned. 'Did your father truly believe the Grail existed?'

Thomas was about to give a vigorous affirmative, but paused, remembering. For much of the time his father had been a wry, amused and clever man, but there had been other times when he had been a wild, shrieking creature, struggling with God and desperate to make sense of the sacred mysteries. 'I think,' Thomas said carefully, 'that he did believe in the Grail.'

'Of course he did,' Mordecai said suddenly, 'how stupid of me! Of course your father believed in the Grail because he believed that he possessed it!'

'He did?' Thomas asked. He was utterly confused now.

'Nehemiah was more than the Tirshatha of Judaea,' the doctor said, 'he was cupbearer to Artaxerxes. He says so at the beginning of his writings. "I was the King's cupbearer." There.' He pointed to a line of Hebrew script. '"I was the King's cupbearer." Your father's words, Thomas, taken from Nehemiah's story.'

Thomas stared at the writing and knew that Mordecai was right. That was his father's testimony. He had been cupbearer to the greatest King of all, to God Himself, to Christ, and the phrase confirmed Thomas's dreams. Father Ralph had been the cupbearer. He had possessed the Grail. It did exist. Thomas shivered.

'I think' – Mordecai spoke gently – 'that your father believed he possessed the Grail, but it seems unlikely.'

'Unlikely!' Thomas protested.

'I am merely a Jew,' Mordecai said blandly, 'so what can I know

of the saviour of mankind? And there are those who say I should not even speak of such things, but so far as I understand Jesus was not rich. Am I right?'

'He was poor,' Thomas said.

'So I am right, he was not a rich man, and at the end of his life he attends a *seder*.'

'A *seder*?'

'The Passover feast, Thomas. And at the *seder* he eats bread and drinks wine, and the Grail, tell me if I am wrong, was either the bread dish or the wine goblet, yes?'

'Yes.'

'Yes,' Mordecai echoed and glanced off to his left where a small fishing boat rode the broken swell. There had been no sign of the *Saint-Esprit* all morning, and none of the smaller boats they passed showed any interest in the *Pentecost*. 'Yet if Jesus was poor,' Mordecai said, 'what kind of *seder* dish would he use? One made of gold? One ringed with jewels? Or a piece of common pottery?'

'Whatever he used,' Thomas said, 'God could transform.'

'Ah yes, of course, I was forgetting,' Mordecai said. He sounded disappointed, but then he smiled and gave Thomas the book. 'When we reach wherever we are going,' he said, 'I can write down translations of the Hebrew for you and I hope it helps.'

'Thomas!' Sir Guillaume bellowed from the stern. 'We need fresh arms to bail water!'

The caulking had not been finished and the *Pentecost* was taking water at an alarming rate and so Thomas went down into the bilge and handed up the pails to Robbie who jettisoned the water over the side. Sir Guillaume had been pressing Villeroy to go north and east again in an attempt to run past Caen and make Dunkirk, but Villeroy was unhappy with his small sail and even more unhappy with the leaking hull. 'I have to put in somewhere soon,' he growled, 'and you have to buy me a sail.'

They dared not call into Normandy. It was well known throughout the province that Sir Guillaume had been declared a traitor and if the *Pentecost* was searched – and it was probable on this smuggling coast that she would be – then Sir Guillaume would be discovered. That left Brittany and Sir Guillaume was eager to make Saint-Malo or Saint-Brieuc, but Thomas protested from the bilge that he and

Will Skeat would be considered enemies by the Breton authorities who, in those towns, held allegiance to Duke Charles who was struggling against the English-backed rebels who reckoned Duke Jean was Brittany's true ruler. 'So where would you go?' Sir Guillaume demanded. 'England?'

'We'll never make England,' Villeroy said unhappily, looking at his sail.

'The islands?' Thomas suggested, thinking of Guernsey or Jersey.

'The islands!' Sir Guillaume liked that idea.

This time it was Villeroy who objected. 'Can't do it,' he said bluntly and explained that the *Pentecost* was a Guernsey boat and he had been one of the men who helped capture her. 'I take her into the isles,' he said, 'and they'll take her back and me with her.'

'For God's sake!' Sir Guillaume snarled. 'Then where do we go?'

'Can you make Tréguier?' Will Skeat asked and everyone was so astonished he had spoken that for a few heartbeats no one responded.

'Tréguier?' Villeroy asked after a while, then nodded. 'Like as not,' he said.

'Why Tréguier?' Sir Guillaume demanded.

'It was in English hands last I heard,' Skeat said.

'Still is,' Villeroy put in.

'And we've got friends there,' Skeat went on.

And enemies, Thomas thought. Tréguier was not just the closest Breton port in English hands, but also the harbour closest to La Roche-Derrien where Sir Geoffrey Carr, the Scarecrow, had gone. And Thomas had told Brother Germain that he was headed for the same small town, and that would surely mean de Taillebourg would hear of it and follow. And perhaps Jeanette was there too, and suddenly, though Thomas had been saying for weeks that he would not go back, he desperately wanted to reach La Roche-Derrien.

For it was there in Brittany, he possessed friends, old lovers and enemies he wanted to kill.

PART THREE

Brittany, Spring 1347

The King's Cupbearer

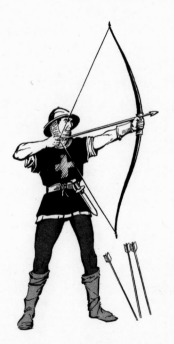

Jeanette Chenier, Comtesse d'Armorique, had lost her husband, her parents, her fortune, her house, her son and her royal lover, and all before she was twenty years old.

Her husband had been lost to an English arrow and had died in agony, weeping like a child.

Her parents had died of the bloody flux and their bedclothes had been burned before they were buried near the altar of St Renan's church. They had left Jeanette, their only remaining child, a small fortune in gold, a wine-shipping business and the great merchant's house on the river in La Roche-Derrien.

Jeanette had spent much of the fortune on equipping ships and men to fight the hated English who had killed her husband, but the English won and thus the fortune vanished.

Jeanette had begged help from Charles of Blois, Duke of Brittany and her dead husband's kinsman, and that was how she had lost her son. The three-year-old Charles, named for the duke, had been snatched from her. She was called a whore because she was a merchant's daughter and thus unworthy to be an aristocrat and Charles of Blois, to show Jeanette how much he despised her, had raped her. Her son, now the Count of Armorica, was being raised by one of Charles of Blois's loyal supporters to ensure that the boy's extensive lands stayed sworn to the house of Blois. So Jeanette, who had lost her fortune in the attempt to make Duke Charles the undisputed ruler of Brittany, learned a new hatred and found a new lover, Thomas of Hookton. She fled north with him to the English army in Normandy and there she had caught the eye of Edward of Woodstock, Prince of Wales, and so Jeanette had

abandoned Thomas. But then, fearing that the English would be crushed by the French in Picardy and that the victorious French would punish her for her choice of lover, she had fled again. She had been wrong about the battle, the English had won, but she could not go back. Kings, and the sons of Kings, did not reward fickleness and so Jeanette Chenier, dowager Countess of Armorica, had gone back to La Roche-Derrien to find she had lost her house.

When she had left La Roche-Derrien she had been deeply in debt and Monsieur Belas, a lawyer, had taken the house to pay those debts. Jeanette, on her return, possessed money enough to pay all she owed, for the Prince of Wales had been generous with jewels, but Belas would not move from the house. The law was on his side. Some of the English who occupied La Roche-Derrien showed sympathy for Jeanette, but they did not interfere with the decision of the court and it would not have mattered overmuch if they had, for everyone knew the English could not stay in the small town for long. Duke Charles was gathering a new army in Rennes and La Roche-Derrien was the most isolated and remote of all the English strongholds in Brittany, and when Duke Charles snapped up the town he would reward Monsieur Belas, his agent, and scorn Jeanette Chenier whom he called a whore because she was not nobly born.

So Jeanette, unable to claim back her house, found another, much smaller, close to La Roche-Derrien's southern gate and she confessed her sins to the priest at St Renan's church, who said she had been wicked beyond man's measure and perhaps beyond God's measure as well; the priest promised her absolution if she would sin with him and he hoisted up his robes and reached for her, then cried aloud as Jeanette kicked him. She continued to take mass at St Renan's, for it was her childhood church and her parents were buried beneath the painting of Christ emerging from the tomb with a golden light about His head, and the priest dared not refuse her the sacrament and dared not meet her eyes.

Jeanette had lost her servants when she fled north with Thomas, but she hired a fourteen-year-old girl to be her kitchen maid and the girl's idiot brother to draw water and collect firewood. The Prince's jewels, Jeanette reckoned, would last her a year and

something would turn up by then. She was young, she was truly beautiful, she was filled with anger, her child was still a hostage and she was inspired by hatred. Some in the town feared she was mad because she was much thinner than when she had left La Roche-Derrien, but her hair was still raven-black, her skin as smooth as the rare silk that only the wealthiest could afford and her eyes were big and bright. Men came and begged her favours, but were told they could not speak to her again unless they brought her the shrivelled heart of Belas the lawyer and the shrivelled prick of Charles of Blois. 'Bring them both to me in reliquaries,' she told them, 'but bring me my son alive.' Her anger repelled men and some of them spread the tale that she was moon-touched, perhaps a witch. The priest of St Renan's confided to the other clergy in the town that Jeanette had tried to tempt him and he spoke darkly of bringing in the Inquisition, but the English would not permit it for the King of England refused to let the torturers of God work their dark arts in his possessions. 'There's enough grumbling,' Dick Totesham, commander of the English garrison in La Roche-Derrien said, 'without bringing in damned friars to stir up trouble.'

Totesham and his garrison knew that Charles of Blois was raising an army that would attack La Roche-Derrien before marching on to besiege the other English strongholds in Brittany, and so they worked hard to make the town's walls higher and to build new ramparts outside the old. Local farm labourers were whipped to the work. They were forced to push barrowloads of clay and rock, they drove timbers into the soil to make palisades and they dug ditches. They hated the English for forcing them to work without pay, but the English did not care for they had to defend themselves and Totesham pleaded with Westminster to send him more men and on the feast of St Felix, in the middle of January, a troop of Welsh archers landed at Tréguier, which was the small harbour an hour and a half's walk upriver from La Roche-Derrien, but the garrison's only other reinforcements were a few knights and men-at-arms who were down on their luck and came to the small town in hope of plunder and prisoners. Some of those knights came from as far away as Flanders, lured by false rumours of the riches to be had in Brittany, and another six men-at-arms arrived from northern England, led by a malevolent, raw-faced man who carried a whip

and a heavy load of grudges, and they were La Roche-Derrien's last reinforcements before the *Pentecost* came to the river.

La Roche-Derrien's garrison was small, but Duke Charles's army was large and grew even larger. Spies in English pay told of Genoese crossbowmen arriving at Rennes in companies a hundred strong, and of men-at-arms riding from France to swear fealty to Charles of Blois. His army swelled and the King of England, apparently careless of his garrisons in Brittany, sent them no help. Which meant that La Roche-Derrien, smallest of all the English fortress towns in Brittany and the one closest to the enemy, was doomed.

Thomas felt strangely unsettled as the *Pentecost* slipped between the low rocky outcrops that marked the mouth of the River Jaudy. Was it a failure, he wondered, to be coming back to this small town? Or had God sent him because it was here that the enemies of the Grail would be seeking him? That was how Thomas thought of the mysterious de Taillebourg and his servant. Or perhaps, he told himself, he was merely nervous of seeing Jeanette again. Their history was too tangled, there was too much hate mixed with the love, yet he did want to see her and he was worried she would not want to see him. He tried and failed to conjure a picture of her face as the incoming tide carried the *Pentecost* into the river's mouth, where guillemots spread their ragged black wings to dry above rocks fretted with white foam. A seal raised its glistening head, stared indignantly at Thomas and then went back to the depths. The river-banks came closer, bringing the smell of land. There were boulders and pale grass and small wind-bent trees, while in the shallows there were sinuous fish traps made from woven willow stakes. A small girl, scarce more than six years old, used a stone to knock limpets from the rocks. 'It's a poor supper, that,' Will Skeat remarked.

'It is, Will, it is.'

'Ah, Tom!' Skeat smiled, recognizing the voice. 'You never had limpets for supper!'

'I did!' Thomas protested. 'And for breakfast too.'

'A man who speaks Latin and French? Eating limpets?' Skeat grinned. 'You can write, ain't that so, Tom?'

'Good as a priest, Will.'

'I reckon we should send a letter to his lordship,' Skeat said, meaning the Earl of Northampton, 'and ask for my men to be shipped here, only he won't do that without money, will he?'

'He owes you money,' Thomas said.

Skeat frowned at Thomas. 'He does?'

'Your men have been serving him these last months. He has to pay for that.'

Skeat shook his head. 'The Earl was never slow to pay for good soldiers. He'll be keeping their purses full, I'll be bound, and if I want them here I'll have to persuade him to let them go and I'll have to pay their passages too.' Skeat's men were contracted to fight for the Earl of Northampton who, after campaigning in Brittany, had joined the King in Normandy and now served him near Calais. 'I'll have to pay passage for men and horses, Thomas,' Skeat went on, 'and unless things have changed since I got slapped about the head that won't be cheap. Won't be cheap. And why would the Earl want them to leave Calais? They'll have a bellyful of fighting come springtime.'

The question was a good one, Thomas thought, for there surely would be some vicious fighting near Calais when the winter ended. So far as Thomas knew the town had not fallen, but the English had surrounded it and the French King was said to be raising a great army that would attack the besiegers in springtime.

'There'll be plenty of fighting here come spring,' Thomas said, nodding at the riverbank, which was very close now. The fields beyond the banks were fallow, but at least the barns and farmhouses still stood for these lands fed La Roche-Derrien's garrison and so they had been spared the pillage, rape and fire that had crackled across the rest of the dukedom.

'There'll be fighting here,' Skeat agreed, 'but more in Calais. Maybe you and I should go there, Tom?'

Thomas said nothing. He feared Skeat could no longer command a band of men-at-arms and archers. His old friend was too prone to forgetfulness or to sudden bouts of vagueness and melancholy, and those attacks were made worse by the times when Skeat seemed like his old self – except he never was *quite* like the old Will Skeat who had been so swift in war, savage in decision and

241

clever in battle. Now he repeated himself, became confused and was too frequently puzzled – as he was now by a guardboat flying England's red cross on its white field that pulled downstream towards the *Pentecost*. Skeat frowned at the small craft. 'Is he an enemy?'

'Flying our flag, Will.'

'He is?'

A mail-clad man stood up in the rowboat's bows and hailed the *Pentecost*. 'Who are you?'

'Sir William Skeat!' Thomas shouted back, using the name that would be most welcome in Brittany.

There was a pause, maybe of incredulity. 'Sir William Skeat?' the man called back. 'Will Skeat, you mean?'

'The King knighted him,' Thomas told the man.

'I keep forgetting that myself,' Skeat said.

The portside oarsmen backed water so that the guard boat turned in the tide alongside the *Pentecost*. 'What are you carrying?' the man asked.

'Empty!' Thomas shouted.

The man stared up at the ragged, scorched, doubled sail. 'You had trouble?'

'Off Normandy.'

'Time those bastards were killed once and for all,' the man grumbled, then gestured upriver to where Tréguier's houses smeared the sky with their woodsmoke. 'Tie up outboard of the *Edward*,' he ordered them. 'There's a harbour fee you'll have to pay. Six shillings.'

'Six shillings?' Villeroy exploded when he was told. 'Six bloody shillings! Do they think we pull money off the seabed in nets?'

Thus Thomas and Will Skeat came back to Tréguier where the cathedral had lost its tower after Bretons who supported Charles of Blois had fired crossbows at the English from its summit. In retaliation the English had pulled the tower down and shipped the stone to London. The little harbour town was scantily populated now for it had no walls and Charles of Blois's men sometimes raided the warehouses behind the quay. Small ships could go all the way upriver to La Roche-Derrien, but the *Pentecost* drew too much water and so she tied herself alongside the English cog and then a dozen

men in red-crossed jupons came aboard to take the harbour fee and look for contraband or else a healthy bribe to persuade them to ignore whatever they might discover, but they found neither goods nor bribe. Their commander, a fat man with a weeping ulcer on his forehead, confirmed that Richard Totesham still commanded at La Roche-Derrien. 'He be there,' the fat man said, 'and Sir Thomas Dagworth commands in Brest.'

'Dagworth!' Skeat sounded pleased. 'He's a good one, he is. So's Dick Totesham,' he added to Thomas, then looked puzzled as Sir Guillaume emerged from the forecabin.

'It's Sir Guillaume,' Thomas said in a low voice.

''Course it is,' Skeat said.

Sir Guillaume dropped the saddlebags on the deck and the chink of coins drew an expectant gaze from the fat man. Sir Guillaume met his gaze and half drew his sword.

'Reckon I be going,' the fat man said.

'Reckon you do,' Skeat said with a chuckle.

Robbie heaved his baggage onto the deck, then stared across the waist of the *Edward* to where four girls were gutting herrings and chucking the offal into the air where gulls snatched it in mid flight. The girls strung the gutted fish on long poles that would be placed in the smokers at the quay's end. 'Are they all as pretty as that?' Robbie asked.

'Prettier,' Thomas said, wondering how the Scot could see the girl's faces under their bonnets.

'I'm going to like Brittany,' Robbie said.

There were debts to be paid before they could leave. Sir Guillaume paid off Villeroy and added enough cash to buy a new sail. 'You might do well,' he advised the big man, 'to avoid Caen for a while.'

'We'll go on down to Gascony,' Villeroy said. 'There's always trade in Gascony. Maybe we'll even poke on down to Portugal?'

'Perhaps,' Mordecai spoke shyly, 'you would let me come?'

'You?' Sir Guillaume turned on the doctor. 'You hate goddamn ships.'

'I have to go south,' Mordecai said wearily, 'to Montpellier first of all. The further south a man is, the friendlier the people. I would rather suffer a month of sea and cold than meet Duke Charles's men.'

'Passage to Gascony' – Sir Guillaume offered Villeroy a gold coin – 'for a friend of mine.'

Villeroy glanced at Yvette, who shrugged, and that persuaded the big man to agree. 'You're welcome, doctor,' he said.

So they said farewell to Mordecai and then Thomas and Robbie, Will Skeat and Sir Guillaume and his two men-at-arms went ashore. A boat was going upstream to La Roche-Derrien, but not till later in the day and so the two men-at-arms were left with the baggage and Thomas led the others along the narrow track that followed the river's western bank. They wore mail and carried weapons for the local peasantry were not friendly to the English, but the only men they passed were a dozen drab labourers pitch-forking dung from two carts. The men paused to watch the soldiers pass, but said nothing. 'And by this time tomorrow,' Thomas commented, 'Charles of Blois will know we've arrived.'

'He'll be quaking in his boots,' Skeat said with a grin.

It began to rain as they reached the bridge which led into La Roche-Derrien. Thomas stopped under the arch of the protective barbican on the bank opposite the town and pointed upstream to the ramshackle quay where he and Skeat's other archers had sneaked into La Roche-Derrien on the night it first fell to the English. 'Remember that place, Will?' he asked.

''Course I remember,' Skeat said, though he looked vague and Thomas did not say more.

They crossed the stone bridge and hurried down the street to the house by the tavern that had always been Richard Totesham's headquarters and Totesham himself was just sliding out of his saddle as they arrived. He turned and scowled at the newcomers, then recognized Will Skeat and stared at his old friend as though he had seen a ghost. Skeat looked blankly back and his lack of recognition troubled Totesham. 'Will?' the garrison commander asked. 'Will? Is it you, Will?'

A look of astonished delight animated Skeat's face. 'Dick Totesham! Of all the folk to meet!'

Totesham was puzzled that Skeat should be surprised to meet him in a garrison he commanded, but then he saw the emptiness in his old friend's eyes and frowned. 'Are you well, Will?'

'I had a bash on the head,' Skeat said, 'but a doctor cobbled me

together again. Things get blurred here and there, just blurred.'

The two clasped hands. They were both men who had been born penniless and become soldiers, then earned the trust of their masters and gained the profits of prisoners ransomed and property plundered until they were wealthy enough to raise their own bands of men, which they hired to the King or to a noble and so became richer still as they ravaged more enemy lands. When the troubadours sang of battle they named the King as the fighting hero, and extolled the exploits of dukes, earls, barons and knights, but it was men like Totesham and Skeat who did most of England's fighting.

Totesham clapped Skeat good-naturedly on the shoulder. 'Tell me you've brought your men, Will.'

'God knows where they are,' Skeat said. 'I haven't laid eyes on them in months.'

'They're outside Calais,' Thomas put in.

'Dear God.' Totesham made the sign of the cross. He was a squat man, grey-haired and broad-faced, who held La Roche-Derrien's garrison together by sheer force of character, but he knew he had too few men. Far too few men. 'I've a hundred and thirty-two men under orders,' he told Skeat, 'and half of those are sick. Then there's fifty or sixty mercenaries who might or might not stay till Charles of Blois arrives. Of course the townsfolk will fight for us, or most of them will.'

'They will?' Thomas interrupted, astonished at the claim. When the English had captured the town the previous year the town's people had fought bitterly to defend their walls, and when they had lost they had been subjected to rape and plunder, yet now they supported the garrison?

'Trade's good,' Totesham explained. 'They've never been so rich! Ships to Gascony, to Portugal, to Flanders and to England. Making money, they are. They don't want us to leave, so yes, some will fight for us and it'll help, but it's not like having trained men.'

The other English troops in Brittany were a long way to the west so when Charles of Blois came with his army, Totesham would have to hold the small town for two or three weeks before he could expect any relief and, even with the inhabitants' help, he doubted he could do it. He had sent a petition to the King at Calais begging that more men be sent to La Roche-Derrien. 'We are far from help,'

his clerk had written to Totesham's dictation, 'and our enemies gather close about.' Totesham, seeing Will Skeat, had assumed that Skeat's men had arrived in answer to his petition and he could not hide his disappointment. 'You'll write to the King yourself?' Totesham asked Will.

'Tom here can write for me.'

'Ask for your men to be sent,' Totesham urged. 'I need three or four hundred more archers, but your fifty or sixty would help.'

'Tommy Dagworth can't send you any?' Skeat asked.

'He's as hard pressed as I am. Too much land to hold, too few men and the King won't hear of us surrendering a single acre to Charles of Blois.'

'So why doesn't he send reinforcements?' Sir Guillaume asked.

'Because he ain't got men to spare,' Totesham said, 'which is no reason for us not to ask.'

Totesham took them inside his house where a fire blazed in a big hearth and his servants brought jugs of mulled wine and plates of bread and cold pork. A baby lay in a wooden cradle by the fire and Totesham blushed when he admitted it was his. 'Newly married,' he told Skeat, then ordered a maid to take the baby away before it began crying. He flinched when Skeat took off his hat to reveal his scarred, thick-ridged scalp, then he insisted on hearing Will's story, and when it was told he thanked Sir Guillaume for the help the Frenchman had given his friend. Thomas and Robbie got a cooler welcome, the latter because he was Scottish and the former because Totesham remembered Thomas from the previous year. 'You were a bloody nuisance,' Totesham said bluntly, 'you and the Countess of Armorica.'

'Is she here?' Thomas asked.

'She came back, aye.' Totesham sounded guarded.

'We can go back to her house, Will,' Thomas said to Skeat.

'No you can't,' Totesham said firmly. 'She lost the house. It was sold to pay her debts and she's been screaming about it ever since, but it was sold fair and square. And the lawyer who bought it has paid us a quittance to be left in peace and I don't want him disturbed, so the two of you can find yourself space at the Two Foxes. Then come and have supper.' This invitation was to Will Skeat and to Sir Guillaume and pointedly not to Thomas or Robbie.

Thomas did not mind. He and Robbie found a room to share in the tavern called the Two Foxes and afterwards, as Robbie had his first taste of Breton ale, Thomas went to St Renan's church, which was one of the smallest in La Roche-Derrien, but also one of the wealthiest because Jeanette's father had endowed it. He had built a bell tower and paid to have fine pictures painted on its walls, though by the time Thomas reached St Renan's it was too dark to see the Saviour walking on Galilee's water or the souls tumbling down to their fiery hell. The only light in the church came from some candles burning on the altar where a silver reliquary held St Renan's tongue, but Thomas knew there was another treasure beneath the altar, something almost as rare as a saint's silent tongue, and he wanted to consult it. It was a book, a gift from Jeanette's father, and Thomas had been astonished to find it there, not just because the book had survived the fall of the town – though in truth not many soldiers would seek books for plunder – but because there was any book in a small church in a Breton town. Books were rare and that was St Renan's treasure: a bible. Most of the New Testament was missing, evidently because some soldiers had taken those pages to use in the latrines, but all of the Old Testament remained. Thomas threaded his way through the black-dressed old ladies who knelt and prayed in the nave and he found the book beneath the altar and blew off the dust and cobwebs, then put it beside the candles. One of the women hissed that he was being impious, but Thomas ignored her.

He turned the stiff pages, sometimes stopping to admire a painted capital. There was a bible in St Peter's church in Dorchester and his father had possessed one, and Thomas must have seen a dozen in Oxford, but he had seen few others and, as he searched the pages, he marvelled at the time it must take to copy such a vast book. More women protested his annexation of the altar and so, to placate them, he went a few steps away and sat cross-legged with the heavy book on his lap. He was now too far from the candles and found it hard to read the script, which was mostly ill done. The capitals were pretty, suggesting they had been done by a skilled hand, but most of the writing was cramped and his task was made no easier by his ignorance of where to look in the huge book. He began at the end of the Old Testament, but did not find

what he wanted and so he leafed back, the huge pages crackling as he turned them. He knew what he sought was not in the Psalms so he turned those pages fast, then slowed again, seeking words out of the ill-written script and then, suddenly, the names jumped from the page. 'Neemias Athersatha filius Achelai', 'Nehemiah the Governor, son of Hachaliah'. He read the whole passage, but did not find what he sought, and so he leafed still further back, page by stiff page, knowing he was close, and there, at last, it was.

'Ego enim eram pincerna regis.'

He stared at the phrase, then read it aloud. '"Ego enim eram pincerna regis."'

'For I was the King's cupbearer.'

Mordecai had thought Father Ralph's book was a plea to God to make the Grail true, but Thomas did not agree. His father did not want to be the cupbearer. No, the notebook was a way of confessing and of hiding the truth. His father had left a trail for him to follow. Go from Hachaliah to the Tirshatha and realize that the Governor was also the cupbearer: ego enim eram pincerna regis. 'Was', Thomas thought. Did that mean his father had lost the Grail? It was more likely that he knew Thomas would only read the book after his death. But Thomas was certain of one thing: the words confirmed that the Grail did exist and his father had been its reluctant keeper. I was the King's cupbearer; let this cup pass from me; the cup makes me drunk. The cup existed and Thomas felt a shiver go though his body. He stared at the candles on the altar and his eyes blurred with tears. Eleanor had been right. The Grail existed and it was waiting to be found and to put the world right and to bring God to man and man to God and peace on earth. It existed. It was the Grail.

'My father,' a woman said, 'gave that book to the church.'

'I know he did,' Thomas said, then he closed the bible and he turned to look at Jeanette and he was almost frightened to see her in case she was less beautiful than he remembered, or perhaps he feared the sight of her would engender hatred because she had abandoned him, but instead he felt tears in his eyes when he saw her face. 'Merle,' he said softly, using her nickname. It meant Blackbird.

'Thomas.' Her voice was toneless, then she flicked her head towards an old woman dressed and veiled in black. 'Madame

248

Verlon,' Jeanette said, 'who is nervous of life, told me that an English soldier was stealing the bible.'

'So you came to fight the soldier?' Thomas asked. A candle guttered to his right, its flame flickering as fast as a small bird's heart.

Jeanette shrugged. 'The priest here is a coward and would not challenge an English archer, so who else would come?'

'Madame Verlon can rest safe,' Thomas said as he put the bible back under the altar.

'She also said' – Jeanette's voice had a quaver in it – 'that the man stealing the bible had a big black bow.' Which was why, she implied, she had come herself instead of sending for help. She had guessed it was Thomas.

'At least you did not have to come far,' Thomas said, gesturing to the side door which led into the yard of Jeanette's father's house. He was pretending not to know that she had lost the house.

Her head jerked back. 'I do not live there,' she said curtly, 'not now.'

A dozen women were listening and they stepped nervously back as Thomas came towards them. 'Then perhaps, madame,' he said to Jeanette, 'you will let me escort you home?'

She nodded abruptly. Her eyes seemed very bright and big in the candlelight. She was thinner, Thomas thought, or perhaps that was the darkness in the church shadowing her cheeks. She had a bonnet tied under her chin and a great black cloak that swept on the flagstones as she followed him to the western door. 'You remember Belas?' she asked him.

'I remember the name,' Thomas said. 'Wasn't he a lawyer?'

'He is a lawyer,' Jeanette said, 'and a thing of bile, a creature of slime, a cheat. What was that English word you taught me? A tosspot. He is a tosspot. When I came home he had bought the house, claiming it was sold to pay my debts. But he had bought the debts! He promised to look after my business, waited till I was gone, then took my house. And now I am back he won't let me pay what I owed. He says it is paid. I said I would buy the house from him for more than he paid, but he just laughs at me.'

Thomas held the door for her. Rain was spitting in the street. 'You don't want the house,' he told her, 'not if Charles of Blois comes back. You should be gone by then.'

'You're still telling me what to do, Thomas?' she asked and then, as if to soften the harshness of her words, she took his arm. Or perhaps she put her hand through his elbow because the street was steep and slippery. 'I will stay here, I think.'

'If you hadn't escaped from him,' Thomas said, 'Charles was going to marry you to one of his men-at-arms. If he finds you here he'll do that. Or worse.'

'He already has my child. He has already raped me. What more can he do? No' – she clutched Thomas's arm fiercely – 'I shall stay in my little house by the south gate and when he rides into the town I will sink a crossbow quarrel in his belly.'

'I'm surprised you haven't put a quarrel into Belas's belly.'

'You think I would hang for a lawyer's death?' Jeanette asked and gave a short, hard laugh. 'No, I shall save my death for the life of Charles of Blois and all Brittany and France will know he was killed by a woman.'

'Unless he returns your child?'

'He won't!' she said fiercely. 'He answered no appeals.' She meant, Thomas was sure, that the Prince of Wales, maybe the King as well, had written to Charles of Blois, but the appeals had achieved nothing, and why should they? England was Charles's most bitter enemy. 'It's all about land, Thomas,' she said wearily, 'land and money.' She meant that her son, who at three years old was the Count of Armorica, was the rightful heir to great swathes of western Brittany that were presently under English occupation. If the child were to give fealty to Duke Jean, who was Edward of England's candidate to rule Brittany, then the claim of Charles of Blois to sovereignty of the duchy would be seriously weakened and so Charles had taken the child and would keep him till he was of an age to swear fealty.

'Where is Charles?' Thomas asked. It was one of the ironies of Jeanette's life that her son had been named after his great-uncle in an attempt to win his favour.

'He is in the Tower of Roncelets,' Jeanette said, 'which is south of Rennes. He is being raised by the Lord of Roncelets.' She turned on Thomas. 'It's almost a year since I've seen him!'

'The Tower of Roncelets,' Thomas said, 'it's a castle?'

'I've not seen it. A tower, I suppose. Yes, a castle.'

'You're sure he's there?'

'I'm sure of nothing,' Jeanette said wearily, 'but I received a letter which said Charles was there and I have no reason to doubt it.'

'Who wrote the letter?'

'I don't know. It was not signed.' She walked in silence for a few paces, her hand warm on his arm. 'It was Belas,' she said finally. 'I don't know that for sure, but it must be. He was goading me, tormenting me. It is not enough that he has my house and Charles of Blois has my child, Belas wants me to suffer. Or else he wants me to go to Roncelets knowing that I would be given back to Charles of Blois. I'm sure it was Belas. He hates me.'

'Why?'

'Why do you think?' she asked scornfully. 'I have something he wants, something all men want, but I won't give it to him.'

They walked on through dark streets. Singing sounded from some taverns, and somewhere a woman screamed at her man. A dog barked and was silenced. The rain pattered on thatch, dripped from the eaves and made the muddy street slippery. A red glow slowly appeared ahead, growing as they came closer until Thomas saw the flames of two braziers warming the guards on the south gate and he remembered how he and Jake and Sam had opened that gate to let in the English army. 'I promised you once,' he said to Jeanette, 'that I would fetch Charles back.'

'You and I, Thomas,' Jeanette said, 'made too many promises.' She still sounded weary.

'I should start keeping some of mine,' Thomas said. 'But to reach Roncelets I need horses.'

'I can afford horses,' Jeanette said, stopping by a dark doorway. 'I live here,' she went on, then looked into his face. He was tall, but she was very nearly the same height. 'The Count of Roncelets is famous as a warrior. You mustn't die to keep a promise you should never have made.'

'It was made, though,' Thomas said.

She nodded. 'That is true.'

There was a long pause. Thomas could hear a sentry's footsteps on the wall. 'I—' he began.

'No,' she said hastily.

'I didn't . . .'

'Another time. I must get used to your being here. I'm tired of men, Thomas. Since Picardy . . .' She paused and Thomas thought she would say no more, but then she shrugged. 'Since Picardy I have lived like a nun.'

He kissed her forehead. 'I love you,' he said, meaning it, but surprised all the same that he had spoken the thought aloud.

For a heartbeat she did not speak. The reflected light from the two braziers glinted red in her eyes. 'What happened to that girl?' she asked. 'That little pale thing who was so protective of you?'

'I failed to protect her,' Thomas said, 'and she died.'

'Men are such bastards,' she said, then turned and pulled the rope that lifted the latch of the door. She paused for a moment. 'But I'm glad you're here,' she said without looking back, and then the door was shut, the bolt slid home and she was gone.

Sir Geoffrey Carr had begun to think his foray to Brittany was a mistake. For a long time there had been no sign of Thomas of Hookton and once the archer arrived he had made little effort to discover any treasure. It was mysterious and all the time Sir Geoffrey's debts were growing. But then, at last, the Scarecrow discovered what plans Thomas of Hookton was hatching. That new knowledge took Sir Geoffrey to Maître Belas's house.

Rain poured on La Roche-Derrien. It was one of the wettest winters in memory. The ditch beyond the strengthened town wall was flooded so it looked like a moat, and many of the River Jaudy's water meadows resembled lakes. The streets of the town were sticky with mud, men's boots were thick with it and women went to market wearing awkward wooden pattens that slipped treacherously on the steeper streets and still thick mud was smeared on the hems of their dresses and cloaks. The only good things about such rain was the protection it offered against fire and, for the English, the knowledge that it would make any siege of the town difficult. Siege engines, whether catapults, trebuchets or guns, needed a solid base, not a quagmire, and men could not assault through a marsh. Richard Totesham was said to be praying for more rain and giving thanks every morning that dawned grey, heavy and damp.

'A wet winter, Sir Geoffrey,' Belas greeted the Scarecrow, then gave his visitor a covert inspection. A raw and ugly face, he thought, and while Sir Geoffrey's clothes were of a fine quality, they had also been made for a fatter man which suggested that either the Englishman had recently lost weight or, more likely, the clothes had been taken from a man he had killed in battle. A coiled whip hung at his belt, which seemed a strange accoutrement, but the lawyer never presumed to understand soldiers. 'A very wet winter,' Belas went on, waving the Scarecrow into a chair.

'It's a pissing wet winter,' Sir Geoffrey snarled to cover his nervousness, 'nothing but rain, cold and chilblains.' He was nervous because he was not certain that this thin and watchful lawyer was as sympathetic to Charles of Blois as tavern rumour suggested, and he had been forced to leave Beggar and Dickon in the courtyard below and he felt vulnerable without their protective company, especially as the lawyer had a great hulking attendant who was dressed in a leather jerkin and had a long sword at his side.

'Pierre protects me,' Belas said. He had seen Sir Geoffrey glancing at the big man. 'He protects me from the enemies all honest lawyers make. Please, Sir Geoffrey, sit yourself.' He gestured again at a chair. A small fire burned in the hearth, the smoke vanishing up a newly made chimney. The lawyer had a face as hungry as a stoat and pale as a grass-snake's belly. He was wearing a black gown and a black cloak edged with black fur and a black hat with flaps that covered his ears, though he now pushed one flap up so he could hear the Scarecrow's voice. '*Parlez-vous français?*' he asked.

'No.'

'*Brezoneg a ouzit?*' the lawyer enquired and, when he saw the dumb incomprehension on the Scarecrow's face, shrugged. 'You don't speak Breton?'

'I just told you, didn't I? I don't talk French.'

'French and Breton are not the same language, Sir Geoffrey.'

'They're not bloody English,' Sir Geoffrey said belligerently.

'Indeed they are not. Alas, I do not speak English well, but I learn fast. It is, after all, the language of our new masters.'

'Masters?' the Scarecrow asked. 'Or enemies?'

Belas shrugged. 'I am a man of, how do you say? Of affairs. A man of affairs. It is not possible, I think, to be such and not to make

253

enemies.' He shrugged again, as if he spoke of trivialities, then he leaned back in his chair. 'But you come on business, Sir Geoffrey? You have property to convey, perhaps? A contract to make?'

'Jeanette Chenier, Countess of Armorica,' Sir Geoffrey said bluntly.

Belas was surprised, but did not show it. He was alert, though. He knew well enough that Jeanette wanted revenge and he was ever watchful for her machinations, but now he pretended indifference. 'I know of the lady,' he admitted.

'She knows you. And she don't like you, *Monsieur* Belas,' Sir Geoffrey said, making his pronunciation of the name sound like a sneer. 'She don't like you one small bit. She'd like to have your collops in a skillet and kindle a fierce fire under them.'

Belas turned to the papers on his desk as though his visitor was being tedious. 'I told you, Sir Geoffrey, that a lawyer inevitably makes enemies. It is nothing to worry about. The law protects me.'

'Piss on the law, Belas.' Sir Geoffrey spoke flatly. His eyes, curiously pale, watched the lawyer, who pretended to be busy sharpening a quill. 'Suppose the lady got her son back?' the Scarecrow went on. 'Suppose the lady takes her son to Edward of England and has the boy swear fealty to Duke Jean? The law won't stop them chopping off your collops then, will it? One, two, snip, snip and stoke the fire, lawyer.'

'Such an eventuality,' Belas said in apparent boredom, 'could have no possible repercussions for me.'

'So your English ain't bad, eh?' Sir Geoffrey sneered. 'I don't pretend to know the law, monsieur, but I know folk. If the Countess gets her son then she'll go to Calais and see the King.'

'So?' Belas asked, still pretending carelessness.

'Three months' – Sir Geoffrey held up three fingers – 'four, maybe, before your Charles of Blois can get here. And she might be in Calais in four weeks' time and back here with the King's piece of parchment inside eight weeks, and by then she'll be valuable. Her son has what the King wants and he'll give her what she wants, and what she wants is your collops. She'll bite them off with her little white teeth and then she'll skin you alive, monsieur, and the law won't help you. Not against the King, it won't.'

Belas had been pretending to read a parchment, which he now released so that it rolled up with a snap. He stared at the Scarecrow, then shrugged. 'I doubt, Sir Geoffrey, that what you describe is likely to happen. The Countess's son is not here.'

'But suppose, monsieur, just suppose, that a party of men is readying themselves to go to Roncelets and fetch the little tosspot?'

Belas paused. He had heard a rumour that just such a raid was being planned, but he had doubted the rumour's truth for such tales had been told a score of times and come to nothing. Yet something in Sir Geoffrey's tone suggested that this time there might be some meat on the bone. 'A party of men,' Belas responded flatly.

'A party of men,' the Scarecrow confirmed, 'that plans to ride to Roncelets and watch until the little darling is taken out for his morning piddle and then they'll snatch him, bring him back here and put your collops in the frying pan.'

Belas unrolled the parchment and pretended to read it again. 'It is hardly surprising, Sir Geoffrey,' he said carelessly, 'that Madame Chenier conspires for the return of her son. It is to be expected. But why should you bother me with it? What harm can it do me?' He dipped the newly sharpened quill in his ink pot. 'And how do you know about this planned raid?'

'Because I ask the right questions, don't I?' the Scarecrow answered.

In truth the Scarecrow had heard rumours that Thomas planned a raid on Rostrenen, but other men in the town had sworn that Rostrenen had been picked over so often that a sparrow would die of starvation there now. So what, the Scarecrow had wondered, was Thomas really doing? Sir Geoffrey was certain that Thomas was riding to find the treasure, the same treasure that had taken him to Durham, but why would it be at Rostrenen? What was there? Sir Geoffrey had accosted one of Richard Totesham's deputies in a tavern and bought the man ale and asked about Rostrenen and the man had laughed and shaken his head. 'You don't want to ride on that nonsense,' he told Sir Geoffrey.

'Nonsense?'

'They ain't going to Rostrenen. They're going to Roncelets. Well, we don't know that for certain,' the man had continued, 'but the

Countess of Armorica is up to her pretty neck in the whole business, so that means it must be Roncelets. And you want my advice, Sir Geoffrey? Stay out of it. They don't call Roncelets the wasp's nest for nothing.'

Sir Geoffrey, more confused than ever, asked more questions and slowly he came to understand that the *thesaurus* Thomas sought was not thick golden coins, nor leather bags filled with jewels, but instead was land: the Breton estates of the Count of Armorica, and if Jeanette's little son swore allegiance to Duke Jean, then the English cause in Brittany was advanced. It was a treasure in its way, a political treasure: not so satisfying as gold, but it was still valuable. Quite what the land had to do with Durham the Scarecrow did not know. Perhaps Thomas had gone there to find some deeds? Or a grant made by a previous duke? Some lawyer's nonsense, and it did not matter; what mattered was that Thomas was riding to seize a boy who could bring political muscle to the King of England, and Sir Geoffrey had then wondered how he could benefit from the child and for a time he had toyed with the wild idea of kidnapping the boy and taking him to Calais himself, but then he had realized there was a far safer profit to be made by simply betraying Thomas. Which was why he was here, and Belas, he suspected, was interested, but the lawyer was also pretending that the raid on Roncelets was none of his business and so the Scarecrow decided it was time to force the lawyer's hand. He stood and pulled down his rain-soaked jerkin. 'You ain't interested, monsieur?' he asked. 'So be it. You know your business better than I do, but I know how many are going to Roncelets and I know who leads them and I can tell you when they're going.' The quill was no longer moving and drips of ink were falling from its tip to blot the parchment, but Belas did not notice as the Scarecrow's harsh voice ground on. 'Of course they ain't told Mr Totesham what they're doing, on account that officially he'd disapprove, which he might or he might not, I wouldn't know, so he thinks they're going to burn some farms near Rostrenen, which maybe they will and maybe they won't, but whatever they say and whatever Master Totesham might believe, I know they're going to Roncelets.'

'How do you know?' Belas asked quietly.

'I know!' Sir Geoffrey said harshly.

Belas put down the pen. 'Sit,' he ordered the Scarecrow, 'and tell me what you want.'

'Two things,' Sir Geoffrey said as he sat again. 'I came to this damned town to make money, but we're having thin pickings, monsieur, thin pickings.' Very thin, for English troops had been pillaging Brittany for months and there were no farms within a day's ride that had not been burned and robbed, while to ride further afield was to risk strong enemy patrols. Beyond the walls of its fortresses Brittany was a wilderness of ambush, danger and ruin and the Scarecrow had quickly discovered that it would be a hard landscape in which to make a fortune.

'So money is the first thing you want,' Belas said acidly. 'And the second?'

'Refuge,' Sir Geoffrey said.

'Refuge?'

'When Charles of Blois takes the town,' the Scarecrow said, 'then I want to be in your courtyard.'

'I cannot think why,' Belas said drily, 'but of course you will be welcome. And as for money?' He licked his lips. 'Let us first see how good your information is.'

'And if it is good?' the Scarecrow asked.

Belas considered for a moment. 'Seventy *écus*?' he suggested. 'Eighty, perhaps?'

'Seventy *écus*?' The Scarecrow paused to convert it into pounds, then spat. 'Just ten pounds! No! I want a hundred pounds and I want them in English-struck coin.'

They settled on sixty English pounds, to be paid when Belas had proof that Sir Geoffrey was telling him the truth, and that truth was that Thomas of Hookton was leading men to Roncelets and they were leaving on the eve of Valentine's Feast which was just over two weeks away.

'Why so long?' Belas wanted to know.

'He wants more men. He's only got half a dozen now and he's trying to persuade others to go with him. He's telling them there's gold to be had at Roncelets.'

'If you want money,' Belas asked acidly, 'why don't you ride with him?'

'Because I'm seeing you instead,' Sir Geoffrey answered.

Belas leaned back in his chair and steepled his pale, long fingers. 'And that is all you want?' he asked the Englishman. 'Some money and refuge?'

The Scarecrow stood, bending his head under the room's low beams. 'You pay me once,' he said, 'and you'll pay me again.'

'Perhaps,' Belas said evasively.

'I give you what you want,' Sir Geoffrey said, 'and you'll pay me.' He went to the door, then stopped because Belas had called him back.

'Did you say Thomas of Hookton?' Belas asked and there was an undeniable interest in his voice.

'Thomas of Hookton,' the Scarecrow confirmed.

'Thank you,' Belas said, and he looked down at a scroll he had just unrolled and it seemed he found Thomas's name written there for his finger checked and he smiled. 'Thank you,' he said again and, to Sir Geoffrey's astonishment, the lawyer took a small purse from a chest beside his desk and pushed it towards the Scarecrow. 'For that news, Sir Geoffrey, I do thank you.'

Sir Geoffrey, back down in the courtyard, found he had been given ten pounds of English gold. Ten pounds for just mentioning Thomas's name? He suspected there was much more to learn about Thomas's plans, but at least he had gold in his pocket now, so the visit to the lawyer had been profitable and there was the promise of more lawyer's gold to come.

But it was still bloody raining.

Thomas persuaded Richard Totesham that instead of writing another plea to the King they should appeal to the Earl of Northampton who was now among the leaders of the army besieging Calais. The letter reminded his lordship of his great victory in capturing La Roche-Derrien and stressed that achievement might all be for naught if the garrison was not reinforced. Richard Totesham dictated most of the words and Will Skeat put a cross beside his name at the foot of the letter which claimed, truthfully enough, that Charles of Blois was assembling a new and mighty army in Rennes.

'Master Totesham,' Thomas wrote, 'who sends your lordship humble greetings, reckons that Charles's army already numbers a thousand men-at-arms, two times that number in crossbowmen and other men besides, while in our garrison we have scarce a hundred healthy men, while your kinsman, Sir Thomas Dagworth, who is a week's march away, can raise no more than six or seven hundred men.'

Sir Thomas Dagworth, the English commander in Brittany, was married to the Earl of Northampton's sister and Totesham was hoping that family pride alone would persuade the Earl to avoid a defeat in Brittany, and if Northampton were to send Skeat's archers, just the archers and not the men-at-arms, it would double the number of bowmen on La Roche-Derrien's walls and give Totesham a chance to resist a siege. Send the archers, the letter pleaded, with their bows, their arrows, but without their horses and Totesham would send them back to Calais when Charles of Blois was repulsed. 'He won't believe that,' Totesham grumbled, 'he'll know I'll want to keep them, so make sure he knows it's a solemn promise. Tell him I swear on Our Lady and on St George that the archers will go back.'

The description of Charles of Blois's army was real enough. Spies in English pay sent the news which, in truth, Charles was eager for his enemies to learn for the more La Roche-Derrien's garrison was outnumbered the lower its hopes would be. Charles already had close to four thousand men, more were coming every week, and his engineers had hired nine great siege engines to hurl boulders at the walls of the English towns and fortresses in his duchy. La Roche-Derrien would be attacked first and few men gave it a hope of lasting longer than a month.

'It is not true, I trust,' Totesham said sourly to Thomas when the letter was written, 'that you have designs on Roncelets?'

'On Roncelets?' Thomas pretended not to have heard of the place. 'Not Roncelets, sir, but Rostrenen.'

Totesham gazed at Thomas with dislike. 'There's nothing at Rostrenen,' the garrison commander said icily.

'I hear there's food there, sir,' Thomas said.

'Whereas' – Totesham continued as if Thomas had not spoken – 'the Countess of Armorica's son is said to be held at Roncelets.'

'Is he, sir?' Thomas asked disingenuously.

'And if it's a swiving you want,' – Totesham ignored Thomas's lies – 'then I can recommend the brothel behind St Brieuc's chantry.'

'We're riding to Rostrenen,' Thomas insisted.

'And none of my men will ride with you,' Totesham said, meaning none that took his wages, though that still left the mercenaries.

Sir Guillaume had agreed to ride with Thomas, though he was uncomfortable about the prospects for success. He had bought horses for himself and his two men but he reckoned they were of poor quality. 'If it comes to a chase out of Roncelets,' he said, 'we'll be trounced. So take a lot of men to put up a decent fight.'

Thomas's first instinct had been to ride with just a handful of others, but a few men on bad horses would be easy bait. More men made the expedition safer.

'And why are you going anyway?' Sir Guillaume demanded. 'Just to get into the widow's skirts?'

'Because I made a promise to her,' Thomas said, and it was true, though Sir Guillaume's reason had the more truth. 'And because,' Thomas went on, 'I need to let our enemies know that I'm here.'

'You mean de Taillebourg?' Sir Guillaume asked. 'He knows already.'

'You think so?'

'Brother Germain will have told him,' Sir Guillaume said confidently, 'in which case I reckon your Dominican is already in Rennes. He'll come for you in good time.'

'If I raid Roncelets,' Thomas said, 'they'll hear of me. Then, I can be sure they'll come.'

By Candlemas he knew he could rely on Robbie, on Sir Guillaume and his two men-at-arms and he had found seven other men who had been lured by the rumours of Roncelets' wealth or by the prospect of Jeanette's good opinion. Robbie wanted to leave straightaway, but Will Skeat, like Sir Guillaume, advised Thomas to take a larger party. 'This ain't like northern England,' Skeat said, 'you can't run for the border. You get caught, Tom, and you'll need a dozen good men to lock shields and break heads. Reckon I ought to come with you.'

'No,' Thomas said hastily. Skeat had his lucid moments, but too often was vague and forgetful, though now he tried to help Thomas

by recommending other men to go on the raid. Most turned the invitation down: the Tower of Roncelets was too far off, they claimed, or the Lord of Roncelets was too powerful and the odds against the raiders too great. Some were frightened of offending Totesham who, fearing to lose any of his garrison, had decreed that no raids should go farther than a day's ride from the town. His caution meant there was little plunder to be had and it was only the poorest mercenaries who, desperate for anything they could turn into cash, offered to ride with Thomas.

'Twelve men is enough,' Robbie insisted. 'Sweet Christ, but I've been on enough raids into England. My brother and I once took a herd of cattle from Lord Percy with just three other men and Percy had half the county searching for us. Go in fast and come out quicker. Twelve men is enough.'

Thomas was almost convinced by Robbie's fervent words, but he worried that the odds were still too uneven and the horses too badly conditioned to allow them to go swiftly in and come out quicker. 'I want more men,' he told Robbie.

'If you go on dithering,' Robbie told him, 'the enemy will hear about you. They'll be waiting for us.'

'They won't know where to wait,' Thomas said, 'or what to think.' He had spread a score of rumours about the raid's purpose and hoped that the enemy would be thoroughly confused. 'But we'll go soon,' he promised Robbie.

'Sweet God, but who's left to ask?' Robbie demanded. 'Let's ride now!'

But that same day a ship came to Tréguier and three more Flemish men-at-arms rode into the garrison. Thomas found them that night in a tavern by the river's edge. The three complained how they had been in the English lines at Calais, but there was too little fighting there and thus few prospects of wealthy prisoners. They wanted to try their luck in Brittany and so they had come to La Roche-Derrien. Thomas spoke to their leader, a gaunt man with a twisted mouth and with two fingers missing from his right hand, who listened, grunted an acknowledgement and said he would think about it. Next morning all three Flemings came to the Two Foxes tavern and said they were willing to ride. 'We came here to fight,' their leader, who was called Lodewijk, said, 'so we go.'

'So let's leave!' Robbie urged Thomas.

Thomas would have liked to recruit still more men, but he knew he had waited long enough. 'We'll go,' he told Robbie, then he went to find Will Skeat and made the older man promise to keep an eye on Jeanette. She liked and trusted Skeat and Thomas was confident enough to leave his father's notebook in her keeping. 'We shall be back,' he told her, 'in six or seven days.'

'God be with you,' Jeanette said. She clung to Thomas for an instant. 'God be with you,' she said again, 'and bring me my son.'

And next dawn, in a mist that pearled their long mail coats, the fifteen horsemen rode.

Lodewijk – he insisted it was Sir Lodewijk though his two companions sniggered whenever he did – refused to speak French, claiming that the language made his tongue sour. 'It is a people of filth,' Lodewijk maintained, 'the French. Filth. The word is good, *ja*? Filth?'

'The word is good,' Thomas agreed.

Jan and Pieter, Sir Lodewijk's companions, spoke only in guttural Flemish spiced with a handful of English curses they must have learned near Calais.

'What's happening in Calais?' Thomas asked Sir Lodewijk as they rode south.

'Nothing. The town is . . . what you say?' Sir Lodewijk made a circling motion with his hand.

'Surrounded.'

'*Ja*, the town is goddamn surrounded. By the English, *ja*? And by . . .' He paused, uncertain of the word he wanted, then pointed to a stretch of waterlogged ground that lay east of the road. 'By that.'

'Marshes.'

'*Ja*! By bloody marshes. And the goddamn bloody French, they are on . . .' Again he was lost for words, so jabbed his mailed finger at the lowering sky.

'Higher ground?' Thomas guessed.

'*Ja*! Bloody high ground. Not so bloody high, I think, but higher. And they . . .' He put a hand over his eyes, as if shading them.

'Stare?'

'*Ja*! They stare at each other. So nothing is happens but they and we gets bloody wet. Pissing wet, *ja*?'

They got wet later that morning when the rains swept in from the ocean. Great curtains of grey lashed the deserted farmlands and upland heaths where the trees were permanently bent towards the east. When Thomas had first come to Brittany this had been a productive land of farms, orchards, mills and grazing, but now it was blasted naked. The fruit trees, untended, were thick with bull-finches, the fields were choked with weeds and the pastures tangled with couch grass. Here and there a few folk still tried to scratch a living, but they were constantly being forced to La Roche-Derrien to work on the ramparts and their harvests and livestock were forever being stolen by English patrols. If any such Bretons were aware of the fifteen horsemen they took care to hide themselves and so it seemed as though Thomas and his companions rode through a deserted country.

They rode with one spare horse. They should have had more because only the three Flemings were mounted on good stallions. Sea voyages usually had a bad effect on horses, but Sir Lodewijk made it plain their journey had been unusually quick. 'Bloody winds, *ja*?' He whirled his hand and made a whooshing noise to suggest the strength of the winds which had brought the destriers through in such fine fettle. 'Quick! Bloody quick!'

The Flemings were not only well mounted, but well equipped. Jan and Pieter had fine mail hauberks while Sir Lodewijk had his chest, both thighs and one arm protected by good plate that was strapped over a leather-backed mail haubergeon. The three wore black surcoats with a broad white stripe running down front and back, and all had undecorated shields, though Sir Lodewijk's horse's trapper displayed a badge showing a knife dripping blood. He tried to explain the device, but his English could not cope and Thomas was left with the vague impression that it was the mark of a trading guild in Bruges. 'The butchers?' he suggested to Robbie. 'Is that what he said? Butchers?'

'Bloody butchers don't make war. Except on pigs,' Robbie said. He was in a fine mood. Raiding was in his blood and he had heard stories in La Roche-Derrien's taverns of the plunder that could be stolen if a man was willing to break Richard Totesham's rule and

ride further than a day's journey from the town. 'The trouble in the north of England,' he told Thomas, 'is that if it's worth stealing then it's behind big bloody walls. We scratch up some cattle now and then, and a year ago I stole a fine horse off my Lord Percy, but there's not any gold and silver to be had. Nothing that you'd call real plunder. The Mass vessels are all wood or pewter or clay, and the poor boxes are poorer than the poor. And ride too far south and the bastards will be waiting for you on the way home. I hate bloody English archers.'

'I'm a bloody English archer.'

'You're different,' Robbie said, and he meant it for he was puzzled by Thomas. Most archers were country born, the sons of yeomen or smiths or bailiffs, while a few were the sons of labourers, but none in Robbie's experience was well born, which Thomas plainly was for he spoke French and Latin, he was confident in the company of lords and other archers deferred to him. Robbie might look like a wild Scottish fighter, but he was the son of a gentleman and nephew to the Knight of Liddesdale, and thus he regarded archers as inferior beings who, in a properly arranged universe, could be ridden down and slaughtered like game, but he liked Thomas. 'You're just bloody different,' he said. 'Mind you, when my ransom's paid and I'm safe home, I'll come back and kill you.'

Thomas laughed, but it was forced laughter. He was nervous. He put the nervousness down to being in the unfamiliar position of leading a raid. This was his idea, and it had been his promises that brought most of these men on the long ride. He had claimed that Roncelets, being so far from any English stronghold, lay in unplundered country. Snatch the child, he had promised them, and they could then pillage as much as they wished or at least until the enemy woke up and organized a pursuit, and that promise had persuaded men to follow him and the responsibility of it weighed on Thomas. He also resented worrying. His ambition, after all, was to be the leader of a war band like Will Skeat had been before his injury, and what hope did he have of being a good leader if he fretted over a little raid like this? Yet fret he did, and he worried most of all that he might not have anticipated everything that could go wrong; and the men who had joined him gave him small consolation for, except for his friends and the newly arrived Flemings,

they were the poorest and least well equipped of all the adventurers who had come to La Roche-Derrien in search of wealth. One of them, a quarrelsome man-at-arms from western Brittany, became drunk on the first day and Thomas discovered he had two water skins filled with a fierce apple spirit. He broke both skins, whereupon the enraged Breton drew his sword and attacked Thomas, but he was too drunk to see properly and a knee to his groin and a thump over the head put him down hard. Thomas took the man's horse and left him groaning in the mud, which meant he was down to fourteen men. 'That will have helped,' Sir Guillaume said cheerfully.

Thomas said nothing. He deserved to be mocked, he thought.

'No, I mean it! You knock a man down one day and you might do it again. You know why some men are bad leaders?'

'Why?'

'They want to be liked.'

'That's bad?' Thomas asked.

'Men want to admire their leaders, they want to fear them, and above all they want them to be successful. What does being liked have to do with any of that? If the leader is a good man he will be liked and if he's not, he won't, and if he is a good man and a bad leader then he is better off dead. You see? I am full of wisdom.' Sir Guillaume laughed. He might be down on his luck, his manor lost and fortune gone, but he was riding to a fight and that cheered him. 'The good thing about this rain,' he said, 'is that the enemy won't expect you to be riding in it. It's stay-at-home weather.'

'They'll know we've left La Roche-Derrien,' Thomas said. He was certain that Charles of Blois had as many spies in the town as the English had in Rennes.

'He won't know yet,' Sir Guillaume said. 'We're travelling faster than any message can go. Anyway, while they know we've left La Roche-Derrien, they don't know where we're going.'

They rode south in hope that the enemy would think they were planning to scavenge the farms near Guingamp, then late in the first day they turned eastwards and climbed into a high, empty country. The hazels were in blossom and rooks were calling from the bare elm tops, signs that the year was turning away from winter.

They camped in a deserted farm, sheltered by low scorched stone walls, and before the last glimmer of dusk faded they had a good augury when Robbie, rooting about in the ruins of the barn, discovered a leather bag half buried beside the broken wall. The exorbitant rain had washed the earth away above the bag which held a small silver plate and three handfuls of coins. Whoever had buried the money must have thought the coins too heavy to carry or else had feared being robbed during their exile from the house.

'We, how do you say?' Sir Lodewijk made a chopping motion with his hand as if he cut up a pie.

'Share?'

'*Ja!* We share?'

'No,' Thomas said. That had not been the agreement. He would have preferred to have shared, for that was how Will Skeat had treated spoils, but the men who rode with him wanted to keep whatever they found.

Sir Lodewijk bridled. 'It is how we do it, *ja*? We share.'

'We don't share,' Sir Guillaume said harshly, 'it's been agreed.' He spoke in French and Sir Lodewijk reacted as though he had been struck, but he understood well enough and just turned and walked away.

'Tell your Scottish friend to watch his back,' Sir Guillaume said to Thomas.

'Lodewijk's not so bad,' Thomas said, 'you just don't like him because he's Flemish.'

'I hate the Flemish,' Sir Guillaume agreed, 'they're dull, stupid porkwits. Like the English.'

The small argument with the Flemings did not fester. Next morning Sir Lodewijk and his companions were cheerful and, because their horses were much fresher and fitter than any others, they volunteered, with much broken English and elaborate hand signals, to ride ahead as scouts and all day their black and white surcoats appeared and reappeared far ahead and each time they waved the main party on, signalling that there was no danger. The deeper they went into enemy territory the greater the risk, but the Flemings' watchfulness meant that they made good progress. They were weaving a path either side of the main highway that ran east and west along Brittany's spine, a road flanked by deep woods, which

hid the raiders from the few people who travelled on the road. They saw only two drovers with their skinny cattle and a priest leading a band of pilgrims who walked barefoot, waved tattered branches and sang a dirge. No pickings there.

Next day they went south again. They were now entering a country where the farms had escaped English raiders and so the people were unafraid of horsemen and the pastures were filled with ewes and their newborn lambs, many of which had been torn to bloody scraps because the men of Brittany were too busy hunting each other and so the foxes thrived and the lambs died. Shepherds' dogs barked at the grey-mailed men, and now Thomas no longer had the Flemings ride ahead, but instead he and Sir Guillaume led the horsemen and, if challenged, they answered in French, claiming to be supporters of Charles of Blois. 'Where's Roncelets?' they constantly asked and at first found no one who knew, but as the morning wore on they discovered a man who had at least heard of the place, then another who said his father had once been there and he thought it was beyond the ridge, the forest and the river, and then a third who gave them precise directions. The tower, he said, was no more than a half-day's journey away at the far end of a long wooded ridge that ran between two rivers. He showed them where to ford the nearer river, told them to follow the ridge crest southwards and then bowed his head in thanks for the coin Thomas gave him.

They crossed the river, climbed the ridge and rode south. Thomas knew they must be close to Roncelets when they stopped for the third night, but he did not press on for he reckoned it would be better to come to the tower in the dawn and so they camped under beech trees, shivering because they dared not light a fire, and Thomas slept badly because he was listening to the strange things crackle and rustle deep in the woods and he feared those noises might be made by patrols sent out by the Lord of Roncelets. Yet no patrols found them. Thomas doubted there were any patrols except in his imagination, yet still he could not sleep and so, very early, while the others snored, he blundered through the trees to where the ridge's flank fell steeply away and he stared into the night in hope of seeing a glimmer of light cast from the battlements of the Tower of Roncelets. He saw nothing, but he heard sheep bleating

piteously further down the slope and he guessed that a fox had got among the lambs and was slaughtering them.

'The shepherd's not doing his job.' Someone spoke in French and Thomas turned, thinking it was one of Sir Guillaume's men-at-arms, but saw, in the small moonlight, that it was Sir Lodewijk.

'I thought you wouldn't use French?' Thomas said.

'There are times when I do,' Sir Lodewijk said and he strolled to stand beside Thomas and then, smiling, he rammed a makeshift club into Thomas's belly and when Thomas gasped and bent over the Fleming slammed the broken branch over his head and then kicked him in the chest. The attack was sudden, unexpected and overwhelming. Thomas was fighting for breath, half doubled over, staggering, and he tried to straighten and claw at Sir Lodewijk's eyes, but the club hit him a resounding blow on the side of the head and Thomas was down.

The Flemings' three horses had been tied to trees a small way from the others. No one had thought that strange and no one had remarked that the beasts had been left saddled and no one woke as the horses were untethered and led away. Sir Guillaume alone stirred when Sir Lodewijk collected his pieces of plate armour. 'Is it dawn?' he asked.

'Not yet,' Sir Lodewijk answered in soft French, then carried his armour and weapons out to the wood's edge where Jan and Pieter were lashing Thomas's wrists and ankles. They slung him belly down on a horse's back, tied him to the beast's girth strap and then took him eastwards.

Sir Guillaume woke properly twenty minutes later. The birds were filling the trees with song and the sun was a hint of light in the misted east.

Thomas had vanished. His mail coat, his arrow bag, his sword, his helmet, his cloak, his saddle and his big black bow were all still there, but Thomas and the three Flemings were gone.

Thomas was taken to the Tower of Roncelets, a foursquare, unadorned fortress that reared from an outcrop of rock high above a river bend. A bridge, made of the same grey stone as the tower,

carried the high road to Nantes across the river and no merchant could move his goods across the bridge without paying dues to the Lord of Roncelets whose banner of two black chevrons on a yellow field flew from the tower's high ramparts. His men wore the black and yellow stripes as a livery and were inevitably called *guêpes*, wasps. This far east in Brittany the folk spoke French rather than Breton and their tower was nicknamed the Guêpier, the wasp's nest, though on this late winter's morning most of the soldiers in the village wore plain black liveries rather than the waspish stripes of the Lord of Roncelets. The newcomers were quartered in the little cottages that lay between the Guêpier and the bridge and it was in one of those cottages that Sir Lodewijk and his two companions rejoined their comrades. 'He's up in the castle' – Sir Lodewijk jerked his head towards the tower – 'and God help him.'

'No trouble?' a man asked.

'No trouble at all,' Sir Lodewijk said. He had drawn a knife and was cutting off the white stripes that had been sewn onto his surcoat. 'He made it easy for us. A stupid bloody Englishman, eh?'

'So why do they want him?'

'God knows and who cares? All that matters is that they've got him and the devil will have him soon.' Sir Lodewijk yawned hugely. 'And there's a dozen more of them out in the woods so we're riding out to find them.'

Fifty horsemen rode westwards from the village. The sound of their hooves and their curb chains and creaking leather armour was loud, but quickly faded when they rode into the ridge's thick woods. A pair of kingfishers, startling blue, whipped up the river and vanished in shadows. Long weeds waved in the current where a flash of silver showed that the salmon were returning. A girl carried a pail of milk down the village street and wept because in the night she had been raped by one of the black-liveried soldiers and she knew it was futile to complain for no one would protect her or even make a protest on her behalf. The village priest saw her, understood why she was weeping, and reversed his course so he would not have to face her. The black and yellow flag on the Guêpier's ramparts flapped in a small gust of wind, then hung limp. Two young men with hooded falcons perched on their arms rode out of the tower and turned south. The great door grated shut

behind them and the sound of the heavy locking bar dropping into its brackets could be heard throughout the village.

Thomas heard it too. The sound shuddered through the rock on which the Guêpier was built and reverberated up the winding stair to the long, bare room where he had been taken. Two windows lit the chamber, but the wall was so thick and the embrasures so deep that Thomas, who was chained between the windows, could not see through either of them. An empty hearth stood on the opposite wall, the stones of its chimney hood stained black. The floor's wide wooden boards were scarred and worn by too many nail-studded boots and Thomas guessed this had been a barrack room. It probably still was, but now it was needed as his prison and so the men-at-arms had been ordered out and Thomas carried in and manacled to the iron ring set into the wall between the two windows. The manacles encircled his wrists and held them behind his back and were connected to the iron ring in the wall by three feet of chain. He had tested the ring, seeing if he could shift it or perhaps snap a link of the chain, but all he did was hurt his wrists. A woman laughed somewhere in the tower. Feet sounded on the circular stairs beyond the door, but no one came into the room and the footsteps faded.

Thomas wondered why the iron ring should have been cemented into the wall. It seemed an odd thing to have so high up the tower where no horse would ever need to be tied. Maybe it had been placed there when the castle had been built. He had watched once as men hauled stones to the top of a church tower and they had used a pulley attached to a ring like this one. It was better to think of the ring and of stones and of masons making the tower than to reflect on his idiocy in being so easily captured, or to wonder what was about to happen to him, though of course he did wonder about that and nowhere in his imagination was the answer comforting. He tugged on the ring again, hoping that it had been there a long time and that the mortar that bedded it would have been weakened, but all he did was break the skin of his wrists on the manacles' sharp edges. The woman laughed again and a child's voice sounded.

A bird flew in one of the windows, fluttered for a few heartbeats and then vanished again, evidently rejecting the room as a nesting site. Thomas closed his eyes and softly recited the prayer of the

Grail, the same prayer that Christ had uttered in Gethsemane: *'Pater, si vis, transfer calicem istum a me.'* Father, if you're willing, take this cup from me. Thomas repeated the prayer over and over, suspecting it was a waste of breath. God had not spared his own son the agony of Golgotha so why would He spare Thomas? Yet what hope did he have without prayer? He wanted to weep for his own naïveté in thinking he could ride here and somehow snatch the child from this stronghold that stank of woodsmoke, horse dung and rancid fat. It had all been so stupid and he knew he had not done it for the Grail, but to impress Jeanette. He was a fool, such a damned fool, and like a fool he had walked into his enemy's trap and he knew he would not be ransomed. What value did he have? So why was he even alive? Because they wanted something from him and just then the door to the room opened and Thomas opened his eyes.

A man in a monk's black robe carried two trestles into the room. He had untonsured hair, suggesting he was a lay servant to a monastery. 'Who are you?' Thomas asked.

The man, who was short and had a slight limp, gave no answer, but just placed the two trestles in the centre of the floor and, a moment later, brought in five planks that he laid across the trestles to make a table. A second untonsured man, similarly robed in black, entered the room and stared at Thomas. 'Who are you?' Thomas asked again, but the second man was as silent as the first. He was a big man with bony ridges over his eyes and sunken cheeks and he inspected Thomas as if he were appraising a bullock at slaughter time.

'Are you going to make the fire?' the first man asked.

'In a minute,' the second man said and he pulled a short-bladed knife from a sheath at his belt and walked towards Thomas. 'Stay still,' he growled, 'and you don't get hurt.'

'Who are you?'

'No one you know and no one you'll ever know,' the man said, then he seized the neck of Thomas's woollen jerkin and, with one savage cut, slit it down the front. The blade touched, but did not break Thomas's skin. Thomas pulled back, but the man simply followed him, slashing and tugging at the torn cloth until Thomas's chest was naked, then he slit down the sleeves and pulled the jerkin

away so that Thomas was naked from the waist up. Then the man pointed at Thomas's right foot, 'lift it,' he ordered. Thomas hesitated and the man sighed. 'I can make you do it,' he said, 'and that will hurt, or you can do it yourself and it won't hurt.'

He pulled off both of Thomas's boots, then cut the waist of his breeches.

'No!' Thomas protested.

'Don't waste your breath,' the man said, and he sawed and tugged and ripped with the blade until he had cut through the breeches and could pull them away to leave Thomas shivering and naked. Then the man scooped up the boots and torn clothes and carried them out of the room.

The other man was carrying things into the room and placing them on the table. There was a book and a pot, presumably of ink, because the man placed two goose feathers beside the book and a small ivory-handled knife to trim the quills. Then he put a crucifix on the table, two large candles like those that would grace the altar of a church, three pokers, a pair of pincers and a curious instrument that Thomas could not see properly. Last of all he put two chairs behind the table and a wooden bucket within Thomas's reach. 'You know what that's for, don't you?' he asked, knocking the bucket with his foot.

'Who are you? Please!'

'Don't want you to make a mess on the floor, do we?'

The bigger man came back into the room carrying some kindling and a basket of logs. 'At least you'll be warm,' he said to Thomas with evident amusement. He had a small clay pot filled with glowing embers that he used to light the kindling, then he piled on the smaller logs and held his hands to the growing flames. 'Nice and warm,' he said, 'and that's a blessing in winter. Never known a winter like it! Rain! We should be building an ark.'

A long way off a bell tolled twice. The fire began to crackle and some of the smoke seeped out into the room, perhaps because the chimney was cold. 'What he really likes,' the big man who had laid the fire said, 'is a brazier.'

'Who?' Thomas asked.

'He always likes a brazier, he does, but not on a wooden floor. I told him.'

273

'Who?' Thomas demanded.

'Don't want to burn the place down! Not a brazier, I told him, not on a wooden floor, so we had to use the hearth.' The big man watched the fire for a while. 'That seems to be burning proper, don't it?' He heaped a half-dozen larger logs on the fire and then backed away. He gave Thomas a casual look, shook his head as if the prisoner was beyond help and then both men left the room.

The firewood was dry and so the flames blazed high, fast and fierce. More smoke billowed into the room and gusted out of the windows. Thomas, in a sudden spurt of rage, dragged at the manacles, heaving with all his archer's strength to pull the iron ring from the wall, but all he achieved was to cut the iron gyves further into his bleeding wrists. He stared up at the ceiling, which was simply planks over beams, presumably the floor of the chamber above. He had heard no footsteps up there, but then there came the sound of feet just beyond the door and he stepped back to the wall.

A woman and a small child came in. Thomas crouched to hide his nakedness and the woman laughed at his modesty. The child laughed too and it took Thomas a few seconds to realize that the boy was Jeanette's son, Charles, who was gazing at him with interest, curiosity, but no recognition. The woman was tall, fair-haired, very pretty and very pregnant. She wore a pale blue dress that was belted above her swollen belly and was trimmed with white lace and little loops of pearls. Her hat was a blue spire with a brief veil that she pushed away from her eyes to see Thomas better. Thomas drew up his knees to hide himself, but the woman brazenly crossed the room to stare down at him. 'Such a pity,' she said.

'A pity?' Thomas asked.

She did not elaborate. 'Are you really English?' she demanded and looked peeved when Thomas did not answer. 'They're making a rack downstairs, Englishman. Windlasses and ropes to stretch you. Have you ever seen a man after he's been racked? He flops. It's amusing, but not, I think, for the man himself.'

Thomas still ignored her, looking instead at the small boy who had a round face, black hair and the fierce dark eyes of Jeanette, his mother. 'You remember me, Charles?' Thomas asked, but the boy just stared at him blankly. 'Your mother sends you greetings,' Thomas said and saw the surprise on the boy's face.

'Mama?' Charles, who was almost four, asked.

The woman snatched at Charles's hand and dragged him away as though Thomas carried a contagion. 'Who are you?' she asked angrily.

'Your mother loves you, Charles,' Thomas told the wide-eyed boy.

'Who are you?' the woman insisted, and then turned as the door was pushed open.

A Dominican priest came in. He was gaunt, thin and tall with short grey hair and a fierce face. He frowned when he saw the woman and child. 'You should not be here, my lady,' he said harshly.

'You forget, priest, who rules here,' the pregnant woman retorted.

'Your husband,' the priest said firmly, 'and he will not want you here, so you will leave.' The priest held the door open and the woman, whom Thomas assumed to be the Lady of Roncelets, hesitated for a heartbeat and stalked out. Charles looked back once, then was dragged out of the room just before another Dominican entered, this one a younger man, small and bald, with a towel folded over one arm and a bowl of water in his hands. He was followed by the two robed servants who walked with folded hands and downcast eyes to stand beside the fire. The first priest, the gaunt one, closed the door, then he and his fellow priest walked to the table.

'Who are you?' Thomas asked the gaunt priest, though he suspected he knew the answer. He was trying to remember that misted morning in Durham when he had seen de Taillebourg fight Robbie's brother. He thought it was the same man, the priest who had murdered Eleanor or else ordered her death, but he could not be certain.

The two priests ignored him. The smaller man put the water and towel on the table, then both men knelt. 'In the name of the Father and of the Son and of the Holy Ghost,' the older priest said, making the sign of the cross, 'amen.' He stood, opened his eyes and looked down at Thomas who was still crouching on the pitted floorboards. 'You are Thomas of Hookton,' he said formally, 'bastard son of Father Ralph, priest of that place?'

'Who are you?'

'Answer me, please,' the Dominican said.

Thomas stared up into the man's eyes and recognized the terrible strength in the priest and knew that he dared not give in to that strength. He had to resist from the very first and so he said nothing.

The priest sighed at this display of petty obstinacy. 'You are Thomas of Hookton,' he declared, 'Lodewijk says so. In which case, greetings, Thomas. My name is Bernard de Taillebourg and I am a friar of the Dominican order and, by the grace of God and at the pleasure of the Holy Father, an Inquisitor of the faith. My brother in Christ' – here de Taillebourg gestured at the younger priest, who had settled at the table where he opened the book and picked up one of the quills – 'is Father Cailloux, who is also an Inquisitor of the faith.'

'You are a bastard,' Thomas said, staring at de Taillebourg, 'you're a murdering bastard.'

He might have spared his breath for de Taillebourg showed no reaction. 'You will stand, please,' the priest demanded.

'A motherless murdering bastard,' Thomas said, making no move.

De Taillebourg made a small gesture and the two servants ran forward and took Thomas by his arms and dragged him upright and, when he threatened to collapse, the bigger one slapped him hard in the face, stinging the bruise left by the blow Sir Lodewijk had given him before dawn. De Taillebourg waited till the men were back beside the fire. 'I am charged by Cardinal Bessières,' he said tonelessly, 'to discover the whereabouts of a relic and we are informed that you can assist us in this matter, which is deemed to be of such importance that we are empowered by the Church and by Almighty God to ensure that you tell us the truth. Do you understand what that means, Thomas?'

'You killed my woman,' Thomas said, 'and one day, priest, you're going to roast in hell and the devils will dance on your shrivelled arse.'

De Taillebourg again showed no reaction. He was not using his chair, but standing tall and arrow-thin behind the table on which he rested the tips of his long, pale fingers. 'We know,' he said, 'that your father might have possessed the Grail, and we know that he gave you a book in which he wrote his account of that most precious thing. I tell you that we know of these matters so that you do not

waste our time or your pain by denying them. Yet we shall need to know more and that is why we are here. You understand me, Thomas?'

'The devil will piss in your mouth, priest, and shit in your nostrils.'

De Taillebourg looked faintly pained as if Thomas's crudity was tiresome. 'The Church grants us the authority to question you, Thomas,' he continued in a mild voice, 'but in her infinite mercy she also commands that we do not shed blood. We may use pain, indeed it is our duty to employ pain, but it must be pain without bloodshed. This means we may employ fire' – his long pale fingers touched one of the pokers on the table – 'and we may crush you and we may stretch you and God will forgive us for it will be done in His name and in His most holy service.'

'Amen,' Brother Cailloux said and, like the two servants, made the sign of the cross. De Taillebourg pushed all three of the pokers to the edge of the table and the smaller servant ran across the room, took the irons and plunged them into the fire.

'We do not employ pain lightly,' de Taillebourg said, 'or wantonly, but with prayerful regret and with pity and with a tearful concern for your immortal soul.'

'You're a murderer,' Thomas said, 'and your soul will sear in hell.'

'Now,' de Taillebourg continued, apparently oblivious to Thomas's insults, 'let us start with the book. You told Brother Germain in Caen that your father wrote it. Is that true?'

And so it began. A gentle questioning at first to which Thomas gave no answers for he was consumed by a hatred for de Taillebourg, a hatred fed by the memory of Eleanor's pale and blood-laced body, yet the questioning was insistent and unceasing, and the threat of an awful pain was in the three pokers that heated in the fire, and so Thomas persuaded himself that de Taillebourg knew some things and there could be very little harm in telling him others. Besides, the Dominican was so very reasonable and so very patient. He endured Thomas's anger, he ignored the abuse, he expressed again and again an unwillingness to employ torture and said he only wanted the truth, however inadequate and so, after an hour, Thomas began to answer the questions. Why suffer, he asked himself, when he did not possess what the Dominican

wanted? He did not know where the Grail was, he was not even certain that the Grail existed and so, hesitantly at first, and then more willingly, he talked.

There was a book, yes, and much of it was in strange languages and scripts and Thomas claimed to have no idea what those mysterious passages meant. As for the rest he admitted a knowledge of Latin and agreed he had read those parts of the book, but he dismissed them as vague, repetitive and unhelpful. 'They were just stories,' he said.

'What kind of stories?'

'A man received his sight after looking at the Grail and then, when he was disappointed in its appearance, he lost his sight again.'

'God be praised for that,' Father Cailloux interjected, then dipped the quill in ink and wrote down the miracle.

'What else?' de Taillebourg asked.

'Stories of soldiers winning battles because of the Grail, stories of healings,' Thomas said.

'Do you believe them?'

'The stories?' Thomas pretended to think, then nodded. 'If God has given us the Grail, father,' he said, 'then it will surely work miracles.'

'Did your father possess the Grail?'

'I don't know.'

So de Taillebourg asked him about Father Ralph and Thomas told how his father had walked the stony beach at Hookton wailing for his sins and sometimes preaching to the wild things of the sea and the sky.

'Are you saying he was mad?' de Taillebourg asked.

'He was mad with God,' Thomas said.

'Mad with God,' de Taillebourg repeated, as though the words intrigued him. 'Are you suggesting he was a saint?'

'I think many saints must have been like him,' Thomas replied cautiously, 'but he was also a great mocker of superstitions.'

'What do you mean?'

'He was very fond of St Guinefort,' Thomas said, 'and called on him whenever some minor problem occurred.'

'Is it mockery to do that?' de Taillebourg asked.

'St Guinefort was a dog,' Thomas said.

'I know what St Guinefort was,' de Taillebourg said testily, 'but are you saying God could not use a dog to effect His sacred purposes?'

'I am saying that my father did not believe a dog could be a saint, and so he mocked.'

'Did he mock the Grail?'

'Never,' Thomas answered truthfully, 'not once.'

'And in his book' – de Taillebourg suddenly reverted to the earlier subject – 'did he say how the Grail came to be in his possession?'

For the last few moments Thomas had been aware that there was someone standing on the other side of the door. De Taillebourg had closed it, but the latch had been silently lifted and the door pushed gently ajar. Someone was there, listening, and Thomas assumed it was the Lady of Roncelets. 'He never claimed that the Grail was in his possession,' he countered, 'but he did say that it was once owned by his family.'

'Once owned,' de Taillebourg said flatly, 'by the Vexilles.'

'Yes,' Thomas replied and he was sure the door moved a fraction.

Father Cailloux's pen scratched on the parchment. Everything Thomas said was being written down and he remembered a wandering Franciscan preacher at a fair in Dorchester shouting at the people that every sin they ever committed was being recorded in a great book in heaven and when they died and went to the judgement before God the book would be opened and their sins read out, and George Adyn had made the crowd laugh by calling out that there was not enough ink in Christendom to record what his brother was doing with Dorcas Churchill in Puddletown. The sins, the Franciscan had angrily retorted, were recorded in letters of fire, the same fire that would roast adulterers in the depths of hell.

'And who is Hachaliah?' de Taillebourg asked.

Thomas was surprised by the question and hesitated. Then he tried to look puzzled. 'Who?'

'Hachaliah,' de Taillebourg repeated patiently.

'I don't know,' Thomas said.

'I think you do,' de Taillebourg declared softly.

Thomas stared at the priest's strong, bony face. It reminded him of his father's face for it had the same grim determination, a hard-jawed inwardness which hinted that this man would not care what

others thought of his behaviour because he justified himself only to God. 'Brother Germain mentioned the name,' Thomas said cautiously, 'but what it means I don't know.'

'I don't believe you,' de Taillebourg insisted.

'Father,' Thomas said firmly, 'I do not know what it means. I asked Brother Germain and he refused to tell me. He said it was beyond someone of my wits to understand.'

De Taillebourg stared at Thomas in silence. The fire roared hollow in the chimney and the big servant shifted the pokers as one of the logs collapsed. 'The prisoner says he doesn't know,' de Taillebourg dictated to Father Cailloux without taking his gaze from Thomas. The servants put more logs on the fire and de Taillebourg let Thomas stare at the pokers and worry about them for a moment before he resumed his questioning. 'So,' the Dominican asked, 'where is the book now?'

'In La Roche-Derrien,' Thomas said promptly.

'Where in La Roche-Derrien?'

'With my baggage,' Thomas said, 'which I left with an old friend, Will Skeat.' That was not true. He had left the book in Jeanette's keeping, but he did not want to expose her to danger. Will Skeat, even with a damaged memory, could look after himself better than the Blackbird. 'Sir William Skeat,' Thomas added.

'Does Sir William know what the book is?' de Taillebourg asked.

'He can't even read! No, he doesn't know.'

There were other questions then, scores of them. De Taillebourg wanted to know the story of Thomas's life, why he had abandoned Oxford, why he had become an archer, when he had last made confession, what had he been doing in Durham? What did the King of England know of the Grail? What did the Bishop of Durham know? The questions went on and on until Thomas was faint from hunger and from standing, yet de Taillebourg seemed indefatigable. As evening came on and the light from the two windows paled and darkened he still persisted. The two servants had long looked rebellious while Father Cailloux kept frowning and glancing at the windows as if to suggest that the time for a meal was long past, but de Taillebourg did not know hunger. He just pressed and pressed. With whom had Thomas travelled to London? What had he done in Dorset? Had he searched for the Grail in Hookton?

Brother Cailloux filled page after page with Thomas's answers and, as the evening wore on, he had to light the candles so he could see to write. The flames of the fire cast shadows from the table legs and Thomas was swaying with fatigue when at last de Taillebourg nodded. 'I shall think and pray about all your answers tonight, Thomas,' he said, 'and in the morning we shall continue.'

'Water,' Thomas croaked, 'I need water.'

'You shall be given food and drink,' de Taillebourg said.

One of the servants removed the pokers from the fire. Father Cailloux closed the book and gave Thomas a glance which seemed to have some sympathy. A blanket was fetched and with it came a meal of smoked fish, beans, bread and water, and one of Thomas's hands was unmanacled so he could eat it. Two guards, both in plain black surcoats, watched him eat, and when he was done they snapped the manacles back about his wrist and he sensed a pin being pushed through the clasp to secure it. That gave him hope and when he was left alone he tried to reach the pin with his fingers, but both the gyves were deep bracelets and he could not reach the clasp. He was trapped.

He lay back against the wall, huddled in the blanket and watching the dying fire. No heat crossed the room and Thomas shivered uncontrollably. He contorted his fingers as he tried to reach the clasp of the manacles, but it was impossible and he suddenly moaned involuntarily as he anticipated the pain. He had been spared torture this day, but did that mean he had escaped it altogether? He deserved to, he thought, for he had mostly told the truth. He had told de Taillebourg that he did not know where the Grail was, that he was not even certain it existed, that he had rarely heard his father speak of it and that he would rather be an archer in the King of England's army than a seeker of the Grail. Again he felt a terrible shame that he had been captured so easily. He should have been on his way back to La Roche-Derrien by now, riding home to the taverns and the laughter and the ale and the easy company of soldiers. There were tears in his eyes and he was ashamed of that too. Laughter sounded from deep in the castle and he thought he could hear the sound of a harp playing.

Then the door opened.

He could only see that a man had come into the room. The visitor

was wearing a swathing black cloak that made him appear a sinister shadow as he crossed to the table where he stopped and stared down at Thomas. The fire's dying timbers were behind the man, edging his tall cloaked figure with red, but illuminating Thomas. 'I am told,' the man said, 'that he did not burn you today?'

Thomas said nothing, just huddled under the blanket.

'He likes burning people,' the visitor said. 'He does like it. I have watched him. He shudders as the flesh bubbles.' He went to the fire, picked up one of the pokers and thrust it into the smouldering embers before piling new logs over the dying flames. The dry wood burned quickly and, in the flaring light, Thomas could see the man for the first time. He had a narrow, sallow face, a long nose, a strong jaw and black hair swept back from a high forehead. It was a good face, intelligent and hard, then it was shadowed as the man turned away from the fire. 'I am your cousin,' he said.

A stab of hatred coursed through Thomas. 'You're Guy Vexille?'

'I am the Count of Astarac,' Vexille said. He walked slowly towards Thomas. 'Were you at the battle by the forest of Crécy?'

'Yes.'

'An archer?'

'Yes.'

'And at the battle's end,' Guy Vexille said, 'you shouted three words in Latin.'

'*Calix meus inebrians*,' Thomas said.

Guy Vexille perched on the edge of the table and gazed at Thomas for a long time. His face was in shadow so Thomas could see no expression, only the faint glimmer of his eyes. '*"Calix meus inebrians"*,' Vexille said at last. 'It is the secret motto of our family. Not the one we show on our crest. You know what that is?'

'No.'

'*"Pie repone te"*,' Guy Vexille said.

'*"In pious trust"*,' Thomas translated.

'You're strangely well educated for an archer,' Vexille said. He stood and paced up and down as he spoke. 'We display *"pie repone te"*, but our real motto is *"calix meus inebrians"*. We are the secret guardians of the Grail. Our family has held it for generations, we were entrusted with it by God, and your father stole it.'

'You killed him,' Thomas said.

'And I am proud of that,' Guy Vexille said, then suddenly stopped and turned to Thomas. 'Were you the archer on the hill that day?'

'Yes.'

'You shoot well, Thomas.'

'That was the first day I ever killed a man,' Thomas said, 'and it was a mistake.'

'A mistake?'

'I killed the wrong one.'

Guy Vexille smiled, then went back to the fire and pulled out the poker to see its tip was a dull red. He pushed it back into the heat. 'I killed your father,' he said, 'and I killed your woman in Durham and I killed the priest who was evidently your friend.'

'You were de Taillebourg's servant?' Thomas asked, astonished. He had hated Guy Vexille because of his father's death. Now he had two more deaths to add to that hatred.

'I was indeed his servant,' Vexille confirmed. 'It was the penance put on me by de Taillebourg, the punishment of humility. But now I am a soldier again and charged with recovering the Grail.'

Thomas hugged his knees under the blanket. 'If the Grail has so much power,' he asked, 'then why is our family so powerless?'

Guy Vexille thought about the question for a moment, then shrugged. 'Because we squabbled,' he said, 'because we were sinners, because we were not worthy. But we shall change that, Thomas. We shall recover our strength and our virtue.' Guy Vexille stooped to the fire and took the poker from the flames and swept it like a sword so that it made a hissing sound and its red-hot tip seared an arc of light in the dim room. 'Have you thought, Thomas,' he asked, 'of helping me?'

'Helping you?'

Vexille paced close to Thomas. He still swung the poker in great scything cuts so that the light trailed like a falling star to leave wispy lines of smoke in the dark room. 'Your father,' he went on, 'was the elder brother. Did you know that? If you were legitimate, you would be Count of Astarac.' He dropped the poker's tip so that it was close to Thomas's face, so close that Thomas could feel the scorching heat. 'Join me,' Guy Vexille said intensely, 'tell me what you know, help me retrieve the book and go with me on the quest

for the Grail.' He crouched so that his face was at the same height as Thomas's. 'Bring glory to our family, Thomas,' he said softly, 'such glory that you and I could rule all Christendom and, with the power of the Grail, lead a crusade against the infidel that will leave them writhing in agony. You and I, Thomas! We are the Lord's anointed, the Grail guardians, and if we join hands then for generations men will talk of us as the greatest warrior saints that the Church ever knew.' His voice was deep, even, almost musical. 'Will you help me, Thomas?'

'No,' Thomas said.

The poker came close to Thomas's right eye, so close that it loomed like a great sullen sun, but Thomas did not twitch away. He did not think his cousin would plunge the poker into his eye, but he did think Guy Vexille wanted him to flinch and so he stayed still.

'Your friends got away today,' Vexille said. 'Fifty of us rode to catch them and somehow they avoided us. They went deep into the trees.'

'Good.'

'But all they can do is retreat to La Roche-Derrien and they'll be trapped there. Come the spring, Thomas, we shall close that trap.' Thomas said nothing. The poker cooled and went dark, and Thomas at last dared to blink. 'Like all the Vexilles,' Guy said, taking the poker away and standing, 'you are as brave as you are foolish. Do you know where the Grail is?'

'No.'

Guy Vexille stared at him, judging that answer, then shrugged. 'Do you think the Grail exists, Thomas?'

Thomas paused, then gave the answer he had denied to de Taillebourg through all the long day. 'Yes.'

'You're right,' Vexille said, 'you're right. It does exist. We had it and your father stole it and you are the key to finding it.'

'I know nothing of it!' Thomas protested.

'But de Taillebourg won't believe that,' Vexille said, dropping the poker onto the table. 'De Taillebourg wants the Grail as a starving man wants bread. He dreams of it. He moans in his sleep and he weeps for it.' Vexille paused, then smiled. 'When the pain becomes too much to bear, Thomas, and it will, and when you are wishing

284

that you were dead, and you will, then tell de Taillebourg that you repent and that you will become my liege man. The pain will stop then, and you will live.'

It had been Vexille, Thomas realized, who had been listening outside the door. And tomorrow he would listen again. Thomas closed his eyes. *Pater,* he prayed, *si vis, transfer calicem istem a me.* He opened his eyes again. 'Why did you kill Eleanor?' he asked.

'Why not?'

'That is a ridiculous answer,' Thomas snarled.

Vexille's head snapped back as if he had been struck. 'Because she knew we existed,' he said, 'that's why.'

'Existed?'

'She knew we were in England, she knew what we wanted,' Guy Vexille said. 'She knew we had spoken to Brother Collimore. If the King of England had learned that we were searching for the Grail in his kingdom then he would have stopped us. He would have imprisoned us. He would have done to us what we are doing to you.'

'You think Eleanor could have betrayed you to the King?' Thomas asked, incredulous.

'I think it was better that no one knew why we were there,' Guy Vexille said. 'But do you know what, Thomas? That old monk could tell us nothing except that you existed. All that effort, that long journey, the killings, the Scottish weather, just to learn about you! He didn't know where the Grail was, couldn't imagine where your father might have hidden it, but he did know about you and we have been seeking you ever since. Father de Taillebourg wants to question you, Thomas, he wants to make you cry with pain until you tell him what I suspect you cannot tell him, but I don't want your pain. I want your friendship.'

'And I want you dead,' Thomas said.

Vexille shook his head sadly, then stooped so that he was near to Thomas. 'Cousin,' he said quietly, 'one day you will kneel to me. One day you will place your hands between my hands and you will pledge your allegiance and we shall exchange the kiss of lord and man, and thus you will become my liege man and we shall ride together, beneath the cross, to glory. We shall be as brothers, I promise it.' He kissed his fingers then laid the tips on Thomas's

cheek and the touch of them was almost like a caress. 'I promise it, brother,' Vexille whispered, 'now goodnight.'

'God damn you, Guy Vexille,' Thomas snarled.

'*Calix meus inebrians,*' Guy Vexille said, and went.

Thomas lay shivering in the dawn. Every footstep in the castle made him cringe. Beyond the deep windows cockerels crowed and birds sang and he had an impression, for what reason he did not know, that there were thick woods outside the Tower of Roncelets and he wondered if he would ever see green leaves again. A sullen servant brought him a breakfast of bread, hard cheese and water and, while he ate, the manacles were unpinned and a wasp-liveried guard watched him, but the gyves were again fixed onto his wrists as soon as he had finished. The bucket was carried away to be emptied and another put in its place.

Bernard de Taillebourg arrived shortly after and, while his servants revived the fire and Father Cailloux settled himself at the makeshift table, the tall Dominican greeted Thomas politely. 'Did you sleep well? Was your breakfast adequate? It's colder today, isn't it? I've never known a winter as wet. The river flooded in Rennes for the first time in years! All those cellars under water.'

Thomas, cold and frightened, did not respond and de Taillebourg did not take offence. Instead he waited as Father Cailloux dipped a quill in the ink, then ordered the taller servant to take Thomas's blanket away. 'Now,' he said when his prisoner was naked, 'to business. Let us talk about your father's notebook. Who else is aware of the book's existence?'

'No one,' Thomas said, 'except Brother Germain and you know about him.'

De Taillebourg frowned. 'But, Thomas, someone must have given it to you! And that person is surely aware of it! Who gave it to you?'

'A lawyer in Dorchester,' Thomas lied glibly.

'A name, please, give me a name.'

'John Rowley,' Thomas said, making the name up.

'Spell it, please,' de Taillebourg said and after Thomas had obeyed the Inquisitor paced up and down in apparent frustration. 'This Rowley must have known what the book was, surely?'

'It was wrapped in a cloak of my father's and in a bundle of other old clothes. He didn't look.'

'He might have done.'

'John Rowley,' Thomas said, spinning his invention, 'is old and fat. He won't go searching for the Grail. Besides, he thought my father was mad, so why would he be interested in a book of his? All Rowley's interested in is ale, mead and mutton pies.'

The three pokers were heating in the fire again. It had started to rain and gusts of cold wind sometimes blew drops through the open windows. Thomas remembered his cousin's warning in the night that de Taillebourg liked to inflict pain, yet the Dominican's voice was mild and reasonable and Thomas sensed he had survived the worst. He had endured a day of de Taillebourg's questioning and his answers seemed to have satisfied the stern Dominican who was now reduced to filling in the gaps of Thomas's story. He wanted to know about the lance of St George and Thomas told how the weapon had hung in Hookton's church and how it had been stolen and how he had taken it back at the battle outside the forest of Crécy. Did Thomas believe it was the real lance? de Taillebourg asked and Thomas shook his head. 'I don't know,' he said, 'but my father believed it was.'

'And your cousin stole the lance from Hookton's church?'

'Yes.'

'Presumably,' de Taillebourg mused, 'so that no one would realize he sailed to England to search for the Grail. The lance was a disguise.' He thought about that and Thomas, not feeling the need to comment, said nothing. 'Did the lance have a blade?' de Taillebourg asked.

'A long one.'

'Yet, surely, if this was the lance that killed the dragon,' de Taillebourg observed, 'the blade would have melted in the beast's blood?'

'Would it?' Thomas asked.

'Of course it would!' de Taillebourg insisted, staring at Thomas as though he were mad. 'Dragon's blood is molten! Molten and fiery.' He shrugged as if to acknowledge that the lance was irrelevant to his quest. Father Cailloux's pen scratched as he tried to keep up with the interrogation and the two servants stood by the fire, scarcely bothering to hide their boredom as de Taillebourg looked for a new subject to explore. He chose Will Skeat for some reason and asked about his wound and about his memory lapses. Was Thomas really sure Skeat could not read?

'He can't read!' Thomas said. He sounded now as though he were reassuring de Taillebourg and that was a measure of his confidence. He had begun the previous day with insults and hate, but now he was eagerly helping the Dominican towards the end of the interrogation. He had survived.

'Skeat can't read,' de Taillebourg said as he paced up and down 'I suppose that's not surprising. So he won't be looking at the notebook you left in his keeping?'

'I'll be lucky if he doesn't use its pages to wipe his arse. That's the only use Will Skeat has for paper or parchment.'

De Taillebourg gave a dutiful smile then stared up at the ceiling. He was silent for a long time, but at last shot Thomas a puzzled look. 'Who is Hachaliah?'

The question took Thomas by surprise and he must have shown it. 'I don't know,' he managed to say after a pause.

De Taillebourg watched Thomas. The room was suddenly tense; the servants were fully awake and Father Cailloux was no longer writing, but gazing at Thomas. De Taillebourg smiled. 'I'm going to give you one last chance, Thomas,' he said in his deep voice. 'Who is Hachaliah?'

Thomas knew he must brazen it out. Get past this, he thought, and the interrogation would be done. 'I'd never heard of him,' he said, doing his best to sound guileless, 'before Brother Germain mentioned his name.'

Why de Taillebourg seized on Hachaliah as the weak point of Thomas's defences was a mystery, but it was a shrewd seizure for if the Dominican could prove that Thomas knew who Hachaliah was then he could prove that Thomas had translated at least one of the Hebrew passages in the book. He could prove that Thomas

289

had lied through the whole interrogation and he would open whole new areas of revelation. So de Taillebourg pressed hard and when Thomas continued with his denials the priest beckoned to the servants. Father Cailloux flinched.

'I told you,' Thomas said nervously, 'I really don't know who Hachaliah is.'

'But my duty to God,' de Taillebourg said, taking the first of the red-hot pokers from the tall servant, 'is to make sure you are not telling lies.' He looked at Thomas with what appeared to be sympathy, 'I don't want to hurt you, Thomas. I just want the truth. So tell me, who is Hachaliah?'

Thomas swallowed. 'I don't know,' he said, then repeated it in a louder voice, 'I don't know!'

'I think you do,' de Taillebourg said, and so the pain began. 'In the name of the Father,' de Taillebourg prayed as he placed the iron against the bare flesh of Thomas's leg, 'and of the Son and of the Holy Ghost.' The two servants held Thomas down and the pain was worse than he could have believed and he tried to twist away from it, but he could not move and his nostrils were filled with the stench of burning flesh and still he would not answer the question for he thought that by revealing his lies he would open himself to more punishment. Somewhere in his shrieking head he believed that if he persisted in the lie then de Taillebourg must believe him and he would cease to use the fire, but in a competition of patience between torturer and prisoner the prisoner has no chance. A second poker was heated and its tip traced down Thomas's ribs. 'Who is Hachaliah?' de Taillebourg asked.

'I've told you —'

The red-hot iron was put to his chest and drawn down to his belly to leave a line of burning, puckered, raw flesh and the wound was instantly cauterized so it left no blood and Thomas's scream echoed from the high ceiling. The third poker was waiting and the first was being reheated so that the pain did not need to stop, and then Thomas was turned onto his burned belly and the strange device which he had not been able to recognize when it was first put on the table was placed over a knuckle of his left hand and he knew it was an iron vice, screw-driven, and de Taillebourg tightened the screw and the pain made Thomas jerk and scream again. He

lost consciousness, but Father Cailloux brought him back to his senses with the towel and cold water.

'Who is Hachaliah?' de Taillebourg asked.

Such a stupid question, Thomas thought. As if the answer was important! 'I don't know!' He moaned the words and prayed that de Taillebourg would believe him, but the pain came again and the best moments, other than pure oblivion, were when Thomas drifted in and out of consciousness and it seemed that the pain was a dream – a bad dream, but still only a dream – and the worst moments were when he realized it was not a dream and that his world was reduced to agony, pure agony, and then de Taillebourg would apply more pain, either tightening a screw to shatter a finger or else placing the hot iron on his flesh.

'Tell me, Thomas,' the Dominican said gently, 'just tell me and the pain will end. It will end if you just tell me. Please, Thomas, you think I enjoy this? In the name of God, I hate it so tell me, please, tell me.'

So Thomas did. Hachaliah was the father of the Tirshatha, and the Tirshatha was the father of Nehemiah.

'And Nehemiah,' de Taillebourg asked, 'was what?'

'Was the cup bearer to the King,' Thomas sobbed.

'Why do men lie to God?' de Taillebourg asked. He had put the finger-vice back on the table and the three pokers were all in the fire. 'Why?' he asked again. 'The truth is always discovered, God ensures that. So, Thomas, after all, you did know more than you claimed and we shall have to discover your other lies, but let us talk first, though, about Hachaliah. Do you think this citation from the book of Esdras is your father's way of proclaiming his possession of the Grail?'

'Yes,' Thomas said, 'yes, yes, yes.' He was hunched against the wall, his broken hands manacled behind him, his body a mass of pain, but perhaps the hurt would end if he confessed all.

'But Brother Germain tells me that the Hachaliah entry in your father's book,' de Taillebourg said, 'was written in Hebrew. Do you know Hebrew, Thomas?'

'No.'

'So who translated the passage for you.'

'Brother Germain.'

'And Brother Germain told you who Hachaliah was?' de Taillebourg asked.

'No,' Thomas whimpered. There was no point in lying for the Dominican would doubtless check with the old monk, but the answer opened a new question that, in turn, would reveal other areas where Thomas had lied. Thomas knew that, but it was too late to resist now.

'So who did tell you?' de Taillebourg asked.

'A doctor,' Thomas said softly.

'A doctor,' de Taillebourg repeated. 'That doesn't help me, Thomas. You want me to use the fire again? What doctor? A doctor of theology? A physician? And if you asked this mysterious doctor to explain the significance of the passage, was he not curious why you wished to know?'

So Thomas confessed it was Mordecai, and admitted that Mordecai had looked at the notebook and de Taillebourg thumped the table in the first display of temper he had shown in all the long hours of questioning. 'You showed the book to a Jew?' He hissed the question, his voice incredulous. 'To a Jew? In the name of God and of all the precious saints, what were you thinking? To a Jew! To a man of the race that killed our dear Saviour! If the Jews find the Grail, you fool, they will raise the Antichrist! You will suffer for that betrayal! You must suffer!' He crossed the room, snatched a poker from the fire, and brought it back to where Thomas huddled against the wall. 'To a Jew!' de Taillebourg shouted and he scored the poker's glowing tip down Thomas's leg. 'You foul thing!' he snarled over Thomas's screams. 'You are a traitor to God, a traitor to Christ, a traitor to the Church! You are no better than Judas Iscariot!'

The pain went on. The hours went on. It seemed to Thomas that there was nothing left but pain. He had lied when there had been no pain and so now all his previous answers were being checked against the measure of agony he could endure without losing consciousness.

'So where is the Grail?' de Taillebourg demanded.

'I don't know,' Thomas said and then, louder, 'I don't know!' He watched the red-hot iron come to his skin and by now he was shrieking before it even touched.

The screaming did no good because the torture went on. And on. And Thomas talked, telling all he knew, and he was even tempted to do as Guy Vexille had suggested and beg de Taillebourg to let him swear allegiance to his cousin, but then, somewhere in the red horror of his torment, he thought of Eleanor and kept silent.

On the fourth day, when he was quivering, when even a twitch of de Taillebourg's hand was enough to make him whimper and beg for mercy, the Lord of Roncelets came into the room. He was a tall man with short bristling black hair and a broken nose and two missing front teeth. He was wearing his own waspish livery, the two black chevrons on yellow, and he sneered at Thomas's scarred and broken body. 'You didn't bring the rack upstairs, father.' He sounded disappointed.

'It wasn't necessary,' de Taillebourg said.

The Lord of Roncelets prodded Thomas with a mailed foot. 'You say the bastard's an English archer?'

'He is.'

'Then cut off his bow fingers,' Roncelets said savagely.

'I cannot shed blood,' de Taillebourg said.

'By God, I can.' Roncelets pulled a knife from his belt.

'He is my charge!' de Taillebourg snapped. 'He is in God's hands and you will not touch him. You will not shed his blood!'

'This is my castle, priest,' Roncelets growled.

'And your soul is in my hands,' de Taillebourg retorted.

'He's an archer! An English archer! He came here to snatch the Chenier boy! That's my business!'

'His fingers have been shattered by the vice,' de Taillebourg said, 'so he's an archer no longer.'

Roncelets was placated by that news. He prodded Thomas again. 'He's a piece of piss, priest, that's what he is. A piece of feeble piss.' He spat on Thomas, not because he hated Thomas in particular, but because he detested all archers who had dethroned the knight from his rightful place as king of the battlefield. 'What will you do with him?' he asked.

'Pray for his soul,' de Taillebourg said curtly and when the Lord of Roncelets was gone he did exactly that. It was evident he had finished his questioning for he produced a small vial of holy oil and he gave Thomas the final rites of the church, touching the oil to

his brow and to his burned breast and then he said the prayers for the dying. '*Sana me, Domine,*' de Taillebourg intoned, his fingers gentle on Thomas's brow, '*quoniam conturbata sunt ossa mea.*' Heal me, Lord, for my bones are twisted with pain. And when that was said and done Thomas was carried down the castle stairs into a dungeon sunk into a pit in the rock crag on which the Guêpier was built. The floor was the bare black stone, as damp as it was cold. His manacles were removed as he was locked in the cell and he thought he must go mad for his body was all pain and his fingers were shattered and he was no longer an archer for how could he draw a bow with broken hands? Then the fever came and he wept as he shivered and sweated and at night, when he was half sleeping, he gibbered in his nightmares; and he wept again when he woke for he had not endured the torture, but had told de Taillebourg everything. He was a failure, lost in the dark, dying.

Then, one day, he did not know how many days it was since he had been taken down to the Guêpier's cellars, de Taillebourg's two servants came and fetched him. They put a rough woollen shirt on him, pulled dirty woollen breeches over his soiled legs and then they carried him up to the castle yard and threw him into the back of an empty dung cart. The tower's gate creaked open and, accompanied by a score of men-at-arms in the Lord of Roncelets's livery and dazzled by the pale sun light, Thomas left the Guêpier. He was hardly aware of what was happening, he just lay on the dirty boards, hunched in pain, the stink of the cart's usual cargo sour in his nostrils, wanting to die. The fever had not gone and he was shaking with weakness. 'Where are you taking me?' he asked, but no one answered; maybe no one even heard him for his voice was so feeble. It rained. The cart rumbled northwards and the villagers crossed themselves and Thomas drifted in and out of a stupor. He thought he was dying and he supposed they were taking him to the graveyard and he tried to call out to the cart's driver that he still lived, but instead it was Brother Germain who answered him in a querulous voice, saying he should have left the book with him in Caen. 'It's your own fault,' the old monk said and Thomas decided he was dreaming.

He was next aware of a trumpet calling. The cart had stopped and he heard the flapping of cloth and looked up and saw that one

of the horsemen was waving a white banner. Thomas wondered if it was his winding sheet. They wrapped a baby when it came into the world and they wrapped a corpse when it went out and he sobbed because he did not want to be buried, and then he heard English voices and he knew he was dreaming as strong hands lifted him from the remnants of dung. He wanted to scream, but he was too weak, and then all sense left him and he was unconscious.

When he woke it was dark and he was in another cart, a clean one this time, and there were blankets over him and a straw mattress beneath him. The cart had a leather cover on wooden half-hoops to keep out the rain and sunlight. 'Will you bury me now?' Thomas asked.

'You're talking nonsense,' a man said and Thomas recognized Robbie's voice.

'Robbie?'

'Aye, it's me.'

'Robbie?'

'You poor bastard,' Robbie said and stroked Thomas's forehead. 'You poor, poor bastard.'

'Where am I?'

'You're going home, Thomas,' Robbie said, 'you're going home.'

To La Roche-Derrien.

He had been ransomed. A week after his disappearance and two days after the rest of the raiding party had returned to La Roche-Derrien a messenger had come to the garrison under a flag of truce. He brought a letter from Bernard de Taillebourg that was addressed to Sir William Skeat. Surrender Father Ralph's book, the letter said, and Thomas of Hookton will be delivered back to his friends. Will Skeat had the message translated and read to him, but he knew nothing of any book so he asked Sir Guillaume if he had any idea what the priest wanted and Sir Guillaume spoke to Robbie who, in turn, talked to Jeanette and next day an answer went back to Roncelets.

Then there was a fortnight's delay because Brother Germain had to be fetched from Normandy to Rennes. De Taillebourg insisted

on that precaution because Brother Germain had seen the book and he could confirm that what was exchanged for Thomas was indeed Father Ralph's notebook.

'And so it was,' Robbie said.

Thomas stared up at the ceiling. He vaguely felt it had been wrong to exchange him for the book, even if he was grateful to be alive, to be home and among his friends.

'It was the right book,' Robbie went on with indecent relish, 'but we added some stuff to it.' He grinned at Thomas. 'We copied it all out first, of course, and then we added some rubbish to mislead them. To confuse them, see? And that shrivelled old monk never noticed. He just pawed at the book like a starving dog given a bone.'

Thomas shuddered. He felt as if he had been stripped of pride, strength and even manhood. He had been utterly humiliated, reduced to a shivering, whining, twitching thing. Tears ran down his face though he made no sound. His hands hurt, his body hurt, everything hurt. He did not even know where he was, only that he had been brought back to La Roche-Derrien and carried up a steep flight of stairs to this small chamber under a roof's steep rafters where the walls were roughly plastered and a crucifix hung at the head of the bed. A window screened with opaque horn let in a dirty brown light.

Robbie went on telling him about the false entries they had added to Father Ralph's book. It had been his idea, he said, and Jeanette had copied out the book first, but after that Robbie had let his imagination run wild. 'I put some of it in Scots,' he boasted, 'how the Grail is really in Scotland. Have the bastards searching the heather, eh?' He laughed, but could see that Thomas was not listening. He went on talking anyway, and then another person came into the room and wiped the tears from Thomas's face. It was Jeanette.

'Thomas?' she asked, 'Thomas?'

He wanted to tell her that he had seen and spoken to her son, but he could not find the words. Guy Vexille had said Thomas would want to die while he was being tortured and that had been true, but Thomas was surprised to find it was still true. Take a man's pride, he thought, and you leave him with nothing. The worst

memory was not the pain, nor the humiliation of begging for the pain to stop, but the gratitude he had felt towards de Taillebourg when the pain did stop. That was the most shameful thing of all.

'Thomas?' Jeanette asked again. She knelt by the bed and stroked his face. 'It's all right,' she said softly, 'you're safe now. This is my house. No one will hurt you here.'

'I might,' a new voice said and Thomas shook with fear, then turned to see that it was Mordecai who had spoken. Mordecai? The old doctor was supposed somewhere in the warm south. 'I might have to reset your finger and toe bones,' the doctor said, 'and that will be painful.' He put his bag on the floor. 'Hello, Thomas. I do hate boats. We waited for the new sail and then when they'd finished sewing it up they decided there wasn't enough caulking between the planks and when that was corrected they decided the rigging needed work and so the wretched boat is still sitting there. Sailors! All they ever do is talk about going to sea. Still, I shouldn't complain, it gave me the time to concoct some new material for your father's notebook and I rather enjoyed doing that! Now I hear you need me. My dear Thomas, what have they done to you?'

'Hurt me,' Thomas said and they were the first words he had spoken since he had come to Jeanette's house.

'Then we must mend you,' Mordecai said very calmly. He peeled the blanket back from Thomas's scarred body and, though Jeanette flinched, Mordecai just smiled. 'I've seen worse come from the Dominicans,' he said, 'much worse.'

So Thomas was again tended by Mordecai and time was measured by the clouds passing beyond the opaque window and the sun climbing ever higher in the sky and the noise of birds plucking straw from the thatch to make their nests. There were two days of awful pain when Mordecai brought a bone-setter to rebreak and splint Thomas's fingers and toes, but that pain went after a week and the burns on his body healed and the fever passed. Day after day Mordecai peered at his urine and declared it was clearing. 'You have the strength of an ox, young Thomas.'

'I have the stupidity of one,' Thomas said.

'Just brashness,' Mordecai said, 'just youth and brashness.'

'When they . . .' Thomas began and flinched from remembering

297

what de Taillebourg had done. 'When they talked to me,' he said instead, 'I told them you had seen the notebook.'

'They can't have liked that,' Mordecai said. He had taken a spool of cord from a pocket of his gown and now looped one end of the line around a spur of wood that protruded from an untrimmed rafter. 'They can't have liked the thought of a Jew being curious about the Grail. They doubtless thought I wanted to use it as a pisspot?'

Thomas, despite the impiety, smiled. 'I'm sorry, Mordecai.'

'For telling them about me? What choice did you have? Men always talk under torture, Thomas, that is why torture is so useful. It is why torture will be used so long as the sun goes on circling the earth. And you think I am in more danger now than I was? I'm Jewish, Thomas, Jewish. Now, what do I do with this?' He was speaking of the cord, which now hung from the rafter and which he evidently wished to attach to the floor, but there was no obvious anchor point.

'What is it?' Thomas asked.

'A remedy,' Mordecai said, staring helplessly at the cord, then at the floor. 'I was ever unpractical with matters like this. A hammer and nail, you think?'

'A staple,' Thomas suggested.

Jeanette's idiot servant boy was sent out with careful instructions and managed to find the staple that Mordecai asked Thomas to hammer into the floorboard, but Thomas held up his crooked right hand with its fingers bent like claws and said he could not do it, so Mordecai clumsily banged the staple in himself and then tightened the cord and tied it off so that it stretched taut from floor to ceiling. 'What you must do,' he said, admiring his handiwork, 'is pluck it like a bowcord.'

'I can't,' Thomas said in panic, holding up his crooked hands again.

'What are you?' Mordecai asked.

'What am I?'

'Ignore the specious answers. I know you're an Englishman and I assume you're a Christian, but what are you?'

'I was an archer,' Thomas said bitterly.

'And you still are,' Mordecai said harshly, 'and if you are not an

archer then you are nothing. So pluck that cord! And keep on plucking it until your fingers can close on it. Practise. Practise. What else do you have to do with your time?'

So Thomas practised and after a week he could tighten two fingers opposite the thumb and make the cord reverberate like a harp string, and after another week he could bend the fingers of both hands about the cord and he plucked it so vigorously that it finally broke under the strain. His strength was coming back and the burns had healed to leave puckered welts where the poker had scored his skin, but the wounds in his memory did not heal. He would not talk of what had been done to him for he did not want to remember it, instead he practised plucking the cord until it snapped and then he learned to grip a quarterstaff and fought mock battles in the house yard with Robbie. And, as the days had lengthened out of winter, he went for walks beyond the town. There was a windmill on a slight hill that lay not far from the town's eastern gate and at first he could hardly manage the climb because his toes had been broken in the vice and his feet felt like unyielding lumps, but by the time April had filled the meadows with cowslips he was walking confidently. Will Skeat often went with him and though the older man never said much his company was easy. If he did talk it was to grumble about the weather or complain because the food was strange or, more likely, because he had heard nothing from the Earl of Northampton. 'You think we should write to his lordship again, Tom?'

'Maybe the first letter didn't reach him?'

'I never did like things written down,' Skeat said, 'it ain't natural. Can you write to him?'

'I can try,' Thomas said, but though he could pluck a bowcord and hold a quarterstaff or even a sword he could not manage the quill. He tried but his letters were scratchy and uncontrolled and in the end one of Totesham's clerks wrote the letter, though Totesham himself did not think the message would do any good.

'Charles of Blois will be here before we get any reinforcements,' he said. Totesham was awkward with Thomas, who had disobeyed him by riding to Roncelets, but Thomas's punishment had been far more than Totesham would have wanted and so he felt sorry for the archer. 'You want to carry the letter to the Earl?' he asked Thomas.

299

Thomas knew he was being offered an escape, but he shook his head. 'I'll stay,' he said, and the letter was entrusted to a shipmaster who was sailing the next day.

The letter was a futile gesture and Totesham knew it for his garrison was almost certainly doomed. Each day brought news of the reinforcements reaching Charles of Blois, and the enemy's raiding parties were now coming within sight of La Roche-Derrien's walls and harassing the forage parties that searched the countryside for any cattle, goats and sheep that could be driven back to the town to be slaughtered and salted down. Sir Guillaume enjoyed such foraging raids. Since losing Evecque he had become fatalistic and so savage that already the enemy had learned to be wary of the blue jupon with its three yellow hawks. Yet one evening, coming home from a long day that had yielded only two goats, he was grinning when he came to see Thomas. 'My enemy has joined Charles,' he said, 'the Count of Coutances, God damn his rotten soul. I killed one of his men this morning and I only wish it had been the Count himself.'

'Why's he here?' Thomas asked. 'He's not a Breton.'

'Philip of France is sending men to help his nephew,' Sir Guillaume said, 'so why won't the King of England send men to oppose him? He thinks Calais is more important?'

'Yes.'

'Calais,' Sir Guillaume said in disgust, 'is the arsehole of France.' He picked a shred of meat from between his teeth. 'And your friends were out riding today,' he went on.

'My friends?'

'The wasps.'

'Roncelets,' Thomas said.

'We fought half a dozen of the bastards in some benighted village,' Sir Guillaume said, 'and I put a lance clean through a black and yellow belly. He was coughing afterwards.'

'Coughing?'

'It's the wet weather, Thomas,' Sir Guillaume explained, 'it gives men a cough. So I left him alone, killed another of the bastards, then went back and cured his cough. I cut his head off.'

Robbie rode with Sir Guillaume and, like him, amassed coins taken from dead enemy patrols, though Robbie also rode in hope

of meeting Guy Vexille. He knew that name now because Thomas
had told him that it was Guy Vexille who had killed his brother
just before the battle outside Durham and Robbie had gone to
St Renan's church, put his hand on the altar's cross and sworn
revenge. 'I shall kill Guy Vexille and de Taillebourg,' he vowed.

'They're mine,' Thomas insisted.

'Not if I get to them first,' Robbie promised.

Robbie had found himself a brown-eyed Breton girl called Oana
who hated to leave his side and she came with him whenever he
walked with Thomas. One day, as they set out for the windmill,
she appeared with Thomas's big black bow.

'I can't use that!' Thomas said, frightened of it.

'Then what bloody use are you?' Robbie asked and he patiently
encouraged Thomas to draw the bow and praised him as his strength
returned. The three of them would take the bow to the windmill
and Thomas would drive arrows into the wooden tower. The shots
were feeble at first for he could scarcely pull the cord halfway and
the more power he exerted the more treacherous his fingers seemed
to be and the more wayward his aim, but by the time the swallows
and swifts had magically reappeared above the town's roofs he
could pull the cord all the way back to his ear and put an arrow
through one of Oana's wooden bracelets at a hundred paces.

'You're cured,' Mordecai told him when Thomas told him that
news.

'Thanks to you,' Thomas said, though he knew it was not only
Mordecai, any more than it was the friendship of Will Skeat or of
Sir Guillaume or of Robbie Douglas that had helped him recover.
Bernard de Taillebourg had wounded Thomas, but those bloodless
wounds of God had not just been to his body, but to his soul, and
it was on a dark spring night when the lightning was flickering
in the east that Jeanette had climbed to her attic. She had not left
Thomas until the town's cockerels greeted the new dawn and if
Mordecai understood why Thomas was smiling the next day he
said nothing, but he noted that from that moment on Thomas's
recovery was swift.

Thereafter Thomas and Jeanette talked every night. He told her
of Charles and of the look on the boy's face when Thomas had
mentioned his mother; Jeanette wanted to know everything about

that look and she worried that it meant nothing and that her son had forgotten her, but eventually she believed Thomas when he said the boy had almost wept when he heard news of her. 'You told him I loved him?' she asked.

'Yes,' Thomas said, and Jeanette lay silent, tears in her eyes, and Thomas tried to reassure her, but she shook her head as if there was nothing Thomas could say that would console her. 'I'm sorry,' he said.

'You tried,' Jeanette said.

They wondered how the enemy had known Thomas was coming and Jeanette said that she was sure that Belas the lawyer had had a hand in it. 'I know he writes to Charles of Blois,' she said, 'and that horrid man, what did you call him? *Épouvantail*?'

'The Scarecrow.'

'Him,' Jeanette confirmed, '*l'épouvantail*. He talks to Belas.'

'The Scarecrow talks to Belas?' Thomas asked, surprised.

'He lives there now. He and his men live in the storehouses.' She paused. 'Why does he even stay in the town?' Others of the mercenaries had slipped away to find employment where there was some hope of victory rather than stay and endure the defeat that Charles of Blois threatened.

'He can't go home,' Thomas said, 'because he has too many debts. He's protected from his creditors so long as he's here.'

'But why La Roche-Derrien?'

'Because I'm here,' Thomas said. 'He thinks I can lead him to treasure.'

'The Grail?'

'He doesn't know that,' Thomas said, but he was wrong because the next day, while he was alone at the windmill and shooting arrows at a wand he had planted a hundred and fifty paces away, the Scarecrow and his six men-at-arms came riding out of the town's eastern gate. They turned off the Pontrieux road, filed through a gap in the hedge and spurred up the shallow slope towards the mill. They were all in mail and all with swords except for Beggar who, dwarfing his horse, carried a morningstar.

Sir Geoffrey reined in close to Thomas, who ignored him to shoot an arrow that just brushed the wand. The Scarecrow let the coils of his whip ripple to the ground. 'Look at me,' he ordered Thomas.

Thomas still ignored him. He took an arrow from his belt and put it on the string, then jerked his head aside as he saw the whip snake towards him. The metal tip touched his hair, but did no damage. 'I said look at me,' Sir Geoffrey snarled.

'You want an arrow in your face?' Thomas asked him.

Sir Geoffrey leaned forward on his saddle's pommel, his raw red face twisted with a spasm of anger. 'You are an archer' – he pointed his whip handle at Thomas – 'and I am a knight. If I chop you down there's not a judge alive who would condemn me.'

'And if I put an arrow through your eye,' Thomas said, 'the devil will thank me for sending him company.'

Beggar growled and spurred his horse forward, but the Scarecrow waved the big man back. 'I know what you want,' he said to Thomas.

Thomas hauled the string back, instinctively corrected for the small wind rippling the meadow's grass, and released. The arrow made the wand quiver. 'You have no idea what I want,' he told Sir Geoffrey.

'I thought it was gold,' the Scarecrow said, 'and then I thought it was land, but I never understood why gold or land would take you to Durham.' He paused as Thomas shot another arrow that hissed a hand's breadth past the distant wand. 'But now I know,' he finished, 'now at last I know.'

'What do you know?' Thomas asked derisively.

'I know you went to Durham to talk with the churchmen because you're seeking the greatest treasure of the Church. You're looking for the Grail.'

Thomas let the bowcord slacken, then looked up at Sir Geoffrey. 'We're all looking for the Grail,' Thomas said, still derisive.

'Where is it?' Sir Geoffrey growled.

Thomas laughed. He was surprised the Scarecrow knew about the Grail, but he supposed that gossip in the garrison had probably let everyone in La Roche-Derrien know. 'The best questioners of the Church asked me that,' he said, holding up one crooked hand, 'and I didn't tell them. You think I'll tell you?'

'I think,' the Scarecrow said, 'that a man searching for the Grail doesn't lock himself into a garrison that only has a month or two to live.'

'Then maybe I'm not looking for the Grail,' Thomas said and shot another arrow at the wand, but this shaft was warped and the arrow wobbled in flight and went wide. Above him the great sails of the mill, furled about their spars and tethered by ropes, creaked as a wind gust tried to turn them.

Sir Geoffrey coiled the whip. 'You failed the last time you rode out. What happens if you ride again? What happens if you ride after the Grail? And you must be going soon, before Charles of Blois gets here. So when you ride you're going to need help.' Thomas, incredulous, realized that the Scarecrow had come to offer him help, or perhaps Sir Geoffrey was asking for help. He was in La Roche-Derrien for only one reason, treasure, and he was no nearer to it now than he had been when he first accosted Thomas outside Durham. 'You daren't fail again,' the Scarecrow went on, 'so next time take some real fighters with you.'

'You think I'd take you?' Thomas asked, astonished.

'I'm an Englishman,' the Scarecrow said indignantly, 'and if the Grail exists I want it in England. Not in some scab of a foreign place.'

The sound of a sword scraping from its scabbard made the Scarecrow and his men turn in their saddles. Jeanette and Robbie had come to the meadow with Oana at Robbie's side; Jeanette had her crossbow cocked and Robbie, as though he did not have a care in the world, was now slashing the tops from thistles with his uncle's sword. Sir Geoffrey turned back to Thomas. 'What you don't need is a damned Scotchman,' he said angrily, 'nor a damned French bitch. If you look for the Grail, archer, look for it with loyal Englishmen! It's what the King would want, isn't it?'

Again Thomas did not answer. Sir Geoffrey hung the whip on a hook attached to his belt, then jerked his reins. The seven men cantered down the hill, going close to Robbie as if tempting him to attack them, but Robbie ignored them. 'What did that bastard want?'

Thomas shot at the wand, brushing it with the arrow's feathers. 'I think,' he said, 'that he wanted to help me find the Grail.'

'Help you!' Robbie exclaimed. 'Help you find the Grail? Like hell. He wants to steal it. That bastard would steal the milk from the Virgin Mary's tits.'

'Robbie!' Jeanette said, shocked, then aimed her crossbow at the wand.

'Watch her,' Thomas said to Robbie. 'She'll close her eyes when she shoots. She always does.'

'Damn you,' Jeanette said, then, unable to help it, closed her eyes as she pulled the trigger. The bolt slapped out of the groove and miraculously clipped the top six inches from the wand. Jeanette looked at Thomas triumphantly. 'I can shoot better than you with my eyes closed,' she said.

Robbie had been on the town's walls and had seen the Scarecrow accost Thomas and so he had come to help, but now, with Sir Geoffrey gone, they sat in the sun with their backs against the mill's wooden skirt. Jeanette was staring at the town's wall which still showed the scars where the English-made breach had been repaired with a lighter-coloured stone. 'Are you really nobly born?' she asked Thomas.

'Bastard born,' Thomas said.

'But to a nobleman?'

'He was the Count of Astarac,' Thomas said, then laughed because it was strange to think that Father Ralph, mad Father Ralph who had preached to the gulls on Hookton's beach, had been a count.

'So what's the badge of Astarac?' Jeanette asked.

'A yale,' Thomas told her, 'holding a cup,' and he showed her the faded silver patch on his black bowstave that was engraved with the strange creature that had horns, cloven hooves, claws, tusks and a lion's tail.

'I'll have a banner made for you,' Jeanette said.

'A banner? Why?'

'A man should display his badge,' Jeanette said.

'And you should leave La Roche-Derrien,' Thomas retorted. He kept trying to persuade her to leave the town, but she insisted she would stay. She doubted now she would ever get her son back and so she was determined to kill Charles of Blois with one of her crossbow's bolts, which were made of dense yew heartwood tipped with iron heads and fledged, not with feathers, but with stiff pieces of leather inserted into slits cut crosswise into the yew and then bound up with cord and glue. That was why she practised so

assiduously, for the chance to cut down the man who had raped her and taken her child.

Easter came before the enemy arrived. The weather was warm now. The hedgerows were full of nestlings and the meadows echoed with the shriek of partridges and on the day after Easter, when folk ate up the remnants of the feast that had broken their Lenten fast, the dreaded news at last arrived from Rennes.

That Charles of Blois had marched.

More than four thousand men left Rennes under the white ermine banner of the Duke of Brittany. Two thousand of them were cross-bowmen, most wearing the green and red livery of Genoa and bearing the city's badge of the Holy Grail on their right arms. They were mercenaries, hired and prized for their skill. A thousand infantrymen marched with them, the men who would dig the trenches and assault the broken walls of the English fortresses, and then there were over a thousand knights or men-at-arms, most of them French, who formed the hard armoured heart of Duke Charles's army. They marched towards La Roche-Derrien, but the real aim of the campaign was not to capture the town, which was of negligible value, but rather to draw Sir Thomas Dagworth and his small army into a pitched battle in which the knights and men-at-arms, mounted on their big armoured horses, would be released to smash their way through the English ranks.

A convoy of heavy carts carried nine siege machines, which needed the attentions of over a hundred engineers who understood how to assemble and work the giant devices that could hurl boulders the size of beer barrels further than a bow could drive an arrow. A Florentine gunner had offered six of his strange machines to Charles, but the Duke had turned them down. Guns were rare, expensive and, he believed, temperamental, while the old mechanical devices worked well enough if they were properly greased with tallow and Charles saw no reason to abandon them.

Over four thousand men left Rennes, but far more arrived in the fields outside La Roche-Derrien. Country folk who hated the English joined the army to gain revenge for all the cattle, harvests,

property and virginity their families had lost to the foreigners. Some were armed with nothing more than mattocks or axes, but when the time came to assault the town such angry men would be useful.

The army came to La Roche-Derrien and Charles of Blois heard the last of the town's gates slam shut. He sent a messenger to demand the garrison's surrender, knowing the request was futile, and while his tents were pitched he ordered other horsemen to patrol westwards on the roads leading to Finisterre, the world's end. They were there to warn him when Sir Thomas Dagworth's army marched to relieve the town, if indeed it did march. His spies had told Charles that Dagworth could not even raise a thousand men. 'And how many of those will be archers?' he asked.

'At most, your grace, five hundred.' The man who answered was a priest, one of the many who served in Charles's retinue. The Duke was known as a pious man and liked to employ priests as advisers, secretaries and, in this case, as a spymaster. 'At most five hundred,' the priest repeated, 'but in truth, your grace, far fewer.'

'Fewer? How so?'

'Fever in Finisterre,' the priest answered, then smiled thinly. 'God is good to us.'

'Amen to that. And how many archers are in the town garrison?'

'Sixty healthy men, your grace' – the priest had Belas's latest report – 'just sixty.'

Charles grimaced. He had been defeated by English archers before, even when he had so outnumbered them that defeat had seemed impossible, and, as a result, he was properly wary of the long arrows, but he was also an intelligent man and he had given the problem of the English war bow a deal of thought. It was possible to defeat the weapon, he thought, and on this campaign he would show how it could be done. Cleverness, that most despised of soldierly qualities, would triumph, and Charles of Blois, styled by the French as the Duke and ruler of Brittany, was undeniably a clever man. He could read and write in six languages, spoke Latin better than most priests and was a master of rhetoric. He even looked clever with his thin, pale face and intense blue eyes, fair beard and moustache. He had been fighting his rivals for the dukedom almost all his adult life, but now, at last, he had gained the

ascendancy. The King of England, besieging Calais, was not reinforcing his garrisons in Brittany while the King of France, who was Charles's uncle, had been generous with men, which meant that Duke Charles at last outnumbered his enemies. By summer's end, he thought, he would be master of all his ancestral domains, but then he cautioned himself against over-confidence. 'Even five hundred archers,' he observed, 'even five hundred and sixty archers can be dangerous.' He had a precise voice, pedantic and dry, and the priests in his entourage often thought he sounded very like a priest himself.

'The Genoese will swamp them with bolts, your grace,' a priest assured the Duke.

'Pray God they do,' Charles said piously, though God, he thought, would need some help from human cleverness.

Next morning, under a late spring sun, Charles rode around La Roche-Derrien, though he kept far enough away so that no English arrow could reach him. The defenders had hung banners from the town walls. Some of the flags displayed the English cross of St George, others the white ermine badge of the Montfort Duke that was so similar to Charles's own device. Many of the flags were inscribed with insults aimed at Charles. One showed the Duke's white ermine with an English arrow through its bleeding belly, and another was evidently a picture of Charles himself being trampled under a great black horse, but most of the flags were pious exhortations inviting God's help or displaying the cross to show the attackers where heaven's sympathies were supposed to lie. Most besieged towns would also have flaunted the banners of their noble defenders, but La Roche-Derrien had few nobles, or at least few who displayed their badges, and none to match the ranks of the aristocrats in Charles's army. The three hawks of Evecque were displayed on the wall, but everyone knew Sir Guillaume had been dispossessed and had no more than three or four followers. One flag showed a red heart on a pale field and a priest in Charles's entourage thought it was the badge of the Douglas family in Scotland, but that was a nonsense for no Scotsman would be fighting for the English. Next to the red heart was a brighter banner showing a blue and white sea of wavy lines. 'Is that . . .' Charles began to ask, then paused, frowning.

'The badge of Armorica, your grace,' the Lord of Roncelets answered. Today, as Duke Charles circled the town, he was accompanied by his great lords so that the defenders would see their banners and be awed. Most were lords of Brittany; the Viscount Rohan and the Viscount Morgat rode close behind the Duke, then came the lords of Châteaubriant and of Roncelets, Laval, Guingamp, Rougé, Dinan, Redon and Malestroit, all of them mounted on high-stepping destriers, while from Normandy the Count of Coutances and the lords of Valognes and Carteret had brought their retainers to do battle for the nephew of their King.

'I thought Armorica was dead,' one of the Norman lords remarked.

'He has a son,' Roncelets answered.

'And a widow,' the Count of Guingamp said, 'and she's the traitorous bitch flying the banner.'

'A pretty traitorous bitch, though,' the Viscount Rohan said, and the lords laughed for they all knew how to treat unruly but pretty widows.

Charles grimaced at their unseemly laughter. 'When we take the town,' he ordered coldly, 'the dowager Countess of Armorica will not be hurt. She will be brought to me.' He had raped Jeanette once and he would rape her again, and when that pleasure was done he would marry her off to one of his men-at-arms who would teach her to mind her manners and to curb her tongue. Now he reined in his horse to watch as more banners were hung from the ramparts, all of them insults to him and his house. 'It's a busy garrison,' he said drily.

'Busy townspeople,' the Viscount Rohan snarled. 'Busy goddamn traitors.'

'Townsfolk?' Charles seemed puzzled. 'Why would the townsfolk support the English?'

'Trade,' Roncelets answered curtly.

'Trade?'

'They're becoming rich,' Roncelets growled, 'and they like it.'

'They like it enough to fight against their lord?' Charles asked in disbelief.

'A disloyal rabble,' Roncelets said dismissively.

'A rabble,' Charles said, 'that we shall have to impoverish.' He

spurred on, only checking his horse when he saw another nobleman's banner, this one showing a yale flourishing a chalice. So far he had not seen a single banner that promised a great ransom if its lord was captured, but this badge was a mystery. 'Whose is that?' he asked.

No one knew, but then a slim young man on a tall black horse answered from the rear of the Duke's entourage. 'The badge of Astarac, your grace, and it belongs to an imposter.' The man who had answered had come from France with a hundred grim horsemen liveried in plain black and he was accompanied by a Dominican with a frightening race. Charles of Blois was glad to have the black-liveried men in his army, for they were all hard and experienced soldiers, but he did feel somewhat nervous of them. They were somehow too hard, too experienced.

'An imposter?' he repeated and spurred on. 'Then we do not need to worry ourselves about him.'

There were three gates on the town's landward side and a fourth, opening onto the bridge, facing the river. Charles planned to besiege each of those gates so that the garrison would be trapped like foxes with their earths stopped. 'The army,' he decreed when the lords returned to the ducal tent, which had been raised close to the windmill that stood on the slight hill to the east of the town, 'will be divided into four parts, and one part will face each gate.' The lords listened and a priest copied down the pronouncement so that history would have a true record of the Duke's martial genius.

Each of the four divisions of Charles's army would outnumber any relief force that Sir Thomas Dagworth could gather, but, to make himself even more secure, Charles ordered that the four encampments were to surround themselves with earthworks so that the English would be forced to attack across ditches, banks, palisades and thorn hedges. The obstacles would conceal Charles's men from the archers and give his Genoese crossbowmen cover while they rewound their weapons. The ground between the four encampments was to be cleared of hedges and other obstacles to leave a bare wilderness of grass and marsh.

'The English archer,' Charles told his lords, 'is not a man who will fight face to face. He kills from a distance and he hides behind hedges, thus frustrating our horses. We shall turn that tactic against

him.' The tent was big, white and airy, and the smell inside was of trampled grass and men's sweat. From beyond the canvas walls came the sound of dull thudding as the engineers used wooden mallets to assemble the biggest of the great siege engines.

'Our men,' Charles further decreed, 'will stay within their own defences. We shall thus make four fortresses that will stand at the four gates of the town and if the English send a relief force then those men will have to attack our fortresses. Archers cannot kill men they cannot see.' He paused to make sure those simple words were understood. 'Archers,' he said again, 'cannot kill men they cannot see. Remember that! Our crossbows will be behind banks of earth, we will be screened by hedges and hidden by palisades, and the enemy will be out in the open where they can be cut down.'

There were growls of agreement for the Duke made sense. Archers could not kill invisible men. Even the fierce Dominican who had come with the soldiers in black looked impressed.

The midday bells rang from the town. One, the loudest, was cracked and gave a harsh note. 'La Roche-Derrien,' the Duke continued, 'does not matter. Whether it falls or not is of little consequence. What matters is that we draw our enemy's army out to attack us. Dagworth will probably come to protect La Roche-Derrien. When he arrives we shall crush him and once he is broken then only the English garrisons will be left and we shall take them one by one until, at summer's end, all Brittany is ours.' He spoke slowly and simply, knowing it was best to spell out the campaign for these men who, though they were tough as rams, were not renowned as thinkers. 'And when Brittany is ours,' he went on, 'there will be gifts of land, of manors and of strongholds.' A much louder growl of approbation sounded and the listening men grinned for there would be more than land, manors and castles as the rewards of victory. There would be gold, silver and women. Lots of women. The growl turned into laughter as the men realized they were all thinking the same thing.

'But it is here' – Charles's voice called his audience to order – 'that we make our victory possible, and we do it by denying the English archer his targets. An archer cannot kill men he cannot see!' He paused again, looking at his audience and he saw them

311

nodding as the simple truth of that assertion at last penetrated their skulls. 'We shall all be in our own fortress, one of four fortresses, and when the English army comes to relieve the siege they will attack one of those fortresses. That English army will be small. Fewer than a thousand men! Suppose, then, that it begins by attacking the fort I shall make here. What will the rest of you do?'

He waited for an answer and, after a while, the Lord of Roncelets, as uncertain as a schoolboy giving a response to his master, frowned and made a suggestion. 'Come to help your grace?'

The other lords nodded and smiled agreement.

'No!' Charles said angrily. 'No! No! No!' He waited, making sure they had understood the simple word. 'If you leave your fortress,' he explained, 'then you offer the English archer a target. It is what he wants! He will want to tempt us from behind our walls to cut us down with his arrows. So what do we do? We stay behind our walls. *We stay behind our walls.*' Did they understand that? It was the key to victory. Keep the men hidden and the English must lose. Sir Thomas Dagworth's army would be forced to assault earth walls and thorn hedges and the crossbowmen would spit them on quarrels and when the English were so thinned that only a couple of hundred remained on their feet the Duke would release his men-at-arms to slaughter the remnant. 'You do not leave your fortresses,' he insisted, 'and any man who does will forfeit my generosity.' That threat sobered the Duke's listeners. 'If even one of your men leaves the sanctuary of the walls,' Charles continued, 'we shall make sure that you will not share in the distribution of land at the end of the campaign. Is that plain, gentlemen? Is that plain?'

It was plain. It was simple.

Charles of Blois would make four fortresses to oppose the four gates of the town and the English, when they came, would be forced to assault those newly made walls. And even the smallest of the Duke's four forts would have more defenders than the English had attackers, and those defenders would be sheltered, and their weapons would be lethal, and the English would die and so Brittany would pass to the House of Blois.

Cleverness. It would win wars and make reputations. And once

Charles had shown how to defeat the English here he would defeat them through all France.

Because Charles dreamed of a crown heavier than Brittany's ducal coronet. He dreamed of France, but it must begin here, in the flooded fields about La Roche-Derrien, where the English archer would be taught his place.

In hell.

The nine siege engines were all trebuchets, the largest of them capable of throwing a stone weighing twice the weight of a grown man for almost three hundred paces. All nine had been made at Regensburg in Bavaria and the senior engineers who accompanied the gaunt machines were all Bavarians who understood the intricacies of the weapons. The two biggest had throwing beams over fifty feet long and even the two smallest, which were placed on the far bank of the Jaudy to threaten the bridge and its barbican, had beams thirty-six feet long.

The biggest two, which were named Hellgiver and Widowmaker, were placed at the foot of the hill on which the windmill stood. In essence each was a simple machine, merely a long beam mounted on an axle like a giant's balance or a child's see-saw, only one end of the see-saw was three times longer than the other. The shorter end was weighted with a huge wooden box that was filled with lead weights, while the longer end, which actually threw the missile, was attached to a great windlass which drew it down to the ground and so raised the ten tons of lead counterweights. The stone missile was placed in a leather sling some fifteen feet long, which was attached to the longer arm. When the beam was released so that the counterweight slammed down, the longer end whipped up into the sky and the sling whipped even faster and the boulder was released from the sling's leather cradle to curve through the sky and crash down onto its target. That much was simple. What was hard was to keep the mechanism greased with tallow, to construct a winch strong enough to haul the long beam down to the ground, to make a container strong enough to thump down again and again and not spill the ten tons of lead weights and, trickiest of all, to

fashion a device strong enough to hold the long beam down against the weight of the lead yet capable of releasing the beam safely. These were the matters on which the Bavarians were experts and for which they were paid so generously.

There were many who said that the Bavarians' expertise was redundant. Guns were much smaller and hurled their missiles with greater force, but Duke Charles had applied his intelligence to the comparison and decided on the older technology. Guns were slow and prone to explosions that killed their expensive gunners. They were also painfully slow because the gap between the missile and the gun's barrel had to be sealed to contain the powder's force and so it was necessary to pack the cannon ball about with wet loam, and that needed time to dry before the powder could be ignited, and even the most skilful gunners from Italy could not fire a weapon more than three or four times a day. And when a gun fired it spat a ball weighing only a few pounds. While it was true that the small ball flew with a velocity so great that it could not even be seen, nevertheless the older trebuchets could throw a missile of twenty or thirty times the weight three or four times in every hour. La Roche-Derrien, the Duke decided, would be hammered the old-fashioned way, and so the little town was surrounded by the nine trebuchets. As well as Hellgiver and Widowmaker, there was Stone-Hurler, Crusher, Gravedigger, Stonewhip, Spiteful, Destroyer and Hand of God.

Each trebuchet was constructed on a platform made of wooden beams and protected by a palisade that was tall and stout enough to stop any arrow. Some of the peasants who had joined the army were trained to stand close to the palisades and be ready to throw water over any fire arrows that the English might use to burn the fences down and so expose the trebuchets' engineers. Other peasants dug the ditches and threw up the earthen banks that formed the Duke's four fortresses. Where possible they used existing ditches or incorporated the thick blackthorn hedges into the defences. They made barriers of sharpened stakes and dug pits to break horses' legs. The four parts of the Duke's army ringed themselves with such defences and, day after day, as the walls grew and the trebuchets took shape from the pieces transported on the wagons, the Duke had his men practise forming their lines of battle. The Genoese

crossbowmen manned the half-finished walls while behind them the knights and men-at-arms paraded on foot. Some men grumbled that such practices were a waste of time, but others saw how the Duke intended to fight and they approved. The English archers would be baffled by the walls, ditches and palisades and the crossbows would pick them off one by one, and finally the enemy would be forced to attack across the earth walls and the flooded ditches to be slaughtered by the waiting men-at-arms.

After a week of back-breaking work the trebuchets were assembled and their counterpoise boxes had been filled with great pigs of lead. Now the engineers had to demonstrate an even subtler skill, the art of dropping their great stones one after the other onto the exact same spot of the wall so that the ramparts would be battered away and a path opened into the town. Then, once the relieving army was defeated, the Duke's men could assault La Roche-Derrien and put its treasonous inhabitants to the sword.

The Bavarian engineers selected their first stones carefully, then trimmed the length of the slings to affect the range of their machines. It was a fine spring morning. Kestrels soared, buttercups dotted the fields, trout were rising to the mayflies, the wild garlic was blossoming white and pigeons flew through the new leaves of the green woods. It was the loveliest time of the year and Duke Charles, whose spies told him that Sir Thomas Dagworth's English army had yet to leave western Brittany, anticipated triumph. 'The Bavarians,' he told one of his attendant priests, 'may begin.'

The trebuchet named Hellgiver shot first. A lever was pulled that extracted a thick metal pin from a staple attached to the long arm of Hellgiver's beam. Ten tons of lead dropped with a crash that could be heard in Tréguier, the long arm whipped up and the sling whirled at the arm's end with the sound of a sudden gale and a boulder arched into the sky. It seemed to hang for a moment, a great stone lump in the kestrel-haunted sky, and then, like a thunderbolt, it fell.

The killing had begun.

The first stone, thrown by Hellgiver, crashed through the roof of a dyer's house close to St Brieuc's church and took off the heads of an English man-at-arms and the dyer's wife. A joke went through the garrison that the two bodies were so crushed together by the boulder that they would go on coupling throughout eternity. The stone which killed them, a rock about the size of a barrel, had missed the eastern ramparts by no more than twenty feet and the Bavarian engineers made adjustments to the sling and the next stone thumped just short of the wall, spewing up filth and sewage from the ditch. The third boulder hit the wall plumb and then a monstrous thump announced that Widowmaker had just shot its first missile and one after the other Stone-Hurler, Crusher, Grave-digger, Stonewhip, Spiteful, Destroyer and Hand of God added their contributions.

Richard Totesham did his best to blunt the assault of the trebu-chets. It was evident that Charles was attempting to make four breaches, one on each side of the town, and so Totesham ordered vast bags to be sewn and stuffed with straw and the bags were placed to cushion the walls, which were further protected by baulks of timber. Those precautions served to slow the process of making the breaches, but the Bavarians were sending some of their missiles deep into the town and nothing could be done to shield the houses from those plunging boulders. Some townsfolk argued that Tote-sham should construct a trebuchet of his own and try to break the enemy's machines, but he doubted there was time and instead a giant crossbow was fashioned from ships' spars that had been brought upstream from Tréguier before the siege began. Tréguier

316

was now deserted for, lacking walls, its inhabitants had either come to La Roche-Derrien for shelter, fled to sea in their ships or gone over to Charles's camp.

Totesham's springald was thirty feet in width and shot a bolt eight feet long propelled by a cord made from braided leather. It was cocked by means of a ship's windlass. It took four days to make the weapon and the very first time they tried to use it the spar-arm broke. It was a bad omen, and there was an even worse one next morning when a horse drawing a cart of night soil broke free from its harness and kicked a child in the head. The child died. Later that day a stone from one of the smaller trebuchets across the river plunged into Richard Totesham's house and brought down half the upper floor and very nearly killed his baby. Over a score of mercenaries tried to desert the garrison that night and some must have got clean away, others joined Charles's army and one, who had been carrying a message for Sir Thomas Dagworth concealed in a boot, was caught and beheaded. Next morning his severed head, with the letter fixed between his teeth, was hurled into the town by the trebuchet called the Hand of God and the spirits of the garrison plummeted even further.

'I am not sure,' Mordecai told Thomas, 'whether omens can be trusted.'

'Of course they can.'

'I should like to hear your reasons. But show me your urine first.'

'You said I was cured,' Thomas protested.

'Eternal vigilance, dear Thomas, is the price of health. Piss for me.'

Thomas obeyed, Mordecai held the liquid up to the sun, then dipped a finger in it and dabbed it onto his tongue. 'Splendid!' he said. 'Clear, pure and not too saline. That is a good omen, is it not?'

'That's a symptom,' Thomas said, 'not an omen.'

'Ah.' Mordecai smiled at the correction. They were in the small back yard behind Jeanette's kitchen where the doctor watched the house-martins bringing mud to their new nests beneath the eaves. 'Enlighten me, Thomas,' he said with another smile, 'on the matter of omens.'

'When our Lord was crucified,' Thomas said, 'there was darkness in daytime and a curtain in the temple was torn in two.'

'You are saying that omens are secreted at the very heart of your faith?'

'And yours too, surely?' Thomas asked.

Mordecai flinched as a boulder crunched down somewhere in the town. The sound reverberated, then there was another splintering crash as a weakened roof or floor gave way. Dogs howled and a woman screamed. 'They're doing it deliberately,' Mordecai said.

'Of course,' Thomas said. Not only was the enemy sending boulders to fall on the tight small houses of the town, but they sometimes used the trebuchets to lob the rotting corpses of cattle or pigs or goats to splatter their filth and stench through the streets.

Mordecai waited till the woman had stopped screaming. 'I don't think I believe in omens,' he said. 'We suffer some bad luck in the town and everyone assumes we are doomed, but how do we know there is not some ill fortune afflicting the enemy?'

Thomas said nothing. Birds squabbled in the thatch, oblivious that a cat was stalking just below the roof ridge.

'What do you want, Thomas?' Mordecai asked.

'Want?'

'What do you want?'

Thomas grimaced and held out his right hand with its crooked fingers. 'For these to be straight.'

'And I want to be young again,' Mordecai said impatiently. 'Your fingers are mended. They are misshapen, but mended. Now tell me what you want.'

'What I want,' Thomas said, 'is to kill the men who killed Eleanor. To bring Jeanette's son back. Then to be an archer. Just that. An archer.' He wanted the Grail too, but he did not like to talk of that with Mordecai.

Mordecai tugged at his beard. 'To kill the men who killed Eleanor?' he mused aloud. 'I think you'll do that. Jeanette's son? Maybe you will do that too, though I don't understand why you wish to please her. You don't want to marry Jeanette, do you?'

'Marry her!' Thomas laughed. 'No.'

'Good.'

'Good?' Thomas was offended now.

'I have always enjoyed talking with alchemists,' Mordecai said,

'and I have often seen them mix sulphur and quicksilver. There is a theory that all metals are composed of those two substances, did you know? The proportions vary, of course, but my point, dear Thomas, is that if you put quicksilver and sulphur into a vessel, then heat it, the result is very often calamitous.' He mimed an explosion with his hands. 'That, I think, is you and Jeanette. Besides, I cannot see her married to an archer. To a king? Yes. To a duke? Maybe. To a count or an earl? Certainly. But to an archer?' He shook his head. 'There is nothing wrong with being an archer, Thomas. It's a useful skill in this wicked world.' He sat silent for a few heartbeats. 'My son is training to be a doctor.'

Thomas smiled. 'I sense a reproof.'

'A reproof?'

'Your son will be a healer and I'm a killer.'

Mordecai shook his head. 'Benjamin is training to be a physician, but he would rather be a soldier. He wants to be a killer.'

'Then why—' Thomas stopped because the answer was obvious.

'Jews cannot carry weapons,' Mordecai said, 'that is why. No, I meant no reproof. I think, as soldiers go, Thomas, that you are a good man.' He paused and frowned because another stone from one of the bigger trebuchets had slammed into a building not far away and, as the echoing crash subsided, he waited for the screams. None came. 'Your friend Will is a good man, too,' Mordecai went on, 'but I fear he's no longer an archer.'

Thomas nodded. Will Skeat was cured, but not restored. 'It would have been better, I sometimes think—' Thomas began.

'If he had died?' Mordecai finished the thought. 'Wish death on no man, Thomas, it comes soon enough without a wish. Sir William will go home to England, no doubt, and your Earl will look after him.'

The fate of all old soldiers, Thomas thought. To go home and die on the charity of the family they served. 'Then I'll go to the siege of Calais when all this is over,' Thomas said, 'and see if Will's archers need a new leader.'

Mordecai smiled. 'You won't look for the Grail?'

'I don't know where it is,' Thomas said.

'And your father's book?' Mordecai asked. 'It didn't help?'

Thomas had been poring over the copy Jeanette had made. He

thought his father must have used some kind of code, though try as he might he could not pierce the code's workings. Or else, in its ramblings, the book was merely a symptom of Father Ralph's troubled mind. Yet Thomas was sure of one thing. His father had believed he possessed the Grail. 'I will look for the Grail,' Thomas said, 'but I sometimes think the only way to seek it is *not* to search for it.' He looked up, startled, as there was a sudden scrabbling sound on the roof. The cat had made a rush and almost lost its footing as birds scattered upwards.

'Another omen?' Mordecai suggested, looking up at the escaping birds. 'Surely a good one?'

'Besides,' Thomas said, 'what do you know of the Grail?'

'I am a Jew. What do I know of anything?' Mordecai asked innocently. 'What would happen, Thomas, if you found the Grail?' He did not wait for an answer. 'Do you think,' he went on instead, 'that the world will become a better place? Is it just lacking the Grail? Is that all?' There was still no answer. 'It's a thing like Abracadabra, is that it?' Mordecai said sadly.

'The devil?' Thomas was shocked.

'Abracadabra isn't the devil!' Mordecai answered, equally shocked. 'It's simply a charm. Some foolish Jews believe if you write it in the form of a triangle and hang it about your neck then you'll not suffer from the ague! What nonsense! The only cure for an ague is a warm poultice of cow dung, but folk will put their trust in charms and, I fear, in omens too, yet I do not think God works through the one or reveals Himself through the other.'

'Your God,' Thomas said, 'is a very long way away.'

'I rather fear he is.'

'Mine is close,' Thomas said, 'and He does show Himself.'

'Then you're fortunate,' Mordecai said. Jeanette's distaff and spindle were on the bench beside him and he put the distaff under his left arm and tried to spin some thread from the wool bundled about its head, but he could make nothing of it. 'You are fortunate,' he said again, 'and I hope that when Charles's troops break in that your God stays close. As for the rest of us, I suppose we're doomed?'

'If they break in,' Thomas said, 'then either take refuge in a church or try and escape by the river.'

'I can't swim.'

'Then the church is your best hope.'

'I doubt that,' Mordecai said, putting down the distaff. 'What Totesham should do,' he said sadly, 'is surrender. Let us all leave.'

'He won't do that.'

Mordecai shrugged. 'So we must die.'

Yet, the very next day, he was given a chance to escape when Totesham said that anyone who did not want to suffer the privations of the siege could leave the town by the southern gate, but no sooner was it thrown open than a force of Charles's men-at-arms, all in mail and with their faces hidden by their helmets' grey visors, blocked the road. No more than a hundred folk had decided to go, all of them women and children, but Charles's men-at-arms were there to say they would not be allowed to abandon La Roche-Derrien. It was not in the besiegers' interest to have fewer mouths for the garrison to feed and so the grey men barred the road and Totesham's soldiers shut the town gate and the women and children were stranded all day.

That evening the trebuchets ceased their work for the first time since the stone had killed the dyer's wife and her lover and, in the strange silence, a messenger came from Charles's encampment. A trumpeter and a white flag announced that he wanted a truce and Totesham ordered an English trumpeter to respond to the Breton and for a white banner to be waved above the southern gate. The Breton messenger waited until a man of rank came to the walls, then he gestured at the women and children. 'These folk,' he said, 'cannot be allowed to pass through our lines. They will starve here.'

'This is the pity your master has for his people?' Totesham's envoy responded. He was an English priest who spoke Breton and French.

'He has such pity for them,' the messenger answered, 'that he would free them of England's chains. Tell your master that he has until this evening's angelus to surrender the town, and if he does he will be permitted to march out with all his weapons, banners, horses, families, servants and possessions.'

It was a generous offer but the priest did not even consider it. 'I will tell him,' the priest said, 'but only if you tell your master that we have food for a year and weapons enough to kill all of you twice over.'

The messenger bowed, the priest returned the compliment and

the parley was over. The trebuchets began their work again and, at nightfall, Totesham ordered the town gates opened and the fugitives were allowed back inside to the jeers of those who had not fled.

Thomas, like every man in La Roche-Derrien, served time on the ramparts. It was tedious work for Charles of Blois took great care to ensure that none of his forces strayed within bowshot of the English archers, but there was some diversion to be had in watching the great trebuchets. They were cranked down so slowly that it seemed the vast beams were hardly moving, but gradually, almost imperceptibly, the big wooden box with its lead weights would rise from behind the protective palisade and the long arm would sink out of sight. Then, when the long arm was winched as low as it could go, nothing would happen for a long time, presumably because the engineers were loading the sling and then, just when it seemed nothing ever would happen, the counterweight would drop, the palisade would quiver, startled birds flash up from the grass and the long arm would slash up, judder, the sling would whip about and a stone arc into the air. The sound would come then, the monstrous crash of the falling counterweight, followed a heartbeat later by the thump of the stone onto the broken ramparts. More straw-filled bags would be thrown onto the growing breach, but the missiles still did their damage and so Totesham ordered his men to begin making new walls behind the growing breaches.

Some men, including Thomas and Robbie, wanted to make a sally. Put together sixty men, they argued, and let them stream out of the town at first light. They could easily overrun one or two of the trebuchets, soak the machines in oil and pitch and throw burning brands into the tangle of ropes and timber, but Totesham refused. His garrison was too small, he argued, and he did not want to lose even a half-dozen men before he needed to fight Charles's men in the breaches.

He lost men anyway. By the third week of the siege Charles of Blois had finished his own defensive works and the four portions of his army were all protected behind earth walls, hedges, palisades and ditches. He had scoured the land between his encampments of any obstacles so that when a relieving army came its archers would have nowhere to hide. Now, with his own encampments fortified and the trebuchets biting ever bigger holes in La Roche-Derrien's

walls, he sent his crossbowmen forward to harass the ramparts. They came in pairs, one man with the crossbow and his partner holding a pavise, a shield so tall, wide and stoutly made that it could protect both men. The pavises were painted, some with holy imprecations, but most with insults in French, English and, in some cases, because the crossbowmen were Genoese, Italian. Their quarrels battered the wall, whistled about the defenders' heads and smacked into the thatch of the houses beyond the walls. Sometimes the Genoese would shoot fire arrows and Totesham had six squads of men who did nothing except chase down fires in thatch and, when they were not extinguishing flames, they hauled water out of the River Jaudy and soaked the thatch roofs that were nearest the ramparts and thus most in danger from the crossbowmen.

The English archers shot back, but the crossbowmen were mostly hidden behind their pavises and, when they did shoot, they exposed themselves for only a heartbeat. Some died all the same, but they were also bringing down archers on the town's walls. Jeanette often joined Thomas on the southern rampart and loosed her bolts from a crenellation by the gate. A crossbow could be fired from a kneeling position so she did not expose much of her body to danger, while Thomas had to stand to loose an arrow. 'You shouldn't be here,' he told her every time and she would mimic his words, then stoop to rewind her bow.

'Do you remember,' she asked him, 'the first siege?'

'When you were shooting at me?'

'Let's hope I'm more accurate now,' she said, then propped the bow on the wall, aimed and pulled the trigger. The bolt smacked into a pavise that was already stuck with feathered English arrows. Beyond the crossbowmen was the earth wall of the closest encampment above which showed the ungainly beams of two trebuchets and, beyond them, the gaudy flags of some of Charles's lords. Jeanette recognized the banners of Rohan, Laval, Malestroit, and Roncelets, and the first sight of that wasplike banner had filled her with anger and then she had cried for the thought of her son in Roncelets's distant tower. 'I wish they'd assault now,' she said, 'and I could put a bolt in Roncelets as well as Blois.'

'They won't attack until they've defeated Dagworth,' Thomas said.

'You think he's coming?'

'I think that's why they're here,' Thomas said, nodding towards the enemy, then he stood, drew the bow and launched an arrow at a crossbowman who had just stepped out from behind his shield. The man ducked back a heartbeat before Thomas's arrow hissed past him. Thomas crouched again. 'Charles knows he can pluck us whenever he wants,' he said, 'but what he really wants is to crush Dagworth.'

For when Sir Thomas Dagworth was crushed there would be no English field army left in Brittany and the fortresses would inevitably fall, one by one, and Charles would have his duchy.

Then, a month after Charles had arrived, when the hedges about his four fortresses were white with hawthorn blossom and the petals were blowing from the apple trees and the banks of the river were thick with iris and the poppies were a brilliant red in the growing rye, there was a drift of smoke in the south-western sky. The watchers on La Roche-Derrien's walls saw scouts riding from the enemy encampment and they knew that the smoke must come from campfires which meant that an army was coming. Some feared it might be reinforcements for the enemy, but they were reassured by others who claimed, truly, that only friends would be approaching from the south-west. What Richard Totesham and the others who knew the truth did not reveal was that any relieving force would be small, much smaller than Charles's army, and that it was coming towards a trap that Charles had made.

For Charles's ploy had worked and Sir Thomas Dagworth had taken the bait.

Charles of Blois summoned his lords and commanders to the big tent beside the mill. It was Saturday and the enemy force was now a short march away and, inevitably, there were hotheads in his ranks who wanted to strap on their plate armour, hoist up their lances and clatter off on horseback to be killed by the English archers. Fools abounded, Charles thought, then dashed their hopes by making it clear that no one except the scouts was to leave any

of the four encampments. 'No one!' He pounded the table, almost upsetting the ink pot belonging to the clerk who copied down his words. 'No one will leave! Do you all understand that?' He looked from face to face and thought again what fools his lords were. 'We stay behind our entrenchments,' he told them, 'and they will come to us. They will come to us and they will be killed.'

Some of the lords looked disgruntled, for there was little glory in fighting behind earth walls and damp ditches when a man could be galloping on a destrier, but Charles of Blois was firm and even the richest of his lords feared his threat that any man who disobeyed him would not share in the distribution of land and wealth that would follow the conquest of Brittany.

Charles picked up a piece of parchment. 'Our scouts have ridden close to Sir Thomas Dagworth's column,' he said in his precise voice, 'and we now have an accurate estimate of their numbers.' Knowing that every man in the tent wanted to hear the enemy's strength, he paused, because he wanted to invest this announcement with drama, but he could not help smiling as he revealed the figures. 'Our enemies,' he said, 'threaten us with three hundred men-at-arms and four hundred archers.'

There was a pause as the numbers were understood, then came an explosion of laughter. Even Charles, usually so pallid, unbending and stern, joined in. It was risible! It was actually impertinent! Brave, perhaps, but utterly foolhardy. Charles of Blois had four thousand men and hundreds of peasant volunteers who, though not actually encamped inside his earthworks, could be relied on to help massacre an enemy. He had two thousand of the finest crossbowmen in Europe, he had a thousand armoured knights, many of them champions of great tournaments, and Sir Thomas Dagworth was coming with seven hundred men? The town might contribute another hundred or two hundred, but even at their most hopeful the English could not muster more than a thousand men and Charles had four times that number. 'They will come, gentlemen,' he told his excited lords, 'and they will die here.'

There were two roads on which they might approach. One came from the west and it was the most direct route, but it led to the far side of the River Jaudy and Charles did not think Dagworth would use that road. The other curled about the besieged town to approach

from the south-east and that road led straight towards the largest of Charles's four encampments, the eastern encampment where he was in personal command and where the largest trebuchets pounded La Roche-Derrien's walls.

'Let me tell you, gentlemen' – Charles stilled the amusement of his commanders – 'what I believe Sir Thomas will do. What I would do if I were so unfortunate as to be in his shoes. I believe he will send a small but noisy force of men to approach us on the Lannion road' – that was the road that came from the west, the direct route – 'and he will send them during the night to tempt us into believing that he will attack our encampment across the river. He will expect us to reinforce that encampment and then, in the dawn, his real attack will come from the east. He hopes that most of our army will be stranded across the river and that he can come in the dawn and destroy the three encampments on this bank. That, gentlemen, is what he will probably attempt and it will fail. It will fail because we have one clear, hard rule and it will not be broken! No one leaves an encampment! No one! Stay behind your walls! We fight on foot, we make our battle lines and we let them come to us. Our crossbowmen will cut down their archers, then we, gentlemen, shall destroy their men-at-arms. But no one leaves the encampments! No one! We do not make ourselves targets for their bows. Do you understand?'

The Lord of Châteaubriant wanted to know what he was supposed to do if he was in his southern encampment and there was a fight going on in another of the forts. 'Do I just stand and watch?' he asked, incredulous.

'You stand and watch,' Duke Charles said in a steely voice. 'You do not leave your encampment. You understand? Archers cannot kill what they cannot see! Stay hidden!'

The Lord of Roncelets pointed out that the skies were clear and the moon nearly full. 'Dagworth is no fool,' he went on, 'and he'll know we've made these fortresses and cleared the land to deny them cover. So why won't he attack at night?'

'At night?' Charles asked.

'That way our crossbowmen can't see their targets, but the English will have enough moonlight to see their way across our entrenchments.'

326

It was a good point that Charles acknowledged by nodding brusquely. 'Fires,' he said.

'Fires?' a man asked.

'Build fires now! Big fires! When they come, light the fires. Turn night into day!'

His men laughed, liking the idea. Fighting on foot was not how lords and knights made their reputations, but they all understood that Charles had been thinking how to defeat the dreaded English archers and his ideas made sense even if they offered little chance for glory, but then Charles offered them a consolation. 'They will break, gentlemen,' he said, 'and when they do I shall have my trumpeter give seven blasts. Seven! And when you hear the trumpet, you may leave your encampments and pursue them.' There were growls of approval, for the seven trumpet blasts would release the armoured men on their huge horses to slaughter the remnants of Dagworth's force.

'Remember!' Charles pounded the table once more to get his men's attention. 'Remember! You do not leave your encampment until the trumpet sounds! Stay behind the trenches, stay behind the walls, let the enemy come to you and we shall win.' He nodded to show he was finished. 'And now, gentlemen, our priests will hear confessions. Let us cleanse our souls so that God can reward us with victory.'

Fifteen miles away, in the roofless refectory of a plundered and abandoned monastery, a much smaller group of men gathered. Their commander was a grey-haired man from Suffolk, stocky and gruff, who knew he faced a formidable challenge if he was to relieve La Roche-Derrien. Sir Thomas Dagworth listened to a Breton knight tell what his scouts had discovered: that Charles of Blois's men were still in the four encampments placed opposite the town's four gates. The largest encampment, where Charles's great banner of a white ermine flew, was to the east. 'It is built around the windmill,' the knight reported.

'I remember that mill,' Sir Thomas said. He ran his fingers through his short grey beard, a habit when he was thinking. 'That's where we must attack,' he said, so softly that he could have been talking to himself.

'It's where they're strongest,' a man warned him.

'So we shall distract them.' Sir Thomas stirred himself from his reverie. 'John' – he turned to a man in a tattered mail coat – 'take all the camp servants. Take the cooks, clerks, grooms, anyone who isn't a fighter. Then take all the carts and all the draught horses and make an approach on the Lannion road. You know it?'

'I can find it.'

'Leave before midnight. Lots of noise, John! You can take my trumpeter and a couple of drummers. Make 'em think the whole army's coming from the west. I want them sending men to the western encampment well before dawn.'

'And the rest of us?' the Breton knight asked.

'We'll march at midnight,' Sir Thomas said, 'and go east till we reach the Guingamp road.' That road approached La Roche-Derrien from the south-east. Since Sir Thomas's small force had marched from the west he hoped that the Guingamp road was the very last one Charles would expect him to use. 'It'll be a silent march,' he ordered, 'and we go on foot, all of us! Archers in front, men-at-arms behind, and we'll attack their eastern fort in the darkness.' By attacking in the dark Sir Thomas hoped he could cheat the crossbowmen of their targets and, better still, catch the enemy asleep.

So his plans were made: he would make a feint in the west and attack from the east. And that was exactly what Charles of Blois expected him to do.

Night fell. The English marched, Charles's men armed themselves and the town waited.

Thomas could hear the armourers in Charles's camp. He could hear their hammers closing the rivets of the plate armour and hear the scrape of stones on blades. The campfires in the four fortresses did not die down as they usually did, but were fed to keep them bright and high so that their light glinted off the iron straps that fastened the frames of the big trebuchets outlined against the fires' glow. From the ramparts Thomas could see men moving about in the nearest enemy encampment. Every few minutes a fire would glow even brighter as the armourers used bellows to fan the flames.

A child cried in a nearby house. A dog whined. Most of Totesham's

small garrison was on the ramparts and a good many of the towns-people were there too. No one was quite sure why they had gone to the walls for the relief army had to be a long way off still, yet few people wanted to go to bed. They expected something to happen and so they waited for it. The day of judgement, Thomas thought, would feel like this, as men and women waited for the heavens to break and the angels to descend and for the graves to open so that the virtuous dead could rise into the sky. His father, he remembered, had always wanted to be buried facing the west, but on the eastern edge of the graveyard, so that when he rose from the dead he would be looking at his parishioners as they came from the earth. 'They will need my guidance,' Father Ralph had said, and Thomas had made sure it had been done as he wished. Hookton's parishioners, buried so that if they sat up they would look eastwards towards the glory of Christ's second coming, would find their priest in front of them, offering them reassurance.

Thomas could have done with some reassurance this night. He was with Sir Guillaume and his two men-at-arms and they watched the enemy's preparations from a bastion on the town's south-east corner, close to where the tower of St Barnabé's church offered a vantage point. The remnants of Totesham's giant springald had been used to make a rickety bridge from the bastion to a window in the church tower and once through the window there was a ladder that climbed past a gaping hole torn by one of the Widowmaker's stones to the tower parapet. Thomas must have made the journey a half-dozen times before midnight because, from the parapet, it was just possible to see over the palisade into the largest of Charles's camps. It was while he was on the tower that Robbie came to the rampart beneath. 'I want you to look at this,' Robbie called up to him, and flourished a newly painted shield. 'You like it?'

Thomas peered down and, in the moonlight, saw something red. 'What is it?' he asked. 'A blood smear?'

'You blind English bastard,' Robbie said, 'it's the red heart of Douglas!'

'Ah. From up here it looks like something died on the shield.'

But Robbie was proud of his shield. He admired it in the moon-light. 'There was a fellow painting a new devil on the wall in St Goran's church,' he said, 'and I paid him to do this.'

329

'I hope you didn't pay him too much,' Thomas said.

'You're just envious.' Robbie propped the shield against the parapet before edging over the makeshift bridge to the tower. He vanished through the window then reappeared at Thomas's side. 'What are they doing?' he asked, gazing eastwards.

'Jesus,' Thomas blasphemed, because something was at last happening. He was staring past the great black shapes of Hellgiver and Widowmaker into the eastern encampment where men, hundreds of men, were forming a battle line. Thomas had assumed that any fight would not start until dawn, yet now it looked as though Charles of Blois was readying to fight in the night's black heart.

'Sweet Jesus,' Sir Guillaume, summoned to the tower's top, echoed Thomas's surprise.

'The bastards are expecting a fight,' Robbie said, for Charles's men were lining shoulder to shoulder. They had their backs to the town and the moon glinted off the espaliers that covered the knights' shoulders and touched the blades of spears and axes white.

'Dagworth must be coming.' Sir Guillaume said.

'At night?' Robbie asked.

'Why not?' Sir Guillaume retorted, then shouted down to one of his men-at-arms to go and tell Totesham what was happening. 'Wake him up,' he snarled when the man wanted to know what he should do if the garrison commander was asleep. 'Of course he's not asleep,' he added to Thomas. 'Totesham might be a bloody Englishman, but he's a good soldier.'

Totesham was not asleep, but nor had he been aware that the enemy was formed for battle and, after he had negotiated the precarious bridge to St Barnabé's tower, he gazed at Charles's troops with his customary sour expression. 'Reckon we'll have to lend a hand,' he said.

'I thought you didn't approve of sorties beyond the wall?' Sir Guillaume, who had chafed under that restriction, observed.

'This is the battle that saves us,' Totesham said. 'If we lose this fight then the town falls, so we must do what we can to win it.' He sounded bleak, then he shrugged and turned back to the tower's ladder. 'God help us,' he said softly as he climbed down into the shadows. He knew Sir Thomas Dagworth's relieving army would be small and he feared it would be much smaller than he dared

imagine, but when it attacked the enemy encampment the garrison had to be ready to help. He did not want to alert the enemy to the likelihood of a sortie from the battered gates and so he did not sound the church bells to gather his troops, but rather sent men through all the streets to summon the archers and men-at-arms to the market square outside St Brieuc's church. Thomas went back to Jeanette's house and pulled on his mail haubergeon, which Robbie had brought back from the Roncelets raid, then he strapped his sword belt in place, fumbling with the buckle because his fingers were still clumsy at such finicky things. He hung the arrow bag on his left shoulder, slid the black bow out of its linen cover, put a spare bowcord in his sallet, then pulled the sallet onto his head. He was ready.

And so, he saw, was Jeanette. She had her own haubergeon and helmet and Thomas gaped at her. 'You can't join the sortie!' he said.

'Join the sortie?' She sounded surprised. 'When you all leave the town, Thomas, who will guard the walls?'

'Oh.' He felt foolish.

She smiled, stepped to him and gave him a kiss. 'Now go,' she said, 'and God go with you.'

Thomas went to the marketplace. The garrison was gathering there, but they were desperately few in number. A tavern-keeper rolled a barrel of ale into the square, tapped it and let men help themselves. A smith was sharpening swords and axes in the light of a cresseted torch that burned outside the porch of St Brieuc's and his stone rang on long steel blades, the sound strangely mournful in the night. It was warm. Bats flickered about the church and dipped into the tangled moon-cast shadows of a house ruined by a trebuchet's direct hit. Women were bringing food to the soldiers and Thomas remembered how, just the year before, these same women had screamed as the English scrambled into the town. It had been a night of rape, robbery and murder, yet now the townsfolk did not want their occupiers to leave and the market square was becoming ever more crowded as men from the town brought makeshift weapons to help the foray. Most were armed with the axes they used to chop their firewood, though a few had swords or spears, and some townsmen even possessed leather or mail armour. They

far outnumbered the garrison and would at least make the sally seem formidable.

'Christ Jesus.' A sour voice spoke behind Thomas. 'What in Christ's name is that?'

Thomas turned and saw the lanky figure of Sir Geoffrey Carr staring at Robbie's shield, which was propped against the steps of a stone cross in the market's centre. Robbie also turned to look at the Scarecrow who was leading his six men.

'Looks like a squashed turd,' the Scarecrow said. His voice was slurred and it was evident he had spent the evening in one of the town's many taverns.

'It's mine,' Robbie said.

Sir Geoffrey kicked the shield. 'Is that the bloody heart of Douglas, boy?'

'It's my badge,' Robbie said, exaggerating his Scottish accent, 'if that's what you mean.' Men all about had stopped to listen.

'I knew you were a Scot,' the Scarecrow said, sounding even more drunk, 'but I didn't know you were a damned Douglas. And what the hell is a Douglas doing here?' The Scarecrow raised his voice to appeal to the assembled men. 'Whose side is bloody Scotland on, eh? Whose side? And the goddamn Douglases have been fighting us since they were spawned from the devil's own arsehole!' The Scarecrow staggered, then pulled the whip from his belt and let its coils ripple down. 'Sweet Jesus,' he shouted, 'but his goddamn family has impoverished good Englishmen. They're goddamn thieves! Spies!'

Robbie dragged his sword free and the whip lashed up, but Sir Guillaume shoved Robbie out of the way before the clawed tip could slash his face, then Sir Guillaume's sword was drawn and he and Thomas were standing beside Robbie on the steps of the cross. 'Robbie Douglas,' Sir Guillaume shouted, 'is my friend.'

'And mine,' Thomas said.

'Enough!' A furious Richard Totesham pushed through the crowd. 'Enough!'

The Scarecrow appealed to Totesham. 'He's a damned Scot!'

'Good God, man,' Totesham snarled, 'we've got Frenchmen, Welshmen, Flemings, Irishmen and Bretons in this garrison. What the hell difference does it make?'

'He's a Douglas!' the Scarecrow insisted drunkenly. 'He's an enemy!'

'He's my friend!' Thomas bellowed, inviting to fight anyone who wished to side with Sir Geoffrey.

'Enough!' Totesham's anger was big enough to fill the whole marketplace. 'We have fight enough on our hands without behaving like children! Do you vouch for him?' he demanded of Thomas.

'I vouch for him.' It was Will Skeat who answered. He pushed through the crowd and put an arm about Robbie's shoulders. 'I vouch for him, Dick.'

'Then Douglas or not,' Totesham said, 'he's no enemy of mine.' He turned and walked away.

'Sweet Jesus!' The Scarecrow was still angry. He had been impoverished by the house of Douglas and he was still poor – the risk he had taken in pursuing Thomas had not paid off because he had found no treasure – and now all his enemies seemed united in Thomas and Robbie. He staggered again, then spat at Robbie. 'I burn men who wear the heart of Douglas,' he said, 'I burn them!'

'He does too,' Thomas said softly.

'Burns them?' Robbie asked.

'At Durham,' Thomas said, his gaze on Sir Geoffrey's eyes, 'he burned three prisoners.'

'You did what?' Robbie demanded.

The Scarecrow, drunk as he was, was suddenly aware of the intensity of Robbie's anger, and aware too that he had not gained the sympathy of the men in the marketplace, who preferred Will Skeat's opinion to his. He coiled the whip, spat at Robbie, and stalked uncertainly away.

Now it was Robbie who wanted a fight. 'Hey, you!' he shouted.

'Leave it be,' Thomas said. 'Not tonight, Robbie.'

'He burned three men?' Robbie demanded.

'Not tonight,' Thomas repeated, and he pushed Robbie hard back so that the Scotsman sat on the steps of the cross.

Robbie was staring at the retreating Scarecrow. 'He's a dead man,' he said grimly. 'I tell you, Thomas, that bastard is a dead man.'

'We're all dead men,' Sir Guillaume said quietly, for the enemy was ready for them and in overwhelming numbers.

And Sir Thomas Dagworth was nearing their trap.

John Hammond, a deputy to Sir Thomas Dagworth, led the feint that came from the west along the Lannion road. He had sixty men, as many women, a dozen carts and thirty horses and he used them to make as much noise as possible once they were within sight of the westernmost of Duke Charles's encampments.

Fires outlined the earthworks and firelight showed in the tiny slits between the timbers of the palisade. There seemed to be a lot of fires in the encampment, and even more blazed up once Hammond's small force began to bang pots and pans, clatter staves against trees and blow their trumpets. The drummers beat frantic-ally, but no panic showed on the earthen ramparts. A few enemy soldiers appeared there, stared for a while down the moonlit road where Hammond's men and women were shadows under the trees, then turned and went away. Hammond ordered his people to make even more noise and his six archers, the only real soldiers in his decoy force, went closer to the camp and shot their arrows over the palisades, but still there was no urgent response. Hammond expected to see men streaming over the river that Sir Thomas's spies had said was bridged with boats, but no one appeared to be moving between the enemy encampments. The feint, it seemed, had failed.

'If we stay here,' a man said, 'they'll goddamn crucify us.'

'They goddamn will,' Hammond agreed fervently. 'We'll go back down the road a bit,' he said, 'just a bit. Back into deeper shadow.'

The night had begun badly with the failure of the feint assault, but Sir Thomas's men, the real attackers, had made better progress than they expected and arrived off the eastern flank of Duke Charles's encampment not long after the decoy group began its noisy diversion three miles to the west. Sir Thomas's men crouched at the edge of a wood and stared across the felled land to the shape of the nearest earthworks. The road, pale in the moonlight, ran

empty to a big wooden gate where it was swallowed up by the makeshift fort.

Sir Thomas had divided his men into two parties that would attack either side of the wooden gate. There was to be nothing subtle in the assault, just a rush through the dark then a swarming attack over the earth wall and kill whoever was discovered on its farther side. 'God give you joy,' Sir Thomas said to his men as he walked down their line, then he drew his sword and waved his party on. They would approach as silently as they could and Sir Thomas still hoped he would achieve surprise, but the firelight on the other side of the defences looked unnaturally bright and he had a sinking feeling that the enemy was ready for him. Yet none showed on the embanked wall and no crossbow quarrels hissed in the dark, and so he dared to let his hopes rise and then he was at the ditch and splashing through its muddy bottom. There were archers to left and right of him, all scrambling up the bank to the palisade. Still no crossbows shot, no trumpet sounded and no enemy showed. The archers were at the fence now and it proved more flimsy than it looked for the logs were not buried deeply enough and they could be kicked over without much effort. The defences were not formidable, and were not even defended for no enemy challenged as Sir Thomas's men-at-arms splashed through the ditch, their swords bright in the moonlight. The archers finished demolishing the palisade and Sir Thomas stepped over the fallen timbers and ran down the bank into Charles's camp.

Except he was not inside the camp, but rather on a wide open space that led to another bank and another ditch and another palisade. The place was a labyrinth! But still no bolts flew in the dark and his archers were running ahead again, though some cursed as they tripped in holes dug to trap horses' hooves. The fires were bright beyond the next palisade. Where were the sentries? Sir Thomas hefted his shield with its device of a wheatsheaf and looked to his left to see that his second party was across the first bank and streaming over the grass towards the second. His own archers pulled at the new palisade and, like the first, it tumbled easily. No one was speaking, no one was shouting orders, no one was calling on St George for help, they were just doing their job, but surely the enemy must hear the falling timbers? But the second palisade was

down and Sir Thomas jostled with the archers through the new gap and there was a meadow in front and a hedge beyond it, and beyond that hedge were the enemy tents and the high windmill with its furled sails and the monstrous shapes of the two biggest trebuchets, all of them lit by the bright fires. So close now! And Sir Thomas felt a fierce surge of joy for he had achieved surprise and the enemy was surely his, and just at that moment the crossbows sounded.

The bolts flickered in from his right flank, from an earth bank that ran between the second earthwork and the hedge. Archers were falling, cursing. Sir Thomas turned towards the crossbowmen who were hidden, and then more bolts came from the thick hedge in front and he knew he had surprised no one, that the enemy had been waiting for him, and his men were screaming now, but at least the first archers were shooting back. The long English arrows flashed in the moonlight, but Sir Thomas could see no targets and he realized the archers were shooting blindly. 'To me!' he shouted. 'Dagworth! Dagworth! Shields!' Maybe a dozen men-at-arms heard and obeyed him, making a cluster who overlapped their shields and then ran clumsily towards the hedge. Break through that, Sir Thomas thought, and at least some of the crossbowmen would be visible. Archers were shooting to their front and their side, confused by the enemy's bolts. Sir Thomas snatched a glance across the road and saw his other men were being similarly assailed. 'We have to get through the hedge,' he shouted, 'through the hedge! Archers! Through the hedge!' A crossbow bolt slammed into his shield, half spinning him round. Another hissed overhead. An archer was twisting on the grass, his belly pierced by a quarrel.

Other men were shouting now. Some called on St George, others cursed the devil, some screamed for their wives or mothers. The enemy had massed his crossbows and was pouring the bolts out of the darkness. An archer reeled back, a quarrel in his shoulder. Another screamed pitiably, hit in the groin. A man-at-arms fell to his knees, crying Jesus, and now Sir Thomas could hear the enemy shouting orders and insults. 'The hedge!' he roared. Get through the hedge, he thought, and maybe his archers would have clear targets at last. 'Get through the hedge!' he bellowed, and some of his archers found a gap closed up with nothing but hurdles and

they kicked the wicker barriers down and streamed through. The night seemed alive with bolts, fierce with them, and a man shouted at Sir Thomas to look behind. He turned and saw the enemy had sent scores of crossbowmen to cut off his retreat and that new force was pushing Sir Thomas's men on into the heart of the encampment. It had been a trap, he thought, a goddamned trap. Charles had wanted him to come into the encampment, he had obliged and now Charles's men were curling about him. So fight, he told himself, fight!

'Through the hedge!' Sir Thomas thundered. 'Get through the damned hedge!' He dodged between the bodies of his men, pounded through the gap and looked for an enemy to kill, but instead he saw that Charles's men-at-arms were formed in a battle line, all armoured, visors down and shields up. A few archers were shooting at them now, the long arrows smacking into shields, bellies, chests and legs, but there were too few archers and the crossbowmen, still hidden by hedges or walls or pavises, were killing the English bowmen. 'Rally on the mill!' Sir Thomas shouted for that was the most prominent landmark. He wanted to collect his men, form them into ranks and start to fight properly, but the crossbows were closing on him, hundreds of them, and his frightened men were scattering into the tents and shelters.

Sir Thomas swore out of sheer frustration. The survivors of the other assault party were with him now, but all of his men were entangled in the tents, tripping on ropes, and still the crossbow bolts slammed through the dark, ripping the canvas as they hurtled into Sir Thomas's dying force. 'Form here! Form here!' he yelled, choosing an open space between three tents, and maybe twenty or thirty men ran to him, but the crossbowmen saw them and poured their bolts down the dark alleys between the tents, and then the enemy men-at-arms came, shields up, and the English archers were scattering again, trying to find a vantage point to catch their breath, find some protection and look for targets. The great banners of the French and Breton lords were being brought forward and Sir Thomas, knowing he had blundered into this trap and been comprehensively beaten, just felt a surge of anger. 'Kill the bastards,' he bawled and he led his men at the nearest enemy, the swords rang in the dark, and at least, now that it was hand to hand, the

crossbowmen could not shoot at the English men-at-arms. The Genoese were hunting the hated English archers instead, but some of the bowmen had found a wagon park and, sheltered by the vehicles, were at last fighting back.

But Sir Thomas had no shelter and no advantage. He had a small force and the enemy a great one, and his men were being forced backwards by sheer pressure of numbers. Shields crashed on shields, swords hammered on helmets, spears came under the shields to tear through men's boots, a Breton flailed an axe, beating down two Englishmen and letting in a rush of men wearing the white ermine badge who shrieked their triumph and cut down still more men. A man-at-arms screamed as axes hacked through the mail covering his thighs, then another axe battered in his helmet and he was silent. Sir Thomas staggered backwards, parrying a sword blow, and saw some of his men running into the dark spaces between the tents to find refuge. Their visors were down and they could hardly see where they were going or the enemy who came to kill them. He slashed his sword at a man in a pig-snout helmet, backswung the blade into a shield striped yellow and black, took a step back to make space for another blow and then his feet were tangled by a tent's guy ropes and he fell backwards onto the canvas.

The knight in the pig-snout helmet stood over him, his plate mail shining in the moon and his sword at Sir Thomas's throat.

'I yield,' Sir Thomas said hurriedly, then repeated his surrender in French.

'And you are?' the knight asked.

'Sir Thomas Dagworth,' Sir Thomas said bitterly and he held up his sword to his enemy who took the weapon and then pushed up his snouted visor.

'I am the Viscount Morgat,' the knight said, 'and I accept your surrender.' He bowed to Sir Thomas, handed back his sword and held out a hand to help the Englishman to his feet. The fight was still going on, but it was sporadic now as the French and Bretons hunted down the survivors, killed the wounded who were not worth ransoming and hammered their own wagons with crossbow bolts to kill the English bowmen who still sheltered there.

The Viscount Morgat escorted Sir Thomas to the windmill where he presented him to Charles of Blois. A great fire burned a few

338

yards away and in its light Charles stood beneath the furled sails with his jupon smeared with blood for he had helped to break Sir Thomas's band of men-at-arms. He sheathed his sword, still bloody, and took off his plumed helmet and stared at the prisoner who had twice defeated him in battle. 'I commiserate with you,' Charles said coldly.

'And I congratulate your grace,' Sir Thomas said.

'The victory belongs to God,' Charles said, 'not to me,' yet all the same he felt a sudden exhilaration because he had done it! He had defeated the English field army in Brittany and now, as certain as blessed dawn follows darkest night, the duchy would fall to him. 'The victory is God's alone,' he said piously, and he remembered it was now very early on Sunday morning and he turned to a priest to tell the man to have a Te Deum sung in thanks for this great victory.

And the priest nodded, eyes wide, even though the Duke had not yet spoken, and then he gasped and Charles saw there was an unnaturally long arrow in the man's belly, then another white-fledged shaft hammered into the windmill's flank and a raucous, almost bestial, growl sounded from the dark.

For though Sir Thomas was captured and his army was utterly defeated, the battle, it seemed, was not quite finished.

Richard Totesham watched the fight between Sir Thomas's men and Charles's forces from the top of the eastern gate tower. He could not see a great deal from that vantage point for the palisades atop the earthworks, the two great trebuchets and the windmill obscured much of the battle, but it was abundantly clear that no one was coming from the other three French encampments to help Charles in his largest fortress. 'You'd think they'd be helping each other,' he said to Will Skeat who was standing next to him.

'It's you, Dick!' Will Skeat exclaimed.

'Aye, it's me, Will,' Totesham said patiently. He saw that Skeat was dressed in mail and had a sword at his side, and he put a hand on his old friend's shoulder. 'Now, you're not going to be fighting tonight, Will, are you?'

'If there's going to be a scrap,' Skeat said, 'then I'd like to help.'

'Leave it to the young ones, Will,' Totesham urged, 'leave it to the young ones. You stay and guard the town for me. Will you do that?'

Skeat nodded and Totesham turned back to stare into the enemy's camp. It was impossible to tell which side was winning for the only troops he could see belonged to the enemy and they had their backs to him, though once in a while a flying arrow would flash a reflection of the firelight as proof that Sir Thomas's men still fought, but Totesham reckoned it was a bad sign that no troops were coming from the other fortresses to help Charles of Blois. It suggested the Duke did not need help, which in turn suggested that Sir Thomas Dagworth did and so Totesham leaned over the inner parapet. 'Open the gate!' he shouted.

It was still dark. Dawn was two hours or more away, yet the

340

moon was bright and the fires in the enemy camp threw a garish light. Totesham hurried down the stairs from the ramparts while men pulled away the stone-filled barrels that had formed a barricade inside the gateway, then lifted the great locking bar that had not been disturbed in a month. The gates creaked open and the waiting men cheered. Totesham wished they had kept silent for he did not want to alert the enemy that the garrison was making a sortie, but it was too late now and so he found his own troop of men-at-arms and led them to join the stream of soldiers and townsmen who poured through the gate.

Thomas went to the attack alongside Robbie and Sir Guillaume and his two men. Will Skeat, despite his promise to Totesham, had wanted to come with them, but Thomas had pushed him onto the ramparts and told him to watch the fight from there. 'You ain't fit enough, Will,' Thomas had insisted.

'If you say so, Tom,' Skeat had agreed meekly, then climbed the steps. Thomas, once he was through the gate, looked back and saw Skeat on the gate tower. He raised a hand, but Skeat did not see him or, if he did, could not recognize him.

It felt strange to be outside the long-locked gates. The air was fresher, lacking the stench of the town's sewage. The attackers followed the road which ran straight for three hundred paces before vanishing beneath the palisade which protected the timber platforms on which Hellgiver and Widowmaker were mounted. That palisade was higher than a tall man and some of the archers were carrying ladders to get across the obstacle, but Thomas reckoned the palisades had been made in a hurry and would probably topple to a good heave. He ran, still clumsy on his twisted toes. He expected the crossbows to start at any moment, but no bolts came from Charles's earthworks; the enemy, Thomas supposed, were occupied with Dagworth's men.

Then the first of Totesham's archers reached the palisade and the ladders went up, but, just as Thomas had reckoned, a whole length of the heavy fence collapsed with a crash when men put their weight on the ladders. The banks and palisades had not been built to keep men out, but to shelter the crossbowmen, but those crossbowmen still did not know that a sortie had come from the town and so the bank was undefended.

Four or five hundred men crossed the fallen palisade. Most were not trained soldiers, but townsmen who had been enraged by the enemy's missiles crashing into their houses. Their women and children had been maimed and killed by the trebuchets and the men of La Roche-Derrien wanted revenge, just as they wanted to keep the prosperity brought by the English occupation, and so they cheered as they swarmed into the enemy camp. 'Archers!' Totesham roared in a huge voice. 'Archers, to me! Archers!'

Sixty or seventy archers ran to obey him, making a line just to the south of the platforms where the two biggest trebuchets were set. The rest of the sortie were charging at the enemy who were no longer formed in their battle line, but had scattered into small groups who were so intent on completing their victory over Sir Thomas Dagworth that they had not been watching behind them. Now they turned, alarmed, as a feral roar announced the garrison's arrival. 'Kill the bastards!' a townsman shouted in Breton.

'Kill!' An English voice roared.

'No prisoners!' another man bellowed, and though Totesham, fearful for lost ransoms, called out that prisoners must be taken, no one heard him in the savage roar that the attackers made.

Charles's men-at-arms instinctively formed a line, but Totesham, ready for it, had gathered his archers and now he ordered them to shoot: the bows began their devil's music and the arrows hissed through the dark to bury themselves in mail and flesh and bone. The bowmen were few, but they shot at close range, they could not miss, and Charles's men cowered behind their shields as the missiles whipped home, but the arrows easily pierced shields and the men-at-arms broke and scattered to find shelter among the tents. 'Hunt them down! Hunt them down!' Totesham released his archers to the kill.

Less than a hundred of Sir Thomas Dagworth's men were still fighting and most of those were the archers who had gone to ground in the wagon park. Some of the others were prisoners, many were dead, while most were trying to escape across the earthworks and palisades, but those men, hearing the great roar behind them, turned back. Charles's men were scattered: many were still hunting down the remnants of the first attack and those who had tried to

resist Totesham's sortie were either dead or fleeing into shadows. Totesham's men now struck the heart of the encampment with the savagery of a tempest. The townsmen were filled with rage. There was no subtlety in their assault, just a lust for vengeance as they swarmed past the two great trebuchets. The first huts they encountered were the shelters of the Bavarian engineers who, wanting no part of the hand-to-hand slaughter that was finishing off the survivors of Sir Thomas Dagworth's assault, had stayed by their billets and now died there. The townsmen had no idea who their victims were, only that they were the enemy, and so they were chopped down with axes, mattocks and hammers. The chief engineer tried to protect his eleven-year-old son, but they died together under a frenzy of blows, and meanwhile the English and Fleming men-at-arms were streaming past.

Thomas had shot his bow with the other archers, but now he sought Robbie whom he had last seen by the two big trebuchets. Widowmaker had been winched down ready to launch its first missile in the dawn and Thomas stumbled over a stout metal spike that protruded a yard from the beam and acted as an anchor for the sling. He cursed, because the metal had hurt his shins, then he climbed onto the trebuchet's frame and shot an arrow above the heads of the men slaughtering the Bavarians. He had been aiming at the enemy still clustered at the foot of the windmill and he saw a man fall there before the gaudy shields came up. He shot again, and realized that his wounded hands were doing what they had always done and were doing it well, and so he plucked a third arrow from the bag and drove it into a firelit shield painted with a white ermine, then the English men-at-arms and their allies were climbing the hill and obscuring his aim so he jumped down from the trebuchet and resumed his search for Robbie.

The enemy was defending the mill stoutly and most of Totesham's men had veered away into the tents where they had more hope of finding plunder. The townsmen, their Bavarian tormentors killed, were following with bloody axes. A man in plate armour stepped from behind a tent and cut at a man with a sword, folding him at the belly, and Thomas did not think, but put an arrow on the cord, drew and loosed. The arrow went through the slit in the enemy's

visor as cleanly as if Thomas had been shooting on the butts at home and moon-glossed blood, glistening like a jewel, oozed from the visor slits as the man fell backwards onto the canvas.

Thomas ran on, stepping over bodies, edging past half-fallen tents. This was no place for a bow, everything was too cramped, and so he slung the yew stave on his shoulder and drew his sword. He ducked into a tent, stepped over a fallen bench, heard a scream and twisted, sword raised, to see a woman on the ground, half hidden by bedding, shaking her head at him. He left her there, went out into the firelit night and saw an enemy aiming a crossbow at the English men-at-arms who attacked the mill. He took two steps and stabbed the man in the small of the back so that his victim arched his wounded spine and twisted and shook. Thomas, dragging the sword free, was so appalled by the noise the dying man made that he hacked the blade down again and again, chopping at the fallen, twitching man to make him silent.

'He's dead! Christ, man, he's dead!' Robbie shouted at him, then snatched at Thomas's sleeve and pulled him towards the mill and Thomas took the bow from his shoulder and shot two men wearing the white ermine badge on their jupons. They had been trying to escape, running down the back side of the hill. A dog streaked across the shoulder of the slope, something red and dripping in its jaws. There were two great bonfires on the hill, flanking the mill, and a man-at-arms fell backwards into one, driven there by the strike of an English arrow. Sparks exploded upwards as he fell, then he began to scream as his flesh roasted inside his armour. He tried to scramble out of the flames, but a townsman thrust him back with the butt of a spear and laughed at the man's desperate squeals. The clash of swords, shields and axes was huge, filling the night, but in the strange chaos there was a peaceful area at the back of the windmill. Robbie had seen a man duck through a small doorway there and he pulled Thomas that way. 'He's either hiding or running away!' Robbie shouted. 'He must have money!'

Thomas was not sure what Robbie was talking about, but he followed anyway; he just had time to sling his bow again and draw the sword a second time before Robbie smashed the door down with his mail-clad shoulder and plunged into the darkness. 'Come here, you English bastard!' he shouted.

'You want to be killed?' Thomas roared at him. 'You're fighting for the goddamn English!'

Robbie swore at that reminder, then Thomas saw a shadow to his right, only a shadow, and he swung his sword that way. It clanged against another sword and Robbie was screaming in the dusty dark and the man was shouting at them in French and Thomas pulled back, but Robbie just slammed his sword down once, twice, and the blade chopped through bone and flesh and there was a crash as an armoured man fell onto the upper millstone. 'What the hell was he saying to me?' Robbie wanted to know.

'He was trying to surrender.' A voice spoke from across the mill and Thomas and Robbie both spun towards the sound, their swords banging against the wooden tangle of joists, beams, cogwheels and axles, and then the unseen man called out again. 'Whoa, boys, whoa! I'm English.' There was a thump as an arrow struck the outside wall. The furled sails tugged against their tethers and made the wooden machinery squeal and shudder. More arrows thumped into the boards. 'I'm a prisoner,' the man said.

'You're not now,' Thomas said.

'I suppose not.' The man climbed over the millstones and pushed open the door and Thomas saw he was middle-aged with grey hair. 'What's happening?' the man asked.

'We're gralloching the devils,' Robbie said.

'Pray God you are.' The man turned and offered his hand to Robbie. 'I'm Sir Thomas Dagworth, and I thank you both.' He drew his sword and ducked out into the moonlit night, and Robbie stared at Thomas.

'Did you hear that?'

'He said thank you,' Thomas said.

'Aye, but he said he was Sir Thomas Dagworth!'

'Then maybe he was?'

'So what the hell was he doing in here?' Robbie asked, before taking hold of the man he had killed and, with much effort and the clank of armour against stone and timber, dragged him to the door where the fires offered light. The man had discarded his helmet and Robbie's sword had split his skull, but under the gore there was the glint of gold and Robbie dragged a chain from beneath the man's breastplate. 'He must have been an important fellow,' Robbie

said, admiring the gold chain, then he grinned at Thomas. 'We'll split it later, eh?'

'Split it?'

'We're friends, aren't we?' Robbie asked, then pushed the gold under his haubergeon before shoving the corpse back into the mill. 'Valuable armour that,' he said. 'We'll come back when it's over and hope no bastard has stolen it.'

There was tangled, bloody horror in the encampment now. Survivors of Sir Thomas Dagworth's attack still fought, notably the archers in the wagon park, but as the town's garrison swept through the tents they released prisoners or brought other survivors out of the dark places where they had been hiding. Charles's crossbowmen, who could have stemmed the garrison's attack, were mostly fighting against the English archers in the wagon park. The Genoese were using their huge pavises as shelters, but the new attackers came from behind and the crossbowmen had nowhere to hide as the long arrows hissed through the night. The war bows sang their devil's melody, ten arrows flying to every quarrel shot, and the crossbowmen could not endure the slaughter. They fled.

The victorious archers, reinforced now by the men who had been among the wagons, turned back to the shelters and tents where a deadly game of hide and seek was being played in the dark avenues between the canvas walls, but then a Welsh archer discovered that the enemy could be flushed out if the tents were set on fire. Soon there were smoke and flames spewing all across the encampment and enemy soldiers were running from the fires onto the arrows and blades of the incendiarists.

Charles of Blois had retreated from the windmill, reckoning his position on the hill made him conspicuous, and he had tried to rally some knights in front of his own sumptuous tent, but an overwhelming rush of townsmen had swept those knights underfoot and Charles watched, appalled, as butchers, coopers, wheelwrights and thatchers massacred their betters with axes, cleavers and reaping hooks. He had hastily retreated into his tent, but now one of his retainers unceremoniously pulled him towards the back entrance. 'This way, your grace.'

Charles shook off the man's hand. 'Where can we go?' he asked plaintively.

'We'll go to the southern camp, sir, and bring men back to help.'

Charles nodded, reflecting that he should have ordered that himself and regretting his insistence that none of his men leave their encampments. Well over half his army was in the other three camps, all of them close by and all of them eager to fight and more than capable of sweeping this disorganized horde aside, yet they were obeying his orders and standing tight while his encampment was put to the sword. 'Where's my trumpeter?' he demanded.

'Sir? I'm here, your grace! I'm here.' The trumpeter had miraculously survived the fight and stayed close to his lord.

'Sound the seven blasts,' Charles ordered.

'Not here!' a priest snapped and, when Charles looked offended, made a hasty explanation. 'It will attract the enemy, your grace. After two blasts they'll be onto us like hounds!'

Charles acknowledged the wisdom of the advice with a curt nod. A dozen knights were with him now and they made a formidable force in this night of fractured battle. One of them peered from the tent and saw flames searing the sky and knew the Duke's tents would be fired soon. 'We must go, your grace,' he insisted, 'we must find our horses.'

They left the tent, hurrying across the patch of beaten grass where the Duke's sentinels usually stood, and then an arrow flickered from the dark to glance off a breastplate. Shouts were suddenly loud and a rush of men came from the right and so Charles retreated to his left, which took him back up the slope towards the firelit windmill, and then a shout announced that he had been seen and the first arrows slashed up the hill. 'Trumpeter!' Charles shouted. 'Seven blasts! Seven blasts!'

Charles and his men, barred from reaching their horses, now had their backs against the mill's apron, which was stuck with scores of white-feathered arrows. Another arrow spitted a man in the midriff, drilling through his mail, piercing his belly and the mail on his back to pin him to the mill's boards, then an English voice roared at the archers to stop shooting. 'It's their Duke!' the man roared, 'it's their Duke! We want him alive! Stop shooting! Bows down!'

The news that Charles of Blois was cornered at the mill prompted

a growl from the attackers. The arrows stopped flying and Charles's battered, bleeding men-at-arms who were defending the hill stared down the slope to see, just beyond the light of the mill's two fires, a mass of dark creatures prowling like wolves. 'God help us,' a priest said in a scared voice.

'Trumpeter!' Charles of Blois snapped.

'Sir,' the trumpeter acknowledged. He had found his instrument's mouthpiece mysteriously plugged by earth. He must have fallen, though he did not remember doing so. He shook the last of the soil out of the silver mouthpiece, then put the trumpet to his mouth and the first blast sounded sweet and loud in the night. The Duke drew his sword. He only had to defend the mill long enough for his reinforcements to come from the other camps and sweep this impertinent rabble into hell. The second trumpet note rang out.

Thomas heard the trumpet, turned and saw the flash of silver by the mill, then he saw the reflection of flamelight rippling off the instrument's bell as the trumpeter raised it to the moon for the third time. Thomas had heard no order to stop shooting arrows and so he hauled his bow's cord back, twitched his left hand up a fraction and released. The arrow whipped over the heads of the English men-at-arms and struck the trumpeter just as he took breath for the third blast and the air hissed and bubbled out of his pierced lung as he spilled sideways onto the turf. The dark prowling things at the hill's base saw the man fall and suddenly charged.

No help came to Charles from the three remaining fortresses. They had heard two trumpet blasts, but only two, and they reckoned Charles must be winning; besides, they had his strict and constantly repeated orders to stay where they were on pain of losing out when the conquered lands were distributed among the victors. So they did stay, watching the smoke boil out of the flames and wondering what happened in the large eastern encampment.

Chaos was happening. This fight, Thomas reckoned, was like the attack on Caen: unplanned, disordered and utterly brutal. The English and their allies had been keyed up, nervous, expecting defeat, while Charles's men had been expecting victory – indeed they had gained the early victory – but now the English nervousness was being turned into a maddened, bloody, vicious assault and the French and Bretons were being harried into terror. A ragged clash

sounded as the English men-at-arms slammed into Charles's men defending the windmill. Thomas wanted to join that fight, but Robbie suddenly pulled at his mail sleeve. 'Look!' Robbie was pointing back into the burning tents.

Robbie had seen three horsemen in plain black surcoats and with them, on foot, a Dominican. Thomas saw the white and black robes and followed Robbie through the tents, trampling over a collapsed spread of blue and white canvas, past a fallen standard, running between two fires and then across an open space that whirled with smoke and burning scraps of flying cloth. A woman with a dress half torn away screamed and ran across their path and a man scattered fire with his boots as he pursued her into a turf-roofed hut. For a moment they lost sight of the priest, then Robbie saw the black and white robes again: the Dominican was trying to mount an unsaddled horse that the men in black surcoats held for him. Thomas drew his bow, let the arrow fly and saw it bury itself up to its feathers in the horse's breast; the beast reared up, yellow hooves flailing, and the Dominican fell backwards. The men in black surcoats galloped away from the bow's threat and the priest, abandoned, turned and saw his pursuers and Thomas recognized de Taillebourg, God's torturer. Thomas screamed a challenge and drew the bow again, but de Taillebourg ran towards some remaining tents. A Genoese crossbowman suddenly appeared, saw them, raised his weapon and Thomas let the cord go. The arrow slashed the man's throat, spilling blood down his red and green tunic. The woman screamed inside the shelter, then was abruptly silenced as Thomas followed Robbie to where the Inquisitor had disappeared among the tents. The door flap of one was still swinging and Robbie, sword drawn, thrust the canvas aside and ducked into what proved to be a chapel.

De Taillebourg was standing at the altar with its white Easter frontal. A crucifix stood on the altar between two flickering candles. The camp outside was an uproar of screams and pain and arrows, of horses whimpering and men shouting, but it was oddly calm in the makeshift chapel.

'You bastard,' Thomas said, drawing his sword and advancing on the Dominican, 'you goddamn stinking turd-faced piece of priestly shit.'

Bernard de Taillebourg had one hand on the altar. He raised the other to make the sign of the cross. '*Dominus vobiscum*,' he said in his deep voice. An arrow scraped over the tent's roof with a high-pitched scratching sound and another whipped through a side wall and span down behind the altar.

'Is Vexille with you?' Thomas demanded.

'God's blessings on you, Thomas,' de Taillebourg said. He was fierce-faced, stern, eyes hard, and he made the sign of the cross towards Thomas, then stepped back as Thomas raised the sword.

'Is Vexille with you?' Thomas demanded again.

'Can you see him?' the Dominican asked, peering about the chapel, then smiled. 'No, Thomas, he's not here. He's gone into the dark. He rode to fetch help and you cannot kill me.'

'Give me a reason,' Robbie said, 'because you killed my brother, you bastard.'

De Taillebourg looked at the Scotsman. He did not recognize Robbie, but he saw the anger and offered him the same blessing he had given Thomas. 'You cannot kill me,' he said after he had made the sign of the cross, 'because I am a priest, my son, I am God's anointed, and your soul will be damned through all time if you so much as touch me.'

Thomas's response was to lunge his sword at de Taillebourg's belly, forcing the priest hard back against the altar. A man screamed outside, the sound faltering and fading, ending in a sob. A child wept inconsolably, her breath coming in great gasps, and a dog barked frantically. The light of the burning tents was lurid on the chapel's canvas walls. 'You are a bastard,' Thomas said, 'and I don't mind killing you for what you did to me.'

'What I did!' De Taillebourg's anger flared like the fires outside. 'I did nothing!' He spoke in French now. 'Your cousin begged me to spare you the worst and so I did. One day, he said, you would be on his side! One day you would join the side of the Grail! One day you would be on God's side and so I spared you, Thomas. I left you your eyes! I did not burn your eyes!'

'I'll enjoy killing you,' Thomas said, though in truth he was nervous of attacking a priest. Heaven would be watching and the recording angel's pen would be writing letters of fire in a great book.

'And God loves you, my son,' de Taillebourg said gently, 'God loves you. And God chastises whom he loves.'

'What's he saying?' Robbie interrupted.

'He's saying that if we kill him,' Thomas said, 'our souls are damned.'

'Till another priest undamns them,' Robbie said. 'There ain't a sin done on earth that some priest won't absolve if the price is right. So stop talking to the bastard and just kill him.' He advanced on de Taillebourg, sword raised, but Thomas held him back.

'Where's my father's book?' Thomas asked the priest.

'Your cousin has it,' de Taillebourg replied. 'I promise you, your cousin has it.'

'Then where is my cousin?'

'I told you, he rode away to fetch help,' de Taillebourg said, 'and now you must go too, Thomas. You must leave me here to pray.'

Thomas almost obeyed, but then he remembered his pathetic gratitude to this man when he had ceased the torture, and the memory of that gratitude was so shaming, so painful, that he suddenly shuddered and, almost without thinking, swung the sword at the priest.

'No!' de Taillebourg shouted, his left arm cut to the bone where he had tried to defend himself from Thomas's sword.

'Yes,' Thomas said, and the rage was consuming him, filling him, and he cut again and Robbie was beside him, stabbing with his sword, and Thomas swung a third time, but so lavishly that his blade got tangled with the tent roof.

De Taillebourg was swaying now. 'You can't kill me!' he shouted. 'I'm a priest!' He screamed that last word and was still screaming as Robbie chopped Sir William Douglas's sword into his neck. Thomas disentangled his own blade. De Taillebourg, the front of his robes soaked with blood, was staring at him with astonishment, then the priest tried to speak and could not, and the blood was spreading through the weave of his robes with an extraordinary swiftness. He fell to his knees, still trying to speak, and Thomas's sword blow took him on the other side of his neck, and more blood spurted out to slash drops across the white altar frontal. De Taillebourg looked up, this time with puzzlement on his face, then Robbie's last blow killed the Dominican, tearing his windpipe out of his neck.

Robbie had to leap back to avoid the spray of blood. The priest twitched and in his death throes his left hand pulled the blood-drenched frontal off the altar, spilling candles and cross. He made a rattling noise, twitched and was still.

'That did feel good,' Robbie said in the sudden dark as the candles went out. 'I hate priests. I've always wanted to kill one.'

'I had a friend who was a priest,' Thomas said, making the sign of the cross, 'but he was murdered, either by my cousin or by this bastard.' He stirred de Taillebourg's body with his foot, then stooped and wiped his sword blade clean on the hem of the priest's robes.

Robbie went to the tent door. 'My father reckons that hell is full of priests,' he said.

'Then there's one more on his way down there now,' Thomas said. He picked up his bow and he and Robbie went back into the dark where the screams and arrows laced the night. So many tents and huts were now aflame that it might as well have been daylight and in the lurid glare Thomas saw a crossbowman kneeling between two picketed and terrified horses. The crossbow was aimed up the hill to where so many English were fighting. Thomas put an arrow on his cord, drew, and at the very last second, just as he was about to put the arrow through the crossbowman's spine, he recognized the blue and white wavy pattern on the jupon and he jerked his aim aside so that his arrow hit the crossbow instead and knocked it out of Jeanette's hands. 'You'll get killed!' he shouted at her angrily.

'That's Charles!' She pointed up the hill, equally angry with him.

'The only crossbows are with the enemy,' he said to her. 'You want to be shot by an archer?' He picked up her bow by its crank and tossed it into the shadows. 'And what are you goddamn doing here?'

'I came to kill him!' she said, pointing again at Charles of Blois who, with his retainers, was warding off a desperate assault. He had eight surviving knights with him and they were all fighting savagely even though they were hugely outnumbered and every one of them was wounded. Thomas led Jeanette up the slope just in time to see a tall English man-at-arms hack at Charles who caught the blow on his shield and slid his own sword under its rim to stab the Englishman in the thigh. Another man attacked and

was slashed down by an axe, a third pulled one of Charles's retainers away from the mill and hacked at his helmet. There seemed to be a score of Englishmen trying to reach Charles, smashing their shields into his retainer's weapons, thrusting swords and chopping with big war axes.

'Give him room!' an authoritative voice shouted. 'Give him room! Back away! Back away! Let him yield!'

The attackers reluctantly moved back. Charles had his visor up and there was blood on his pale face and more blood on his sword. A priest was on his knees beside him.

'Yield!' a man shouted at the Duke, who seemed to understand because he impulsively shook his head in refusal, but then Thomas put an arrow on his cord, drew and pointed it at Charles's face. Charles saw the threat and hesitated.

'Yield!' another man shouted.

'Only to a man of rank!' Charles called in French.

'Who has rank here?' Thomas called in English, then again in French. One of Charles's remaining men-at-arms slowly collapsed, first to his knees, then onto his belly with a crash of plate armour.

A knight stepped out of the English ranks. He was a Breton, one of Totesham's deputies, and he announced his name to prove to Charles that he was a man of noble birth and then he held out his hand and Charles of Blois, nephew to the King of France and claimant of the Duchy of Brittany, stepped awkwardly forward and held out his sword. A huge cheer went up, then the men on the hill divided to let the Duke and his captor walk away. Charles expected to be given his sword back and looked surprised when the Breton did not make the offer, then the defeated Duke walked stiffly down the hill, ignoring the triumphant English, but suddenly checked for a black-haired figure had stepped into his path.

It was Jeanette. 'Remember me?' she asked.

Charles looked her up and down and flinched as though he had been struck when he recognized the badge on her jupon. Then he flinched again when he saw the anger in her eyes. He said nothing.

Jeanette smiled. 'Rapist,' she said, then spat through his open visor. The Duke jerked his head away, but too late, and Jeanette spat into his face again. He shivered with anger. She was daring him to strike her, but he restrained himself and Jeanette, unable

to do the same, spat a third time. 'Ver,' she said scornfully and walked away to an ironic cheer.

'What's *ver*?' Robbie asked.

'Worm,' Thomas said, then smiled at Jeanette. 'Well done, my lady.'

'I was going to kick his goddamn balls,' she said, 'but I remembered he was wearing armour.'

Thomas laughed, then stepped aside as Richard Totesham ordered a half-dozen men-at-arms to escort Charles back into La Roche-Derrien. Short of capturing the King of France, he was as valuable a captive as any to be had in the war. Thomas watched him walk away. Charles of Blois would now be joining the King of Scotland as England's prisoner and both men would have to raise a fortune if they wished to be ransomed.

'It isn't finished!' Totesham shouted. He had seen the crowd of jeering men following the captured Duke and hurried to pull them away. 'It isn't done! Finish the job!'

'Horses!' Sir Thomas Dagworth called. 'Take their horses!'

The fight in Charles's encampment was won, but not ended. The assault from the town had hit like a storm and driven clean through the centre of Duke Charles's carefully prepared battle line and what was left of his force was now split into small groups. Scores were already dead, and others were fleeing into the darkness. 'Archers!' a shout went up. 'Archers to me!' Dozens of archers ran to the back of the encampment, where the escaping French and Bretons were trying to reach the other fortresses, and the bows cut the fugitives down mercilessly.

'Clean them out!' Totesham shouted. 'Clean them out!' A rough kind of organization had emerged in the shambles as the garrison and the townsmen, augmented by the survivors of Sir Thomas Dagworth's force, hunted through the burning encampment to drive any survivors back to where the archers waited. It was slow work, not because the enemy was making any real resistance, but because men were constantly stopping to pillage tents and shelters. Women and children were pulled out into the moonlight and their men were killed. Prisoners worth a huge ransom were slaughtered in the confusion and darkness. The Viscount Rohan was chopped down, as were the lords of Laval and of Châteaubriant, of Dinan and of Redon.

A grey light glimmered in the east, the first hint of dawn. Whimpering sounded in the burned camp.

'Finish them off?' Richard Totesham had at last found Sir Thomas Dagworth. The two men were on the encampment's ramparts from where they stared at the southern enemy fortress.

'Can't leave them sitting there,' Sir Thomas said, then held out a hand. 'Thanks, Dick.'

'For doing my job?' Totesham responded, embarrassed. 'So let's scour the bastards out of the other camps, eh?'

A trumpet called the English to assemble.

Charles of Blois had told his men that an archer could not shoot a man he could not see, and that was true, but the men of the southern encampment, who formed the second largest portion of Charles's army, were crowding onto their outer rampart in an effort to see what was happening in the eastern encampment about the windmill. They had lit fires to give their own crossbowmen illumination, but those fires now served to outline them as they stood on the earth bank, which had no palisade, and the English archers, given such a target, could not miss. Those archers were in the cleared ground between the encampments, shadowed by the loom of the long earthworks, and their arrows flickered out of the night to strike the watching French and Bretons. Crossbowmen tried to shoot back, but they made the easiest targets for few of them possessed mail, and then, with a roar, the English men-at-arms were charging over the defences and the killing began again. Townsmen, eager for plunder, followed the charge and the archers, seeing the earthwork stripped of defenders, ran to catch up.

Thomas paused on the earth rampart to shoot a dozen arrows into the panicked enemy who had made this encampment where the English siege camp had stood the previous year. He had lost sight of Sir Guillaume and, though he had told Jeanette to go back to the town, she was still with him, but now armed with a sword she had taken from a dead Breton. 'You shouldn't be here!' he snarled at her.

'Wasps!' she called back, and pointed to a dozen men-at-arms

wearing the black and yellow surcoats of the Lord of Roncelets.

The enemy here made small resistance. They had been unaware of the disaster that had overcome Charles, and they had been surprised by the sudden assault from the darkness. The surviving crossbowmen now retreated panicking into the tents and the English again snatched brands from the great fires and hurled them onto the canvas roofs to flare bright and garish in the predawn darkness. The English and Welsh archers had slung their bows and were grimly working their way through the tent lines with axes, swords and clubs. It was another slaughter, fuelled by the prospect of plunder, and some of the French and Bretons, rather than face the screaming mass of maddened men, took to their horses and fled east towards the thin grey light that now leaked a touch of red along the horizon.

Thomas and Robbie headed for the men wearing Roncelets's waspish stripes. Those men had attempted to make a stand beside a trebuchet that had the name Stonewhip painted on its big frame, but they had been outflanked by archers and now they were trying to escape and in the chaos they did not know which way to go. Two of them ran at Thomas and he skewered one with his sword while Robbie stunned the other with a massive blow to his helmet, then a rush of archers swept the men in black and yellow aside and Thomas scabbarded his wet sword and unslung his bow before running into a big unburned tent that stood beside a pole flying the black and yellow banner and there, between a bed and an open chest, was the Lord of Roncelets himself. He and a squire were scooping coins from the chest into small bags and they turned as Thomas and Robbie entered and the Lord of Roncelets snatched up a sword from the bed just as Thomas dragged back the bowcord. The squire lunged at Robbie, but Thomas loosed the arrow and the squire jerked back as if tugged by a massive rope and the blood from the wound in his forehead pattered red on the tent roof. The squire jerked a few times and then was still, and the Lord of Roncelets was still three paces from Thomas when the second arrow was placed on the string. 'Come on, my lord,' Thomas said, 'give me a reason to send you to the devil.'

The Lord of Roncelets looked like a fighter. He had short bristly hair, a broken nose and missing teeth, but there was no belligerence

in him now. He could hear the screams of defeat all about him, he could smell the burning flesh of the men trapped among the tents and he could see the arrow on Thomas's bow that was aimed at his face and he simply held out his sword in instant surrender. 'You have rank?' he asked Robbie. He had not recognized Thomas and, anyway, presumed that any man carrying a bow had to be a commoner.

Robbie did not understand the question, which had been asked in French, and so Thomas answered for him. 'He's a Scottish lord,' Thomas said, exaggerating Robbie's status.

'Then I yield to him,' Roncelets said angrily and threw his sword at Robbie's feet.

'God,' Robbie said, not understanding the exchange, 'but he scared quick!'

Thomas gently released the bowcord's tension and held up the crooked fingers of his right hand. 'It's a good job you surrendered,' he told Roncelets. 'Remember you wanted to cut these off?' He could not help smiling as first recognition, then abject fear showed on Roncelets's face. 'Jeanette!' Thomas shouted, his small victory gained. 'Jeanette!' Jeanette came through the tent flap and with her, of all people, was Will Skeat. 'What the hell are you doing here?' Thomas demanded angrily.

'You wouldn't keep an old friend from a scrap, would you, Tom?' Skeat asked with a grin and Thomas thought he could see his friend's true character in that grin.

'You're an old fool,' Thomas grumbled, then he picked up the Lord of Roncelets's sword and gave it to Jeanette. 'He's our prisoner,' he said, 'yours as well.'

'Ours?' Jeanette was puzzled.

'He's the Lord of Roncelets,' Thomas said, and he could not help another smile, 'and I've no doubt we can squeeze a ransom from him. And I don't mean that cash' – he pointed at the open chest – 'that's ours anyway.'

Jeanette stared at Roncelets and it slowly dawned on her that if the Lord of Roncelets was her prisoner then her son was as good as returned to her. She laughed suddenly, then gave Thomas a kiss. 'So you do keep your promises, Thomas.'

'And you keep good guard of him,' Thomas said, 'because his ransom is going to make us all rich. Robbie, you, me and Will.

We're all going to be wealthy.' He grinned at Skeat. 'You'll stay with her, Will? Look after him?'

'I'll stay,' Will agreed.

'Who is she?' the Lord of Roncelets asked Thomas.

'The Countess of Armorica,' Jeanette answered for him and laughed again when she saw the shock on his face.

'Take him back to the town now,' Thomas told them, and he ducked outside the tent where he found two townsmen searching for plunder among the nearest tents. 'You two!' he snapped at them, 'you're going to help guard a prisoner. Take him back to the town and you'll be well rewarded. Guard him well!' Thomas pulled the two men into the tent. He reckoned the Lord of Roncelets could not escape if Jeanette, Skeat and the two men were watching him. 'Just guard him,' he told them, 'and take him to your old house.' This last was to Jeanette.

'My old house?' she was puzzled.

'You wanted to kill someone tonight,' Thomas said, 'and you can't kill Charles of Blois, so why don't you go and murder Belas?' He laughed at the look on her face, then he and Robbie slammed down the chest lid and covered it with blankets from the bed in hope of hiding it for a few moments and then they went back to the fight.

All through the flame-lit battle Thomas had caught glimpses of men in plain black surcoats and he knew that Guy Vexille must be nearby, but he had not seen him. Now there were shouts and the clash of blades from the encampment's southern edge and Thomas and Robbie ran to see what the commotion was. They saw that a group of horsemen in black surcoats were fighting off a score of English men-at-arms. 'Vexille!' Thomas shouted. 'Vexille!'

'It's him?' Robbie asked.

'It's his men, anyway,' Thomas said. He guessed his cousin had been in the eastern encampment with de Taillebourg and that he had come here in hope of bringing a relief force to Charles's aid, but he had been too late and now his men were fighting a rearguard battle to protect other men who were fleeing.

'Where is he?' Robbie demanded.

Thomas could not see his cousin. He shouted again. 'Vexille! Vexille!'

And there he was. The Harlequin, Count of Astarac, armoured in plate, visor lifted, mounted on a black destrier and carrying a plain black shield. He saw Thomas and raised his sword in an ironic salute. Thomas unslung his bow, but Guy Vexille saw the threat, turned away and his horsemen closed protectively about him. 'Vexille!' Thomas yelled and he ran towards his cousin. Robbie called a warning and Thomas ducked as a horseman swung a blade at him, then he pushed against the horse, smelling leather and sweat, and another horseman banged into him, almost throwing him off his feet. 'Vexille!' he bellowed. He could see Guy Vexille again, only now his cousin was turning back, spurring towards him, and Thomas drew the bowcord, but Vexille held up his right hand to show he had scabbarded his sword and the gesture made Thomas lower the black bow.

Guy Vexille, his visor raised and his handsome face lit by the fires, smiled. 'I have the book, Thomas.'

Thomas said nothing, but just raised the bow again.

Guy Vexille shook his head in reproof. 'No need for that, Thomas. Join me.'

'In hell, you bastard,' Thomas said. This was the man who had killed his father, had killed Eleanor, had killed Father Hobbe, and Thomas drew the arrow fully back and Vexille took a small knife that had been concealed in his shield hand and calmly leaned forward and cut the bowcord. The broken string made the bow jump violently in Thomas's hand and the arrow spewed away harmlessly. The cord had been cut so swiftly that Thomas had been given no time to react.

'One day you'll join me, Thomas,' Vexille said, then he saw that the English archers had at last noticed his men and were beginning to take their toll and so he turned his horse, shouted at his men to retreat and spurred away.

'Jesus!' Thomas swore in frustration.

'*Calix meus inebrians*!' Guy Vexille shouted, then he was lost among the horsemen galloping south. A flight of English arrows followed them, but none struck Vexille.

'Bastard!' Robbie swore at the retreating figure.

A woman's scream sounded from the burning tents.

'What did he say to you?' Robbie asked.

'He wanted me to join him,' Thomas said bitterly. He threw away the slashed cord and took the spare from under his sallet. His clumsy fingers fumbled as he restrung the bow, but he managed to do it on the second try. 'And he said he's got the book.'

'Aye, well, much good that will bloody do him,' Robbie commented. The fight had died and he knelt by a black-dressed corpse and began searching for coins. Sir Thomas Dagworth was shouting for men to assemble at the encampment's western edge to assault the next fortress where some of the defenders, realizing that the battle was lost, were already running away. Church bells were ringing in La Roche-Derrien, celebrating that Charles of Blois had entered the town as a prisoner.

Thomas stared after his cousin. He was ashamed because one small part of him, one small and treacherous part, had been tempted to take the offer. Join his cousin, be back in a family, look for the Grail and harness its power. The shame was sour, like the shame of the gratitude he had felt towards de Taillebourg when the torture ceased. 'Bastard!' he yelled uselessly. *Bastard.*

'Bastard!' It was Sir Guillaume's voice that cut across Thomas's. Sir Guillaume, with his two men-at-arms, was prodding a prisoner in the back with a sword. The captive wore plate armour and the sword scraped on it with every prod. 'Bastard!' Sir Guillaume bawled again, then saw Thomas. 'It's Coutances! Coutances!' He pulled off his prisoner's helmet. 'Look at him!'

The Count of Coutances was a melancholy-looking man, bald as an egg, who was doing his best to appear dignified. Sir Guillaume poked him again. 'I tell you, Thomas' – he spoke in French – 'that this bastard's wife and daughters will have to whore themselves to raise this ransom! They'll be swiving every man in Normandy to buy this gutless bastard back!' He jabbed the Count of Coutances again. 'I'm going to squeeze you witless!' Sir Guillaume roared and then, exultant, marched his prisoner onwards.

The woman screamed again.

There had been many women screaming that night, but something about this sound cut through Thomas's awareness and he turned, alarmed. The scream sounded a third time and Thomas began to run. 'Robbie!' he shouted. 'To me!'

Thomas ran across the remnants of a burning tent, his boots

360

throwing up sparks and embers. He swerved round a smoking brazier, almost tripped on a wounded man who was vomiting into an upturned helmet, ran down an alley between armourers' huts where anvils, bellows, hammers, tongs and barrels full of rivets and mail rings were spilt on the grass. A man in a farrier's apron with blood streaming from a head wound staggered into his path and Thomas shoved him aside to run towards the black and yellow standard that still flew outside the Lord of Roncelets's burning tent. 'Jeanette!' he called. 'Jeanette!'

But Jeanette was a prisoner. She was being held by a huge man who had pressed her spine against the windlass of the trebuchet called Stonewhip that stood just beyond the Lord of Roncelets's tent. The man heard Thomas shouting and looked round, grinning. It was Beggar, all beard and rotted teeth, and he shoved Jeanette hard as she struggled to escape him.

'Hold her, Beggar!' Sir Geoffrey Carr shouted. 'Hold the bitch!'

'The pretty ain't going anywhere,' Beggar said, 'going nowhere, darling,' and he tried to haul up her coat of mail, but it was too heavy and awkward and Jeanette was struggling too frantically.

The Lord of Roncelets, still without his sword, was sitting on Stonewhip's frame. He had a red mark on his face, suggesting he had been struck, and Sir Geoffrey Carr with five other men-at-arms was standing over him. The Scarecrow stared defiantly at Thomas. 'He's my prisoner!' he insisted.

'He belongs to us,' Thomas said, 'we took him.'

'Listen, boy,' the Scarecrow said, his voice still slurred by drink, 'I am a knight and you are a turd. You understand me?' He staggered slightly as he stepped towards Thomas. 'I am a knight,' he said again, louder, 'and you are nothing!' His red face, made lurid by the flames, was twisted in derision. 'You are nothing!' he shouted again, then whipped round to make sure that his men were guarding the Lord of Roncelets. Such a wealthy captive would solve all Sir Geoffrey's problems and he was determined to hold onto him and take the ransom for himself. 'She can't take a captive,' he said, pointing his sword at Jeanette, 'because she's got tits, and you can't take him because you're a turd. But I'm a knight! A *knight*!' He spat the word at Thomas who, goaded by the insults, drew his bow. The new string was slightly too long and he could feel the

lack of power in the black stave because of it, but he reckoned there was enough strength for his purpose. 'Beggar!' the Scarecrow shouted, 'if he looses that bow, kill the bitch.'

'Kill the pretty,' Beggar said. He was drooling spittle, which ran down his big beard as he stroked the mail rings above Jeanette's breasts. She still fought, but he had her bent painfully back across the windlass and she could hardly move.

Thomas kept the bow drawn. The trebuchet's long beam, he saw, had been winched down to the ground though the engineers must have been interrupted before they could load a stone because the great leather sling was empty. A heap of stones stood off to the right and a sudden movement there made Thomas see there was a wounded man leaning against the boulders. The man was trying to stand, but could not. There was blood on his face. 'Will?' Thomas asked.

'Tom!' Will Skeat tried to push himself upright again. 'It's you, Tom!'

'What happened?' Thomas asked.

'Not what I was, Tom,' Skeat said. The two townsmen who had been helping to guard the Lord of Roncelets were dead at Skeat's feet, and Skeat himself seemed to be dying. He was white-faced, feeble and every breath was a struggle. There were tears on his face. 'I tried to fight,' he said pitiably, 'I did try, but I'm not what I was.'

'Who attacked you?' Thomas asked, but Skeat seemed unable to answer.

'Will was just trying to protect me,' Jeanette shouted, then she screamed as Beggar thrust her back so hard that at last she was forced onto the top of the windlass and Beggar could push her mail skirts up. He gabbled excitedly just as Sir Geoffrey roared in anger.

'It's the Douglas bastard!'

Thomas loosed the cord. With a new bowcord he liked to shoot a couple of arrows to discover how the new hemp would behave, but he had no time for such niceties now, he just loosed the arrow and it sliced through the tangles of Beggar's beard to cut his throat, the broad arrow head slitting his gullet as cleanly as a butcher's knife, and Jeanette screamed as the blood spurted across her jupon

362

and face. The Scarecrow bellowed in rage and ran at Thomas who rammed the horn-tipped bowstave into the red face then let the weapon fall as he drew his sword. Robbie ran past him and thrust his uncle's sword at the Scarecrow's belly, but even drunk Sir Geoffrey was quick and he managed to parry the blow and strike back. Two of his men-at-arms were running to help – the others were guarding the Lord of Roncelets – and Thomas saw the two men coming. He went to his left, hoping to put the big frame of Stonewhip between himself and the men wearing Sir Geoffrey's badge of the black axe, but Sir Geoffrey almost cut him off and Thomas gave a desperate backswing with his newly drawn sword that slammed against the Scarecrow's blade with a force that numbed Thomas's arm. The blow rocked the Scarecrow back, then he recovered and leaped forward and Thomas was desperately defending himself as the Scarecrow rained blows down on him. Thomas was no swordsman and he was being beaten down to his knees and Robbie could not help him because he was fending off Sir Geoffrey's two followers, and then there was an almighty crash, a bang that sounded as though the gates of hell had just opened, and the ground shook as the Scarecrow screamed in utter agony. His howl, trailing blood, seared into the sky.

Jeanette had pulled the lever that released the long beam. Ten tons of counterweight had thumped to the ground and the thick metal pin that held the sling had jerked up between Sir Geoffrey's legs and torn a bloody hole from his crotch to his belly. He should have been hurled halfway to the town by the trebuchet's beam, but instead the pin had been trapped in his entrails and he was caught on the beam's end where he writhed in agony, his blood pouring down to the ground.

His men, seeing their master dying, stepped back. Why fight for a man who could offer no reward? Robbie gaped up as the Scarecrow twisted and jerked, and somehow the dying man managed to tear himself free of the great iron stake and he fell, trailing intestines and spraying blood. He hit the ground with a thump, bounced bloodily, yet still he lived. His eyes were twitching and his mouth was drawn back in a snarl. 'Goddamn Douglas,' he managed to gasp before Robbie stepped to him, lifted his uncle's sword, and rammed it down once, straight between the Scarecrow's eyes.

The Lord of Roncelets had watched it all happen with disbelief. Now Jeanette was holding a sword to his face, daring him to run away, and he dumbly shook his head to show that he had no intention of risking his life among the drunken, screaming, savage men who had come out of the night to destroy the greatest army the duchy of Brittany had ever raised.

Thomas crossed to Sir William Skeat, but his old friend was dead. He had been wounded in the neck and he had bled to death on the stone pile. He looked strangely peaceful. A first shaft of the new day's sun cut across the world's edge to light the bright blood at the top of Stonewhip's beam as Thomas closed his mentor's eyes. 'Who killed Will Skeat?' Thomas demanded of Sir Geoffrey's men and Dickon, the young one, pointed at the wreckage of mail, flesh, entrails and bone that had been the Scarecrow.

Thomas inspected the dents in his sword. He must learn to use one, he thought, or else he would die by the sword, then he looked up at Sir Geoffrey's men. 'Go and help the attack on the next fort,' he told them. They stared at him. 'Go!' he snapped and, startled, they ran westwards.

Thomas pointed his sword at the Lord of Roncelets. 'Take him back to town,' he told Robbie, 'and guard him well.'

'What about you?' Robbie asked.

'I'm going to bury Will,' Thomas said. 'He was a friend.' He thought he must shed some tears for Will Skeat, but there were none. Not now, anyway. He sheathed the sword, then smiled at Robbie. 'You can go home, Robbie.'

'I can?' Robbie seemed puzzled.

'De Taillebourg's dead. Roncelets will pay your ransom to Lord Outhwaite. You can go to Eskdale, go home, go back to killing Englishmen.'

Robbie shook his head. 'Guy Vexille lives.'

'He's mine to kill.'

'And mine,' Robbie said. 'You forget he killed my brother. I'm staying till he's dead.'

'If you can ever find him,' Jeanette said softly.

The sun was lighting the smoke of the burning encampments and casting long shadows across the ground where the last of Charles's army abandoned their earthworks and fled towards

Rennes. They had come in their great splendour and now they scuttled away in abject defeat.

Thomas went to the engineers' tents and found a pickaxe, a mattock and a shovel. He dug a grave beside Stonewhip and tipped Skeat into the damp soil and tried to say a prayer, but he could not think of one, and then he remembered the coin for the ferryman and so he went to the Lord of Roncelets's tent and pulled the charred canvas away from the chest and took a piece of gold and went back to the grave. He jumped down beside his friend and put the coin under Skeat's tongue. The ferryman would find it and know from the gold that Sir William Skeat was a special man. 'God bless you, Will,' Thomas said, then he scrambled out of the grave and he filled it in, though he kept pausing in hope that Will's eyes would open, but of course they did not and Thomas at last wept as he shovelled earth onto his friend's pale face. The sun was up by the time he finished and women and children were coming from the town to look for plunder. A kestrel flew high and Thomas sat on the chest of coins and waited for Robbie to return from the town.

He would go south, he thought. Go to Astarac. Go and find his father's notebook and solve its mystery. The bells of La Roche-Derrien were ringing for the victory, a huge victory, and Thomas sat among the dead and knew he would have no peace until he had found his father's burden. *Calix meus inebrians. Transfer calicem istem a me. Ego enim eram pincerna regis.*

Whether he wanted the job or not he was the King's cupbearer, and he would go south.

Historical Note

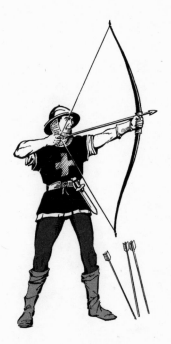

The novel begins with the battle of Neville's Cross. The name of the battle is derived from the stone cross that Lord Neville erected to mark the victory, though it is possible there was another cross already on the site which Lord Neville's memorial replaced. The battle, fought by a large Scottish army against a small scratch force hastily assembled by the Archbishop of York and the northern lords, was a disaster for the Scots. Their King, David II, was captured as described in *Vagabond*, trapped under a bridge. He managed to knock out some of his captor's teeth, but then was subdued. He spent a long time at Bamburgh Castle recovering from his facial wound, then was taken to London and put into the Tower with most of the other Scottish aristocracy captured that day, including Sir William Douglas, the Knight of Liddesdale. The two Scottish Earls who had previously sworn fealty to Edward were decapitated, then quartered, and the parts of their body displayed around the realm as a warning against treachery. Later that year Charles of Blois, nephew to the King of France and would-be Duke of Brittany, joined David II in the Tower of London. It was a remarkable double by the English who will, in another decade, add the King of France himself to the haul.

The Scots invaded England at the request of the French to whom they were allied, and it is probable that David II truly believed England's army was all in northern France. But England had foreseen just this kind of trouble and certain northern lords were charged with staying at home and being ready to raise forces if the Scots ever marched. The backbone of those forces was, of course, the archer, and this is the great age of English (and, to a lesser

extent, Welsh) archery. The weapon used was the longbow (a name that was coined much later) which was a yew bow at least six feet in length with a draw weight of over a hundred pounds (more than double the weight of modern competition bows). It is a mystery why England alone could field armies of lethal archers who did, indeed, become kings of the European battlefield, but the likeliest answer is that mastery of the longbow was an English enthusiasm, practised as a sport in hundreds of villages. Eventually laws were passed making archery practice obligatory, presumably because the enthusiasm was fading. It was, certainly, an extraordinarily difficult weapon to use, requiring immense strength, and the French, though they tried to introduce the weapon into their ranks, never mastered the longbow. The Scots were accustomed to these archers and had learned never to attack them on horseback, but in truth there was no answer to the longbow until firearms were deployed on the battlefield.

Prisoners were important. A great man like Sir William Douglas would only be released on payment of a vast ransom, though Sir William was given early parole to help negotiate the ransom of the King of Scotland and when he failed he dutifully returned to his imprisonment in the Tower of London. The ransoms for men like Charles of Blois and King David II were massive and might take years to negotiate and raise. In David's case the ransom was £66,000, a sum that has to be multiplied at least a hundred times to get even a rough approximation of its modern value. The Scots were allowed to pay it in ten instalments and twenty noblemen had to be surrendered as hostages for the payment before David was released in 1357 by which time, ironically, his sympathies had become entirely pro-English. Sir Thomas Dagworth was officially the captor of Charles of Blois and he sold him to Edward III for the much smaller sum of £3,500, but doubtless it was better to have that money in hand than wait while a larger ransom was collected in France and Brittany. King David's captor had been an Englishman called John Coupland who also sold his prisoner to Edward, in Coupland's case for a knighthood and land.

Charles's defeat at La Roche-Derrien is one of the great unsung English triumphs of the period. Charles had faced archers before and had worked out, rightly as it happened, that the way to defeat

them was to make them attack well-protected positions. What the archer could not see he could not kill. The tactic worked against Sir Thomas Dagworth's assault, but then came Richard Totesham's frenetic sortie from the town and, because Charles had insisted that the four parts of his army stay behind their protective earthworks, he was overwhelmed and the other parts of his army were then defeated in turn. His defeat and capture were an immense shock to his allies, the French, who were failing to relieve the siege of Calais. I must record my debt to Jonathan Sumption whose book, *Trial by Battle*, the first volume of his superb history of the Hundred Years War, was of particular use to me. The errors in the novel are entirely mine, of course, though in the interests of lightening my post bag may I gently point out that Durham Cathedral only possessed two towers in 1347 and that I placed the Hachaliah reference in the book of Esdras, instead of in Nehemiah, because I was using the Vulgate and not the King James Bible.

Liferaft support
Battens 19" dead.

Liferaft

1¼"

19"

VAGABOND